Jack

JACK

Brian Carter

C

CENTURY PUBLISHING

LONDON

First published in Great Britain in 1986 by
Century Hutchinson Ltd
Brookmount House, 62–65 Chandos Place
London WC2N 4NW

ISBN 0 7126 0946 6

Printed in Great Britain by Anchor Brendon Ltd, Tiptree, Essex

The Lord is my shepherd; I shall not want.
He maketh me to lie down in green pastures;
He leadeth me beside the still waters.
He restoreth my soul.

Psalm 23

To all the horses that did not
find their green pastures.

Prologue

A shell descended and the fountain of earth rose, hung for a moment and fell apart. Fumes gusted across the road and the sergeant coughed and drew the corner of his turned-up collar over his mouth.

'Walk on,' the driver said, and the two cart horses who were tandem-hitched to the ambulance strode away.

Twilight closed on the fields. Screened by trees to the west of the Front the British heavies opened up. Then a column of limbers came along the road at speed. Jack stepped aside and sat on an overturned watercart. The first team thundered past, the horses bounding through the mud. The right lead animal was familiar. Its face was white and despite the mud the marbling on its flanks and haunches was rich enough to catch the eye. Jack's scalp prickled. The horse was surging on, filling the air with spray that stank.

'Beth,' he cried. 'Beth.'

And she swung her head and tried to dig in her feet and stop. But Milburn's whip smacked her neck and obedience won. Her stride faltered only to lengthen again.

'Beth,' Jack began to run.

'McKenna,' the sergeant barked. 'Stand still, man, stand still.'

The mud sucked at his legs and brought him to a halt.

'Beth,' he groaned

The lead driver of the next limber team was roaring at him to get out of the way. Then something hard and heavy struck Jack's shoulder and spun him off the road.

'You dingo bugger!' the sergeant grunted, dragging him out of the shell hole. 'Talk about bog Irish! Where were you going, you horrible little Irishman?'

'It was my horse,' Jack gasped. He spat mud and pawed at his eyes. 'My bloody horse. My Beth.'

The sergeant stared at him and nodded.

'A red roan mare. Bethlehem. I helped bring her into the world. She's my horse.'

'No lad,' the sergeant said. 'She's the King's horse. There's nothing you can do about it. Best forget you saw her – if it was her.'

Jack wiped his mouth on his sleeve and spat again. His puttees had uncoiled and were hanging over his boots.

'We don't own anything out here, lad – least of all ourselves.'

'She's mine,' Jack whispered. 'I made her a promise.'

'I made my old lady a promise at the altar but it don't mean a lot now.'

'She's mine,' Jack repeated, and there was a raw, manic certainty in his voice that aborted further comment.

PART ONE

BOY AND FOAL

1

Shortly before dawn Jack McKenna closed the front door of Number Eight Angarrick Terrace behind him and walked the deserted streets of Lansworthy out into the South Devon countryside. The air was heavy with the scents of spring but the birdsong was quieter where the gardens of the seaside town surrendered to pasture and copse. The boy turned up the collar of his jacket against the cold, tugged down the peak of his cap and buried his hands in his trouser pockets. He liked the solitude, the slow ebb of darkness and the ring of his nailed boots on the road. It was the best part of the day or perhaps he just loved beginnings, that warm thrill before mystery subsided into the commonplace.

He was fourteen and not long out of the Board School. 'Irish' Jack they called him, partly because of his accent but mainly because he bounced between wild enthusiasm and cheerfulness – which the Devonians grudgingly admired although they pretended to disapprove. The boy was small, nimble and bright-eyed in a Celtic way that suggested alertness straying into recklessness. His eyes glistened as though he were permanently close to tears. Their blue pallor and a broken nose, which had been repaired in haste, lent his face a comical ferocity.

He stopped by Batterways Bridge and tightened a bootlace. The road smelt of rain and cattle but the wind blowing across the Channel from the continent promised fine weather. It was shaking raindrops out of the hedges on either side as he came up the hill past the brickworks, thinking of the horses on Cider Mill Tor. They would be facing the sea, waiting for the phantom light to erupt into sunrise. The blackbird singing from the cherry tree at Clayland Cross already had sunshine in its voice. Then a cuckoo began to call and the Mary's Haven Road ran along the low line of hills above sleeping farmland with the sea gleaming now on Jack's left.

Hawthorn blossom was palely visible up in the hedge. The wind and last night's showers had scattered little white stars on the road, and the mist clotting the coombes had the same faint glow. Once again excitement squirmed in Jack's stomach. He was going to the horses like the first boy in the first dawn. All creation was assembling around him as spinneys, woods and high-hedged fields lifted grey and ghostly from the mist. He was glad Princess had had her foal and Melody would soon give birth. Working with horses for Chancellor's Emporium was fine but coming to Tor Barton was an adventure. Old Mr Sidney Chancellor, who also loved horses, understood. Pregnant mares and sick animals were sent from Lansworthy stables to the farm which he owned, and Jack had been put under the head carter. The boy was steeped in horselore. Since early childhood he had hung around the stables behind the railway station whenever he had a free moment until he had become part of the place.

Now rooks were breaking from the elms near the cider mill and drifting down Clennon Valley. Jack turned off the road and took the cart-track on to Cider Mill Tor. The weathered limestone pushed a shoulder out of the common and the boy perched on top of it and hugged his knees to his chin. The rooks were below him and the mist was thinning to reveal dawn's cool colours. Six summers ago the bonfire celebrating King Edward VII's coronation had blazed from the hilltop. Jack remembered the brightness and the crowd singing the national anthem. They ought to light a bonfire here every summer, he thought. Bonfires cheer people up.

Over the blossoming apple trees the farmhouse could be seen standing grey under its lichened roof. Beyond the chimneys the water meadows of Clennon Valley were divided by a stream which passed under the Dartmouth Road, cut across the peat bog and found the sea through a culvert in the Great Western Railway embankment. North eastwards and partly screened by Clennon Woods was the sandstone tower of Lansworthy parish church and the rooftops of the higher part of town. Lansworthy was the central nail in the horseshoe formed by St Mary's Bay.

Above a harbour facing south the fashionable holiday resort of Abbot's Quay was parading rows of terraced villas. Across the water at the other end of the horseshoe a crab boat left the little port of Mary's Haven to sail round St Mary's Head under the lighthouse and sea bird loomeries into the English Channel. Gulls winged silently inland and light was spreading along the horizon.

Jack slid off the rock and ran down to the gate that opened onto a meadow. The draught horses cantered up to him, loosing their manes on the air and fluting through their nostrils. He called them by name: 'Mary, Dolly, Captain, Edward, Sunny, Jan.' Mares and geldings jostled around him, lowering long serious faces and wreathing him in the breath of crushed grass. Beneath the heave of life the boy sensed the power of the great animals. It vibrated in bunched muscles and arched necks and shone and rippled on the surface of their bodies. They towered over him and nudged him gently with their muzzles while the new day crept in off the sea.

From the hamlet of Goodrington to Lansworthy cocks began to crow, and Jack felt curiously light-headed. The birdsong had a desperate edge to it as though it did not belong to the morning. He had come through another beginning but the road ran on to somewhere remote and mysterious and his flesh was goose pimpling. In the valley the curlews called, each note holding the moment's sadness.

He left the horses and went down the hillside among the apple trees to the farmhouse and knocked on the side door. The farmer's wife gave him a blank smile and told him to wait. Mrs Maddock never invited any of the workers into her kitchen. According to Trant, the head carter who preferred to be called the horseman, she had gypsy blood and a worse temper than her husband. Jack smiled. It was a case of the pot calling the kettle black and the boy disliked the little carter and his thin, energetic wife with her goitre and knobbly fingers. At least the farmer could laugh and joke even if he was tight-fisted.

3

'Has Melody foaled, missis?' Jack said, taking the jug of tea from Mrs Maddock.

'I don't know,' came the reply and the door closed on the fire's crackle and the song of the caged goldfinch.

Jack cupped his hands around the hot enamel and a plume of fragrance lifted off the tea. He skated across the wet manure in the bullock yard, past the dung heaps and foraging hens to the stables.

On the tack-room walls hung collars, hames, tug chains and halters, and the rest of the harness necessary to keep horses working in the fields. The thick cob walls had been lime-washed and the smell of straw filtered down from the loft above the wooden ceiling.

He marched along the passage with the open stalls on his right. Iona regarded him placidly although she had a mild attack of diarrhoea. Jack put down the jug and crooned the endearments he always saved for the horses. The damp smell of animals and animal living was seamed with the reek of ammonia. In the next stall Princess and her filly foal, Bathsheba, waited to be let out into the paddock. The shire cross lifted her front feet and beat a tattoo of impatience. Every so often her hooves slid and grated through the straw onto the stone floor.

'Hold to, hold to,' the boy said and Princess's ears pricked and her eyes widened but she knew Jack's voice and did not flinch from his touch.

'For Christ's sake,' the carter cried. 'Leave the beasts alone and get in yer with the tea.'

Trant sat on an upturned pail and his wife leaned against Melody's manger, arms folded, her goitre bulging obscenely in the lantern light. She's swallowed the goose's golden egg, Jack thought. It glowed there beneath the taut skin of her throat.

'I forgot the mugs,' he grinned. His chilblains were jumping and he wanted to take off his boots and have a good scratch.

'That doan surprise me,' the carter said. 'They don't call 'ee "Irish" Jack for nort. Bog Irish Jack, the Dublin dawbake.'

'Dingle, Mister. We come from Dingle.'

'Bliddy Dingle dangle Dublin! – tez all the same to me, boy,' Trant hissed. 'Old man Chancellor may think the sun shines out your behind but I idn impressed. Has it happens I've got a cup.

4

Just give us the jug.'

Jack's grin broadened and he bent over Melody and stroked her nose. The carter glared at him, his leathery face wearing an expression of sullen resignation. Every rut and line on his brow was a testament to hard, impoverished outdoor life. Jack puzzled and irritated him. He was the colt that would remain unbroken and the certainty of this stuck in Trant's craw.

The mare lifted and turned her head as the labour pains intensified. She kicked against it but the pain grew worse. Suddenly the waters burst and the foal slid along the birth canal until its hooves and front legs protruded in a sheath of membrane from its mother's hind quarters. The watching boy had witnessed a dozen such births yet the miracle still had the power to move him.

Slowly the parcel of freshly minted life emerged from Melody and the mare lifted her head eager to see the part of herself which would soon be a separate unique creature. One final shudder pushed the foal free. Wrapped in the glittering membrane it flopped onto the straw and Mrs Trant slit the bag and pulled it off the newborn animal while life flowed through the umbilical cord between mother and daughter. Melody turned and manoeuvred until she was able to lick the foal.

Light slanted over the top of the stable doors and fanned out across the ceiling. The windows opposite the stall held some of the sky's gleam.

'Melody,' Jack whispered, dropping to his knees.

The mare drew back her upper lip and bared her teeth at him.

'She'll give you one hell of a nip if you get too close,' said Trant. 'Her's foal proud.'

'She won't hurt me,' the boy smiled. 'I can talk to horses.'

'Pity you can't talk to pigs,' sniffed the carter's wife. 'Or I'd get 'ee to ask farmer to give my old man a rise. A bliddy 'orse is better off than us.'

The boy stooped and taking the foal's head in his hands planted a kiss on her nose.

'Good girl,' Jack crooned. 'Clever Melody. You've got a perfect foal, a roan. Clever girl. Clever girl.'

Despite the almost hysterical warbling and trilling of the songbirds he caught the whisper of bats' wings along the ceiling. In the neighbouring stalls the other horses splashed the hush with their urine. Hidden behind films of moisture something profoundly sad lay in the mare's eyes. Then her lids descended and rose again leaving the brown pupils empty.

'Come away, boy, and let her get on with it,' the carter said. 'Us've got work to do.'

The foal got to her feet and the life cord broke close to her body. Like the mare she was a red roan, finely marked, with white legs and belly. The whiteness climbed her flanks, marbled her thighs and touched parts of her shoulders. Nearly every inch of her bay coat carried a dusting of white hairs. Her face right up to the eyes was white and there were white streaks in her mane and tail.

'Her's a 'ansome little sod,' Trant admitted. 'Her sire was a carriage horse and she won't have a lot of bulk.'

For a moment she stood wobbling and swaying on legs that threatened to buckle. But Melody was upright now and nudging the foal towards her udder. Soon she was sucking and Mrs Trant wiped the tail of belly cord with iodine. All is well, thought the boy, closing his eyes above an enormous yawn. The foal greedied the rich first milk and Melody began ridding herself of afterbirth.

'What's her name, mister?' said Jack.

'Bethlehem,' the carter said, blowing out the lantern.

'Old man Chancellor came up with it weeks ago. If her'd been a he her would be called Joshua. The boss likes his bible.'

Then Jack was left to water and feed the mare. The sun rose and turned the cobwebs on the windows to gold. Slowly the morning flooded Bethlehem's consciousness but uncertainty tugged her up against her mother's flanks. Melody munched the chafed straw and oats Jack had put in the manger. The steam of her breath poured from her nostrils and the corners of her mouth.

Outside the stables the farm was coming to life. The milkers and teamsters had arrived and the yard was full of cattle. Bethlehem's nostrils dilated.

The chestnut trees behind the stables were whispering and dark shapes of birds flickered across the sun dazzle on the window. Everything fascinated the foal. She returned Jack's gaze not vacantly like a newborn human baby but as a creature that had stepped out of another existence with its senses and intelligence orchestrated to a fine awareness of the world.

6

2

The warm weather prevailed and the mares and foals were turned out permanently into the paddock. Under the chestnut trees next to the stables was a linhay where they could shelter if it rained. But the sun shone and most nights were clear and starry.

Now Bethlehem was caught between love of mother and the wonder of everything around her. Running with Bathsheba through the moonlight was more than a game; and when the foals were tired they stood together on the sloping field looking across the bay. The sky leapt up from the horizon and arched over them, and the moon which was not yet full hung above the sea. Stars were scattered east and west of the meridian, and the stellar glow ran away into silences lit by the light of other stars.

After dark Bethlehem walked through pockets of animal warmth full of scent: the comforting smell of her dam, Princess's smell, the scent of Bathsheba, and other smells which puzzled her. When she smelt Bathsheba the image of the foal grew behind her eyes but the stink of fox in the paddock corner was as mysterious as the moths thudding softly against her head. Sometimes she woke to find dew forming on leaves and grass blades. Then she lay motionless listening to what the night had to say, drawing comfort from the sound of Melody breathing beside her. Always it seemed the curlews were awake and ready to call. Their whistles of two syllables faded into bubbling trills as she returned once more to sleep. But the interlude of nothingness was over quickly and Iona came swishing through the grass while light spread across the water meadows.

One afternoon the boy put Bethlehem in a head collar and despite her protests led her around the paddock. It was the first step in schooling the foal to the harness. After shaking her head and prancing on hind legs for a moment she trotted away with Jack in tow, clinging to the halter.

'Her thinks her's boss,' Trant said. 'Later on us'll put her straight. Doan make a fuss of her, boy, or you'll have trouble when her's full-growed. A spoilt horse is worse than useless.'

Jack bent to pluck bits of bramble off the foal's fetlocks and the long white hairs, or 'feather' as it was known, spreading over her hooves. Bethlehem blew fluttering sighs. Like the other horses she responded to human kindness. In her simplicity she accepted without suspicion the attention lavished on her and her kind. So she watched Jack grooming Melody, brushing the mare down until she glowed. Gnats swarmed around the foal's head and as the day advanced flies zoomed in to worry her eyes and the corners of her mouth. Then she did half a dozen circuits of the paddock with Bathsheba beside her, flicking her hind legs and playfully nipping her companion's neck. Iona and Princess joined in but Melody paced up and down under the chestnut trees.

'Her's still on heat,' said Trant. 'But her won't be gwain to the stallion to be covered – oh no! The old man has arranged for Lazewell's Jim to be brought here.'

The carter spoke as if such a thing was unheard of, although it happened regularly at Tor Barton. But the little man's knowledge of horses impressed Jack and for all his crabbiness he obviously cared about them. When the vet arrived the day before the stallion was due to visit Melody the boy had another demonstration of Trant's expertise.

The vet was a bespectacled Londoner, fresh out of college. The local farmers were busy breaking him in and cataloguing his errors and misfortunes.

'Mother and daughter seem healthy enough, Trant,' he said, rubbing his hands together. 'Mr Maddock tells me the foal was born in the stables. I think it would be better this time of year if the mares were allowed to foal here in the paddock. It's cleaner.' He smiled nervously and added, 'Less chance of infection.'

'I suppose the ditch that was up along the top hedge has vanished,' Trant said, heavily sarcastic. 'Melody would've foaled there for certain and tez just as certain the young horse would've broke a leg tryin' to get out. In any case, 'twas cold and wet when her went into labour. If her had it outdoors the foal would be full of pneumonia and I'd be jawin' to the knacker, not the vet.'

The young man coloured and nodded and Jack grinned. Trant caught the boy's eye and winked. Jack's face was radiant under its shock of black hair.

Out of the sun the swifts came screaming to hawk the sky above Clennon Valley, and doves were moaning on the linhay roof. The whine and hum of insects, the creak of a cart, birdsong, and all the other sounds lifting from the farm entered Bethlehem's knowing. She rolled in the grass and beat the air with her hooves. Amongst the stems were the pale mauve flowers of lady's-smocks. A breeze trailed across the paddock and grass curled at the tips. Where the cow parsley stood in the ditch a yellow-hammer sang.

Bethlehem peered through her lashes and saw the buzzards high over Tor Barton. They swung, tacked and skirled, and passed slowly out of sight.

The patter of chestnut blossom on the linhay roof woke her. Masthead lanterns shone from the bay and the sea glittered to the horizon. An animal burst through the hedge and ran down into the bullock yard. One of the farm dogs began to bark and Bethlehem pressed closer to her mother. The dark green breath of the June night eddied around them.

Less than a mile away Jack lay staring up at the bedroom ceiling, only partly aware of his brothers in the bed beside him and his youngest sister mumbling in her sleep over by the window. The dream had made him sad. He yawned and clasped his hands together behind his head. Silver horses, he thought, struggling to reassemble the dream like a jigsaw puzzle. The tide of shining animals flashed through the darkness and was gone leaving just the ceiling and images too vague to put together.

Number Eight Angarrick Terrace was not a happy house, but the trouble smouldering between husband and wife differed little from the grievances affecting most of the other working-class homes in the neighbourhood. Kevan McKenna was a pub man. His whole life revolved around the sawdust, ale, noise and comradeship of the King William – an inn which the devil it seemed, had placed within easy staggering distance of the terrace.

McKenna had left the Dingle peninsula in the last years of Victoria's reign to join the Irish pick-and-shovel invasion of cities like Liverpool, Birmingham and London. He had drifted to Devon by chance and as soon as he found permanent work with the Great Western Railway had sent for his family. Some of the cheerfulness which his wife had found more attractive than his coarse good looks could still break through the transparent boredom he brought home from the station. Every Friday and Saturday nights especially, he whistled and sang and joked with the children while his mind waltzed ahead to the vivid hours he would soon be spending in the bar. But for the remainder of the week he was morose and dangerous. Empty pockets left him an empty man.

Mrs McKenna hated him quietly and totally. She hated his end-of-week drunkenness and the boredom he carried in his eyes when he was broke. She hated sleeping with him and washing for him and cooking for him. The best years of her life had been squandered on Kevan McKenna, and often she looked in the mirror at the lines of drudgery and despair wondering why she had been born. Perhaps living itself was a kind of martyrdom for poor people and the man she had married, blind to his faults, was her personal cross.

She had five children and looked nearer fifty than thirty-five. Both girls were too young to try her patience but the boys, except her oldest and favourite, Jack, were in and out of trouble. Jack was the eternal Irish paradox, the dreamer attracted to violence, someone who acted on impulse. Now she could hear him creeping along the landing and padding downstairs. Her husband sprawled on his back beside her, breathing through his mouth.

'Choke on your own spit, you old bugger,' Mary McKenna

hissed, and she slipped out of bed.

Downstairs Jack was feeding twigs to the fire in the kitchen range. The candle burnt steadily in its brass holder and the crucifix above the sideboard gleamed like gold.

'God, if you're not the tom cat,' his mother smiled. 'Up and about all hours of the night.'

'I'm going to the farm,' Jack said, tucking his shirt tail into his trousers and retrieving his boots from the regiment of footwear lined up against the fender.

'You'll turn into a horse one day.'

'That would be nice,' said the boy.

'Will you be home for dinner?'

He shrugged and buttoned himself into his waistcoat. The flames leapt and the fire coughed a little smoke across the hearth. Mary McKenna glanced at the crucifix.

'Father Tynan keeps askin' why you're never at Mass, Jack. You've missed three Sundays in a row now.'

'Dad doesn't go.'

'Yes, well, your father's so busy going to hell he can't find time to stop anywhere along the way except the pub. The fool threatened Father Tynan the last time the poor man knocked at our door,' said Mary McKenna.

Jack laughed.

'It's not funny,' she murmured, lifting a hand wearily to her brow.

The boy looked at her and said, 'They call the white waves you see out on the bay when it's stormy, horses – white horses, because they're like stallions with their manes blowing in the wind. I learnt that at school.'

Briefly between the woman and her son flickered the faded image of a white horse and an old man ploughing the side of a great, green hill where cloud shadows raced. Then it was gone and she was beyond weeping for a past which was more distant than the Ireland she would never see again. Drudgery, yes, and hunger but among people who cared and suffered together. All gone, all buried, and nothing to live for but the boy with her hair and eyes.

'When I've got lots of money I'll buy you a pony and trap, Mum, and I'll drive you about like the old Queen.'

'You and your dreams, Jack,' she whispered, kissing him.

'Don't you dream?'

'Not much,' she said. 'And when I do they're only small ones – like having enough money to pay the rent or a new husband to buy me a new skirt.'

'I dream about horses mostly and it's nearly always the same dream. There's this terrible storm and thunder and lightning. And suddenly a big silver horse comes out of the ground. So I get on its back and ride it away, out of the storm followed by lots of other shining horses. Then – something awful happens and I'm scared stiff.'

'You've too much imagination,' his mother said, pushing back his hair with the side of her hand.

'Don't dreams come true? Not ever?'

'Of course they do but sometimes the angels or whoever's job it is to bring a bit of magic into our lives get it wrong. In most fairy tales, for instance, the frog turns into a handsome prince but in my case the prince turned into a frog. You can hear him croaking up there now.'

'But you love him, don't you?' the boy said solemnly.

'Jesus, I married the man didn't I? You don't marry people you don't love. That would be sinful. God knows, Jack, He can see into your heart. He can see everything.'

'Does he watch me on the lav?' asked the boy, his eyes twinkling.

'I doubt it. He'll have more important things to do,' Mrs McKenna laughed. 'Can you picture God up there making moons and suns and things? Is he going to stop in the middle of creating a new star to watch you up the yard with your trousers round your ankles? God's not daft.'

Shortly after sunrise Jack opened the paddock gate and put halters on Melody and the foal. Then he rode the mare and led Bethlehem across the bullock yard. Three of the Maddock children were gathering hens' eggs. They were a scruffy brood, especially the little girls with smears of cattle dung on their bare legs and feet. The boy Arthur was a couple of years younger than Jack. He had buck teeth and a cap that was several sizes too big.

'Where be gwain with they 'orses, Irish?' he grinned. 'They idn yours. They'm old man Chancellor's.'

'Exercise,' announced Jack. 'Trantie wants the foal to get the

12

feel of the road.'

A posse of lean farm cats rubbed against the horses' legs, tails stiff and upright, expecting nothing but half hoping the impossible would happen and they would be fed.

'Kin us come?' bawled one of the girls.

'It's not a joy ride,' Jack said over his shoulder as Melody swung down the lane.

'Us'll tell Dad,' Arthur cried. 'And he'll take a stick to 'ee. You idn s'posed to mess round with they animals. They'm worth money.'

'Go stuff a cabbage in your gob, rabbit face,' Jack growled. 'If I come back there I'll fill it with horse turds.'

'You and who's army, you bliddy foreigner.'

Jack waved a hand contemptuously and let it fall again onto Melody's neck. The broad back rolled under him and the mare's hooves scattered small stones while her shoes sparked on the larger ones. Arching overhead the leaves were silver-edged with sunlight, and dog roses covered the wayside banks. Already swifts and house martins were climbing the morning. The heatwave showed no sign of breaking. Beyond the railway embankment the bay was taking light and colour from the sky. The curlews flapping off the marsh wore their dark summer plumage but their cries were as thin and clear as running water.

He rode away from Clennon past the orchards towards Goodrington and Cider Mill Farm. From the meadow in the bottom of the valley other horses cried out to the mare and foal, and Melody answered them. The whinnying followed them up the cart-track to the road that wound white and dusty towards Dartmouth. Coming up the hill by the quarry Jack could look over flowering fields to the sea. The sight of it all tugged at his innards. Soon he was riding along the downland where larks rose and fell in the hush of distance sketched on haze. Far ahead fields were piled high and quivering, more light than land. At Windy Corner the bridle path ran down a coombe thick with bluebells to the viaduct and marsh behind Broadsands beach. He brought the horses through a gap in the sea wall onto the shingle and took off their harness. Then he undressed and clambered back naked onto the mare. The tide was ebbing and the wet sand above the wavebreak was glazed with light.

Bethlehem took a couple of steps, paused and looked about

her. Waves fizzed slowly over the glare. Crisp ridges of brilliance ran out to the horizon under the flash and whack of gulls' wings. Bethlehem lowered her head and sniffed the bladder-wrack. Her mother was ambling into the light. The foal scuffed through drifts of shells and little sun-baked crabs. The patina of sunshine was suddenly broken by Melody's hooves. She began to trot until she was breasting the waves and Jack screwed up his eyes and gave himself to the floating sensation that had nothing to do with the sea. Holy Mary, Mother of God, he prayed, let me be like the horses. Let me understand them.

Cold water washed over his legs and he gasped. Melody turned and whinnied and was answered by the foal. Together they galloped across the shallows in a cloud of spray. At the end of the beach Jack jumped clear and watched the animals wheel to run back again, their wet coats shining and the mare's mane streaming free. Into the summer heat they went like elements of mirage returning to mirage. The thunder of their hooves and the sight of them flying along the shore would haunt him forever.

'Holy Mary,' he whispered. 'Holy Mother of God.'

They came to him when he called and he took them to the marsh behind the sea wall and rolled with them in the fresh water. Bethlehem gazed curiously at the boy. He was kneeling like a small white horse beside her. Then she breathed a greeting through her nostrils and he hooked an arm round her neck. Dragonflies clicked by and the breeze swept over the scrub willow, whitening the leaves.

'Why did you do it? What on earth possessed you?'

Chancellor ran the tip of his tongue along the fringe of his moustache and looked sideways at Jack. The boy rammed his fist deeper into his trouser pockets, lifted his shoulders and frowned up at the white hairs crowding the old man's nostrils.

'Because the little devil's mazed,' Maddock said, but Chancellor silenced him with an upraised finger.

'I watered and groomed Melody, sir,' Jack said.

'After taking them bathing – you silly young sod,' said Maddock, close to shouting.

'Yes, why the trip to the beach?' Chancellor pressed. His attempt at the middle-class accent only served to draw attention

14

to the broad Devon vowels which were the legacy of a backstreet boyhood.

'I wanted them to have a holiday, sir. And I wanted them to be like they were before we took them over. Foxes and badgers don't have no boss. All animals were free once.'

Maddock sucked in his breath but before he could comment Chancellor dismissed him.

'What will become of you, Jack?'

The old man drew down his eyebrows and thought about it. Sweat trickled from under the brim of his bowler and ran down the vertical creases in his long red face.

'Melody might have caught a chill,' he went on. 'And Beth could have broken a leg galloping along that beach. You must think before you act, son. Think.' He tapped Jack's head with his bunched knuckles.

'They were happy, Mr Chancellor.'

'I'm sure they were. Horses are splendid creatures. Do you know the story of how they came into the world?'

The boy shook his head and slowly drew a finger down his sunburnt nose.

'The Bedouins – those Arabs who live in the desert – say God looked out on creation and saw it was incomplete. So he took a handful of wind and fashioned a mare and a stallion. Now these horses were as swift as the wind, beautiful creatures, strong and brave. When Man asked for their services they gave with loyalty and love and trust. Trust, Jack – trust. It was the way of their kind and it still is.'

'God, yes, sir, yes,' Jack said, passionately. 'When we was in the sea they were like those two Arab horses and I wanted to be like them.'

Chancellor smiled. 'Trant thinks you'll make a good horseman.'

Again the boy shook his head.

'Trant may have a sharp tongue, boy, but he cares about the animals.'

Chancellor removed his hat and used it as a fan. Grey wisps of hair were glued to his forehead but for a man on the weather side of sixty he was remarkably well preserved.

'What's your ambition, Jack?'

'Ambition, sir?'

15

'What do you hope to do with your life?'

'Look after horses, sir. Work for you, sir.'

'That's all?'

'No sir; there's something else.'

'Tell me,' Chancellor said, laying his forearms on top of the gate and smiling at the antics of Bethlehem and Bathsheba.

'I'd like to buy Beth off you one day, Mr Chancellor. I'd have her pullin' my own cart.'

'Selling what?'

'Fish, veg – it don't matter so long as she's mine. And she'll never go to the knackers. Never. She'll have her own field in the summer and a warm stable in the winter. I've already promised her that.'

'Where will the money come from to start your business, Jack?'

'I'm savin', sir. Where did your money come from?'

'Hard work, sweat, a bit of luck and a bank manager who knew a good thing when he saw it. Are you working at the Emporium tomorrow?'

'Yes sir. I'm going out with the coal.'

'And there'll be no more trips to the seaside for mares and foals?'

Jack shrugged and grinned. 'You will sell Beth to me one day won't you, sir.'

'Yes, Jack, I will, if you prove you can take care of her,' the old man said. 'These are prosperous times,' he added, 'and they can only get better. The Empire is growing and Chancellor's is growing with it. What are you like at sums – multiplication, subtraction and all that mumbo jumbo?'

'Hopeless,' said Jack.

'But you know horses. Stick to what you know. In a couple of months the Emporium is shifting premises to become a department store – the biggest between Exeter and Plymouth. Our vans will be delivering as far afield as Kingswear and Dartmouth, Totnes, Newton Abbot and Bovey. One day you could be head horseman and in a sense Beth would be yours.'

'If horses are so special, Mr Chancellor, why have you got one of those motor cars?'

'Ask my son. He bought it,' the old man sighed. 'Noisy temperamental thing, always conking out. Horses aren't like

16

that. You can rely on a mare like old Iona.'

'Iona is a fine name, sir.'

'It was the wife's idea. We went on this Scottish tour and sailed round the Hebrides to Fingal's cave and Iona. Very beautiful, but it didn't measure up to Devon.'

In his passion for the county he forgot his new accent and called it 'Debn'. These lapses were a constant source of embarrassment to his son.

'Can I have a rise, sir?' Jack said suddenly. 'Then I'll be able to get the horse a bit quicker.'

'We'll see,' he said. 'I dislike talking money matters on the Sabbath, McKenna. But we'll see.'

Jack did not want the day to end. He had half a pasty wrapped in muslin and newspaper in his pocket, and from Cider Mill Tor the countryside swam green and seductive all the way to Dartmoor. Keeping to the high ground he walked to the River Dart at Stoke Gabriel. Children were swimming in Mill Pool but he went up river to Hackney Creek and dawdled back to Clennon through lengthening shadows along the Yalberton Road.

It was nearly dark when he had a last look at the horses. Glow worms shone from the laneside above the farm and down in the yard Mrs Maddock and Trant's wife were shooing the fowls into the hen house. The scream of terror took them by surprise. One of the cats ran stiff-legged over the cobbles with a rabbit in its jaws.

'Come yer,' Mrs Trant rasped, and the cat froze and pressed its belly tight to the ground.

Again the rabbit screamed. Mrs Trant stooped, gripped it by the ears and kicked the cat out of the way. When she straightened the rabbit was squirming in her knobbly fist. The woman licked her lips and clamped her free hand to the animal's hindlegs and twisted and wrenched the life out of it.

'You'll have meat in your stew tomorrow,' Mrs Maddock said from a bleak little smile.

'Tez your cat, missus, and your coney,' came the reply. 'Us idn that hard up.'

'Can I have it, Mrs Maddock?' Jack said.

'If her can really spare it,' said the farmer's wife.

Mrs Trant drew her nails delicately over her goitre and tossed the rabbit at Jack's feet. He retrieved it triumphantly and wiped the dust off its fur. Then he grinned up at the women but they turned away, tight-lipped, the resentment crackling between them.

3

His first chore was to take the boys' chamber pot out to the lavatory in the backyard. Michael, who was a year younger than Jack, rolled into the warm hollow left by his brother's body and spread his limbs luxuriously after a cramped night. Monday was washday and Mrs McKenna was boiling the water and pushing clothes into the copper. The downstairs rooms were full of steam.

He ate breakfast by the light of the paraffin lamp, and his mother put the shirts and underclothes to stew while she cut his dinner. Drinking tea from a mug which bore the initials GWR in brown grot lettering, Jack thought about his father. The remains of some streaky bacon and a couple of Woodbine butts lay on the plate at his elbow. Kevan McKenna had left for work at three o'clock. He was a shadowy figure drifting almost casually in and out of family life. He would be there after the evening meal, slumped across the sofa reading the *Daily Mirror*, his face expressionless. Sometimes he was a loud voice in the bedroom or a silhouette filling a pub doorway or a song in the night-time street. Like a privileged lodger he lived on the edge of things. But Jack loved him.

Despite his moods and sarcastic tongue he could be funny when he chose. Full of Saturday beer he would turn a belch into the long drawn-out squeal of a pig and dance around the living-

19

room table on tiptoe. Only Mrs McKenna remained aloof from these antics. Borrowing serenity from the statuette of Our Lady which stood on the sideboard she would crouch by the range and run a gull eye over the wreck she had promised to love, honour and obey.

Outside in the street the sunlight took its texture from the chimney smoke. A goods engine hooted and steam billowed and vanished above the rooftops. Cockerels were crowing. Jack dug his fingers into the neck of his old grey pullover and eased up an inch of shirt collar. Small gangs of men and boys were on their way to work. It was too early in the day for more than a nod between friends; but Winner Street had come to life soon after sunrise. Shopkeepers were sweeping the pavements outside their premises and tradesmen's handcarts rattled by. Wearing his jacket over his apron Charlie Muggridge, the greengrocer, was dressing the open front of his shop, cunningly arranging the best fruit to catch the housewife's eye. His heavy blond moustache had grey streaks in it and he was what he looked – a lady's man gone to seed but still capable of flirtation.

Welsh mutton hung outside the butcher's and Mr Butley's assistants were manhandling pigs' carcasses onto hooks in the windows. The Butleys' eldest boy with his dry cough and old young face scrubbed the doorstep, dipping the brush into the pail and contemplating the suds from the loneliness of ill-health. Jack stopped to gloat over the sausages, pork pies and faggots. Beyond his facsimile another assistant was sprinkling fresh sawdust on the floor.

'Get your snotty little beak off my window, Irish,' the butcher grinned from the doorway.

'Got any spare chops, Mr Butley?' said Jack.

'Yaas – if you've got any spare cash.'

'My uncle's the Duke of Dingle. I come into a fortune when I'm twenty-one – and that's gospel.'

'When the duke dies you can have a thousand chops.'

'Not from you, mister,' Jack laughed. 'When I'm duke I'll be wantin' the quality stuff.'

'Cheeky young sod,' Butley snorted, aiming a playful kick at the boy.

All along the street assistants were tugging down the sun shades. A couple of crows waddled among the pigeons and sparrows outside the baker's and a tramp fixed his desperate eyes on the ground as he dawdled between shops. His dirty brown face and mop of black hair reminded Jack of the fuzzy-wuzzies. When he had passed the pawnbroker's and the saddler's the dark fragrance of ground coffee wafted from the grill above Chancellor's cellars. It had the power to draw people into the Emporium. At that time Chancellor's was large and enterprising in a brash provincial style that reflected the mood of the nation. The black and white façade of the three-storey building was crowned by the proprietor's name. Sidney Chancellor was the classic entrepreneur struggling to rise to a social class he admired. Like the Emporium he was a curious blend of the old fashioned and forward-looking. Trade relied mainly on the Midland business people who took summer villas in Lanswsorthy during the school holidays. From May to September the town was full of wealthy visitors and the store pampered them.

Chancellor's sold a bit of everything – sunblinds, silks, haberdashery, fancy and women's wear, grocery and pro-visions, toys and games, china, glass and linoleum. It boasted millinery and dress counters as well as linen, hardware and soft furnishings in untidy sections rather than departments. To Jack, who had been in and out of the place ever since he could remember, it was an Aladdin's cave cluttered with all sorts of delights. Under ostentatious ceilings and gas lights which were too big, the ladies could sit on cane chairs and thumb through the pattern books or purchase the latest boas and chiffon glacé.

Jack trailed down the alley beside the stores and found most of the other stable boys and carters waiting in the yard. They slouched about among the barrels and boxes, hands in pockets, exchanging the sort of banter he relished. He knew them all. Ingratiating Albert Wotton with his slack jaw and old woman's smile never crossed words with anyone. The Dunsford brothers, Will and Harold, fancied themselves as amateur boxers while quiet Ernie Drew spent most of his free time in the pub. Walter Cooksley had gold hair and a handsome moustache but his stutter made it hard for him to keep a girlfriend.

Nearly all the stable boys were older than Jack. One, Skilly Luscombe, had less sense than a sheep, and everyone said he was 'mazed' or 'looby'. The simpleton's father was 'all beer belly and smut' as Mary McKenna put it, but his heart was supposed to be in the right place. An extravagant show of affection for horses somehow redeemed Fred Luscombe's bullying in the eyes of the sentimental working-class community. The tears would stream down his cheeks if one of the stable cats killed a squab or a sparrow. Yet the same fingers that lovingly stroked the lips of horses were said to have bunched into the first which knocked the wits out of his son. Whenever he lifted a hand Skilly jumped and the other boys giggled. Most of them were hollow-cheeked and wore cast-off clothes. Old Bob Sherwill, the senior carter, regarded them as a necessary evil and although he was a kind, religious man approaching retirement, he had little sympathy for the young. His own childhood had been a treadmill of drudgery and he thought of the boys as ill-equipped little adults needing to be broken to the harness.

Opening the back door he handed out the brooms and went from floor to floor supervising the sweeping and making sure everything was ready for the counter staff. His approval was communicated in slow nods – hence his nickname, Old Bob.

Jack enjoyed the ritualistic start to the day because he would be shut off from the horses and the sun for only a little while. The Emporium was a magnificent dead place full of dead things. Outside in the open air birds flashed and called, and the valerian on the sandstone walls was alive with bees. The song of the thrush was an echo of something in his own heart.

The scavenger's cart put up the pigeons on the corner of Midvale Road. It was pulled by one of the council's bay geldings in a standard issue straw hat. The boys stood and waited for the GWR omnibus to rumble through on its way to Totnes. Across the road a milk horse stamped and a door slammed, and from behind the privet hedge came the clatter of empty cans. Then a goods train hooted and the scent of phlox and wallflowers washed over the bitumen between the rows of brick villas. In the sky light was strengthening.

Behind Dartmouth Road, Station Lane ran parallel to the railway goods depot. It was a shambles of Victorian warehouses, sheds and yards divided by sandstone walls. Fireweed and buddleia grew on the rubble of buildings felled by neglect. Here the co-op, Great Western Railway, Lansworthy Mill and

Chancellor's stabled their horses. Most mornings over a hundred animals left the lane between the shafts of carts or wagons. The mill alone could muster thirty employed in the delivery of provender to farms as far afield as Dittisham on the other side of the River Dart.

The wooden stalls of Chancellor's stables were intersected by a gangway of scrubbed bricks and the horses faced each other over the half-doors. They peered from umber glooms where the smell of dung and harness oil was never absent. Pal, the chestnut three-year-old, had sore shoulders. He stared miserably across at the mare, Magdalene, who had just bitten Fred Luscombe and kicked one of the boys.

'Bad-tempered bitch,' Old Bob called her, and Jack kept his distance, watching the mare's nostrils dilate and her upper lip curl.

'You'm wise, boy,' growled the carter. 'Another snap of they jaws and her'll be travellin' to Germany for sausage meat.'

The other lads remained in the yard to clean the wagons and vans but Jack had horse chores. Soon he was part of the noise and bustle. The carters came staggering along the gangway, water slopping from their pails. Men were whistling, buckets clanked and the animals blew their excitement through their nostrils. Jack went from stall to stall checking the salt-licks while the horses drank and the carters sieved oats into the cribs.

Chancellor's kept a small stud of trotters and walkers to pull carts, vans and wagons loaded with a variety of goods. Mares and geldings lived under the same roof and when the fleet was ready to take to the streets the chestnuts, bays, greys and roans made a fine show. Outstanding among them were the shires with their shining black manes and great, steel-faced shoes. They were immensely strong but for all their beauty and gentleness Jack preferred the half-bred Clydesdales. Lighter-boned and cow-hocked they had the dispositions of angels. Some were the size and build of hackneys.

The horsemaster had slung the harnesses on posts between the stalls. He walked the gangway checking the progress of men and animals. His name was Tom Palfrey and he had fought in the Second Boer War. A tall loose-limbed peasant from the Dartmoor in-county he was still the sunny side of forty. Before speaking he removed his pipe and weighed his words. It was his habit to amble along but when he was harnessing a horse or backing it into the shafts he moved nimbly and quickly.

Once the animals had been watered, fed and groomed they were put in their gears and the bedding-out began. The stable boys struggled to wheel barrow-loads of soiled straw out into the yard, giggling and cursing as their boots slipped on the wet bricks. When the job was done they collected the individual nosebags and took them to the wagons. It was like a military operation but Luscombe soon reduced it to farce.

'You put the collar on Boxer, Skilly,' he said, winking at his audience. ''Bout time you earnt your wages.'

'Tidn no fuss, Dad,' the boy grinned, and he drew a sleeve over his rubbery lips. 'No sir – tidn ort.'

But the collar would not go over the gelding's head and before long whimpers of frustration escaped through Skilly's clenched teeth. It was a curious mewling sound that had most of the onlookers laughing helplessly.

'Leave off, Skilly,' Jack grinned. 'Stop pulling your dad's leg. You know it goes on upside down.'

The simpleton glanced at him, tears streaking his face and his hands trembling.

'Upside down,' Jack repeated, softly. 'Easy as winking'.

Boxer shifted from leg to leg and the swallow nestlings in the loft raised their voices while the parent birds came and went.

So the gelding got his collar and Fred Luscombe twisted it savagely around the right way before fixing the chains to the hames and buckling on the rest of the harness. Then the horse was led out and eased into the shafts.

'Next time you interfere, Irish,' the big man said, 'I'll boot your ass round the yard.'

Jack grinned and shook his head.

'Us've got a new lad startin' soon,' Luscombe continued, 'Ern Lacey's boy; and he's as handy with his fists as you are with your mouth. Step on Arthur Lacey's toes and he'll make you sing.'

'Jack,' the horsemaster called from the stable door. 'Ride with Harold today.'

'Down the coal yard,' Luscombe sneered, and Skilly guffawed and sniffled.

'Get up on the bliddy van, you,' his father barked. 'God! If

24

you idn the world's prize ornament. Get up and shut up.'

But beyond the small talk and malice there was always the incorruptible horses, and their eyes at that early hour seemed full of dreams. Scratching Boxer's nose Jack wondered where they went when they were asleep. Were they the sons and daughters of those first horses God had fashioned from the wind? Could they become part of the night breeze and know a freedom he could only guess at? Palfrey's bull terrier, with half an ear missing and its head terribly scarred from street fighting, butted his knees and pleaded for attention. He crouched and crumpled the dog's good ear. Daws spilt across the roofs and the clank of trucks carried from the shunting yard. Sparrows splashed and twittered in the water troughs.

'Get aboard, son,' Dunsford said.

'Can I take the reins?' said Jack.

'Not yet. Let's bag up and get on the road.'

'Go on, Harold – please.'

'Tidn a game, boy,' came the sharp reply. Then the carter's voice softened. 'Life's not all fun and games. You can't play at work, not here. Palfrey don't stand no messin'.'

Closing his eyes Jack could drift away from the moment. The horse's hooves beat a hypnotic rhythm and in this daydream he was sitting behind Bethlehem twitching the reins, letting the mare take the cart through the summer night. While they bagged coal in the dump next to Queen's Park he kept the dream alive. Between the scrub willow screening the dump were glimpses of sheep grazing on the sports field. He held the sack open and Dunsford shovelled in the coal. It was a dirty, tedious business in the heat and the carter's complaint was heart-felt.

'Thank Christ Chancellor's selling off this side of the business,' he grumbled. 'Palfrey says the old man don't think tez right for a department store to go in for coal delivery. Bliddy coal! I'm sweatin' like a nigger. They rich buggers ought to have a go at this caper. The only time they gets their fingers dirty is whain they stick 'em up their noses.'

'The really rich ones get the butler to do that for them, Harold,' said Jack and the carter laughed.

'Emporium, department store,' he said, sitting on a full bag and lighting a cigarette. 'Twon't make no difference to my wages though Palfrey claims us'll all be getting caps and fancy tunics when Chancellor's goes big next month. Have you seen the new premises in Victoria Street? He've bought three buildings next door to each other; the ironmongers', the boot shop and old Mother Higgs's boarding house. Still,' Dunsford murmured, 'it'll mean more horses and better prospects, I s'pose. And at least us woan have no more coal to bag.'

The sun shone from a cloudless sky. As the cart climbed the hill from the harbour to the villas above fields of flat poll cabbages Jack absently watched the yachts down on the bay. They sailed across his daydream until reality blurred in quiet confusion. Heat was rising off the road and the houses up ahead wobbled like objects seen through flames. Out of this shimmer the watercart passed them but the figure at the reins ignored Dunsford's wave. It was too hot and the working day had only just begun.

4

Then there was the going home after work, sun-flushed and pleasantly tired, wearing the day's grime like the badge of an exclusive male working-class club. At least twice a week he walked to Tor Barton to see Bethlehem and keep the bond alive. Boy and foal shared an affinity which even Trant found difficult to mock. The heatwave had broken but the summer air remained hot and sticky with little rain to wash the smells from the backyards of the terrace.

Jack returned to Lansworthy in the dusk which Devonians call 'dimpsey'. Swifts were still hawking insects while the barn owls cried across Clennon's meadows. It was strange to come back to the solid, urban world as the lamplighter set the lights chuckling into brightness from Dartmouth Road all the way up Fisher Street to the top of Angarrick Terrace and strolled on to become lost in the thickening haze. The bay had also vanished and the water had turned to smoke like the horizon.

Little figures stood under the lamp at the top of the terrace. Behind them were sixteen houses facing each other in two rows across a cobbled cul-de-sac. A hoarding nearly as high as the houses sealed off the end of the terrace and hid the junk yard and the pig that was forced to live in squalid conditions. This creature was the property of Angarrick Pig Club. In the autumn it would be killed and divided among the members.

Now iron hoops were rattling over the cobbles and screams of

27

laughter filled the dusk. Girls in grey smocks and white pinafores ran up and down or gathered near the lamp. Jack's sisters, Blanche and Lily, broke from their gang and sang out his name as they did most evenings when he came home. Dogs barked, women raised their voices to call along the terrace to each other, and cats darted from shadow to lamplight and back again. Neighbours gossiped without leaving their front doorsteps or simply stood taking the air. Then Clubfoot Charlie Emmett, who was fourteen but looked much older, took his ferret for a walk on a bit of string. The boys made lewd guesses about where it might go if the girls didn't watch out. A carthorse trotted down Fisher Street and wherever there was light the ghost moths danced. Darkness closed and shut out the rest of the world.

Number Eight was the last house on the right-hand side. From the front bedroom it was possible to look over the hoarding into the junk yard and sty and watch the pig fattening. Beyond the weeds and garbage was a sandstone wall that kept the poor out of the gardens of middle-class Grosvenor Road. Where the villas slumbered in leafy seclusion there had once been wasteland and a field or two, creating a divide which the taboos of each class had rendered unnecessary. It was easy for the Grosvenor Road residents to pretend the grubby terrace with its noise and poverty, impetigo, rickets and other awful ailments did not exist. Mutual suspicion stood higher than the wall. On the one hand was self-esteem born of comfort and complacency; on the other resentment which rarely surfaced and a sense of inferiority maintained by the absence of hope.

'Eat your supper, Jack,' said Mrs McKenna, 'and I'll get the bath ready. You look like a dervish.'

'Like a monkey,' Michael grinned.

Jack pushed his tongue down behind his lower lip, bent his knees and let his arms dangle loose.

'Mind the wind don't change,' laughed his mother.

Kevan McKenna lifted a blank face from the newspaper, feeling both excluded and neglected.

'If you weren't forever fartin' about with horses,' he taunted, 'you'd be in for your grub at a decent hour.'

'Leave the lad alone and get your head back in that paper,' snapped the woman. When he offended her she tended to go white around the lips. Their conversations rarely extended beyond an exchange of insults.

'Lend us a tanner, Mary,' he retorted, knowing it would raise her hackles.

'Oh yes! For you to piddle against the wall of the King Bill. If they paid you in stout you'd be happy.'

'I earn my beer, woman,' he yawned.

Jack and Michael exchanged grins. The bloaters came hot and dry from the oven where they had lain since early evening, but the rice pudding with a couple of tablespoonsful of condensed milk was worth waiting for. The lamp smoked on the table and Jack sat in his socks, rubbing his feet together to ease his chilblains. Kevan McKenna regarded him from baleful eyes and itched to wipe the cheerfulness off the boy's face. His afternoon nap had left him irritable.

From the scullery came the sound of water splashing into the galvanised iron bath and the husky voice of Mary McKenna singing as she always did when her chores centred on the children.

'Horses,' he said, releasing the word slowly from a sneer. 'Big, stupid brutes. Before I came down to this godforsaken hole I worked in a knacker's yard up in London. That's where they all end up – the knackers. All your Bethlehems and Boxers and Melodies; all the Co-op horses and GW horses and Chancellor's stud; down the bloody knacker's for the chop.

'They won't get Beth,' Jack said. He tilted the big brown earthen teapot and filled his mug.

'Of course they'll get her — and the rest,' said McKenna. 'Even now while she sleeps under the stars the poleaxe is waiting. One day when she's too old to earn money for Chancellor they'll put a hood over her eyes and the axe will fall and she'll shiver all over and drop with a bloody great thud.'

Jack blew into his tea.

'And they don't usually kill them straight off. They put them in a pound. Then they cut off the poor sods' manes before they lead them into the slaughtering yard for the chop. Thump goes the axe and that's that.'

'Not Beth,' Jack whispered, conscious of Michael's eyes on him.

'Why not Beth?' McKenna persisted. 'What's Mr C going to

29

do with her – give her a Christian burial? She will get the hood and the chop and they'll hook up her feet and swing her from the crossbeams like a sack of spuds. Then she'll be flayed and that lovely red and white hide you're always on about will be turned into a cab roof or something. As soon as she's peeled they'll carve off her flesh and put it to boil in the cauldrons. God! The stink is enough to make you throw up. And the catmeat man will smile and rub his hands together. A butchered cart horse can feed all the cats in Lansworthy. Nothing's wasted, Jack. There's mountains of hooves all over the place, waitin' to go to the glue makers with the skins. Who knows but we may buy a sofa one day with some of Beth's tail and mane in the stuffing.

'No, nothing's wasted. Her bones will be broken up for oil or sent away to be made into buttons. Her shoes will finish up on some other horse. Jesus, but you should see them big white nuggets of horse oil ready for the candlemaker. I don't suppose you realise that you go to bed by the light of a burning horse. One night in the future someone will carry a candle made from the oil of your precious Beth upstairs and read while her spirit just melts away.'

'Get in the bath, Jack,' Mary McKenna shouted from the scullery door. 'Take your tea with you.'

She waited until he was gone and stalked over to the table.

'God, what a big man you are,' she whispered, confronting her husband across the debris of the boy's meal. 'Why do you have to pick on him to get at me? I wish you had enough money to be out boozing every night. I wish you had a sovereign for every day of the week so you could booze yourself to death. Boozy old monster.'

McKenna sighed and returned to his paper.

'If I hear you tormentin' that boy again, God as my witness, I'll swing for you,' was the woman's parting shot.

'Tell us what he said,' Blanche pleaded from the darkness of the bedroom.

'No. Go to sleep,' said Michael. 'It would give you night-mares.'

'It would not,' the little girl insisted.

'Just tell me Jack,' Sean whispered.

'Go to sleep,' said Jack. 'No more yap.'

'Is Jack crying, Mike?' asked Lily.

'Jack never cries,' said her brother.

'Anyway,' Jack said, 'Dad didn't mean it. He made it all up.'
He stared at the ceiling.

'Why?' Blanche said.

'I don't know. Go to sleep now.'

Sleep swamped the horror. Soon he found himself floating
through one of those childhood dreams which slip the confines
of geography. It was all magic. There was the horizon and a
dusk that never totally surrendered to darkness. A light to lure,
close enough to touch yet forever out of reach. Other lights
came on and off in the bottom of the sky. They swelled and
burst and vanished; and from the depths of some darkness full
of an old reality he heard Beth crying out to him and saw the
horses emerge from the mist. He was with them, part of them,
part of the mist. The beauty of it all turned to sadness again
when he woke. Through the bedroom wall he heard his mother
saying 'No, no,' in a small, tired voice. His father's angry
rumble was followed by the sound of them grappling in the fight
she never won. 'Please, Kevan. For God's sake, no.' Then the
regular insistent creak of the bedsprings and cries that became
sobs.

Jack covered his ears and waited for the dream to rescue him.

5

Arthur Lacey was too handsome. His near perfect features, long-lashed brown eyes and brown hair found their greatest admirer in himself. He was a tall, slim sixteen-year-old whose reputation as a fist-fighter had received plenty of advance publicity from Fred Luscombe. The Laceys had moved from Abbot's Quay to Lansworthy's St Michael's Road to take over a small fish and chip shop left them by an aunt. Suddenly they were business people and Arthur boasted of his father's independence, claiming he provided a service, like the vet and the dentist. The absurdity did not escape comment.

'Visit Dr Lacey, the potato surgeon,' Jack declared solemnly. 'Let him remove the eyes from your spuds.'

For the first time since he had started work at Chancellor's stables Arthur Lacey felt he was treading close to disaster.

'Watch your lip, Irish,' he rasped.

'Or what?'

'Or I'll button it for you.'

'I thought you were an eye specialist like your dad.'

'How would you like a kick in the balls?'

Jack smiled and said, 'I'm inviting you to try.'

Old Bob intervened but from then on the two boys walked carefully around each other. When the new department store opened all it meant to Jack was more floor space to sweep and new blood in the stables.

'Us should have motor lorries,' Lacey complained. He buckled at the knees under the weight of the loaded wheelbarrow. 'Bliddy horses! They'm nort but trouble.'

'Let the old man hear you speak like that and you'll be out on your ear,' said Luscombe.

'I idn used to playin' nursemaid to a pram full of horse shit,' said the boy. 'How come Irish don't get the rubbish jobs?'

'Because he done the rubbish jobs when he was a tacker,' said Old Bob. 'He could teach 'ee a thing or two about horse management, boy. And he's a bliddy worker. You doan hear him gruntin' and groanin' like you.'

'The Irish were born dung shifters,' Lacey said. 'They'm half donkey.'

'I'm buggered if you haven't got more mouth than a cow's got fanny,' said the old man. 'It'll land 'ee in trouble one day.'

'Not with you though, gran'dad.'

'I can still scat a long streak of piddle like you. Now shift your ass before I plant my toe in it.'

Silent rain washed the perfume from the flower gardens of Grosvenor Road and spread it across the terrace. For most of July cumulo nimbus sailed over Lansworthy Bay and the horses would walk out of the showers to steam in the hot sun. During the lunch hour Jack took off Magdalene's collar and put it to dry so that it would not chafe her.

'Maggie ain't bit you yet, have her, boy?' Albert Wotton grinned, opening his piece and carving off a slice of cheese with his clasp knife. 'Her had Skilly the other day. The loob squealed louder than a maid.'

'Skilly's got such big feet,' murmured Jack. 'God! They're enormous. He comes waddlin' down the gangway like a giant duck. Poor Skilly. Arthur Lacey gives him hell.'

'It's Fred Luscombe's fault. He encourages it. Tidn natural, father baitin' son like that.'

They sat on a couple of meal bags on the wayside verge. The mare stood contentedly in the gateway feeding from her nosebag. It was a good light delivery round and horse, man and boy were happy.

'This is the life, hey Jack,' Wotton sighed. 'We'm as free as a couple of old didakais. I wouldn work in the stores for a sack of gold. Tidn natural. You've got to be out and about. Still, havin' young maids round 'ee all day idn exactly punishment. Actually speakin' to real ladies and smellin' their perfume idn what you might call hard graft. The old King's onto a good thing where the ladies are concerned. Lucky old bugger.'

'Mum thinks he's just a spoilt overfed old pig.'

'Women see things differently than us, boy. Far as I'm concerned the King's all right. Good luck to un. He likes a smoke and a drink and somethin' to warm his bed. There's ort wrong with that.'

Forgetting her nosebag Magdalene swung her head and tried to snap at the flies on her neck. The dark hedgerow trees stood within the patter of raindrops falling from leaf to leaf.

'It was thrush,' Wotton added mysteriously. He was off on one of his bewildering tangents. 'Her hoof was in a terrible state with the frog so sore her must've gone through hell every time her put weight on it. Luscombe had her for a fortnight. If he'd done his job proper he'd have spotted it and Palfrey could have cleaned it up. That's why her was bitin' everyone. Old Bob found out and fetched the vet or Maggie would be carryin' canker.'

'Horses tell you when they're sick,' said the boy. 'Their eyes tell you.'

'He didn't look. He only sees what he wants to see.'

The wheat field sloped down into the slow drift of cloud shadow. Jack and Wotton ate their lunch as the countryside glittered and sank into darkness and emerged again on the surge of sunlight. The mare stamped her feet and waited for the nosebag to be removed. Grass seeds speckled her legs. Jack stroked her flanks, recalling Melody and the foal galloping across the waves.

The road from Longcombe Cross followed high ground to the hamlet of Aish where they delivered a new mangle to Aish House. Another shower fell and forced them to shelter under their oilskins until it had passed. Then the van rolled on beneath massed leaves with the fields holding the hard gleam of sunlight.

One morning before the fleet took to the road a girl appeared at the yard with a message for the horse master. She was a junior from the store and was very self-conscious in the Chancellor 'uniform' of dark, ankle-length grey dress and white apron.

Jack guessed she was fifteen at the most, probably younger. He led one of the geldings out to the van and made a show of squaring the horse up and backing him into the shafts. Then he hooked the back-chain to the ridge bar, fixed the tug chain and coupled the breeching chain. The gelding wore a belly band to prevent the shafts from lifting. When the reins had been passed through the hame rings they were fastened to the bit and Jack told one of the other boys to hold the horse's head until the carter was ready.

It was a smooth, professional performance which the girl watched admiringly. Beside the horse Jack's smallness was exaggerated but the way he danced around the animal was impressive and attractive. He was very much the master of the situation. Sticking his thumbs in his waistcoat pocket he swaggered over to her, grinning so broadly she had to smile. Her hair was the colour of hay and a pair of large green eyes brought a startling, cat-like vitality to a face that was pretty rather than beautiful.

She rubbed the side of her nose with a fingertip and said, 'The old horse knows you'm boss.'

Jack shook his head but the grin would not be dislodged.

'No,' he said, 'Solomon and me are friends. All the horses are my friends.'

'You're Irish aren't you?'

'Irish Jack,' he said, colouring.

'Jack's a nice name. Mine's Kitty. I work up in the store.'

'And you like it?'

'Better than my last job. I was in service.' Her voice dropped. 'And that was awful.'

'Here,' Fred Luscombe bawled across the yard. 'Look at our bantam cock. Cock-a-doodle-doo, Jack. Idn her a prapper lil hen, boy. You watch him, maid – they Irish bantams be lil buggers. Don't go behind the stables with 'ee.'

Skilly's brays of laughter set the other boys going and Lacey was quick to score at Jack's expense. Sweeping off his cap in a deep bow he said, 'Is Irish botherin' you ma'am? You can't trust these foreigners. If he's said anything out of place I'll take a stick to un.'

The horsemaster emerged from one of the sheds behind the vans and ambled up to them.

'Lacey,' he said, pointing the stem of his pipe at the boy.
'Give your tongue a rest and get forking-out.'

'What about Irish, Mr Palfrey?'

'McKenna don't need tellin'. He gets on with the job.'

Lacey's mouth dropped at the corners.

'Wish I had that job, Mr Palfrey. Jawin' with maids idn going
to rupture un.'

The horsemaster's knuckles flicked his ear and Lacey
staggered and skidded on the liquid manure. Then Skilly
hooted over and over until his father told him to shut up. 'Go
and muck out, boy. I'm buggered if that idn all you'm fit for.'

Palfrey's face darkened.

The girl handed him a folded piece of notepaper.

'From the head cashier,' she said. 'There idn no reply, sir.'

Palfrey nodded, stuck the pipe back in his smile and walked
away.

'Bye, Jack,' she said and frowned past him at the other horses
as they were led out.

'Bye-bye, Jack,' Skilly cried and the rest of the lads joined in:
'Bye, Jack — goodbye sweet Jackie boy, bye-bye. Bye-bye.'

'Bloody fools,' Jack laughed.

'Irish is soft on Kitty Widdicombe,' the thin boy from Windy
Corner said derisively.

'But her wudn look twice at Boghopper with his crooked
conk,' crowed Lacey.

'I've seen better faces than your's under dogs' tails,' Jack
said, wondering how the hatred had grown between them.

'Bliddy Catholic.'

'Dung-eater.'

'Dawbake! There's more sense in a spud than you've got
between your ears, you Irish bastard.'

Jack hesitated. The blood hammered at the back of his head
and the retort froze on his lips. He knew he had reached an arid
plateau of emotion where words were redundant. Fortunately
Old Bob bustled out of the harness room barking orders, and
the carters boarded their vehicles. One by one the vans and
wagons rolled out of the yard. The jingle of harness, clatter of
hooves, the rumble and creak of wheels, and the cries of the
horsemen all faded as the fleet dispersed to join the vehicles
which were leaving the other yards. Pigeons drifted from the

roofs into the sunlight and the glare of the whitewashed walls was briefly dappled with small shifting shadows.

Sitting beside Wotton Jack looked up at the highflying gulls. He was thinking of Kitty's eyes and neat little hands. A train left the station, loosing puffs of steam. Then the old woman from the cottage by the railway crossing worked along the lane shovelling horse manure into a pail. Palfrey's dog raked its ribs with a stiff hindleg and gazed after Jack's cart. Silence closed around the stables. The fireweed swayed, swallows flickered in and out of the loft, and the pigeons settled once more on the tiles.

Kitty Widdicombe brought a marvellous charm to Chancellor's Stores. If Jack was close enough to Victoria Street during his lunch hour he paced up and down the pavement opposite the ornate cream and sepia façade, keeping well under the sunshades and praying she would appear. He was slow to realise staff used the delivery entrance at the back. Then one day Ernie Drew spent his noon break in the Crown and Anchor with the cart tucked away behind the pub. The barmaid kept him engrossed and he drank too much.

'Come back near half one, boy,' he said. 'And don't gab about this. Us've got a cushy round. All I want is a bit of time to get acquainted with the lady. I'll keep an eye on Solomon so you can run off and get yourself an ice-cream or somethin'.'

Jack climbed the wall facing the back doors and hid among the lilac leaves, but after twenty minutes Kitty had not appeared so he sauntered down to Station Square. Miraculously she was perched on the edge of the water trough under the lamp at the carriage stand, wearing a white blouse and a straw boater with a black band. And aren't all the angels jealous of her? Jack thought. Warmth rose from his stomach and took his breath away.

'Hello,' he said huskily.

Her eyes lifted full of recognition and she smiled. 'Where are your friends the horses?'

'Out and about. I'm going as far as the seafront.' Then a gush of boldness, 'Have you got time for a bit of a stroll?'

'My friends are supposed to be meeting me here. They'm over the station talking to some of the boys.'

37

'My dad works there,' Jack faltered. They stared silently at each other for a moment. 'You won't be coming down the front, then?' he said at last.

'Yes – I'd like to. Tidn no fun waitin' for they silly maids.'

'You're not walking out with anyone?'

'Mind your own business,' she giggled, lifting her arms and spreading her fingertips to straighten the boater.

They moved off slowly together.

'How come I've never seen you before?' he grinned.

'Us live at Churston and I went to school at Mary's Haven.' Like all locals she pronounced the name 'Marris-havven'.

'How d'you get home a night?'

'Bus, train. But when it's fine I walk.'

'Can I walk with you, Kitty? On the way I'd show you Melody and her foal.'

'More horses,' she laughed. 'Up the store they say you'm horse mazed.'

'One day I'm going to have my own cart and I'll take Bethlehem off old man Chancellor.'

'Who's Bethlehem? – as if I didn know!'

He told the story of the foal's birth and found himself speaking his most private thoughts, dwelling on the dream of the silver horses and the ride in the waves at Broadsands. Kitty was entirely fascinated and would stop and wait while he fumbled for the right words to colour his feelings.

He drifted along the broad, tree-fringed pavement of Lansworthy Road. At either hand were shops under dusty awnings. Old ladies gossiped over tea outside Deller's Café and younger ladies passed with a swish of gowns. How cool and elegant they are, Jack thought, letting a vision of his mother eclipse the moment. One day she would have a white dress and a new parasol and he'd take her and Kitty out in a carriage, like royalty. When Michael got a job she would have three wages coming in. Guiltily he recalled the money he was saving to buy Bethlehem. But it would bring her a new life as well as help him out of the dead end. The watercart rolled by trailing its dim rainbows.

'What you done to your nose?' Kitty asked.

'Broke it — twice. Once fallin' off a horse, the other time, fighting. Old Doctor Burgess, who died last year, was drunk

38

when he set it. That's why it's a bit skew-whiff.'

'It suits you,' she laughed and her voice softened. 'Your hair is as black as coal. Tis so black it've got a blue shine to it, like a jackdaw's wing.'

'My mother's got black hair.'

They crossed the Esplanade onto the green by Lansworthy House. Here and there were scattered groups of nannies with their prams and attendant young men in shirt sleeves. The wealthy holidaymakers picnicked at little tables on the beach. The ladies were well wrapped up, reclining in deckchairs, their parasols held against the sun.

Kitty and Jack sat on the sea wall looking across the sand to the bathing machines and tents on the tideline. Three small boys and a girl scurried along the promenade waving their shrimp nets and calling to each other in excited voices.

'A lot of rich people take the houses above the harbour,' Jack said. 'Some of them were out in India.'

'I know. They come in the store and buy all sorts of expensive things. Most of the girls hate them.'

'I don't,' he said. 'I hope they'll be my best customers when I get the cart.'

'What will you sell, Jack?'

'Fish, I expect. Fresh fish from Mary's Haven market. There's a real demand for crab, lobster and turbot. And in the slack months I'll do logs and veg. A bit of everything.'

'I can't wait to see Beth. Her sounds a little beauty.'

She slid her hand into his own and their fingers dovetailed. It was a sisterly gesture. Half a dozen donkeys carrying an assortment of children trotted along the promenade behind them.

'Would you mind if I kissed you, Kitty?' he said.

'I would,' she laughed. A gentle tug released her hand. 'I've only knowed 'ee five minutes. Do you go round kissin' all the maids?'

He shook his head and his eyes twinkled. 'The horses don't object when I kiss them.'

'I idn no horse,' she giggled, reaching out and squeezing his arm.

'But you'll come to Tor Barton with me this evening?'

When she nodded, a honey-coloured curl escaped from her

boater and fell over her brow.

'You know the Big Tree at the bottom of Fisher Street where it joins Dartmouth Road?' Jack said. 'Whoever finishes work first sits there and waits for the other. Does that suit you?'

Once more the curl bobbed on her forehead.

The evening was sweaty and the smell of the yard hung on the threat of thunder. Skilly wandered about the stables shooing the sparrows from the corn bins. Jack watered and fed the gelding and wisped him down with handfuls of straw to dry his coat. The grey horse stood hardly shifting a hoof, pricking his ears to the sounds coming from the other stalls where his stablemates were also being groomed.

Ernie Drew had brought the van back late, so drunk he could hardly walk, and certainly in no condition to stable an animal. She won't wait, Jack thought. He clenched his teeth on the misery. Cockchafers tapped against the windows and the screams of the swifts flying at rooftop level filled the yard. Solomon turned and looked at him like a great trusting child.

'Hold still, my beauty,' Jack whispered. 'Hold still.'

Beginning behind the horse's ear he kept his forearm rigid and eased the curry comb through the animal's hairs. Every so often he tapped the comb on the rear wall to shake out the dirt. In this manner he worked down the neck and body before tackling the other side and legs, patiently following the lie of the coat. He groomed meticulously according to the drill the horsemaster had developed out of his army service and own experience.

'Where's Drew?' said Palfrey's voice.

'Colic,' Jack grunted.

'And you can cope, boy?'

'Jesus, yes, Mr Palfrey. Me and Solomon are good friends.'

The horsemaster drew on his pipe and the spittle sizzled in the hot bowl.

'Colic, hey?'

'Colic, mister.'

Palfrey sniffed and said, 'We weren't encouraged to use the curry comb in the Transvaal. It was the bristle brush and bags of elbow grease. Bad days, Jack. Poor bloody Boers. They were fine men.'

40

Jack put a soft brush to Solomon's head.

'Right's right, boy,' the horsemaster yawned. 'Don't forget to clean round his eyes and nostrils.'

'I won't, Mr Palfrey.'

Oh God, he thought, she'll be walking through Waterside by now, hating me. God don't let it be like this. Let her be there.

An hour before sunset he washed the grime off his face and dashed out of the yard. But halfway up Station Lane he screwed his face into an expression of despair and stuffed his fists in his pockets. He had to go to the Big Tree, knowing the bench under the giant macrocarpa would be empty. And it was.

6

Old Bob made sure their boots were really clean before letting
them in the store. Compared to the Emporium it was palatial
and the boys and carters spoke in whispers as though they were
attending a church service rather than sweeping out. The
ground floor was divided into spacious departments beneath a
ceiling as ornate as anything the ordinary shopper could expect
to find outside a London music hall. Here the wealthy could
browse through millinery to curtains and soft furnishings with
diversions into silverware, leathergoods, trunks, bags and
haberdashery. A broad staircase led to the first and second floors
and ladies' underwear, china and glass, hosiery, silk,
sunshades, toys and games, and family goods. Beds and
bedsteads, linen, furniture and the boot and shoe department
were in the basement.

The labyrinthine splendour of Chancellor's drew a wide
range of customers from further afield than The Three towns.
All the departments were connected by speaking tubes but one
of the attractions was the cash system. Little containers whizzed
around on wires overhead carrying money to the central cash
department. It was very modern and exciting, 'a temple of West
End sophistication', the *Lansworthy Observer* proclaimed
proudly. Few West Country stores offered such a variety of
stock, and the first week's takings surprised even Sidney

Chancellor.

That morning the sweeping-out finished later than usual because one of the boys was caught stealing from the silver and electro-plate department. The police sergeant was called but when Mr Ormond Chancellor drove in from Roundham he insisted on all the boys being searched. His condescending tone might have been borrowed from an African explorer addressing the natives.

Old Bob registered his disapproval in blunt terms but one by one the boys were questioned and stripped. Sidney Chancellor hurried to the stables as soon as he was informed and tried to repair the damage done by his son. Ormond had never been popular. He was too pompous and high-handed, and his undernourished, mousy moustache bequeathed a sulkiness to a face it was easy to dislike.

'Bloody cheek,' Old Bob said, slamming the door behind him. 'Sorry about that lads. Sticky fingers idn catchin'. That bloody young fool Westmacott will get what he deserves but Mr Ormond had no right to treat 'ee like criminals.'

Yet the delay worked wonderfully on Jack's behalf. She was among the juniors in the delivery yard waiting to go to her department and polish the brass. Lacey saw Jack's face brighten and nudged Skilly.

'Romeo's at it again. When be gwain to get married, Irish? Give un a kiss, Kitty. Us won't watch.' And he broke into song:

> 'Poor little Kitty had only one titty
> to feed the baby on.'

Old Bob bunched his fist and tapped him hard on the back of the head. 'You and your big mouth, Lacey,' he said. 'You could tip a barrlowload of muck in that girt hole.'

'We'm only having a bit of fun,' said Lacey, flashing the old man a savage look. The girls were lowering their faces but their shoulders shook and Kitty's humiliation was complete.

'Bastard Irish,' Lacey hissed under his breath.

'Check they barrels over there, McKenna,' Old Bob winked at Jack. 'See if there's ort for the stables. We'll meet you back at the yard.'

'Jack's like Lazewell's stallion,' laughed Hazel Cundy. 'All he wants is his oats.'

Jack coloured and glanced at Kitty. She was kneeling now to do up a bootlace. Then they were alone and what had happened before had no relevance.

'I waited ages,' she said. 'Ages. I had to go or our mum would've played up. So I caught the bus.' Her voice broke and she whispered, 'Did you come?'

He nodded. 'Drew got drunk and we got back late – too late. I dreamt about you last night.'

Large drops of rain splattered down, drilling holes in the dust. A cloud drifted across the blue.

'I finish at quarter past eight tonight,' she said.

'Whatever happens, Kitty, I'll be at the Big Tree.'

'Promise?'

'God's honour.'

Her thin little body was suddenly graceful and as full of life and beauty as a spring flower.

The day dragged but Ernie Drew had a conscience and made sure the van was back in the yard before the rest of the fleet. Solomon was too tired to be groomed so he was watered, given a light meal and left to himself.

'I hear Lacey is bawlin' you out, boy,' Drew said, working the pump handle for Jack to swill the grime off his hands and face.

'He has a lot to say,' Jack admitted.

'And it don't worry 'ee?'

'No. No more than a horse fartin'.'

Drew laughed and ruffled the boy's hair.

The evening possessed the quality of hallucination. Thunder continued to threaten and the sultry weather persisted. An hour before sunset the heat still shimmered on the road and their boots kicked up the dust. Light streamed through the brim of her straw hat bringing a faint buttercup glow to her face. She was curious about his home and family and spoke of her own life in the farm labourer's cottage at Churston. Her cheerfulness matched his own and her enthusiasm was irresistible.

They left the road beyond the big house next to the railway line and walked into Clennon Valley. Another shower fell, forcing them under his oilskin until it had passed. She kept her face averted but her hair brushed his lips. It had a clean, soapy fragrance and her shoulder beneath the blouse was hard and warm.

Awkwardly they walked on, following the cattle creep across the watermeadows with fields of ripening oats on the hillside. A corncrake was rasping its thin croaks from the reeds.

'That old rape-scrape,' Kitty laughed. 'He's more frog than bird.'

Jack parted the willow herb, foxgloves and nettles for her to climb the bank into the lane. She gathered her skirts and looked very grown-up and feminine. A blackbird fluted its alarm through a hush full of the scent of haystacks. Where the fields met the sky partridges whirred away and Bethlehem's ears pricked forward.

The foal had heard the boy's laughter and stood alert on her long white legs at the paddock gate. Melody and Princess were also curious but Bathsheba lay under the hedge dozing in the last of the day's warmth. Slowly a great black cloud edged over Cider Mill Tor. The rickyard was deserted and bats were squeaking around the outbuildings, picking off winged insects as the falling pressure forced them down.

'Her's a little gem of a sorrel,' Kitty whispered.

'She's grown,' said Jack. 'I've had her on the bit lately.'

'Doan her play up?'

'No, she's used to it now. You just gentle her along.'

The foal laid her chin on the gate and crinkled her nostrils. Dark eyes stared from the flat white face.

'L'il dear,' Kitty murmured, trailing her knuckles across Beth's upper lip, but the foal pulled away and waggled her head.

'Come here, Beth,' Jack said softly and he held out his hands. The voice and smell belonged to a creature whose gentleness was known and sought after by the foal. She took two steps to the right and slid her face deliberately into his palms.

'I idn good enough for her,' Kitty laughed.

'Sure you are. I'm one of the family but she'll get to know you.'

'Beth's brother!' the girl said, taking off her hat and shaking free her curls. 'Will her let me stroke her now?'

'Try. Talk quietly to her.'

The other horses walked up to them and jostled for attention. They had been grazing and the regular, rolling, sideways shift of their lower jaws produced a chomp of the teeth that made the boy and girl grin.

45

'The horses up our farm have got ordinary names,' said Kitty. 'Betty, Punch, Clover, Captain. But Bathsheba and Bethlehem! They make me go all goosepimply. They'm such romantic names.'

'Kitty is romantic enough,' he said.

'Get home do! Kitty's what you call the cat. Have you got a cat, Jack?'

'No. Dad don't like them. We had one once but it pee'd on his best shirt.'

'What did he do?'

'Got rid of it.'

She leaned forward and arched her brows. 'How?'

'Brick round the neck and off the harbour wall in the dark.'

'That's awful,' she said in a small voice.

Beth bumped her muzzle insistently against Jack's chin and he caught hold of one of her ears and drew it through his fingers from base to tip.

'She likes her ears pulled. You try it.'

The honeyed language of horses drifted off Cider Mill Tor and the boy and girl felt the darkness reach across the fields. Beth's eyes held the intense light that springs from innocence but the light in Kitty's eyes was softer. The light of stars and flowers and oceans lit her face although the sun had vanished. Thunder growled and rain began to fall. Another boom ended with a hissing crack and a whine as if the bottom of the sky had exploded. The horizon was trembling. Then lightning played on the darkness and rain hissed into the grass and packed foliage.

Now the foals were galloping wildly round the paddock, heads thrown back and eyes bulging. Everytime the lightning flashed and the thunder clapped they whinnied. Then Bathsheba's feet slipped on the wet grass and she crashed onto her side where she lay kicking her legs. For a moment the rain seemed alive with the huge, grey shapes of horses. They reared and plunged and sent their neighing across the noise of the storm.

'Get in the linhay,' Jack shouted. The gate swung open at his second attempt to free the latch.

'You're soaked,' Kitty cried from beneath the oilskin.

The dark haze of rain bent the foxgloves and hammered into Jack's clothes. Bathsheba was up again and part of the melee,

46

but Iona had gone to the linhay and the mares were calling to their young.

Jack took up a position by the top hedge, afraid the foals would bolt into the ditch. During one of the lulls Bethlehem separated him from the flotsam of her fear and approached quivering. The hands on her neck were firm and the voice breathing in her ear was comforting. Bathsheba joined her and clutching their manes Jack led them to the linhay as another rumbling explosion rocked the hill.

'Poor little things,' Kitty said.

The mares came into the deeper darkness under the roof. The rain drummed and rattled on the tiles and gusted between the stone pillars of the open-sided building. Drops beaded the animals' bodies.

He grabbed a handful of straw and began rubbing Bethlehem down. Kitty needed no encouragement to help dry off Bathsheba.

'Wish I had a farthing for every time I've done this,' she grinned, and Jack gave her one of his broadest smiles.

'You'm like a drowned rat,' she said softly.

He took off his cap and ran his fingers through his hair. He could not say what he wanted to say. The sky was brightening and the thunder was suddenly mufflled and the storm moved on. Then the rain ceased and the wind was shaking the spent downpour off the chestnut trees.

They finished wisping down the foals and turned their attention to the mares. The light of sky gleamed once more on leaves and grasses, and the patter of raindrops across the rooftiles set the horses jumping. Trant came up the paddock with the farmer and Arthur Maddock.

'What's on then, Irish?' the carter said. His small, inquisitive eyes strayed from boy to girl and back again, repeatedly. But his voice was friendly and despite his nature he let his appreciation show.

'We brought the animals in out out of the rain, mister,' said Jack. 'I was showin' Kitty the foals when the storm broke.'

'Lucky you were about, boy,' the carter said. 'I was down yonder with the farrier. The bullocks got out and us had a hell of a job catching 'em what with the thunder and lightning.'

'Are you one of Charlie Widdicombe's maids from

47

Churston?' Maddock enquired. 'Does your father work for Ted Avinall on the big estate?'

She nodded.

'He'll be wondering where you'm to. You'd best see her down the lane, Irish,' he added, measuring the boy with his glance. 'I won't forget what you did for the horses.'

Arthur Maddock grinned.

'Rub down they mares,' said his father. 'And try to pretend you idn daft.'

Mrs Trant was at the gate, her shawl pulled round her shoulders and her head turned away, unwilling to meet Jack's eyes.

'She doesn't like me,' he said.

'Her doan like anyone. Her and that girt lump.'

They came down the lane, jumping the puddles.

'Mum will have a fit when her sees the state of my dress.'

'You couldn't help getting caught in the storm.'

'That ornament Arthur Maddock'll tell,' she said miserably. 'Mother don't like me walkin' out with boys. Her says I'm too young.'

Jack searched for words but found none. Kitty caught his hand and squeezed it.

'I idn too young, Jack. I'm fifteen in September.'

'You're older than me,' he smiled.

They splashed into a glittering nightfall. The pale greenish light of glow-worms shone from the hedge bottoms and silence closing in had a sad ache to it.

'Wednesday's my half day,' she said.

'You're lucky. Look, Kitty' – on emotion that washed away clumsiness – 'I'd like to meet you every night and walk you home.'

'You'd soon tire of it,' she laughed. 'If you really think I'm worth it we could see each other Wednesdays, Saturdays and Sundays. The other days I'm nearly always dead on my feet.'

'Like now?'

'No. Today was special and I doan have many special days. Being with you is fun. Most of the other girls think Lacey's the cat's whiskers but he idn. He's full of himself like that young Mr Ormond – him and his soft white woman's hands. He's always touchin' us. God, he makes my flesh creep.'

Her eyes met his own and the fair lashes descended.

'I finish early Saturday,' he said.

'Saturday's late turn,' she sighed.

'But we could have some chips and I could come home with you on the train.'

'You idn just sayin' that, Jack?'

'No,' he said solemnly.

'Mum and Dad go down the pub Saturday nights,' she continued.

'And Sunday?'

'Don't you go to church or Sunday School?'

He shook his head. 'Lately I've been givin' it a miss.'

'You won't go to Hebn,' she laughed.

'The Blue Hungarian Band is playing in the main shelter on Lansworthy Green Saturday night.'

'I've never heard them,' said Kitty. 'I can see you after dinner on Sunday. I'll come into town on the 2 o'clock bus.'

'I wish every day was Sunday.'

'So do I. I didn use to but now . . .' She let the sentence go unfinished in a sigh.

The wet road was deserted and they stood alone at the bus stop.

'And you liked Beth?' said the boy.

'I loved her. Wouldn it be nice if she was ours, Jack? Us could ride off somewhere wonderful on your cart.'

'You and me and Beth.'

She narrowed her eyes and inhaled slowly through her nostrils.

'I'm glad we met.'

'So am I,' he said.

'You can kiss me if you want to,' she said, taking off her hat and holding up her face, eyes and mouth firmly closed. Jack wrapped his arms around her, planted the kiss and held her close. She responded briefly before placing her hands on his chest and gently pushing him away.

'Your shirt's wet through and you'm shaking,' she whispered. 'If you don't get to bed you'll have pneumonia.'

'I'll run home when the bus has gone.'

They kissed again and her own frail little body was quivering too, and the colour had risen in her cheeks.

49

A blackbird was singing but the lowing of cattle on Sugar Loaf Hill died to a hush. The wind dropped and the sea turned to glass. Then the last bus came and departed with her on the top deck, waving until the bend hid her from view. Running home his body came alive. Overhead the stars flared away and the moon sent his shadow flowing before him. The trance was complete: stars, moon, puddles of light, the rise and fall of his feet. He was not running at all. He was gliding along keeping faith with something older than language, like the horses God had conjured from the wind.

The children circled the hurdy-gurdy at the top of the terrace, laughing and chatting as music filled the dusk. Behind the hoarding the pig was grunting to itself and gleams of rosy lamplight lit the back windows. Jack fastened the top button of his Norfolk jacket and straightened his tie.

'You're late out this evening, Jack,' said Mary McKenna. 'And I can't remember the last time I saw you with your hair brushed.'

'He's sweet on Kitty Widdicombe,' Michael blurted.

'Who's she when she's at home?' frowned the boys' mother.

'A little scrap of a thing from Churston,' Michael said. 'She works at the store.'

'And you're sneaking off to meet her now,' Mary McKenna went on, half mockingly.

Jack laughed. 'I'm not sneaking. I'm walking.'

'You're too young to be courtin' the girls,' she said in a voice suggesting the contrary. 'Those Chancellor hussies are on the road to ruin showin' their ankles like them scarlet women who hang around the King.'

'King Piggy the VIIth,' Sean giggled.

'Eatin' chips with a nice girl at Dimeo's won't have me sproutin' horns. But if it's sin I can always go to confession and ask God's forgiveness. Sorry, Lord – I have sinned. I ate chips with Kitty Widdicombe.'

'With or without scribbles?' Michael said gravely, referring to the little crisp pieces of fried batter the children prized as much as their chips.

'Well, you are growing up Jack,' his mother sighed and her fingers swiftly raked his hair. 'That's better. I can't bear you

50

looking so damned neat and tidy.'

When he had gone she told the boys not to mention Kitty to their father.

'The old bugger would make Jack's life hell if he found out,' she said.

The mirror confirmed things she was half way to accepting. Only her eyes and hair held shadows of their former beauty. And himself was out boozing in his new coker! A bloody watch chain slung across his waistcoat but no watch in the pocket. That had gone just before last Christmas to the pawn shop. Whenever the holidays came around Kevan McKenna made up 'a bundle for uncle', most of which was never redeemed. Holidays were heavy booze days. It was all worry, and now Jack was chasing the girls. A chill touched her heart at the thought of a stranger taking her place. It wasn't fair – all the sacrifice and love and someone else gets the lad while I age and slip into the background. No longer a marvellous, perfect soul deserving worship, but a jealous, heartbroken old creature. There ought to be a knacker's yard for worn-out neglected mothers.

But the mood soon passed and she was singing when Blanche and Lily ran in off the street.

Chips, peas and scribbles became a regular feature of their Saturday nights, although if it was too warm they settled for ice cream from the hokey-pokey cart. But those first Saturdays in the steamy little café up Winner Street past Lansworthy Mills' shop, the smell of boiled pigs knuckles wafting around them, were particularly cosy and intimate. They drank ginger beer and chattered like long-established lovers, sharing secrets and hopes, joys and sorrows with a candour maturity prohibits.

Over the road the pub doors and windows were open and men were singing. The warm, malty fragrance of beer drifted on the night air.

'It'll rain when the fair comes,' Kitty said. 'It always does on Regatta.'

'Not this year.'

Keeping a little apart they strolled along Palace Avenue into Victoria Street. Kitty looked up at Chancellor's and said, 'I wish Monday would never come.'

'Are you unhappy there?'

51

'No – of course not. It's a bit boring but a thousand times better than being in service. That was terrible. Awful. They treated me worse'n a donkey. All that cleaning, polishing, mending and lugging till I was asleep on my feet, dog-tired and too miserable to cry.'

Blind to everything except each other a pair of lovers stepped from a shop doorway.

'At first it was exciting, going to work in the Big House. But those people,' she shivered. 'They pretended we was invisible. His Lordship was the worst. My dad grinds his teeth when he doffs his cap to that nasty old man. The ladies who shop in our store usually give me a smile. Tidn bad, I suppose.'

'What would you really like to do?'

'Something worthwhile. I wish I knew more about things. They didn teach us much at school, but I wanted to learn.'

Then she smiled into his face. 'I'd like to be married to you, Jack. Us would do lots of exciting things together.'

There was a dance at Deller's Café and the strains of a waltz crept up Lansworthy Road. Behind the gold glowing curtains the silhouettes sailed by like the ghosts of some impossibly distant adult world. Other children sat on the wall outside, watching and listening.

'We'll go there one day,' said Jack.

A chaffeur-driven motor car cruised down the street and nearing the green they could hear more colourful music. The Blue Hungarian Concert Band was coming to the end of its rendering of 'Fingal's Cave'. Jack and Kitty sat on the wall overlooking the beach. Lovers lay embracing on the sand and laughter carried across the water. The lights of steam yachts and cargo ships anchored in the bay shifted to the pulse of the ocean. She turned and smiled at him. Her lips still tasted of salt and vinegar. Now the concert band was playing something romantic and foreign which put her in mind of rose gardens and nightingales. Jack was riding the sorrel mare. His sabre flashed and he looked so handsome in the uniform of a Hussar Officer. Right out of the kiss he galloped to snatch her up and carry her off to a thrilling new life.

7

Most Sunday mornings the Salvation Army band marched down Fisher Street and stopped at the entrance to the terrace as if that particular neighbourhood needed redemption more than sleep. The thump of the bass drum drove Mrs Endacott wild and she would send her gormless thirty-year-old son, Moony, out to disrupt proceedings. But Moony liked the music and would caper round the players singing snatches of hymns, his heavy, blue-jowled face one vast beam of pleasure.

Mrs McKenna and Jack's brothers and sisters went to sung Mass in the chapel of the seminary for young priests at the top of St Mary's Hill. She was tired of trying to persuade Jack to attend although the priest's constant references to his absence were aggravating. But if religion did not offer solutions to her personal problems it was a consolation. The service resurrected girlhood days which had not opened and closed in despair.

The small Catholic community rejoiced in its geographical ascendancy over the Anglicans. The chapel sat on the hill amongst fields with the white statue of the Virgin gleaming on its rooftop as close as possible to God. Leaving the grounds for the walk home the congregation gazed across the houses to the tower of the parish church. The town had grown up around this old building and the streets close at hand carried clues to their origin in their names: Winner Street (Vineyard Street), Church

Street, Well Street. The newer parts of Lansworthy lay towards the railway and the seafront.

From Cider Mill Tor the white statue of Our Lady was visible against the haze of Abbot's Quay. Standing on the tor Jack could hear the parish church bells ring out to answer the bells of Collaton, Stoke Gabriel, Churston and Mary's Haven. The slow drift of cloud and cloud shadow were elements of the Sabbath calm. Flocks of small birds shrilled above the ripening grain where young swallows hunted. Great dark elms presided over the patchwork of silver and tawny fields.

Immediately below the rock the grass was full of poppies and when he called, the horses cantered through the red flowers. The mares and foals had been put in with the farm horses. They milled around the tor until he jumped down to pet them. Bethlehem bowed her head so that he could pass his comb through her mane and speak softly to her. Then Melody intruded and her nose had to be scratched. All the animals wanted attention but Bethlehem pursued him, speaking with her eyes. And when she rolled in the grass the geldings joined her, their thrashing hooves severing the poppies and scattering them like drops of blood.

He carried the image home.

'Father Tynan is worryin' me to death,' said Mrs McKenna. She drew her upper lip down over the lower one and sighed. 'I want you at Mass next Sunday and I swear I'll get your dad to kick your ass up the road if you object. It's bad enough having one godless brute for a lodger.'

'Will it really make you happy, Mum?' he smiled.

'Yes,' she replied and unpinned her hat and laid it carefully on the table.

'The parable of the prodigal, Jack. Home to God. I can't keep makin' excuses every time you mooch off. You can't be lookin' after horses every Sunday.'

'But I never left God. He made the horses and I was with them just now. He's everywhere and everything.'

'Then you won't mind meeting Him up the hill once in a while.'

Michael grinned. The other children were quarrelling in the scullery. The smell of the roast cooking in the oven always made Sunday a warm lazy day.

'It will make me happy, Jack,' she added with the hardness gone from her voice. 'I can't look the Father in the face. He's expectin' you at the seminary this afternoon for a chat.'

'Then he'll be disappointed.'

'By God he won't!'

'By the Mother of God, he will.'

'It's more important for you to traipse off with that little Widdicome wench?'

'It is – Father Tynan isn't like a proper priest. He's English and he makes me feel uncomfortable.'

'God's listening, Jack.'

She unbuttoned her coat and draped it over the back of a chair.

'Does He want me to speak up?'

Her hand caught him hard on the side of the head. 'You won't blaspheme in this house, lad. And you'll go up that hill this afternoon even if I have to drag you on a lead like a dog.'

'I'd rather see him now.'

'Well you can't. He's with the Marist Sisters.'

'The nuns wouldn't mind.'

'Jesus! You're so bloody wilful! But you'll be up the seminary, two o'clock sharp.'

'I may be a bit late. One of the horses is sick and I promised old man Chancellor I'd look in on her.'

'You'll come to church when I'm dead I suppose – and you are puttin' me in the grave, you and him upstairs.'

He met Kitty's bus and left her to wait for him on a bench in Victoria Park while he ran to the seminary. Father Tynan was out in the walled garden among the soft fruit cages and plum trees. A fresh fall of rain had left its scent on the dry earth.

The most unpleasant characteristics of age had been distilled to caricature in the priest. His speech was slow and measured and folds of tired turkey flesh couched his eyes. The old man's eyebrows had collapsed and his cheeks sagged. It was a face registering the pain of trying to pin down a thought and translate it into words. The conversation became a monologue and might have gone on all afternoon if the boy had not promised to attend the next sung Mass.

'I'd have promised to tear out my toenails just to escape and

55

get back to you,' Jack said.

'You woan get, you know — whatever it is?' said Kitty. 'What the Pope did to Henry VIII.'

'No,' he laughed. 'I won't get excommunicated.'

'Can Catholics marry Protestants, Jack?'

'Some do,' he said.

Her eyes rolled and from a conspiratorial whisper she said, 'Idn religion boring? And Sunday school! No one ever laughs in church. Tis all so glum.'

'I did once. Father Tynan fell over trying to get up from the altar and reminded me of Dad when he was pokin' the fire after a bellyful of beer. He tipped and nearly stuck his head in the flames.'

'What happened when you laughed in church?'

'In the chapel up there. Everyone looked and my mother tanned my ass till it was like a bit of raw liver when she got home.'

'You're a wicked one, Jack. The devil has got his eye on you.'

A ladybird landed on her cheek and he flicked it off.

'The world's full of lovely things and funny things,' he said. 'And most of the time I seem to be the only one who sees them.'

After tea he walked her home as far as Windy Corner and kissed her good night. The breeze died to a hush broken by his footfalls. Turning once he found her waving and for a moment the evening was cheerless. Solitude had a way of making him look into himself but he was unwilling to succumb to the mood. He thrust his hands in his pockets and thought of Beth while his depression faded and he returned to the moment. A buzzard swung down the coombe that ran through oaks and ash to the sea. Then a dozen or so gulls passed in a silent file overhead.

The lane carried him between fields of wheat and cabbages into dusk. High up where the blue deepened swifts were shrilling, and coming over the brow of the hill to begin the descent into Waterside Jack saw the lights of Lansworthy and Abbot's Quay. The air was soft and warm, and clouds of gnats hung between the hedges.

Dusk possessed an unnatural calm. Birds and farm animals were silent and still, and once again his mind was flying before him to Cider Mill Tor. The horses would be standing there, watching the stars grow out of haze. His pace quickened. Across the coombe lanterns shone from the yard of Tor Barton Farm and he could hear men's voices.

Maddock, his son Arthur, Trant and a labourer were rounding up some bullocks which had stampeded into the spaces between the outbuildings and were blocking the lane leading to the paddock. Jack ran up the hill towards the cider mill and headed off a couple of strays. By the time he had driven them back to the yard everything seemed to be under control.

'Did 'ee see Beth?' Maddock growled.

Jack shook his head, looking from man to man.

'Her's away up yonder somewhere – thank's to that bliddy ornament.' The farmer swung his stick at Arthur. 'Drove the bullocks like one of they bliddy cowboys – whoopin' his head off. And early on he went and left the paddock gate open. Beth and Sheba was in the lane. Us got Sheba but Beth must be halfway to Stoke Gabriel by now.'

Lantern light twinkled on Arthur's buck teeth. He was grinning to cover his embarrassment but the farmer's stick rattled on his skull and fetched up a yell of agony.

'I'll find her,' Jack said, crouching to take off his boots. His stomach heaved.

'Take a head halter, boy,' said Maddock. 'Soon as I've saddled one of the mares I'll follow 'ee. Her woan go far.'

Beth ran to the crossroads the other side of the mill and stopped. Panic no longer gripped her and already she was missing her mother. The lane behind her led back to all that was familiar and secure but as she was about to turn towards home a mongrel came hurtling out of a nearby cottage garden to snarl and snap around her legs.

Beth galloped along the Mary's Haven Road towards Tweenaway and, meeting some labourers who had been drinking cider, bolted down to Yalberton. Pacing nervously in the direction of Stoke Gabriel she had a confrontation with the motor bus and went racing off into a side lane that led to the hamlet of Aish. By now she was totally disorientated and frightened. The tops of the hedges arched to entwine and create a tunnel of foliage. Then it opened suddenly onto a narrow road and she was trotting uphill under pine trees. Three children hurried from a wayside house and tried to trap her against the garden wall, but Beth swerved and swung onto a cart-track. She was lathered and miserable. The starry sky showed in blinks between branches and leaves. Cattle lowed, ghost moths fluttered about her head. The night was hostile.

Jack received directions first from the drunks, then from a woman who had left the Stoke Gabriel bus at Yalberton. The children at Aish giggled when he came padding up the lane in his bare feet, clutching the halter, but he got the information he wanted and set off down the track which led to the duck marsh and the River Dart.

The fragrance of the countryside washed over him. Every so often he trod on a stone and winced, stumbled and hobbled on. Near Aish Farm the track was blocked by a timber wagon. To the left a footpath followed the edge of the marsh and soon he was lengthening his stride in the dew-drenched grass where the smudges of fresh hoofprints could be seen.

Long before Jack reached Aish, Beth was trotting along the path beside the marsh, starting whenever a duck flopped down into the reeds among the shallows. Before her the hills were silhouetted black against the sky. On each side the valley climbed wooded slopes to the glow of twilight. Where the path met the river and swung abruptly downstream it was blocked by cattle. To Beth's right was a sluice, steeply banked with mud and fed by a narrow stream that flowed into the river. Beyond it was Aish Quay and the hulk of an old sand barge. Beth slithered down the bank and the mud oozed around her hocks. Desperately she splashed through the stream to find herself in deeper mud and struggling to free herself she keeled over on her side. A final effort left her with hind legs submerjed and her body at an awkward angle, neck and head held rigidly clear of the morass. A whinny faded to a snuffle of despair. Then she lay motionless, breathing deeply, before the next jolt of panic had her thrashing about.

The moon was rising above the hills on the far side of the Dart as Jack reached the sluice. Cattle walked up to him inquisitively, but he had seen Beth and squelched down the bank to join her. She looked at him, the mud caking around her lips and nostrils.

'What have you been up to, my little darling?' he whispered.

The mud was cold and thigh deep. He crouched and floundered through it. Beth's neck arched and she ran her

58

tongue over her muzzle. For a gut-constricting moment he thought they were in quicksand but he managed to reach her and wrap his arms round her neck, swallowing his fear.

'Lie still,' he murmured, putting the halter on her head and knowing with a sinking of the heart that he would not be able to drag her clear. All he could do was stand there holding up her head until help arrived. It was a chilling prospect.

Ten minutes later he realised his strength would give out and he began to yell for help, but no one came and presently he fell silent. Trying to pull Beth up the bank was an idea he quickly rejected. Then on a sudden surge of horror he noticed that the stream seemed to have stopped flowing and had become a little wider. The tide was coming in.

'Mother of God preserve us,' he breathed. He would have to leave her and go for assistance while she was still able to keep her head out of the mud. But no sooner had he released the halter and turned to go than Beth was snuffling in alarm. A dreadful slow motion crawl brought him to the stream.

'And would I leave you?' he grunted, looking over his shoulder. 'I never will. Never.'

The mud on the stream bed was ankle deep and his feet were slipping on slimy pebbles. Relief brought the savage half-snarl, half-smile to his face. He splashed upstream until the channel shelved to deeper water. The bank beyond was gentle and grassy.

Returning to Beth he stood over her and said, 'Get up girl, come on, now. Come on. Up, up.'

The foal's front legs beat at the mud and her body twisted and heaved.

'Up, Beth. Come on, girl – you can do it. Come on, my darling.'

He tugged the halter rope but she sank back again unable to free her hind legs. Once more his command drilled through her distress, and she rolled onto her back, right over until she was standing. Before she lost her balance as the mud sucked at her limbs he jerked her head around and she managed a couple of awkward steps and flopped onto her side. His voice inspired immediate response and the next staggering bound brought her almost to the water's edge. Now the mud was shallower and a high stepping action of the legs sent Beth crashing into the stream. Jack took her head in his hands. She was quivering and the moonlight touching her muddy coat gave it a metallic sheen.

'Good girl,' the boy smiled.

Beth regarded him from a gaze that was no longer perplexed. Although she was cold, wet and dirty she had lost her fear, and her trust in Jack was absolute.

He led her into the flood water that was brackish and together they swam to the bank and clambered out. Then he ran before her holding the rope and making her trot to get warm until they reached a linhay below Aish Farm. Here he ripped up some old meal sacks for cloths to dry her off, and there was enough straw piled in the corner to twist into wisps. His own discomfort was ignored in his anxiety to prevent her catching cold. When the grooming was over he stripped and tied a meal bag round his waist like a kilt.

Beth shivered in spasms so he made her lie down in the straw and covered her body with sacks. Then he curled up beside her, close enough to take her breath on his face. Her eyes were open and they held some of the moonlight which crept through the doorway. Her breathing was easy, regular, and she had stopped shivering. Outside an owl called. Jack closed his eyes, thinking of the Celtic warriors who lay down in the ferns with their horses in that far off time when men were more animal than human. And he was with his horse, and what was to be was the great adventure they would share together.

The following Wednesday the Venners of Number Fifteen lost their young daughter Florence. She died of tuberculosis and the curtains were drawn in all the terrace houses until she was buried. There was no laughter on the cobbles after dark for many evenings. Moony Endacott, who had worshipped the thin, mousy-haired little girl, was inconsolable. He sat on the front doorstep with his head in his hands, rocking back and forth. The pair of black funeral horses stamped and blew while the coffin was brought out to the hearse. It was a plain unpolished coffin bearing two simple wreaths. The women and children followed it to the cemetery and Moony's wailing sent tears rolling down faces which hard-living had set firm and seemingly impervious to sorrow.

Shortly after the funeral Wotton and Jack brought the smart

blue van to Sidney Chancellor's villa on Roundham Head overlooking the harbour and the bay. Chancellor's eldest grand-daughter was soon to be married and the van was loaded with a variety of fancy goods, ranging from passementerie to bales of silk. Carrying the items up to the tradesmen's door was a lengthy business, for the back gardens were vast.

The white-pillared portico of Morning House caught the sun which was breaking through the thinnest of sea mists. Moisture glittered on the lawns. The black gabled house with its mullioned windows, tall chimneys and pointed tower, faced east – hence its name. Chancellor had added a conservatory full of grapes, orchids, tropical flowers and climbing figs to the south side. A hedge of macrocarpa and beech protected the lawns and flower gardens from the winter winds. In the centre of the largest lawn was a flagpole around which the Chancellors, their guests, an assortment of children and dogs, and a pony were gathered. Bees thrummed on the scent of honeysuckle.

This was the scene that greeted Jack after the housemaid had told him the master wished to see him. The boy wiped his hands on his apron and stuffed his cap in his trouser pocket so he would not have to lift it to fools like Ormond Chancellor.

'Come over here, Jack,' Mr Sidney said warmly.

Years later when Jack pieced together the incident it seemed everything had been orchestrated to embellish the girl's beauty. A faint mother-of-pearl luminosity flowed over her pink dress. Her straw hat was trimmed with flowers and tied at the chin with a pink ribbon. Masses of glossy brown hair tumbled over her shoulders as she extended an arm and patted the pony's nose. The well-dressed boy clutching the reins smiled indulgently. Jack recognised him as Ormond Chancellor's young son, Rupert. Boys and girls of similar age looked on while their parents stood a little apart. The Daubenys from the villa next door were visiting their neighbours.

Sidney Chancellor beckoned Jack and added, 'Have a look at the pony – a good look.'

The boys whispered among themselves, eyeing him as they might have inspected an unusual animal. Their light summer flannels and air of refinement made him uneasy. For the first time in his life he was conscious of his poverty. Even his sunburnt face and arms set him apart, like a bloody redskin, he

61

thought, dragged down from the hill to amuse the white men. But there was something about the girl in the pink dress that he had detected in a few of the juniors at Chancellor's, an animal sexuality, blatant and self-absorbed.

'Miss Daubeny's father is considering buying the mare. It's the young lady's birthday tomorrow.'

Jack nodded and stole another glance at the girl.

'Would you buy the pony?' Chancellor persisted.

'I would not, sir.'

'Why?' the girl demanded.

'She's a bit cock-throttled and goes back at the knee.'

'What!' She uttered a dry little laugh and wrinkled her nose like a cat sneezing.

Mr Daubeny turned enquiringly to Chancellor.

'The brute's got a neck like a fowl,' said the old man. 'It's not pronounced but Irish Jack would spot it instantly.'

'And she does go back at the knee,' Daubeny murmured, frowning at the slightly concave joints.

'Well, I still think she's gorgeous,' the girl said peevishly.

'Isn't that the best reason for having her?' Jack grinned.

An embarrassed silence greeted the remark.

'Run along then, Jack,' said Sidney Chancellor.

The boy coloured and grinned down at his boots for a moment before departing.

'I do wish you'd stop showing off McKenna, father,' Ormond said. 'You parade him like a clever ape.'

'Because I like him. He's got tremendous spirit and he lives for the horses. What does Helen think of him?'

He smiled but the girl in the pink dress could not conceal her displeasure.

'His fingernails were dirty,' she said. 'Is he a gypsy or something?'

'Irish,' laughed her brother Edward.

'Aren't they all the same?' the girl said.

'The Irish certainly have a way with the animals,' Mr Daubeny admitted. 'When we were in India the Irish troopers practically talked fluent horse.'

'Yet they have such difficulty with the King's English,' Ormond observed.

'Does all this mean you'll not buy the pony, father?' Helen

said. 'Oh that horrid boy! He's so ugly and my pony is beautiful.'

'And cock-throttled,' smiled Edward.

'Cock-throttled or not I love her,' his sister exclaimed passionately.

'Then she's yours, Helen,' Mr Daubeny said and the girl flung herself into his arms.

'Come down the yard one morning, Helen,' said old Mr Chancellor. 'We have some fine shires. Or better still I'll get McKenna to show you our little red roan foal up at the farm. She and the boy have struck up a close relationship. My head carter speaks very highly of the lad.'

'And Trant isn't exactly generous when it comes to praising a fellow creature,' Rupert Chancellor said. 'But I'm with you, Grandfather, McKenna is a strange little Arab, very likeable and genuine.'

'Horses are delicious,' Helen sighed. She was radiant and excessively spoilt, Rupert decided.

Bethlehem stood in a daydream. The gnats swarmed around her head and contentment flooded her eyes. Trant also handled her gently but although his voice was calm there was never any love in it. The sudden, erratic flight of a butterfly across her face set her nerves jumping and she shifted sideways. But Jack was crooning and closing her eyes she saw the small white horseboy rolling in the water. Arching her neck she turned and looked at him. His fingers untangled the feather fringing her hooves. Then he was pressing his lips together to make soft, mewing noises. The evening grass whispered around them and for a moment she felt the cold mud drag at her legs as the past hardened to clarity in her mind. It was like drifting out of her body and looking down upon herself. There were the banks of the sluice gleaming under moonlight and the foal Bethlehem was thrashing about with the fear returning on a knife edge. But the horseboy always came to lead her back to the good place and the good times.

Now another memory rose to cancel out the image of mud, and she was no longer afraid. Again the moon shone through the linhay door and every time she woke he was lying beside her, calm and still in the straw.

63

The halter and bit were part of the game they played. He would click his tongue and she would trot. When he murmured 'hold-to' she paced slowly about, champing on the bit but feeling no need to fight it. The harness had been presented to her by the boy who came across the hush of sunset to groom her. The comb with the broad teeth separated the hairs of her mane and tail while light faded and the world blurred. Then the valley would vanish under mist and darkness which brought the scents of the countryside into full life.

Always at that hour Bathsheba sought her out and on calm nights they gazed over the bay waiting for the magic to begin. And Jack would often join them. The shift of the stars played upon his mind. All the constellations were reduced to mere glow-worms by unimaginable distance. He felt things in the blood, nameless things which the horses shared. The moon edging up from the sea was always huge and artificially bright. Bethlehem stared at it, hardly breathing. Everything but the moon vanished from her consciousness. Beyond the radiance boy and foal knew something was waiting. Maybe it was a place or just a feeling, an intense joy like love. They would recognise it when they were part of it.

8

Rain gusted across the stooked corn, then the easterlies produced a settled spell and wasps clung to the apples where the trees bowed under Cider Mill Hill. Out of the wind it was very hot. The smell of the pigsty at the top of the terrace was overwhelming and the people who would soon be eating the animal were its strongest critics. 'That stinking pig' became a catch-phrase for frustration or irritability.

'You hardly ever go out with your brothers,' Mrs McKenna said, hooking herself to Jack's arm and noting how he had grown.

'Sean and Mike get on fine without me,' he said.

They strolled down Winner Street chased by the echoes of sung Mass. Blanche skipped along the pavement clapping her hands to lift the sparrows and pigeons from the grain-litter outside the stores of Lansworthy Mills.

'I like doin' things alone,' the boy continued.

'Or with that girl,' his mother said. She puckered up her face.

A motor car full of laughing young people swung out of Palace Avenue and roared past them leaving the dust swirling.

'Off on a jaunt,' Mrs McKenna said. 'When are you going to take me on a jaunt, Jack? It would be nice to get out of this hole for a change.'

'One day I'll take you out in a carriage, Mum. I will. On my life I will.'

His sincerity amused her and she smiled. 'The only coach ride I'll get will be the black one.'

Then seeing the hurt on his face she squeezed his arm.

Fisher Street ran under high-walled gardens and fruit trees.

'That stinkin' pig,' sighed Mary McKenna. 'You can smell him a mile away. Well,' she added, 'I suppose you'll be off to see the ladies.'

'What ladies?' Michael cried over his shoulder.

'Melody, Bathsheba and Bethlehem, and all the other four-legged lovelies.'

'I've never seen an ugly horse,' said Jack. 'Even the old, worn-out ones are beautiful.'

'But do horses think so?' said Mary McKenna. 'Maybe some of them think Beth is ugly.'

'They don't have a beautiful and an ugly,' the boy said. 'They're in a state of grace. Horses aren't vain like us.'

'Because they've got no minds or souls.'

'They know who's kind and who's not. They hate pain and love fine weather. When you turn them loose they run to each other and gallop around together. And they get lonely like we do. Perhaps they see things we can't see. Sometimes it's in their eyes, like you're lookin' into one of those peep shows.'

'Do they go to heaven?' Blanche asked.

'I don't know,' Jack smiled. 'If heaven's all hymn singin' and prayin' and no horses I don't want to go.'

'God – if you're not a throwback to your Great Uncle Michael,' laughed Mrs McKenna. 'He could turn most things into poetry and he knew all about the past when no one spoke English. He was forever on about talkin' horses, birds, heroes and stuff.'

'Most of the time they keep quiet,' the boy said.

Sean wrinkled his nose. 'That old pig smells somethin' awful.'

'Don't blame the animal. It's probably your father,' said Mary McKenna. 'I left the bedroom windows open when we came out. I'm not having the whole house smellin' like a brewery.'

The end of summer had its own aroma of living things past their prime. The nettles against the walls in Chancellor's yard exhaled a faint rankness whose echoes could be found in the hogweed and first rotting windfalls. But the watercart still sprayed the streets and swallows quartered those parts of the sky the swifts had left vacant.

Bethlehem's world was the hillside field roofed with sunlit sky or starry darkness. Her mane was no longer the tight crest it had been at birth and the shaggy hair on her fetlocks was luxuriant and white. She seldom strayed far from her dam and the other mares. It was reassuring to see their great heads silhouetted against the clouds and hear the whinny of the farm horses at loosing-out time. The starling and sparrow flocks continued to sweep over the stubble and long shadows stalked the meadows. Every once in a while the birds were forced up by Maddocks's youngest boy who sauntered down the avenues of stooked barley whirling his clapper.

A little blood had crept into the bramble leaves and dew lingered in shaded field corners. Bethlehem sought the mare's udder and was suckled. Melody cropped the grass that was settling gently into stillness.

Before night drew in the horses circled the tor, then with heads lowered they came to Iona, although her anguish puzzled them. Breathing in slow shudders the old shire closed her teeth on the clover and pulled away a mouthful. She was waiting for something which at first had puzzled her. Gradually it became clear. A man's voice whispered 'Iona, Iona', and there was a warmth in the words and a special kindness. It was *his* voice, the voice of the carter who had looked after her for ten summers. But staring through her thoughts she saw only the dark countryside and the sea. He was not there, but he would come and put her in the harness. Then they would go together along the streets until the evening grooming. Now she was not weary or distressed. Bathsheba approached her, fluttering the contact call from dew-wet nostrils. The foals lifted their heads to the mare for her serenity lay on the night and they wished to be part of it.

Chancellor's staff outing began well enough. Three wagons were planked-out and the shires had their tails plaited and were paraded in the show brasses. They moved out of Lansworthy pulling their cargoes of high-spirited employees to follow the

67

long country road to Becky Falls. At the Dartmoor beauty spot sandwiches, scones and cream were eaten and washed down with cider. Jack could not get Kitty alone but the company was merry and he was content to sit drinking medium sweet from the jar. Lacey became objectionable as the cider loosened his tongue. His remarks made some of the older women blush but the men encouraged him and he staggered about laughing and joking, usually at Skilly's expense.

Fred Luscombe had his eye on the sixteen-year-old Cundy girl who had the face of a pre-Raphaelite princess and the body of a mature woman. The day was warm and sunny and several holiday romances bloomed. Then Jack noticed Kitty and Lacey were missing but before he could get to his feet they emerged from the bushes to a chorus of hoots. Lacey came and leered down at Jack.

'I tell'ee what, Irish – her doan know how to kiss. There's more warmth in a dead duck's ass.'

'Cut that out,' Old Bob said. 'Us won't have that filthy talk with ladies present.'

'Where be 'em to?' the boy giggled and some of the stable lads laughed. But the carters had seen the frown on Old Bob's face and kept quiet.

'No more scrumpy for that ornament,' said Ernie Drew.

'I can hold my liquor,' Lacey slurred. 'Spoonin' makes you thirsty and I've got the world's biggest thirst.'

Jack glanced at Kitty but she sat cross-legged, her hands in her lap and her head bowed. Lacey rocked quietly on his heels and tapped his fists together.

'Bog Irish's bumpkin idn much cop when it comes to romancin',' he laughed. 'But Bog Irish idn a lot of cop either.'

'Lacey,' Old Bob growled.

'Let 'em get on with it, Bob,' Ernie Drew interjected. 'It'll clear the air.'

'Mr Sidney won't like it,' said the old man.

'Mr Sidney idn here,' someone remarked.

Jack was quivering and the tin mug rattled against his teeth when he drank the remains of his cider. Lacey's grin twisted into a sneer.

'You'm all a-tremble, boy,' he breathed. 'Say sorry and your Uncle Arthur won't do ort.'

68

'Sorry for what?'

'Sorry you'm Bog Irish and bog stupid.'

Jack put down the mug and got to his feet.

'Leave him alone, Lacey,' cried one of the women. 'You bliddy bully – you're bigger than him.'

'Tis time Irish showed us he idn all wind and pee,' said Fred Luscombe.

Balling his fists again Lacey took a step back.

'Are you apologising, Irish?'

Jack grinned.

'Hit the bugger,' Luscombe grated. 'Drop un, Arthur.'

'Yes, hit me, Arthur,' Jack whispered, and on a lurch of fear and panic Lacey realised the grin was not a real grin at all; it was a disguised snarl concealing something intrinsically animal. The pale blue eyes steadily returning his gaze were devoid of fear.

'Just – just watch it, Irish,' he began, and Jack caught him with a right and a left delivered at remarkable speed which made him grunt and spit blood.

'I bit my tongue,' he mumbled. 'You – you – '

'Don't say it,' Jack said, lifting a finger and wagging it in Lacey's face.

'My tongue.' Crimson froth bubbled between vertical strands of saliva.

'If you had kept your mouth shut nothing would have happened,' said Old Bob.

Lacey pressed a handkerchief to his lips and began to sob, but his opponent was walking away towards the waterfall.

'It idn finished,' Lacey shouted.

'You and your mouth,' said Ernie Drew, baffled by the boy's stupidity.

They took the end doors off the wagons and Jack sat with his legs dangling. Shortly before the homeward journey began Kitty joined him, and he smiled at her.

'Do 'ee want to know what happened?' she whispered.

He nodded and took her hand.

'I had to go behind the bushes or – or I would've wet myself. Then he was there on the path waitin' for me. I couldn get past and when I tried to dodge he caught me hold and gave me a kiss. It wadn nice, Jack. It wadn like it is when us do it.'

69

He wrapped an arm round her shoulders. The wagon wheels rumbled over the stony road under the dark, limp foliage, and the music of the harness jingled along with them. Up ahead they were singing and someone in their wagon took up the tune.

'Midst pleasures and palaces, wherever you may roam,
Be it ever so humble there's no place like home . . .

The road fell away behind them and was lost in dust haze.

Yet Lacey retained most of his cronies despite his poor performance at Becky Falls. Then Jack was made aware of the exclusiveness of the tightly knit stable-boy community, and his lack of status. 'Bloody Irish', 'Bloody stingy old Jew', and 'that smelly pig' were different ways of saying the same thing.

'I was cider-puggled,' Lacey explained.

'Get home do!' Old Bob snorted. 'You was yellow.'

'It made me giddy.'

'And gutless,' remarked Ernie Drew.

'Bliddy scrumpy,' Lacey muttered. But on August Bank Holiday Monday he and Skilly and a couple of the more daring stable boys were passing the jug again in the park. The fair jerked Angarrick Terrace out of its summer torpor. Laughing gangs of teenagers went to the green arm in arm while their mothers trailed behind with the toddlers, gossiping all the way down to the swings, booths, stalls and carousels which had sprung up beneath the big wheel. The men would gravitate more gradually from the King Bill to the beer tent and pub-crawl home that evening to deposit the last of their senses in the local.

The genteel visitors pretended to be absorbed in the Regatta although Edward Daubeny impressed the youths gathered at the coconut shy.

'He spends an awful lot of time in the school nets,' Rupert Chancellor explained ruefully as his friend collected his third coconut.

On an impulse the tall, good-looking Daubeny boy presented the prize to the nearest girl. It was graciously accepted and he found himself staring into a startling pair of eyes. Their owner also possessed a mass of blonde hair and a broad, pretty face.

'Who was that?' he asked as they strolled back to the

promenade and the Chancellor party.

'One of the Widdicombe girls,' said Rupert. 'Her sister works at the store. I don't know what she does – something rural I suppose. They live at Churston. She's rather stunning isn't she?'

'Rather,' Edward grinned. Greenish-gold eyes, he thought, and such dark lashes.

The cannon signalling the start of the coxed fours took him by surprise and he jumped. The skiffs were cutting across the water towards the red marker buoy off Hollicombe Head when he hoisted himself onto the sea wall. Out on the bay the sailing dinghies slowly tacked together, scrounging wind from a breeze that was hardly strong enough to unhook the dandelion seeds. The steam yachts anchored a mile or so offshore swung at anchor, now broadside, now bow on, responding to the flooding tide. Cries gusted along the shore. A swimmer launched herself from a bathing machine and kicked up white splashes. Spent sunshine lofted from the sand, warping the figures under the pier.

'Tis so dark and cold,' Kitty shuddered. 'They say bats live up beneath they floorboards.'

Footsteps ringing on the pier above them sounded eerie, and all the convoluted wrought iron where pillars met woodwork in the half-darkness was like the vaulting of some awful dungeon.

She caught his hand and dragged him out into the sunlight that smelt of wet dogs and ladies' perfume.

'Have you ever been roller skatin', Jack?'

'No,' he laughed. 'I'd need wheels on my backside.'

'You can do it on the pier,' she said. 'I've only been on it once.'

He pushed his fingers into his pocket and teased the warm, heavy coins. They would bring him a week closer to owning Beth. But Kitty was lovely with her breath of apples and eyes greener than spring leaves.

'Come on,' he said. 'Let's go up there.'

'But I've only got a tanner!'

He jingled his loose change and winked. Then she screwed up her eyes and laughed and kissed him. Out of the heat shimmer women emerged like white flames in some slow, mysterious dance.

71

The thunder of the fairground steam-organs coloured the moment. Jack and Kitty joined the crowd pouring up the steps into the brilliantly lit pavilion. The wealthy, who lived most of their lives in public, moved about sedately wearing smiles and an air of spiritual fatigue. But on the roller-skating rink the young of all classes mingled unselfconsciously and carried the mood to the theatre where the pierrots were performing. Helen Daubeny surfaced for a moment from a field of flower-trimmed hats. She was laughing helplessly. Then the crowd closed around her once more and she was gone.

The pier was a causeway running high above everyday life. Along it the holiday masses moved in both directions. Out on the end, in a cream and gold pavilion, Mrs Baker was playing the harmonium. It was salon music, varnished with respectability.

'We'd have more fun watchin' mud dry,' Jack whispered.

'But her's very good,' Kitty giggled.

'No funeral would be the same without her.'

Solemn now she said, 'Idn you ever scared God will strike 'ee down dead for the things you say?'

He shrugged. 'Dad says a lot worse. He hates the church and reckons the priests are the curse of Ireland. I suppose it was the time he spent in Dublin drinkin' with atheists and such.'

'Atheists!' she said, her voice low and full of horror.

'Atheists,' he smiled. 'Bogie men. Quick – let's get out in the sun before they grab us.'

She sat side-saddle on the gold and scarlet horse. The steam-organ started up and the carousel went round with all the other gold and scarlet horses rising and falling under the canopy. Kitty's eyes closed tight on her laughter. Then she was waving and vanishing and the horses undulated by until Kitty was back again. Big frightened eyes stared from the painted heads of the carousel animals. They fixed on him until the broad wavy bands of gold and scarlet blurred and deposited him at the brink of dizziness. Bursting from a fog of colour Melody and her foal abandoned the roundabout and cantered off along the shore. Behind them the rainbows dissolved and silence spread over the water. The sun going down was colder and duller than the moon.

Jack shivered and folded his hands at the base of his head.

'Are you all right?' said Kitty's voice.

On a rush of noise the fairground reassembled around him and he smiled at her. Gold light swung across her face. Over her shoulder the carousel horses continued to see-saw as they cut their circle of brilliance like creatures escaped from mythology. Mist had softened the sunlight.

'Jack?'

Reaching out he took her hand.

9

Then the ghost moths danced around the lamps and the Three Towns slowly vanished under dusk. The fairground was a cauldron of noise and lights filtering through Kevan McKenna's alcoholic trance. A final stout in the beer tent had lifted him to the plateau of dazed well-being which his cronies shared. They strolled along the familiar holiday trail stopping at their favourite pubs: the Crown and Anchor, the Globe, the Oldenburgh, before finishing up in the King Bill. By this time nausea was gaining ground and McKenna's slack mouth and halflidded eyes betrayed his slack mind. This did not prevent him bringing an equally drunk companion home for supper. Both men were rocking on their heels ready to drop, and Mary McKenna had no difficulty persuading the unwelcome guest to leave.

'Get some shut-eye, Kev,' he slurred, ricocheting off the wall into the darkness. 'Get your head down, pal.'

Farewells were exchanged until Mary McKenna dragged her husband inside and shut the door.

'Look at the state of you,' she said. 'You ought to be sleepin' with the pig.'

He threw off his cap and jacket. 'I will be in a minute. Gi' us a kiss, Mary – my rose of Tralee.'

'You've more chance of becoming the next pope than getting a kiss off me.'

Jack and Michael glanced at each other and tried to hide their laughter.

'Bloody funny, isn't it,' McKenna roared. 'You've all ganged up on me – all of you. Wife, sons, daughters.'

'And isn't that terrible, you being a saint and the perfect father?' sneered Mary McKenna.

He glared at her and flopped into the armchair.

'You won't beat me, woman.' And bending to unlace a boot and kick it off he was sick.

'Damned waster,' Mary McKenna hissed. The veins stood out dark on her forehead when it caught the lamplight. 'You damned filthy brute. Tomorrow I'm going to apologise to the pig for even suggestin' he could spend a night in your company.'

McKenna pushed himself up and stood contemplating the pool of vomit. His ankle turned and he lurched and placed a foot in the gruel of Guinness, whisky and half-digested whelks. It had to be the one without the boot the boys noted, subsiding into the throes of helpless, silent laughter.

'That's it – paddle in your own puke, you old fool,' said Mary McKenna, her eyes smouldering. 'Your best clothes are ruined.'

'I'm warnin' you woman,' he shouted but she shook her rosary in his face as though he were a werewolf, and turned to the boys.

'Get upstairs, now. Don't argue, just go.'

'Let them stay and share the bottle,' McKenna said, his voice sinking to a whisper. 'Where is the bottle, Mary?'

'You'll not have another drink, Kevan.'

'And who'll stop me?'

'You'll never get to work in the morning.'

'Don't be so bloody daft. I'll have a little nightcap while you go and warm my side of the bed.'

'Over my dead body!'

'Bloody right. That's just about it. Pokin' a corpse. Jesus! but you make love like the priest's watchin' you.'

'God,' she breathed and buried her face in her hands. 'You can say that in front of the boys? Have you so little regard for my feelings?'

He sat and tugged off the other boot.

'Go to bed, please,' Mary McKenna said, and she looked at Jack.

'They'll stay and drink,' the man persisted. 'There's a bottle of light ale in my jacket pocket. Have one yourself, woman.'

'If you open that bottle I'll swing for you, Kevan. By Our Lady I will.'

McKenna staggered to his feet again. Crumbs of vomit had clotted on his moustache. With a low, animal grunt of rage he punched her and broke the skin under her eye. He was about to deliver another blow when Jack tripped him and brought him crashing down. His attempts to rise reminded Jack of a boxer he had seen felled in the fairground booth. The drink which had inflamed him was becoming an anaesthetic.

'Where the hell am I going, Mary?' he sobbed. 'What's it all about? Why are we here? Why?'

Then, on a burst of defiance, 'I'll fix you, you bitch. Jesus I will.' And he went to sleep, flat on his back, an arm crooked behind his head.

'Leave him there,' said Mary McKenna. 'He can sort himself out in the morning.' She fingered the lump that was closing her eye.

'It was the drink,' Jack said, lamely.

'It always is. Knowing why you've got cancer doesn't make the pain go away.'

'Shall I clean up the mess, Mam?' said Michael.

'You will not. It'll remind him of his behaviour when he's sober.'

She smoothed down her dress and stared at the ceiling for a moment. 'I wish to God I'd never set eyes on him. If it wasn't for you and the girls I'd be off tomorrow.'

'Off where?' said Jack. His father was snoring.

'Home. Slea Head, the mountains, the bay – just home. Being near the dead who cared would be enough.'

Once more her eyes settled on him. 'Go to bed, Jack. It'll be all right now.'

Sometime later, through the bedroom wall, her sobbing dredged new depths of despair and misery.

'One day I'm going to kill him,' Michael whispered.

'It's not him, it's the booze,' said Jack.

The ceiling was waiting like a canvas to be painted with his dreams. The stains left by winter damp had shrunk and the elephant's head had turned into a turkey.

'Jack,' Michael said softly. 'What did he mean about Father Tynan watchin' them kiss and – and – ?'

'He wanted to hurt her.'

'Why?'

'The drink turns him nasty.'

'Then why does he drink?'

'They all do it. There's the work and there's the pub. Nothing else.'

'Will it be like that for us?'

'Not for me. I'll have Beth.'

'What'll I have?'

'You're a brainy little bugger. You'll get by if you cut out the fartin'. Another one like that and you can sleep in the coal shed.'

'Hark who's talking!' Michael laughed.

Through the silence her sobbing made the darkness ache. Jack gazed at the ceiling. Next to the turkey was a horse's head. 'Beth,' he whispered. Tomorrow he would visit her. The sobbing continued and he gritted his teeth. If you love someone how can you hurt them? He drew a deep breath and let it go on a sigh, thinking of Kitty's flower-scented hair. Fragments of painful intensity came together behind his eyes. Stillness froze to a silence more terrifying than the dread of amputation. His heart had stopped. I'm dead, cried a voice. The cry drifted across the red motionless landscapes of silence and Kitty was crouching over him covering his face with primroses and apple blossom. But why was the girl in the pink dress sinking into the grass? Help me take it off, she said. Not with the priest watching, said his voice. Hide under the grass. Touch me, kiss me. Do to me what the stallion does to the mare. Go on now, go on. The grass heads swayed against the sky, brushing the hot sweet sickness of wanting her. Father Tynan's shadow fell across them like the shadow of a great black bird. Hail Mary, full of grace. Beneath the girl's lashes such a hunger for all the wicked things. He pushed her up onto Melody's back and sat behind her, pressing his nakedness against her sun-warmed flesh. Then he woke and sat up, dry-mouthed. Michael was whimpering in his sleep. Reaching out Jack found the boy's head with his fingers and stroked it.

'Quiet now,' he crooned. 'It's only a dream.'

And maybe everything's a dream, he thought. Closing his

eyes he opened them again onto darkness. The front door clicked shut and his father's boots rang on the cobbles. Jack tried to curl once more into sleep but the cocks were crowing before it came, and Michael was shaking him before he had time to enjoy it. He swung his legs over the edge of the bed and sat yawning and scratching. Moony was feeding the pig, answering the animal's grunts with his own oinks of greeting. Over the rooftops poured the juicy song of the starlings and the prolonged hooting of a train. Drizzle was misting the window.

Kevan McKenna washed in the scullery and changed reluctantly into his working clothes. The reek of vomit set him retching. His head swam and he groaned as nausea climbed his throat; but he got out of the house and walked unsteadily through the darkness to the railway station. Every so often the ground lifted a fell beneath him and he had to stop and set his legs apart. The drizzle swirled around the lanterns in the goods yard. Rails and trucks gleamed and the damp smell of steam drifted across his hangover. He was sweating. The shunter's pole was greasy in his fist but the trucks were on the move as the Saddle Tank engine warmed to the work. McKenna groaned. Somehow he controlled the nausea and swung the pole with the hook on the end to lift the chain and connect the two wagons. Then his name was called.

Giddiness nudged him into a new dimension of misery. The darkness dissolved, leaving only the drizzle gusting down into his hungover cerebral murk.

'McKenna. For Christ's sake – McKenna.'

The alcohol broke from his pores and trickled through his chest hair. That bloody woman, he thought. Her mother had hated him – her and her savage looks spoiling the wedding. Mary ought to have been a nun. He ducked under the chains and was confronted by another line of trucks. They were trundling gently along the rails and he waited for a gap wide enough to dodge between them. Then the ground heaved but he was already stumbling and fighting to keep his footing. He cleared the near rail and skidded on the sleeper. Something darker than the darkness loomed above him. McKenna screamed and clawed at the wagon. His arms clamped onto metal and he was lifted and carried gently up against the buffer

78

he knew was waiting behind him. The moment of searing agony and disbelief ended almost instantly in nothingness as he was sandwiched between the metal discs. Heels clipping the sleepers he was dragged along until the wagons separated, leaving his crushed and mangled body on the tracks.

So the black horses and black carriage returned to Angarrick Terrace. It was one of those grey, misty days created for funerals. The horses paced over the cobbles with the pig snuffling and grunting behind the hoarding and Jack's sisters weeping tears of genuine grief. But their mother's eyes remained dry.

She stood at the graveside, white-faced, staring out of her thoughts into somewhere beyond the occasion, like a gull dreaming. Earth pattered onto the coffin and Kevan McKenna was no more than an emptiness around his children's hearts. After a week his boots vanished from the fender.

The kitchen clock clipped away at Jack's distress. Often his mother trespassed on his thoughts but said nothing. And hadn't her sobbing been done alone, night after night, in the bedroom? He considered the complexity of it all. She was beyond tears, yet sadness prevailed. The evenings were drawing in and they sat around the fire with the brasswork twinkling and gold light on the move. Sean and the girls were chatting at the table, and Michael was out. Jack watched his mother darning socks. When their glances met they smiled. The fire lent her face a glowing youthfulness which would not survive the night. The black eye rendered it even more pathetic.

The girls were put in her bedroom and Jack had his own bed by the window. When the moon rose above the terrace a small rectangle of light projected the pattern of the lace curtains onto the ceiling. Lying there he let grief churn up the memories. Then the hooting of the trains had a new significance.

10

'Folk don't seem real to me,' he said. 'People are sort of dream things – even Mam.'

'And me?' Kitty said.

'Yes. Something from a nice dream.'

'Like the horses?'

'No. They're always real. I suppose it's because I touch them and stroke them. I know their shape, the way they're made. People don't touch each other enough.'

'You put your arm round me and catch hold my hand,' she said. 'And you kiss me.'

'Like we're part of a dream,' he said. 'It's not a bad thing, Kitty. I can't help what I feel.'

Leaves shook against the sky, branches swung, twigs bent and swayed. He tugged a handful of berries off the hawthorn tree. All outside, he thought. Everything's outside of me – the whole world. And what's Dad now? Nothing daft like the white marble angels up the cemetery. Misery knotted in his stomach and he brought his teeth together.

'Don't be unhappy,' Kitty pleaded.

Clouds were piling up along the base of the evening sky which the sun and moon shared. Smoke from the stubble fires wreathed the valley as thousands of starlings settled screaming in the ash trees above Cider Mill Tor. When the birds had fallen silent the horses could be heard calling in the dusk.

'You get so dirty on the farm,' Mary McKenna said with nothing but affection in her voice. 'You were the proper little man when you were down Chancellor's yard. He could have sent any of the boys to Tor Barton.'

'Beth's nearly weaned,' said Jack as if it were sufficient explanation for his move to the farm.

'Beth, Beth, Beth,' laughed the woman, and she slit the rabbit open and scooped out the entrails. A pink and grey mess oozed between her fingers onto the newspaper.

'You can bring that girl home you know. Pretty Kitty. I won't eat her.'

The skin was peeled off the carcass in one long easy pull, like someone removing a stocking, Jack thought.

'Can I have a dog, Mam – and a cat?'

'A little kitty?' she mocked, and he grinned.

'They got collie pups out the farm – and kittens.'

'I had a dog once,' she said, folding the newspaper round the innards. 'Dando. He was old when I met your father. I couldn't bring him to England. Poor Dando.'

She shivered and muttered a swift little prayer. 'Put some coal on the fire, Jack. I don't know what we'll do when that lot's gone. Your dad used to bring home a couple a hundredweight of Newcastle Bright every month. He was good at things like that.'

The door flew open and the girls waltzed in, their shadows leaping as the candles guttered. Maybe he was there, a shadow among shadows, Kevan McKenna, mute now but wanting to say I love you, Jack. I always loved you and your mother. Maybe the long owl-cry of the goods train was himself calling from the grave.

Jack bent over the fire and tried to blot out the horror. Crushed between two trucks! Mother of God! Mother of God! Bang your thumb with a hammer and it hurts like hell. To die like that! But his mother no longer sobbed herself to sleep and the owls crying from the darkness did not really sound like the trains. When the world stopped and the fairground lights went out the horses ran together, tossing their heads and spreading their manes.

'I doan need no extra help,' Trant sniffed. 'Maddock's eldest boy is always handy if us wants ort. The way old Chancellor fusses over you he must have Irish blood.'

The boy walked in a lively way that suggested great stores of energy; and from the hopelessness of his own increasingly arthritic middle age Trant glimpsed another boy running through the mists of a long vanished evening. But he had never possessed Jack's vitality.

'The old man told me no one knows as much about horses as you, mister,' Jack said. 'I want to learn everthing about them.'

'Do 'ee now?' Trant said, melting before the boy's enthusiasm.

'Then I can buy Beth one day.'

'Her's a sweet-tempered little animal,' said the carter. 'So's Bathsheba. Didn they learn 'ee down Station Lane? I thought Palfrey was the cat's whiskers.'

'He is,' Jack said. 'But all the horses are full grown and I only know a bit about the breaking and training.'

'Tidn no game.'

'It's all I want to do, Mr Trant. The old man says I have to watch you and do what you tell me.

'And report back,' the carter sneered, allowing his inner ugliness to cast a shadow on the moment.

'I don't carry tales,' Jack said quietly.

'Anyway,' Trant continued. 'I'm sorry about your dad. Have 'ee asked the old man for a rise?'

Jack nodded and smiled. 'He saw to that without me pesterin' him.'

'I ought to chuck in farmwork and get down the yard,' said Trant. 'There's no money up yer.'

The September sun warmed his shoulders but the shadows creeping across the yard were pale. In the corner by the tip-cart the little tabby she-cat toyed with the broken, dusty body of a slow-worm. At the granite trough the shire geldings slavered and blew. It was one of those calm mornings of dew and spider-spin. Now and then a windfall thudded down in the orchard and a robin sang his short sad song. Mrs Trant was hanging out the washing and he gave her a good morning which she ignored. The woman's determination to dislike him was puzzling. It's got to be the goitre, Jack thought. Her ugliness affected everthing she did.

82

The tabby cat stood on its hindlegs and sank its claws into the lichen-encrusted gatepost and stretched. The bullock yard was steaming when one of the carters led down Melody and Princess and began to put them in their gears.

'Check the foals and take Melody up the orchard,' said Trant.'There's bagged apples to haul. When us've got a load us'll take 'em up over to the mill.'

Starlings enveloped the hill, and the foals who were desperate for their mothers reacted nervously. They galloped around, showing their teeth and whinnying.

'Whoa girl,' Jack called. 'Whoa Beth.'

The flat white face was lowered and he tugged at her ears, one at a time, until her breathing became quiet and regular. Bathsheba pushed her muzzle against his shoulder and he spoke to the foals while his hands calmed them. Bethlehem's forelocks fell over her eyes. His smell and unhurried movements pleased her. Love flowed through his fingers into her body. Somehow he was part of the living world like the wind, rain and sun and the grass which was to eat and sleep in. Other humans came and went but left nothing of themselves in her blood.

Now he was standing close to her, running a hand down her rump and hind leg to the silky feather. His shoulder pressed against her and he was lifting her foot and scraping the bottom of the hoof. The hoof-pick cleared away the clotted dung and winkled out small stones. Then he was smearing oil on the hoof horn.

Trant voiced his approval. 'Pamper her but doan spoil her. Talk to her all the time you'm groomin', boy. Brush, comb and yap.'

'What's going to happen to Iona, mister?'

'Nothing, as far as I know. Her's up yonder.'

'I mean when she's really old.'

'Her is really old, boy. Give her a few more summers and her'll beg us to cart her off to the knackers.'

'Why does it always end like that? After all they give us.'

'Listen,' Trant said gruffly, tensing his features. 'At the end of their lives old horses suffer. When us puts 'em down us do 'em a kindness. They can't sit round like old folk smokin' and jawin' and being looked after. They'd suffer. So we give 'em death like we give 'em bran mash on Sundays. Tis part of the

83

service, part of our duty. We've got to help them along – just like the old man helped you along.'

'Helped me along where?' Jack frowned.

'Away from the goods yard,' said Trant. 'He told Maddock Beth would help 'ee get over what happened to your dad.'

The sunset colours of the horse chestnut leaves spread all down the valley. At first light the bottom of Clennon was a sea of cobwebs weighed under dew. Slowly the mist lifted and the last of the swallows hawked the pond at Cider Mill Farm. In the flower gardens of Roundham the bush roses bloomed. Below the tor the hedges were clustered with hips, haws and sloes.

Gradually the misery faded and towards the end of the month Jack came to work whistling. As usual Bethlehem was standing at the gate above the orchard, and for Jack she was the first foal in the first dawn of creation. He called from the smoke of his breath and the foal moved in imitation of her dam's measured pace. The early morning wetness had slicked down the hairs of her fetlocks. Although a roan's coat never shines Beth's held the faint sheen of health and her hooves scuffed through the grass and fallen leaves. Beside her Bathsheba swung from side to side, rubbing her chin on the top bar of the gate. Restlessly the geldings waited as the carters sauntered up the track to the tor.

Melody and Princess went unwillingly from their daughters and the foals cried after them. Later they stood each side of Iona as if the mare's warmth offered more than solace. A squirrel bent the hazel whips in the hedge, its redness holding the flush of autumn sunlight. How can I see into things? Jack thought. How can I see into hearts? The eyes revealed a little but there were places inside people and animals which remained more mysterious than the Amazon jungle. Yet the white statue of the Virgin in the moonlit sky was so beautiful, and the sheep folded now behind hurdles under Cider Mill Tor were like old angels put out to grass.

The other men kept mostly to themselves. There was a good deal of back-biting but their quiet lunch breaks suited Jack. Most of the labourers were content to work silently. The animals provided enough companionship, he thought, sitting sideways on Melody and riding her down the track. The mares were tied together at their bits but only until the yard was reached. Behind the cow house Trant was ready to put Princess

84

in the shafts of the tip-cart and haul logs. The boy was told to cart manure.

'Don't push Melody,' Trant said. 'Her's with foal again and Beth's givin' her a hard time. Walk her easy, boy.'

The sun flashed on the prongs of the dung fork and the sounds of the yard hedged in his thoughts. Liquid mud and manure formed a delta between the stables and milking sheds. It was criss-crossed with little rivers of urine. When the pigs fell silent he could hear the heifers chewing the cud and the far-off barking of the collies following the plough. The moments blurred behind the jingle and creak of the cart. Great flocks of birds passed across noons lulled by the bees humming around the ivy blossom on the stable walls.

The stubble was vanishing. At the end of the furrow the shires turned under the cloud of their body steam and plodded back across the field. Long slabs of earth glinted and crumbled in the sun. The red soil took on a purplish gleam. It was speckled with gulls and rooks. Shortly after midday Maddock brought the team back to the stables. They wore the lather of hard work and welcomed the opportunity to cool down. Jack fed and watered them, smiling when they snorted the dust off the chafed oats he had tipped into the mangers. Then he brushed them, gave them another small meal and permitted them to slake their thirst at the trough.

The equinoctial gales washed over Clennon Valley. Leaves and birds filled the sky and the wood was roaring. Dark, rain-lashed evenings made the stables seem especially warm and cosy. The wind buffetted the roof sending the dust of hay and straw drizzling down from the loft. Then the smoking flame of the lantern had phantoms leaping along the walls and the horses tossed their heads and stamped their nervousness. For Jack it was the finest hour. The animals stood at their hay-racks and golden gleams danced on the partitions between the stalls. Yoked to farm implements the horses were great mute machines but at dusk they nuzzled the stable gloom and breathed a majesty into the building. Loosed from their gears they snapped playfully at each other and Jack spoke to them, his voice thick with emotion. A slow arching of their necks brought their heads down to peer into his face. Beneath polished hides the tremor and quake of muscle magicked the light alive. Standing before the geldings he could picture heavy horses striding across the fields of Genesis. Perhaps his father had reached that place. Perhaps dying was a flight back towards the first sunrise.

11

His mother withdrew into religion like a nun and Father Tynan became a frequent visitor to Angarrick Terrace. But Jack could never take to the middle-class priest whose eyes sought out the top corners of the room whenever he spoke at length. It made the boy uncomfortably conscious of what the home lacked – or maybe, he thought, the old man was talking to God.

Mary McKenna's devoutness irritated her eldest son at first but soon her joy began to shine through everything she did. Sensing their restlessness she suggested the whole family went mushrooming on Cider Mill Tor. The Sunday morning was misty when they left and the bush roses of Grosvenor Road filled the air with fragrance.

'The secret,' she said, 'is to stay one jump ahead of the tinkers. Give them a chance and they'll clear a field in an hour.'

They walked stooping among the sheep, gathering the small white button mushrooms. Blanche pressed one to her nose and sniffed the stony scent.

'I love 'em,' she sighed.

Hidden by the mist, leaves were falling from the hedgerow trees and whispering down the brambles. The girls sometimes pushed their hands through spiders' webs and withdrew them again uttering little gasps of horror. The mist thinned except in the valley where it lay in a mass. Birds broke across the blood red silence of the sun as it edged up. The bay was filling with light.

'Like Ireland,' murmured the woman. She was happy standing at the centre of her brood. Yet her mind flew back to a girlhood autumn. Hills crowded together above wild uplands and they were returning from Tralee. Donovan's Mills, the market place, her father bleary from over-work and travel. Flat Sliahb an Iolair and pointed Cruach Mhartham rising over the boggy wastes, the fields and gorse. Mount Brandon dark under cloud.

She muttered a prayer and sucked back the sob that suddenly caught in her throat. Forever hills lifting from distance and sunset waiting out to sea like the Last Judgement. But it had never been so attractive when she was actually there.

Jack smiled. She was a girl again in her best shawl. Beyond her profile the buzzards were aloft and tugging at the silence, crying their cat calls.

'Where's the foal?' Michael asked.

'Down in the paddock,' said Jack. 'In a couple of weeks they'll take her from Melody.'

'How cruel!' Blanche cried.

'The mare's going to have another,' Jack said patiently. 'Beth is old enough to feed herself. She'd be sucking for a year if we let her and it would be rotten for Melody. Beth never stops pestering her.'

'Does the terrace piggy have a mum?' Blanche said.

'All animals have mothers, darling,' said Mary McKenna, folding the child in her arms.

'Didn't piggy's mum cry when they took him away from her?'

''Course not,' said Sean. 'The people who owned the big pig ate her. That's what pigs are for. They don't cry when their young ones go off.'

'But it does seem awful,' shivered Mary McKenna, 'breeding creatures just to be eaten. You'd think the Almighty would organise things better than that.'

'From sty to pie,' Michael grinned.

'Why don't we eat horses?' said Blanche.

'The French and Germans do,' said her mother. 'Those foreigners!'

'Roast gee-gee,' Michael said. 'Shire chops. A bit of cold

88

Clydesdale and chips.'

'Roast gee-gee!' Lily giggled.

'Beth and chips,' said Sean, nudging his brother.

'Horses are magic,' Jack said. 'God made them out of the wind. You can't eat the wind.'

Kitty never joked about the animals which were casting their shadows into her own life. She had seen the happiness spread over Jack's face whenever Bethlehem answered his call. Often she imagined it was just the three of them – girl, boy and foal marooned on the edge of everyone else's world. Her fifteenth birthday had left her feeling closer to womanhood than childhood. Yet looking in the mirror she wondered sometimes what he saw in her. 'My little primrose,' her dad called her. A pale little thing, all elbows and eyes. Hazel Cundy, who had large breasts, would stand in the millinery department staring so intently at her she felt like a butterfly pinned to a board. Hazel liked Jack and nearly all Chancellor's girls thought he was worth a second glance. Lovely ugly, Edith Wotton called him.

His love letters were touching:

Sweet Kitty, will you always love me like I love you? I cut our names into the chestnut tree behind the linhay in Beth's paddock today and put a big heart round them. Our names will be there years from now when we're growed up. That makes me feel good. Jack loves Kitty, always. Your eyes are like the foal's eyes, only green. I lay fifteen kisses on them. One for every year of your life. Love, Jack.

PS See you at the Big Tree tomorrow.

Yes, she thought, sitting on the top deck of the bus – love Jack. And he was at the stop, his jackdaw hair lifting in the wind. The rain slanting out of a squall over the bay left the sky clean enough and clear enough to accommodate the doves winging inland from the sea cliffs.

'You're like a little old married couple,' Mary McKenna reproached him. 'Boys of your age should be out with their pals.'

For once his grin annoyed her and she needed no prompting to vent her spleen. 'Those Widdicombes are a funny lot. The father's Labour. Your dad told how he was down the green at

89

some sort of political rally and Charlie Widdicombe was bawlin'
for better working conditions. 'Workers of the world unite' and
all that crazy rubbish.'

'Kitty thinks he's wonderful,' Jack said.

'Well, if he don't keep his mouth shut he'll be out of a job and
out on the street.'

'That isn't fair.'

'You don't bite the hand that feeds you. The man's looking
for trouble – and so's his eldest girl. Mrs Vosper saw her over
Abbot's Quay with those suffragettes. Votes for women! Jesus!
That would change nothing. We'd still have the King, Porker
VII, and the steps wouldn't scrub themselves and the vote
wouldn't turn the mangle or black the bloody range. It's a game
for rich ladies.'

'King Porker VII!' Michael laughed. 'You'll end up in the
Tower if you go round spoutin' treason, Mother.'

'Well,' she said. 'Votes, and everybody equal! Moony
Endacott takin' tea with Ormond Chancellor! Me and the
Queen of Spain at Ascot. Fred Luscombe strollin' down the
West End to the Café Royal.'

Jack scraped the mud from his hobnails and flicked it off the
knife into the fire. Michael winked at him as he laced his own
boots and tightened them. He was working at the railway
station and their mother was better off than she had been when
McKenna was providing. Jack's savings, which he called the
Horse Fund and kept in a toffee tin in the bedroom, were
growing. The family ate meat twice a week and Mary noted with
a mixture of pride and alarm how her young ones were growing
out of their clothes. Jack seemed to be shooting up.

'Take care of yourself,' she said briskly. Rain pecked at the
window. 'God, but your're a proper scarecrow in that old
overcoat!'

'It keeps out the cold.'

Breakfast warmth filled even the far corners of the kitchen.
Mrs McKenna had begun scalding milk to make the cream,
and, woken by all the activity, Blanche came downstairs
dragging a doll, bumping its head from step to step.

'Lucky I didn't fetch you downstairs like that, young lady,
when you were a tot,' her mother smiled.

'We thought you did, Mam,' said Michael.

'You'll be soaked by the time you get to Tor Barton, Jack,' said Mary McKenna in a changed voice. 'We've some of the GW money left and Mrs Freathy in Number Five wants to sell her bicycle. Poor John. They say it's bronchitis but we know what it is. Anyway she's findin' it hard to make ends meet. Do you want the bicycle, Jack?'

'I could dip into the Horse Fund.'

'You will not. I won't get the white dress and the carriage ride if you don't become your own man.'

She wrapped his sandwiches and tilted her head to take his kiss.

'I'd like a bicycle,' said Michael.

'It'll belong to the family,' Jack said. 'Like the bath tub and the mangle.'

'But you won't be fightin' to decide whose turn it is on the mangle,' their mother said tartly.

'There's men's work and there's women's work,' Michael replied. Like a little replica of his father, Mary thought, her heart beating cold.

The boys walked up the terrace together. The rain had stopped and Moony was addressing his friend the pig behind the hoarding.

'That Moony,' Michael laughed. 'Have you seen him lately? They shaved his head to get rid of the lice.'

'I like him,' said Jack.

'He's a ha'penny short of a shilling.'

'So what? He's as good as gold and as trusting as a dog.'

'Jesus – you're a funny bugger, Jack. There's a lot of the priest in you.'

Back to the farm stables on a morning awash with grey light. Partridges glided over the plough. The swallows had gone but the sun climbing above the mist of noon swept the red admirals to the buddleia behind the farmhouse. A heron beat down the valley where the three-year-old steers were being driven from the pastures to the market. Around the fields men were hedging. Metal hacked at hazel and ash, dropped the saplings with a swish, and they were woven into the pattern of the countryside. Elsewhere the horses were put to work. Their passage up and down the land measured the day and when it was done the smell of it all lay on their bodies; old leaves, bruised soil, rain, something taken from the sky and the wind. He could comb it out of them after work only to rediscover it rising from the countryside as he walked home.

One morning the hunt met at Yalberton for the cubbing and ran a good line onto Tor Barton. Jack was helping sort through the sheep clinging to his clothes. The riders were chattering in high confident voices.

The prime Hampshire Down ewes. There were foxes in the copse below the farm and Jack had seen young ones ranging across Clennon at first light. All at once the lane was full of hounds and horses, flashes of black and hunting pink. The boy stood with mud and dung oozing over his boots, and the stink of sheep clinging to his clothes. The riders were chattering in high confident voices.

'Open the gate,' the master brayed. 'Jump to it, lad.'

Jack touched his cap and nodded. The pack was already streaming between the bars, giving tongue and getting under the horses' feet. Some became temporarily trapped when the gate swung back on its hinges but the riders pressed through, knee to knee, jostling each other and staring fixedly ahead. Mounted on ponies behind the cavalry charge were Edward Daubeny, young Rupert Chancellor and Helen.

Edward drew rein and smiled. 'Hello. What are you up to?'

'It's what the ram's up to, not me.'

'The tupping,' Rupert explained.

Helen Daubeny blushed.

'Stand up wind, Jack,' Rupert added laughingly. 'You smell awful high. Go on, there's a good chap.'

'Sheep,' Jack said, and he sniffed his sleeve.

'Do hurry, Edward,' said Helen Daubeny, and she looked aghast at Jack.

'How's Beth?' Edward went on.

'We'll be separatin' her and her mother soon.'

'Edward,' Helen said with an impatient toss of the head.

'May we come and see her one Sunday?' said the Daubeny boy.

'She'd like that.'

'Must be off now. Have fun with the sheep.'

'Bastards,' Maddock growled when they were alone. 'But you

used your head son. So long as you say yes sir, no sir, three bags full, sir, everything will be alright.'

The fox is born free though, Jack thought. He doesn't 'yes sir' anyone. The boy knew what was happening. The yelping horn and clamour of the pack told everything. He could see the bloody carcass being swung above the hounds. Something had gone forever from the world but the ewes were placing their noses to the tup's hindquarters in their eagerness to sample his potency.

Evening deepened the blackness of the Big Tree's foliage and they sat beneath it waiting for Kitty's bus.

'It's shame Beth has to be taken from her mother,' she said. 'You ought to hear the cows bawlin' for their calves when they'm parted. Their hearts must break.'

'She'll have Iona and Bathsheba for company. Everything has to grow up, Kitty.'

His arm encircled her waist and he tried to kiss her neck but was pushed away.

'I don't like that, Jack. It's what the sailors do to them awful women on the fish quay at Mary's Haven. If you want to be rude you'd better take Hazel Cundy home.'

'Rude?' he laughed. 'You let me kiss your eyes, and ears. So what's rude about kissin' your neck?'

She stroked the creases out of her skirt and stared miserably down at her hands.

'I don't like it. I know what it means.'

'I'll never do it again, Kitty. You don't hate me, do you?'

''Course not. I couldn stop lovin' you no more than you could stop lovin' that foal.'

Dusk smelled sharply of bonfires. The bus rumbled up the smoking street, its sidelamps blazing. Kitty jumped aboard and turned to wave to him. He lifted an arm and let it drop again. Lights were on in downstairs windows offering scenes from other people's lives: children laughing, men in shirt sleeves and braces reading newspapers, a woman turning up a lamp, a cat curled on a windowsill.

Loneliness hollowed his stomach. He wanted to belong to all the human warmth. A station rank cab clattered by, the cabby clicking his tongue at the horse. Jack was cold. He tugged the collar his coat up round his ears as darkness silted the streets and the stars hardened into brilliance. Gulls flying to their roosting places cackled softly. Kitty's fragrance was still on his fingers but thoughts of Helen Daubeny became a curious, exciting ache.

Instead of walking home directly he went to Roundham Head across the meadows on the cliff top. Cattle trailed after him. The view of the bay to St Mary's Head and the lighthouse was spectacular. Rising with the moon the tide set the lights of the schooners gently swaying. But he was intimidated by the vastness of the universe. It reached into him to menace and bewilder. Then he was skirting the cabbage fields and trotting down the lane to Morning House.

Hoisting himself over the front wall he pushed through the shrubbery to the edge of the lawn. The drawing-room curtains were closed on the sound of a piano and a woman's voice singing something unattractive in German. Now and again the shapes of young ladies were silhouetted but Helen Daubeny did not materialise and after a while Jack began to feel foolish. He returned to the street and dawdled home. Hazel Cundy was eclipsing Helen. Hazel was attainable and she would not kiss and tell. But why was Kitty eternally there beyond lust, waiting to redeem him with her purity? Into the confessional of her green eyes. He quickened his step. Moon daisies around her hat. Yes, and the blouse with the starched white cuffs would look so fine in the carriage beside his mother's white dress. Jack smiled.

The ladies would holds hands and chat beneath their parasols. Beth's harness would jingle and her white mane lift and fan out.

'You're late,' said Mary McKenna, setting the meal before him. 'Careful,' she added. 'The plate's hot. Where have you been?'

'Walking.'

'With Kitty?'

'By myself. I had something to think out.'

He liked the sameness of evenings at home: the shift of coal on the fire, the click of his mother's knitting needles making the clock sound ponderous. Michael slept at the table, his dark curly head resting on his arms. Sean and the girls were playing upstairs, and their thumps on the floor and muffled bursts of laughter set him thinking of his father fighting to get out of his trousers on a Saturday night. He tried to bring Kevan McKenna's face into focus but nothing happened. The craneflies tiptoed grotesquely along the picture rail and the tawny owls screeched to each other across the chimneys. Jack got up and stretched. To vanish off the face of the earth and leave nothing behind was awful. What would God make of his father's atheism? The priest had been very po-faced at the graveside as if he knew the late deceased was in for a hard eternity.

Jack went to the front door and stood on the step. The Vosper girls and Moony were still playing under the lamp but the pig was silent.

'You'll catch your death standing round in just your socks,' said his mother, joining him. 'What are you thinking about?'

'Nothin' much – you know, all sorts of stupid things like what's going on among the stars. Why are the horses like they are and why are we like we are? Is Dad up there looking into my head, seeing what I think?'

'Looking up at us more likely,' she murmured. 'Dancin' on the red hot coals, his socks smoulderin' and him teaching the devil new swear words. Do you miss him?'

'Not as often as I should. Is that wrong, Mum?'

'No. You can't tell your heart how to behave. It has a will of its own.'

Above the chimneys, where the stars winked and twitched or stood in blue silence, lay a loneliness no heart could endure. He thought of the horses asleep in the linhay and the dead fox cub stiffening among the brambles under the hedge. His mother's gastric juices gurgled. Closing the door she led him back to the kitchen. Tea was poured and the clock regained control of the evening, but whenever one of the children rushed in the flames leapt and gold puddled the ceiling and walls.

The ravishing beauty of the night continued to draw his thoughts. He quarried into the jacket potato and filled the small, steaming pockets of fragrance with butter. Everyone was pleasantly drowsy but unwilling to go to bed.

'Sing to us, Mam,' Blanche pleaded.

'Yes sing,' Lily said, hardly able to keep her eyes open.

The three youngest children sat on the hearth at their mother's feet.

'And what shall I sing?' smiled Mary McKenna.

"Acushla',' said Jack.

'Yes, yes,' Blanche cried. "Acushla Mine'.'

'It's always that old song,' their mother said but she sang in her low, husky voice:

> Acushla mine, the singing birds are calling,
> The call of love that's meant for lovers true;
> Tis Autumn time, and where the leaves are falling
> Alone I wait, to beg a word with you.

Lovers true, Jack reflected guiltily. It was possible to conjure up the vision before he went to sleep. Kitty's sun-coloured hair and her flowing white dress. She came sailing on horseback over the dazzle of a summer day autumn could never touch.

Perhaps it was the autumn cancelling out personal sadness with its vast decay. Ploughing was over and lines of women worked along the far side of the valley lifting potatoes. The apples had been pressed, the corn stacked, and the gelding's belly hair had been clipped. Then after breakfast on a bright frosty morning some of the men from the terrace Pig Club began to drag the squealing animal to Vosper's yard. Lifting the bedroom curtains Blanche and Sean pressed their faces to the window. One of the men was tugging the nose halter holding the pig's jaws together; another was pushing at its rump. The pig had dug its feet into the cobbles in an attempt to delay the inevitable of which it was acutely aware. Another helper jabbed a goad into the groove behind the pig's ear. Everyone was laughing except Moony and he was crying.

'They'll hit him on the head with a big hammer,' Sean said, and his voice broke. 'I seen it last time. Then the pig stops screamin' and – and –'

'And what?' the little girl whispered.

'They cut his throat and all the blood poures out.'

Soon the pig and the men were out of sight but the screaming continued for a long time. Finally when it stopped there was a numb silence.

Blanche raised eyes rounded by horror and said, 'Can we see

the dead piggy, Sean?'

He nodded and caught her hand.

'Piggy looked funny,' she giggled. 'He was trying to go backwards.'

'Hurry up,' Sean said. 'We're missin' the fun. They open him and take out his insides.'

'Why?'

'For us to eat.'

'Poor piggy,' she said absently, pulling on her boots.

'He's not piggy anymore. He's pork and bacon and crackling and hog's pudding.'

The mist which cleared quickly from the terrace clung to the valley floor. Invisible cattle lowed on the invisible water meadows and the sun crept over the trees like smoke. The smell of frying bacon made Jack hungry as he crossed the bullock yard.

'There's a couple of uncut colts down yonder,' Trant said. He held the bit halter in fingers which were like a mess of gnarled roots. 'They at Cider Mill idn particular about their animals. Doanee let Princess near 'em. Us doan want no rubbish bred 'ere.'

Men's voices were sifted through the cowshed cob and passing the half-doors Jack heard the hiss, spurt and purr of milk filling the pails. Curlews called on their flight over the hill to the mudflats of the River Dar.

'Time us got Beth away from her mother, boy,' the horseman continued. 'Both they foals can stand on their own feet now. I've spoke to Palfrey and he's arranged for the mares to do some light work on the streets. Best the separation be complete. The youngsters won't like it much to start with but they'll get used to it.'

'Aren't I goin' back to Station Lane, mister?'

'Do 'ee want to?'

'Not for a bit.'

'That pal of yours, Arthur Lacey, was up yer last Sunday with the Cundy maid. He left the gate open and Iona got out. I expect you'll be glad to get back with him.'

Jack grinned.

Melody sensed what was happening. She and Princess jerked at the halters and cried repeatedly to their young. The foals ran

97

up and down the lower hedge, shrilling their misery while the mares' anguished whinnying faded into the distance.

'I woan need 'ee for a while,' Trant told the boy. 'Go up the paddock and see if everything's all right.'

Gnats clouded the labyrinths of light among the blackthorn branches. Everything was still. The foal studied his approach, trying to puzzle out her predicament from his looks and actions. But Bathsheba reared on her hind legs and beat the air with flailing hooves. The animals were snuffling and snorting as he opened the gate. Then they set off in a frantic gallop around the paddock until panic abated and he was permitted to go up to them.

Beth's grave face was lowered to his fingers. The nostrils rounded to take in his smell. Cobwebs clung to her feather and he stooped to remove them, while she stood motionless, breathing quietly now. Her ears twitched forward whenever a chestnut fell onto the linhay roof leaving its spiky shell gaping on the tiles. He took out his handerchief and wiped round her eyes and nostrils. Beth gently nuzzled his shoulder. Moving around her he drew his hands one after the other down her coat, stroking her while he crooned endearments.

PART TWO

CHANCELLOR'S MARE

12

Where the ash trees stood against the sky gaps appeared and branches were showing. Sometimes the dew lay from one dawn to the next and the grass in the field corners was perpetually wet. Then the mist rolled in and the foals stood side by side as the sky settled on them, dusting their coats with points of brilliance no bigger than money spiders. Those were occasions when recollection of her mother sharpened to pain and Bethlehem paced down to the gate expecting to see Melody coming out of the bullock yard weary from the day's work.

Leaves continued to fall, the wind blew and after rain the sun shone; yet Bethlehem always felt she was walking through shadow. The stoniest sound in the world was his footsteps retreating down the lane. Darkness took him as it took the hill and the valley. Where did everything go? Why did the sun vanish after dusk? Why did the birds stop singing?

The year was turning, and, rasping through the dead hogweed, the wind had nothing comforting to say. In a short space of time a south-western shift of air brought more fog and rain. Then the labourers worked with sacks slung round their shoulders, and waists, hating the land and what it was doing to them.

Mist carried up Clennon Valley. Lights dimmed to blaze again and vanish. The wind faded and fog hung motionless.

Then the hill was an island and light sparked on the grass and dead leaves. Bethlehem dropped her head to sniff the glitter. A stagbeetle lumbered over the flattened stems carrying minute spheres of moisture on its carapace. Farmwork was continuing all around the tor as morning brightened to noon and the mist vanished. The faint, mouldy reek of the saltmarsh and wet farmland filled her nostrils. Cows cruised across a shallow sea of whiteness but there was more life in the sky than in the fields. The wintering flocks of starlings and pigeons had been joined by rooks, gulls and Scandinavian thrushes.

Dusk closed with the swift descent of night and the barn owls ghosted over the water meadows past the stream where the heron fished. Returning to the stable Bethlehem heard the curlews cry in the darkness as they flew from the Teign estuary to the River Dart. The golden moons of winter shone through the stall window. St Mary's Head lighthouse flared and was noted by foxes and badgers; but Bethlehem slept standing up, unaware that she had become a yearling in January.

Throughout winter the weather altered the face of the landscape. Sudden fog turned everything to vagueness and cattle moving over the brow of the hill looked twice their normal size Yet at the back of these dream episodes the sparrows chirped and the shrill cry of a bird of prey made the heart beat faster. Then the gales were unleashing snow and sleet. On wings buckling at the tips buzzards rode the storms while Jack pushed his bicycle down the cart-track. Sleet fell from a bitter wind and the puddles hardened. Under the grass the soil was like iron and the young horses trod gingerly over it, sniffing at the whiteness which their breath melted.

The thrill of sunrise as light spread to glaze the frost made the morning gallop glorious. Falls of wildfowl and gulls blotted the distances and over everything the wind droned. Standing on the tor Bethlehem and Bathsheba saw the gleam of breakers sweeping across the bay. The pounding of surf blurred to a continuous thunder and the sun would rise from this, offering no warmth.

Congregating in the yard at Station Lane the boys blew on their fingernails, dreading the rounds which would chill them to the marrow. But there was no respite for the sheep huddled against the hedge at the top of the orchard. They were weighed down under sodden fleeces and stood, heads bowed, with misery brimming their eyes. Jack talked to them as if his words could steer them through suffering.

'You'm as mazed as they old muttonheads,' Arthur Maddock mumbled. His scarf was wrapped around the bottom of his face, but he pulled it down to grin.

'You got a bit of toast jammed between your front teeth,' said Jack.

Arthur picked self-consciously at it with a thumbnail.

'Jesus, but it's bloody cold!' Jack added. He thought of the sheep and Moony and Skilly, and all life's victims and scapegoats. Then he smiled.

'Want to ride the bicycle, Arthur? Go on – take it down the yard and try it for size. You'll soon pick it up.'

'You idn jokin', Irish?'

'Just take it easy and don't break anything, including yourself.'

Sleet turned to rain. The downpour streamed off the Roman noses of the shires. Trant ran a hand over his charges, checking their condition but knowing at a glance they were trim enough for anything. Most of the horses had been harnessed for field work but the mare Magdalene, who had been brought to the farm for a rest, was cart-harnessed.

Mounted stiffly on the bicycle Arthur Maddock wobbled across the yard, whooping like a cowboy and followed by his sisters who applauded when he fell off.

'Habn you got no work to do?' Trant growled. The stooping had set his back in a vice of pain.

The rain eased. Blue showed between clouds and the cold intensified. A shower fell, this time of snow. Cider Mill Tor was white. Smoke climbed from the farmhouse chimney and was swept away.

'Beth's in her stall,' Trant went on. 'Bring her out and us'll get on with it.'

The tethering did not appear to upset her. She stood daydreaming but his entry brought a swift change.

'Beth,' he said. 'Beth, my beauty.'

And she raised her head high and fixed her gaze on some far off place that was not part of his world.

103

'Beth.'

Her ears pointed forward and she listened. Bathsheba pulling at her own tether was apprehensive and executed a little sideways shuffle. Beth's movements were alert and eager now. In the corner of the stall the tabby she-cat was uncoiling from sleep.

Jack laid his head on the yearling's neck and murmured the words she loved and expected to hear. She had known he would come. It was the order of things. Before the horses arrived at the Summer Field they were cared for by Man and in return gave their strength. Then they stepped from worklife into the field. So she allowed herself to be led into the yard.

Trant said, 'Let her bide there a bit for she must learn to stand. Once her's in the shafts her'll spend a long time just moochin' about. Tether her for a while. Tidn fair but it's got to be or her will give 'ee hell when her's hauling a cart. Soon as farmer goes up Stuggy Lane with the steers us'll fit a bit to her bridle. Her's a patient little soul and the discipline will come easy.'

Surprised by the sudden locking of his back the horseman groaned.

'Remember to keep praisin' her. Don't rush anything and don't be tempted to spoil her. Without discipline her will be useless. Arthur can do the same for Sheba.'

The yearling had grown but was still leggy. Despite the weather her white mane, tail and feather had the lustre of well-being due to Jack's constant use of the horn comb.

'When you walk her round in her bridle,' Trant said, 'see you don't tug on the bit. Us doan want her to get a hard mouth. Treat an animal firm but kind, Irish, and it'll give 'ee its best. Don't scold her if you lose your temper. Always gentle the animal along. Most boys get bored and expect too much too soon. Horses get round to obeying you in their own time – some sooner than others.

'Do they ever get bored, mister?'

Trant shrugged and winced. 'I shouldn think so. They like routine. Break an animal's routine and it starts to worry.'

'What'll happen to her when I'm down Station Lane?'

'I expect us'll cope. Me and old Gilbert Pike will carry on with her schoolin'. Us'll keep handling her and tethering her and you can walk her about on the bridle until her's ready to be broken in to work.'

'When's that?'

'Not for a while, boy. We'll let her have two more summers grazing.'

He allowed himself the luxury of a smile and added, 'There's no doubt her's going to be a handsome mare. Red roans always look good but Beth's got her mother's nature. Do 'ee still mean to buy her?'

Jack nodded.

'You'd give everything in the world to own her, wouldn 'ee, Irish?'

Again the lively nod and the pale blue eyes lighting up. I'm buggered if you idn like a beady bloody daw, Trant thought, and he grinned and drew his sleeve across his nose. It was difficult to dislike the boy although envy sometimes stood between the carter and sound judgement. But Jack's power over horses was special and the animals loved him. The little devil needed a clip round the ear once in a while for he could act the fool and do some daft stunts. But the father could be blamed for that. Drunken Irish no-good. It was said Mrs McKenna had even gone to the funeral with a black eye. Ruefully Trant remembered his own workhouse childhood and the grey, silent building where his mother had died bringing him into the world. Then the farm near Totnes and the elderly couple who never smiled, never gave him a kind word. Behind all thought the groan of the treadmill.

'Don't let Arthur ride your bicycle in work hours,' he snapped. 'If he falls off and can't do ort his dad'll blame me. Put the bloody machine in the shed and get some hay down from the loft.'

'He's sharp as a green goosegog,' Arthur confided when he joined him in the stables. 'But he idn bad. He always gives us a little bit of something at Christmas.'

'Why's his missus such a mean bugger?'

'Her hates people. Our mum says her was going to marry a farmer out Stoke Gabriel way but he went and wed a publican's daughter instead. Her's full of poison. That's why her's got a lump on her throat. It's the poison.'

Apparently another young horse was coming up to the farm

105

to be prepared for street work. So Bethlehem and Bathsheba would finish wintering in the linhay whose open side had been boarded up.

'Can I have another ride on your bicycle, Irish?' Arthur grinned, and he forced his upper lip down to try and hide his buck teeth. The effect was ludicrous.

'My name is Jack – plain, simple Jack. Yes, you can ride the bicycle. In the dinner break I'll show you how to do it. It's just the balancing.'

But the grass was dead. A chill crept into his heart. The valley was etched in one long, grey furrow, the trees standing stiff and black, some spiky, others like the skeletons of flames. The steady tempo of the surf lifted to the farm. Perhaps the high-circling specks in the sky were buzzards. It did not matter. At times the world fell apart.

Farmer Maddock took him to the salt marsh down by the railway embankment to do some ditching. It was an easy job and he was left to himself for much of the day. As the tide came in the stream met salt water and spilled over its banks to flood the beds of dead sea lavender and arrow grass. A heron balanced on one leg for a moment and then like a Japanese dancer adopted a series of poses in the shallows of the drainage gut. Standing among the hawthorns Jack watched the bird's splay-toed advance. His ears and nose ached with the cold that was making his eyes water.

13

'What pulls the swifts and swallows back to the sun in those foreign lands? I don't know enough about things – the world, animals, birds and stuff. I know what three and three is, and the date of the Battle of Hastings but I don't understand how those birds cross the sky to the warm countries.'

Kitty was solemn. 'Dad says they only teach you enough to get you by. If us got a proper education we'd start questioning everything.'

'Like what?'

'The way things are – them havin' lots; us havin' bugger all. If you lock up a dog in a coal shed all his life all he knows is darkness. According to Dad the Empire idn built on our ships patrolling the Seven Seas or our soldiers fightin' the savages. It's built on our ignorance. We're like dogs in the coal shed. My sister Dora goes white with rage when her gets on her soapbox.'

Jack smiled. 'If your dad keeps blabbin' in public he'll get the push. Old Lord Warborough will have his guts for garters.'

'Don't 'ee ever think of anything except Beth?'

'No. I know what I want. Maybe your dad wants so much he'll end up with nothing.'

'But you've got to fight for what you believe in, Jack.'

'I only want you and Beth. The world can look after itself.'

She shook her head, smiling unhappily.

'Am I stupid for not wantin' much, Kitty?'

'You idn like the rest and that's for certain,' she said.

Sitting up behind Melody on Wotton's cart he recalled the conversation. A fresh snowfall had blanco'd the streets which were criss-crossed with wheel tracks. Lansworthy sparkled under sunlight. The horse's hooves crumped into the stiff whiteness.

'Tez all right on the Christmas cards,' Wotton sniffed.

The uniforms Chancellor had promised had not been forthcoming but the carters had received ankle-length top coats of navy blue serge with massive collars. The boys wore as many old garments as they could get into but the cold still penetrated and the delivery rounds were grim endurance tests. Then stablework, which in summer had seemed boring and sweaty, was eagerly sought by the gang of waifs that trooped despairingly into the yard at first light. During one harsh spell Lacey went absent with slight congestion of the lungs.

'Congestion my backside,' snorted Old Bob and his head rose and fell in slow nods. 'The bugger can't take it.'

Shivering in a wind that howled around the yard the other boys hated Lacey lying warm in bed eating the piping hot faggots and chips his mother would be ferrying up to him. The snowball fights had lost their novelty except for Skilly who continued making a nuisance of himself until Fred Luscombe sent him blubbering into the shed nursing a thick ear. Only the horses seemed immune to the cold.

Carrying water to the stalls was among the most dreaded jobs. Often the skinny fingers clamped to the handles of the pails cracked and bled at the knuckles, and some boys unashamedly wept. But the other chores inside the stables were pleasant enough. The horses drank as their food was prepared. The Clydesdale half-breeds and the rest of the lighter animals consumed less than the shires who pulled the big wagons. These great horses got extra rations. Apart from hay chaff, long hay and oats, each of them ate four pounds of white peas a day as well as linseed cake and oat straw.

While Melody was drinking Jack slotted fresh rock salt into her lick and began bruising the oats. The sparrows sat round the lip of the crib, chirping until there was enough grain litter amongst the bedding for them to feed.

'Us should scat the lil sods,' Harold Dunsford said. 'But they doan eat a lot and they'm all God's creatures like us and the 'orses. They must suffer this weather.'

Now the yard staff breakfasted in one of the empty stalls, sitting in the straw on meal bags. And for Jack it was always a good beginning to the working day although few things could rival the return to the stables at dusk. Then the faces of his companions would glow in the warmth as if they were lit by the anticipation of the hot food and fireside waiting at home.

Loosing Melody from her gears he hung the collar on the peg, padded side facing outwards to dry. Slush and grime had turned her feather grey but he washed it back to whiteness. Palfrey had shown him how to rub sawdust into the wet hair and shake it out leaving the strands to dry.

'Good,' the horsemaster said, blowing smoke from his lips and removing his pipe.

'Good,' Skilly mimicked, following Jack out of the stables.

'Us've got a real little brown-nose,' said the simpleton's father as the work-force streamed from the yard. 'Irish may be stupid but the bugger's sly. He knows how to creep round the important behinds – the old man's, Palfrey's, Maddock's. Yaas, his nose idn only crooked – it's brown.'

Jack stopped dead and turned. 'You've got to be the world's biggest bloody fool, Luscombe.'

His face had tightened round the cheekbones and his eyes stood out.

'What? What — you cheeky little Irish rat!' Luscombe bellowed and he spread his arms wide and crouched, opening and closing his fists. 'Come on then, take a poke at me. I idn Arthur. I idn cider-puggled.'

'You've got a big mouth, mate,' said Harold Dunsford.

'Keep your snout out of this, Dunsford.'

'Lay a finger on the boy and I'll drop you.'

Considering this Luscombe felt his courage desert him and Old Bob took the opportunity to defuse the situation.

'Get home, all of you,' he said. 'You'm worsn a parcel of schoolgirls.'

'I woan forget this, Irish,' Luscombe muttered.

'Look,' Jack said and he grinned. 'Look, mister. The first time you tread on my toes I'll take a dung fork to you. And that's gospel.'

'Gospel,' Skilly cawed. 'Gospel.'

'I'll give you gospel when you get home,' said his father.

'A dung fork for a big pile of dung.' Jack's voice shook.

'Go back to bogland,' Luscombe jeered, and the boy nuzzled the dusk, throwing back his head and closing his eyes.

'Lansworthy is not like London: there's no real poverty here.' Ormond Chancellor broached a subject rarely touched on in the drawing room. 'The Old Age Pension has removed the threat of the workhouse but I don't think business will gain from it. It's the sort of liberal softness the lower classes will latch onto and milk for all it's worth. A lead swinger can gloat over his employer, knowing he'll have enough cash coming in when he's old to keep the wolf from the door. Letting the donkey have the carrot before it has reached its destination seems to me the height of folly.'

Daubeny ran a fingertip lightly over the tiny skin cancers on his cheeks. Too much foreign sun had left his complexion sallow. Unlike the local businessmen present he did not voice agreement. Seated at a table beside the pianola Edward and Rupert Chancellor were flattered to be included in adult male society. Even though Edward thought Ormond's remarks mindless he continued to smile and nod, wondering why his father tolerated the odious snob. Lansworthy certainly was dead in winter. He wished they had more money. Most of his friends who had returned from India lived in Cheltenham. Lansworthy was the worst kind of frontier hill station. Third raters ruled the roost. Why were people in the trade so dull? And the pianola! The boy sighed. But at least Old Chancellor was unpretentious and cheerful, which was more than could be said for the gathering of jumped-up gents' outfitters, hoteliers and glorified pork butchers.

He rose and went to the windows. The wind drove across the lawns, bending the deodar tree, bringing sleet showers to the hills enclosing Lansworthy Bay. A coppery tinge on the horizon foretold of a worsening of the weather. Poor Rupert! thought Edward. Having a father who couldn't stop wallowing in self-esteem.

'Socialism must carry a lot of the blame,' Ormond was saying.

The blame for what? Edward mused. A shambling ursine

110

figure dressed in a patched jacket and ill-fitting velveteens ventured onto the lawn carrying a spade.

'Moony,' said Rupert from a smile. He draped an arm possessively round Edward's shoulders and added, without turning, 'Do you want Moony tramping across the grass, Father?'

'I do not. He was told to keep to the paths.'

Joining the boys he unlatched the window and beckoned to his guests.

'That creature, gentlemen, is your new working man. We employ him to tidy up the garden a few days a week but he's so lazy he can't be bothered to keep to the paths. Go and tell him to get off the lawn now, Rupert. I'll only lose my temper.'

Rupert's hot flush of embarrassment accompanied him into the open air.

'The fool's hobnails are lethal,' Ormond continued. 'It is scandalous to think of that object having the vote, having the power to put others like himself in high office.'

'A sobering thought,' remarked one of his friends.

Moony was shouted off the grass and vanished into the shrubbery. The men retreated to the fireside, the decanters and soda siphons.

'Fear of hunger and the workhouse just about kept the labour force ticking over,' Chancellor relentlessly ploughed on. 'But basically they are a scrounging, workshy, shiftless lot.'

'What about men like Palfrey whom your father admires and constantly refers to as a pillar of society?' Daubeny enquired, rather mischievously his son thought. Soapbox tirades were not encouraged in their household.

'I don't suppose he's saved five guineas in the ten or eleven years he's been with us,' Chancellor snorted. 'Thousands of destitute old people flock to the workhouse because they've never saved a penny, never planned for tomorrow. All their money went on beer and tobacco. If the lower classes were thrifty the workhouse would be empty.'

'Hear hear,' said a voice across the hiss of soda fizzing a generous scotch.

'And you seriously believe the Old Age Pension will dynamite the system?' Daubeny said.

'Yes,' Chancellor blustered. 'Give the masses something for

111

nothing and you have a very dangerous situation.'

'But haven't they earned their pensions? And surely the five or six shillings the old can expect is less than a pathetic gesture?'

Chancellor was intelligent enough to recognize opposition.

'I'm not a hard man, Daubeny,' he said. 'But if we're to maintain decent standards and keep property sacrosanct they have to toe the line.'

His guest smiled. 'I agree up to a point. But a life of drudgery with no hope at the end of it is something too bleak to contemplate.'

'Oh come now! You do not seriously imagine the drudge who cleans your front steps and blacks the range has the sensitive nature of the lady of the house or Helen?'

'Helen! Sensitive?' Edward exclaimed. 'She's as hard as nails.'

'The brute ignorance and stupidity of the lower class is self evident,' Ormond said. 'That sort of bovine mindlessness is beyond redemption. Socialism is therefore an insult to the thinking man.'

Thinking man, Edward reflected. For some curious reason the tall willowy girl from Churston came to mind, and Irish Jack. Both of them had intelligent eyes. Really the situation was far too complex for drawing room drivel. He smiled at Rupert, feeling older than his sixteen years. The pianola rolled out something bland. No, not bland, he decided, as sleet pattered again on the window; vacuous – music created especially for the mediocre.

It was dark when Moony reached the terrace. He had crossed the town fearfully but for once the small boys hunched round the brazier at the station cab rank were too absorbed in the roasting chestnuts to toss abuse his way. The terrace children welcomed him with a mixture of affection and humour. The close-cropped head and and fierce jowls belied his gentleness, but despite his efforts with the razor he forever looked in need of a shave.

'Here,' he said to Blanche and Lily, and he held up the dead flowers he had retrieved from the garbage heap behind Ormond Chancellor's house. 'Pretty flowers for Florence's grave.'

'They're lovely, Moony,' Blanche whispered.

And he laughed and swung her off her feet and around in a circle. Then he set her down as if she were something immensely fragile.

'Poor little Florence,' he said. 'Up there on a cold night like this.'

'She's with God,' Blanche said. 'She's happy now.'

He shook his head and pawed at the tears.

'Don't be sad, Moony,' said Lily and she took his hand.

'Little people are nice,' he said. 'Big people shout at you.'

He went quietly indoors and took off his boots.

'Moony?' his mother called from the scullery.

'Mum,' he bleated. 'I got some pretty flowers for Florence.'

'Go and sit at the table, love,' said the old woman and she climbed the steps up from the scullery with an awkward movement of the hips. Snuff was caked round her nostrils and the lower part of her face was well dusted. Moony entered a kitchen that was lit by a candle and the feeble glow of two or three coals in the grate. The boots his father had worn to work right up to the day he died stood at the fender.

'My eyes hurt,' sighed the old woman. 'I can't see very well at night no more. I idn doing much sewing.'

The plate of stew was nearly all potato and swede. She set it down before him and rested her hands on his shoulders.

'Pity you can't get a proper job, son. It's getting harder to make ends meet. Lord knows what'll happen to you when I'm gone.'

'You won't go, Mum,' he giggled, spooning stew into his grin. 'I woan let 'ee.'

'I idn going to the workhouse and that's for sure,' said Mrs Endacott. 'I'd rather starve to death upstairs.'

'Irish Jack's trying to get me some more gardening, Mum.'

'That boy has a big heart. Twould make all the difference if you could bring in an extra few bob.'

'Doan I look after 'ee, Mum?'

'Course you do, you girt lummock. Eat up and get by the fire. I'll put some more coal on.'

Bending over the hearth she had a blinding recollection of the old man's body swinging from Lansworthy railway bridge. That Christmas Eve had been raw, dark and rainy and she had come walking home after six hours in the kitchen of one of the

113

big houses on the sea front. The homeless pauper, William Pond, had chosen to hang himself rather than knock on the workhouse door.

Gazing into the flames Moony's mother shivered.

'Why does Moony take dead flowers to Florence Venner's grave?' Blanche asked her mother.

'You know he's soft in the head,' said Mary McKenna.

'I like him,' the child said. 'He's kind.'

'How on earth does Mrs Endacott get by?' said Mary McKenna. 'She's all skin and bone and snuff stains as it is. Bless Moony, but he's the millstone round her neck.'

'I asked Mr Palfrey to speak to old Chancellor,' said Jack. 'Moony's good at gardening and there's an awful lot of garden up Roundham.'

'What about the stables, Jack?'

'Lacey and some of the others would give him hell. He'd never stick it.'

'They're not giving you hell are they?'

'How would they do that?'

'Well,' she said, pursing her lips. 'Well, I know you and I know them.'

She folded her knitting needles on the wool in her lap. '*Mioscaise*,' she whispered absently, pronouncing it 'miskish'. 'Boys are mischief, heartache.'

'Mioscaise would be a good name for a horse,' he grinned. 'Mioscaise, son of Beth.'

'Maybe that bloody horse should come and lodge here,' she said, all the dreaminess gone from her voice.

The little red exercise book was opened on the table. Then she took a pencil from her apron pocket and began writing the housekeeping list: 9 ozs tea 4½d., ¾ of dripping 6d., lamp oil 3¼d., 10 lbs of potatoes 5d., greens 2½d., meat 4/9d., bread 1/9d., soap and soda 9d., coal 1/3d., rent 4/-.

Totting it up, although it hardly ever varied from week to week, she murmured, 'I can't see how the Endacotts survive. She can't be saving a penny on her pittance.'

'But we are, aren't we Mum?' said Michael. 'Every payday something goes in the box.'

The nod at the mantelpiece and biscuit tin was unnecessary.

At the mention of The Box every eye lifted gratefully in that direction.

'Are there workhouses in Ireland, Mum?'

'The world is full of spikes. They're everywhere.'

'Don't you want to go home?' Jack said. 'Home to Ireland?'

'And starve? God, boy – what's there for us now except a lot of hungry relatives and English landlords and the memory of how things were?'

But, she thought, there is something marvellously sad about the uprooting of people and their journey out of the homeland. Awful emigration and all the blood-things left behind for time to blur. Nothing with you but a bundle of clothes and a heart so heavy it threatens to burst as soon as you stop crying. The land drops away, the mountains sink into the ocean and your own tears. Then, then – and she drew breath in a swift, broken way with the sob in her throat – the grey sea and the loss. Everything gone and the future cold and cheerless, like Vera Endacott's hearth.

14

When colds kept Wotton and Cooksley at home the horsemaster reluctantly promoted Lacey to carter. Jack, who was in line for the job, was still too young but if it had been left to Palfrey the boy would have taken Melody onto the streets. Luscombe was eager to share Lacey's triumph. The pair stood together in the yard watching the boys muck out on one of those cold, damp February mornings which get into the soul.

'Buck up, Irish,' Lacey jeered. 'Empty that horseshit and let the men get on with the job.'

The warmth in Jack's grin had not reached his eyes and his face had hardened round the cheekbones. He pushed the wheelbarrow to the spoil heap and tipped it.

Harold Dunsford frowned at Lacey. 'You'll never learn, never. One day that little Irish boy will break every bone in your body. But you'll never learn.'

'I was drunk the last time he hit me,' Lacey said, pressing his fists into a greatcoat so large it made him appear puny and shrivelled.

'Here, Lacey,' Old Bob bawled. 'Don't stand around like you'm foreman. Get mucking out with the rest of the boys.'

'But I'm taking the reins today, Mr Sherwill.'

'You may be a carter by name but you'm a muck shifter by nature,' Old Bob grinned. 'Get shovellin'.'

'Why do they all think the sun shines out your ass, McKenna?' said Luscombe as Melody was backed into the shafts.

Jack grinned and shook his head and coughed. Luscombe pressed a finger to his nose and snorted out a cockle of mucus. He had the stony gaze of an abortionist. Yellow crumbs of sleep clotted his lashes and the corners of his eyes. The elbows and lapels of his greatcoat were greasy and his boots were never clean. Mullah the terrier gazed malevolently at him while the greyness rose cold and dark from the sea.

'Get out of it,' Luscombe growled but the dog answered with passion and stood its ground.

The horses were beautiful in the snow. They steamed and danced sideways, swinging their vehicles this way and that until the carters stilled them. A hot excitement gripped the yard. The horses were in command because they gave the impression they were drawing strength from the elements. Palfrey marched up and down before them sucking at his pipe but saying nothing.

Jack watched him from the muzzy depression that presages illness. His right lung hurt and he was sweating. The phlegm was on his chest and no amount of coughing would throw it up.

'Joseph's calling tomorrow,' Old Bob said. 'I'll get un to give you the once over.'

'We doan need the vet, Bob,' said Luscombe. 'He's ready for the knackers.'

It was obvious he was too ill to work. By the time he had walked home he was sticky with sweat and too tired to take off his boots. Wrapped in a towel he sat with his feet in a mustard bath while Mary McKenna put a couple of hot water bottles in his bed. The girls and Sean were told to keep quiet and she went off to get him something from the chemist. Snuggling under the blankets watching the snowflakes flatten and melt on the window was a luxury he had almost forgotten. Above him the damp had bubbled the wallpaper and the elephant's head was back on the ceiling. It was so quiet the mice could be heard running around the roof.

At lunchtime Kitty called but Mrs McKenna did not leave them alone. Woman and girl sat stiffly on hard-backed chairs exchanging the odd smile and glance between chat. Her first visit, Jack thought, and in my bedroom! The strangeness of it all brought the grin back to his face although the pain in his chest was like a hot knife.

'When the phlegm breaks you'll feel better, love,' said his mother. Kitty had gone and the afternoon was losing its light.

'Don't go sending for the doctor,' he said.

'I will if I think it's necessary.'

'Then you'll take the money from the Horse Fund.'

'I will not!'

'Then I'll lie here and die.'

'Mother of God if you're not stubborn enough to do that!'

'We won't need no doctor. I'll shake this off.'

'Your dad used to sweat it out with hot water bottles and whisky.'

'I'll try the whisky before I go to sleep. If that don't work there's Chancellor's new service.'

'New service?'

'Undertaking,' he laughed, coughed and felt the phlegm shift. 'The hearse is bigger and blacker and shinier than the Co-op's. Fit for royalty, I heard Mr Ormond say.'

'Those sort of jokes aren't funny,' his mother sighed. 'Your gran – my mum – used to say there was no heartbreak like the heartbreak of surviving a child.'

'You're forever on about death. So was Dad. It's as if the Irish are in love with it.'

'Back in Ireland the dying and the burial were about the only dignified things that happened to the poor – to folk like us. People take off their hats to the humblest coffin.' She shook her head and tucked in the bed clothes. 'I'm not in love with it but if you've lived with it sittin' across the room like an unwelcome lodger you gossip about it. Have a nap before supper and I'll get you a candle, unless you want to lie up here in the dark.'

'A candle would be nice.'

But among all the patterns on the ceiling there were no horses' heads.

Spring was there beneath the countryside waiting to flood the world. Off Roundham Head the dark figures of crabbers stood in their open boats hauling the pots. The mummified body of a gull lay in the grass that was salt-browned and stringy. Atlantic swells climbed the harbour wall to fall again leaving the stonework glistening.

'You need a shave,' Kitty said, laughing through her surprise. He clamped her in his arms and rubbed his chin against her cheek.

'Don't,' she giggled.

Arm in arm they walked over the meadows to Goodrington Sands.

'You're so small,' he said.

'I idn. You'm getting taller.'

'I won't get much taller,' he said. 'My dad was five nine and Mum's no more than a dwarf.'

'I know. We met, remember, when you had bronch? Sittin' there with her watchin' us was terribly embarrassing. I think I'd die if you come home to our house. Dad's so serious. He expects everyone to share his views. He gets so worked up about politics Mum can hardly stop herself laughing.'

'Lefty' Widdicombe they called him down the yard but Jack did not tell Kitty. According to the Dunsford brothers he was still breathing fire and revolution in the pubs every Saturday. 'I'm surprised old Warborough puts up with it, him being such a blue-blooded Tory,' Harold said.

His lordship's tolerance was short-lived. The estate bailiff dismissed Widdicombe soon after the March sowing. The misery which had left Kitty's face drawn and haggard registered in her voice when she broke the news at their Saturday evening rendezvous.

'Us'll be out on the street,' she faltered. 'God knows who'll put us up. Dad's brothers are in Canada and Mum's family doan want nothing to do with a Socialist. They'm all in tied cottages as it is. Yes I know, you warned me old Warborough would have his guts for garters.'

He shook his head mutely and wrapped his arms around her, but Kitty wriggled free.

'We'm penniless, Jack, and Dad can't keep his mouth shut. Mum's ill with the worry. Surely the truth idn that important? Why won't he hold his tongue?'

She pushed the plate away, poured some salt onto the table and using a fingertip drew a little face. The mouth, Jack noted, was turned down at the corners.

'You will come and live with us,' Jack said. 'Mum likes you.'

119

'All of us? Mother, Dad, me, Dora, and the others?' Her sad smile fell across his heart. 'I can't abandon them, Jack. They all love me. Don't order any tea, please – I don't want anything.'

When she wept the other customers pretended everything was normal although there was sympathy in the odd, furtive glance. No one will do anything, Jack thought. None of them care enough unless misfortune touches them directly. The inertia of his class angered and puzzled him. How easy it would be for them to come together and act together like a big fist. That was the way to deal with bullies. Why hadn't it happened at school? The big buggers and the rich buggers could get away with murder.

'Maybe Mr Sidney will help out,' he said. 'He's a genuine Christian.'

'So's Lord Warborough. He's in church every Sunday.'

'But old man Chancellor tries to do good things all week. I'm hoping he'll give Moony a job.'

'Would us get a house, Jack?'

'I hope so, Kitty. Old Chancellor keeps on about God moving in mysterious ways. They say he eats bits of the bible for breakfast.'

Odd things were becoming clear. Somewhere along the line God had decided the rich were the chosen people or there wouldn't be any workhouses. Why was poverty a sin? So many good poor people went to church and didn't drink or swear or do anything wrong. But they still finished up in the union or the gutter. Not Kitty! Not her and her family. Holy Mother of God he would put Kitty on Beth's back and take her off to the rainbow's end. As the resolution crystallised it fell apart and helplessness returned, but not at the expense of hope. Sidney Chancellor finally extinguished that with a chilling casualness.

'No, no, McKenna,' and from a smile. 'Widdicombe won't do at all. But your friend Moony might fit into the yard.'

'Charlie Widdicombe is a good man, mister.'

'Let me be the judge of that, McKenna. When there's a vacancy in the stables we'll give Moony a chance.'

'He'd be better off gardening.'

'The stables,' Chancellor said. 'My greenhouse is full of sensitive plants. Mucking-out horses isn't quite the same as pruning fig trees or cosseting grapes.'

120

It was raining quietly and sofly as a prelude to spring. The celandines were blooming and daffodils opening beside the pond in Victoria Park.

'Chancellor isn't taking on any more men,' Jack said, and he looked into her eyes.

She smiled and her lower lip trembled.

'Kitty.'

'Yes, Jack. Horses work and they get housed and fed and respected. My dad works and he speaks the truth and he's got nothing.'

'It's not the animals' fault, Kitty.'

'Anyway,' she said, drawing the strings of her purse and looking down at it and up at him, swiftly, 'he's got a job and a cottage near Slapton. The farm is owned by Quakers. We'm lucky I suppose. They'm good bosses.'

'But Slapton's miles away.'

'Miles away from the workhouse.'

'Yes. I'm sorry, I'm sorry. When do you go?'

'Thursday – on the Kingsbridge bus. Dog, cats, us, our bits and pieces.'

'Oh Kitty!'

'Don't worry,' she said. 'I'll be out of the way and you'll soon forget me. You've got the horse.'

Then the words would not rise out of his unhappiness. The rain dripped off the peak of his cap.

'Will you write?' she said in a barely audible whisper.

'You'll have to first because I don't know your new address.'

'Fool,' she laughed. 'But you will, Jack, you will. And you'll come and see me?'

'I don't want you to go. You could carry on working at Chancellor's and go home weekends. There's room for you in our house.'

'My mum wouldn't allow it.'

'No,' he said, his eyes empty.

'Please, dear. I finish early Wednesday. I'd like to go to Tor Barton and say goodbye to Beth and the other horses.'

Her fingertips brushed his eyelashes.

'Don't you ever cry, Jack?'

'No.'

They met under the Big Tree when the rooks were putting

121

the finishing touches to their nests.

'Spring is a bad time for things to end,' he said.

'Do you read stories, Jack?'

'I hardly ever read. Words don't smell of the open air or sing or bleat or moo.'

Over the water meadows the curlews were crying. The March wind lifted the dust behind the harrow and sent it billowing off Cider Mill Tor. Bracing her forelegs Bethlehem came down the hill.

'Her's so lovely,' Kitty whispered.

The white mane stood up and curled and spread. Larks were aloft and singing. Kitty pressed her lips to the warmth of Bethlehem's shoulder.

'Darling,' she wrote a week or so later. 'Us have got a dismal little place about two miles from nowhere. It is very damp and the chimbley smokes. But Mum and Dad are happy. Dora isn't. I have got a job, too, in service. Let us hope it will be better than the last time. I miss Chancellor's and I miss you. Eternal love, Kitty.'

'Makes you think,' said Lacey as Jack dabbed metal polish on the bridle buckle.

'Makes you think what?' Fred Luscombe said, winking.

'Irish has this power over horseflesh but he drives the maids away. They run miles from his crooked conk.'

Jack glanced sideways at him, unsmiling.

'The bird's flown, hasn she, Irish?' Lacey laughed. 'Tidn no good you crying "Here Kitty, Kitty". Her's gone.'

Skilly came capering into the tackroom.

'Here Kitty, Kitty,' he cawed. Like a big stupid parrot, Jack thought. His throat was dry and he had begun to shake. Two or three of the other boys gathered at the door eyed him warily but said nothing.

'Here Kitty, Kitty,' the imbecile cried again.

Jack rose and swivelled in one movement and punched Skilly hard below the belt. He doubled up with a long, staccato inhalation of astonishment and pain.

'You saw that,' Luscombe whispered to the audience. He was slowly unbuckling his belt. 'The bastard attacked Skilly.'

'Skilly asked for it,' someone said. 'Why don't you leave Jack alone and get on with your work.'

'Not this time,' Luscombe said. Skilly was sobbing now and crawling towards the door on his hands and knees. 'That little Irish bastard needs a lesson.'

'And I idn drunk now,' rasped Lacey, rolling up his sleeves.

'He's going to get a good leathering,' Luscombe went on. 'Grab hold of un, Arthur, and I'll lay my belt across his back.'

'Bloody come on then,' Jack said. All the misery and frustration of the past weeks was boiling to black rage in his body but Luscombe ignored the danger signals. The fat man flicked the belt and the buckle caught Jack under the chin, leaving a little blue mark and a swelling. Lacey smiled but Jack stood his ground.

'You doan hit my boy, Irish,' Luscombe was crooning. 'Not my flesh and blood. Oh no, oh no.'

Across his crowing the first swallows of spring darted through the open window to the half-completed nest in the angle of the wall and ceiling. Ducking low Jack sank his head in the fat man's paunch and raked his shins with his boots. A knee to the genitals flopped Luscombe down to writhe and squeal. Despite his own misfortunes Skilly began to giggle. Yet again Lacey realised he had made a terrible mistake. He turned to the other boys but their faces were blank. Before he could say a word Jack was hitting him, brushing aside his flailing arms and standing over him as he crouched and tried to protect his head.

'McKenna,' Palfrey's voice cut through the thumping and grunting. 'McKenna.'

Jack was returning from the numb rapture of violence which negates reason and sluices the heart of its grievances. There was blood on his knuckles. Red streaked Lacey's forehead and ran down his cheeks.

'Outside you lot,' Palfrey rapped. 'Start shifting the meal bags while I have a quiet word with Lacey.'

Luscombe groaned but refused to face the horsemaster.

'Idn it about time you started to act your age?' Palfrey said. 'For Christ's sake grow up.'

'Twadn my fault, Mr Palfrey,' Lacey sobbed. 'He attacked Skilly and Skilly's dad. I tried to stop un. It wadn my fault.'

'You'm the proper hero,' the horsemaster sneered. 'I heard 'ee geeing Irish up but don't worry you're not getting the sack.

Without any help you are turning the yard into your private hell and I'll see you broken as I saw men broken in the army. I won't interfere unless you put the horses in danger. Before long you won't have a friend in town.'

15

Throughout spring and early summer Lacey's unpopularity grew but he clung to what he had. His vanity made it possible for him to walk through contempt unscathed. He never laughed at himself and, like Luscombe, tried to conceal his insecurity behind sneering repartee and ranting. But Hazel Cundy remained dazzled by his good looks. She would pass her fingers through his wavy brown hair while he railed against the world. The brown eyes returning her gaze were moist and tears sprang to them far too often. Yet he had the facility for turning this to his own advantage.

Towards the end of July the Frenchman Bleriot flew the English Channel and at breakfast one morning Lacey told the stable staff he was thinking of becoming an aviator.

'If a Frog can fly the Channel I'm bloody sure an Englishman can do it quicker and better,' he claimed fiercely.

'But wouldn it make your arms ache?' Old Bob asked.

As laughter careered across the yard Harold Dunsford said Arthur was so full of hot air he'd drift over like a balloon.

'I'll show you,' Lacey smiled pityingly. 'One day I'll show you.'

'Show us what?' said Cooksley.

Skilly guffawed. 'His willie. Arthur will show us his willie.'

'Will'ee show us your willie, Arthur?' the Tucker boy from

Windy Corner quipped, and Lacey was glad his enemy was at the farm and not there to revel in his humiliation.

Jack was walking through the long grass on Cider Mill Hill, letting Bethlehem feel the gentle force at the other end of the lead. The yearling shifted the bit against her teeth and swished the flies off her haunches with her tail. Twitching muscles just under her hide kept the insects on the move.

'Can I go down the beach on your bicycle, Jack?' Arthur Maddock called from the paddock.

Jack waved and nodded. Walking several paces behind him Bathsheba whinnied enquiringly.

'You've had your turn,' said the boy and Bethlehem started prancing.

'Good Beth. Beautiful Beth.'

The carters were eating breakfast on the farmhouse steps. Jack brought the yearlings into the yard and saw Trant and the vet entering the stables. The wall-eyed collie rushed out the length of its rope as the horses approached. Bethlehem stopped and waited for Jack's command but Bathsheba leapt frenziedly until a couple of men restrained her.

'Tis the vet,' Pike said. 'They 'orses know when his business involves one of them. They can smell it.'

'Old Iona isn well,' another carter explained. 'If her sees Christmas her'll be lucky.'

'Maybe it's not that serious,' Jack said.

'Vets are expensive, boy. Maddock wouldn call in Josephs for nort.'

'It's a terrible shame,' Jack mumbled.

'Yes it is. Iona is a good animal, a real pleasure to work with,' said Pike. ''Ere,' he went on, staring into the boy's glum face. 'Us mustn't look on the dark side. Vets do their best to save life. So cheer up and grab a bite to eat.'

'He'll be in training,' said the young carter from Three Beaches.

'Training for what?' Pike said.

'The return bout with Luscombe and Lacey.'

'Dang me! If that doan sound like a music hall act,' the old labourer chuckled.

The noises made by the men pattered softly through Bethlehem's stillness. Flies swarmed over the dung on the yard

126

floor and the surface of her body continued to quake and twitch. The sun that kept Trant's joints loose and his temper sweet washed over her. Gold dappled the mud under the elderberry beside the cowshed. Shadows swung like matadors' capes as the breeze stirred the tree tops. Her gaze came to rest on the boy, willing him to turn and take her head in his hands. His eyes were transparent. She could peer into them and see the prairie of light where something neither horse nor boy was waiting. The vision was profound and thrilling.

He tied the halter ropes to a metal ring in the wall and went inside the stables. Maddock and Trant were listening to Josephs. The vet had grown a beard and his appearance had changed considerably. In his black suit and bowler he now looked like a solemn young rabbi.

'What is it, Irish?' Maddock said.

'They say Iona's ill, mister.'

'You doan miss a bloody thing, do you,' said Trant, wiping his hands on his apron. The boy's grin and shake of the head no longer irritated him.

Josephs smiled. 'Nothing is going to happen to the animal.'

'Not yet, anyway,' said Maddock, and the pair of collies at his feet padded up to Jack and tried to thrust their muzzles into his hands. 'This time the old lady fooled me. I thought her had something the other horses could catch.'

'A false alarm,' said Josephs. 'But in her case it could be serious enough.'

'Can I have a look at her, mister?'

'Yes – and I'd welcome a second opinion.'

'You aren't going to put her down?'

'Of course not. Come and run your eye over her.'

Iona recognised him instantly and lifted her head. The snuffled greeting surprised the vet, for until then the old mare had stood silently as if everything outside her discomfort lacked interest. A spasm of shivering had her laying back her ears. Then Jack saw weariness struggling with something else in her eyes. Her glance moved on from face to face and returned to Jack but he felt her mind continuing its travels beyond the cob and tiles. She was breathing in short little gasps.

The shivering stopped.

'What's her pulse like?' Jack said.

127

Josephs coughed into his fist to hide his smile. 'Rapid,' he said, '– like her breathing.'

'And she's got a temperature,' the boy frowned. 'I'll bet money she's constipated as well.'

'Really bound-up,' Trant chuckled.

Jack ran a hand down Iona's neck. 'I'd say she has a fever but the farmer thought it could be something more serious, like influenza, so he called you, mister.'

'Influenza or anthrax,' said Maddock.

Jack looked hard into Iona's eyes. 'There's no spotting and I take it she hasn't been passing blood.' Then he stroked her throat, belly and upper legs.

'No swelling. It isn't anthrax.'

'Now the treatment,' Josephs said.

'Cook her grain and give her half rations, and have plenty of fresh water handy all the time.'

'You've forgotten the warm enemas, twice a day,' the vet added.

'It sounded like Palfrey speaking,' Trant sniffed, and Jack grinned.

'I've learnt a lot from him and you, mister. I don't forget much when it comes to horses.'

'You'll do Sherlock Holmes out of a job,' said Maddock, tugging good-humouredly at the boy's hair. 'I think Iona can be left in your hands. You've plenty of time between playing nursemaid to they yearlings. I want her ready for some light haulage when us've dipped the sheep.'

'The boy learns quickly,' Josephs said. 'Mr Chancellor told me he was bright. I hadn't realised just how bright.'

'Like a daw,' said Trant. 'Jack Daw.'

They walked pensively out into the sunlight.

'He's probably never read a book right through in his life,' the vet continued. 'But he seems able to bring his own observations and what he has picked up from others to bear on a particular problem – unless this is an isolated case?'

'No, Jack's got a way with horses,' said Maddock. 'With Palfrey and co. learnin' him he can't go wrong.'

'But an education would do wonders,' the vet said.

'McKenna knows his place,' Trant said tartly. 'Book learnin' won't alter that. It won't plough a field or put a team in harness.

I've never read a book right through but I can measure a horse's grub with my eye and loose a skittish mare from her gears blindfold.'

Ushering the vet into the farm kitchen Maddock said, 'Trant can't read or write, Mr Josephs. He's a sour-gutted sod but he's had a rough life.'

Josephs sighed. 'I guessed as much as soon as I opened my mouth.'

He sat and waited for the tea to be poured.

'But it's such a shame a boy like McKenna has to finish up in a dead-end job with the rest of the herd.'

'You and old Lefty Widdicombe would get on like a house on fire,' Maddock said.

'In London people are being forced to take men like Widdicombe seriously.'

'Bliddy Socialists,' the farmer sneered. 'I wudn give 'em the dirt from between my toes.'

Josephs tactfully changed the subject.

An important stage in the breaking of the yearlings was getting them accustomed to the weight of the harness. At first it was never the complete gears but enough leather for the young animals to feel they were carrying something other than sunlight. Then Jack and Arthur Maddock led them round the paddock or left them standing like advertisements for patience which the horsemen never took for granted.

Jack's love of Kitty was honed to desperation not only by her absence but through knowing she was unhappy in her job. On her lips the words 'in service' had sounded like a gaol sentence. Standing at the gate watching the young animals playing after they had been released from their gears he recalled Kitty cataloguing the drudgery of the domestic servant's existence. It was agony to think of her working sixteen hours a day at chores she hated while he shared the beauty of life with the yearlings. Every morning he climbed the chestnut tree to look at the names he had carved on the bole.

By the light of the lantern in the stables he wrote: 'Dearest, gentle Kitty. Every day I climb the tree behind the linhay and think of how my heart holds you and your heart holds me. Iona has been ill but she is better now. Beth and Sheba are growing fast. Working on the farm I don't get much time off but when I go down the yard again I will come and see you. Everyone at the store misses you. I am sorry you heard about the little set-to I had with Arthur Lacey and Luscombe. No, I am not in trouble. Don't worry about me. Loving you is all that matters. Keep your chin up. Things will get better. If the moon is out on my way home at night I can see the White Lady of Lansworthy and I ask her to keep an eye on you. Things aren't right without you. All my love, Jack.'

With short steps and much slithering and jostling the wethers came down the lane. The horses were gazing intently at the scene dusk was stealing as if they were committing it to memory. The landscape was faintly freckled with sounds: the cawing of rooks, cattle lifting their voices, moorhens crying. Beth stood under the tor. All the nuances of blue and grey were laid in thin glazes upon distance. Out of this dreamscape birds emerged and became substantial only to retreat again into vagueness. Bumble dors whirred across the meadow and settled on the cow dung. Bats were also on the wing and the air was so still she could hear the muffled bumping of the badgers in their sett under the hedge. Often from the steady rhythm of her heart some of the day's happenings grew again in her mind. The boy was calling her name once more and smiling up at her as he removed the bramble tendril from her fetlock and lifted her feet. A hare lolloped past the horses. The lights on the bay were not reflections of the stars; they were the lanterns of the Mary's Haven fishing fleet returning to harbour.

Further over the water beyond Roundham Head half a dozen warships were anchored.

The corn wagons had brought the harvest to the rickyard and small creatures had taken possession of the stacks. Jack looked at the red soil turning to dust in his hands. Summer was never hard-edged like winter. The ageless farmland sailed through the season under the hum of insects. It was travelling to the place which had no boundaries – emotion made landscape. The mystery left him breathless with an excitement that communicated itself to the yearlings and Iona. There was still fire in the old horse. She let another voice quench the sounds of a day which seemed to last forever. She stood motionless. His

130

agility turned the harnessing into a kind of dance, a celebration of her powers. She was loved and admired and her services were appreciated. Carting half a load of potatoes did not tax her strength. Iona was working again and she knew it was only a matter of time before *he* came back to attend to her needs. The one who had taken her onto the streets summer after summer could smile across the lantern light and whisper the words meant only for her ears.

'Her was young Sid Anning's mare,' Trant said. 'They did the local deliveries back along when Chancellor's wadn so posh.'

The horses puffed into their nosebags as the white-domed cumulus of midday sent the shadows flowing up the far hillsides. Jack waited for the carter to continue.

'Sid died of appendix but her habn forgot him. Horses like Iona don't forget.'

So that's what she's waiting for, Jack thought. He sat on the farmhouse steps tugging the tiny ears of grain off a stem of wild rye. On either side bees were socking into the fuchsias and snapdragons of Maddock's front garden. It was a windy day but Trant was indifferent to the beauty around him. Mournfully he eyed the ploughs, pulling-trees, rollers and harrows which were gathering rust against the milking shed. Mullein and foxgloves stood with fireweed among the implements. In a corner full of nettles the Maddock children were trying to persuade some kittens out of the woodpile.

'Dad will only drown 'em,' sobbed the little girl, but she was ignored.

'You can't go wishing your life away,' Mrs McKenna said when she heard Jack say for the third time that evening how he couldn't wait for autumn.

'I know,' she added, stopping him short as he hastened to explain. 'By then you'll be back at the yard and free to gallivant off to see that girl.'

'She isn't "that" girl: she's Kitty, like you are Mother and not "that" woman.'

'I'm sorry,' she smiled. 'Just don't keep living for tomorrow or you'll have nothing to look back on. The horses take each moment as it comes because they're all precious.'

'Like the moments you spent trying to sort out Dad?' he said in a hard little croak which surprised her. His voice had broken and she found it difficult to take seriously. 'Did you enjoy living through those moments?'

She could not lie to him, nor could she think of an honest reply. Pressing her lips together she returned to the pastry and the flour-whitened table top.

Then the foxgloves had withered and died. Gulls were crying loudly before rain to rival the distant braying of Warborough's peacocks. The aggressive cadences of the thunderstorm rumbled and reverberated over hills. But autumn's rain lacked real sting and for the first time in years there was no Angarrick pig being dragged to the slaughter. The club membership had fallen out over how the choicest meat should be divided.

'I'll miss the pork,' Mary McKenna confessed dreamily. 'The last pig was a little beauty.'

'But he stank out the terrace,' said Blanche.

Taking Solomon onto the streets alone one wet morning and sitting on the tip-cart in his oilskins and sou'wester was the accolade. At the back of Jack's mind while he flicked the reins and set the horse trotting along the Esplanade was the certainty of Sunday's freedom. And Kitty had the afternoon off. I'll see her he sang inside himself as the rain smacked against the oilskin. His eyes clenched on joy so that none of it could escape into the day.

The clop of hooves and the wheels grating and grinding over the cobbles carried him buoyantly through work. He was delivering parcels to guest houses and villas all the way to Abbot's Quay and back through Compton and Marldon. Other vehicles rumbled by: vans and drays, wagons loaded with farm provender, cabs, buses, a coal cart. Clasping the reins was different to taking the lines of horses yoked to farm implements. Between calls his sense of detachment from the rest of the world was total. The horses trotted obediently and Jack dozed and let Kitty occupy his thoughts. Yet whenever they approached the gangs working on the tram lines which would link Abbot's Quay and Lansworthy he was on the alert. Palfrey's creed governed all his dealings with the horses. 'Treat them as green animals who know little about the carrier trade and you and they will always be safe.'

The hogweed held dead, stiff-spoked stars to the gathering

greyness. Death is so strange, Jack thought. He and his horses were alive and breathing, living parts of everything around them. But his father was gone. A door had been slammed in the wind and a flame snuffed out. Where did it all go, the life your heart measured in little, regular thuds? Where did it come from? He recalled Bethlehem's birth and the things he had read in her eyes.

16

The church lifted its tower like a grey, rigid finger proclaiming 'Thou shalt not' to all believers. Behind it light was filling the sky. Across the South Hams mist streamed away and the farmhouses were declaring themselves on hillsides and hilltops.

He passed through a hamlet of half a dozen cottages thrown untidily around another church. The bicycle wheels hissed moistly through the mud, tossing up a fine, red spray. At either hand were hedges, fields and dark, still woods. Then he crossed a bridge, walked his machine up the hill and found himself in that curious limbo where the familiar ends and speculation begins. Halwell was behind him and he was pedalling over high ground to catch the faint, far off clamour of church bells and witness the lift and flocking of birds.

At Cotterbury Forge he stood the bicycle against a gate and picked an ivy leaf from the hedge. Then he put it under his cap and came on to the villge of Strete. A wagon loaded with logs was crawling up the hill behind a pair of of shires. The animals were in bad condition but the man at the business end of the lines looked happy enough. He waved to Jack who let gravity and the gradient take over. Ahead was a breathtaking view of Start Bay, Slapton Sands and Start Point. The mist was still thinning and the sky ascended to great heights in the east.

He raced along the track that was littered with shingle and

pebbles. The fresh water ley was to his right and the sea on the other side. The track ran straight to the hamlet of Torcross, and Kitty was sitting on the wall where the bus stopped. He waved and she stood up. A pregnant woman sullenly regarded him from a doorstep before retreating into her cottage.

'You must be worn out,' Kitty said, taking his kiss on the lips.

He cupped her face in his hands.

'Kitty, Kitty.'

'I idn going to fly away,' she whispered but tears were at the back of her smile, and as he wrapped her in his arms she began to cry bitterly and quietly. His face was wet with her heartbreak when he stood back and produced the ivy leaf.

'Fidelity,' she said. 'An ivy leaf for fidelity and marriage.'

They sat on the wall and the ducks called from the water behind them.

'Did you have to walk far?' he said.

'A mile or so. It was heaven after doing for them at the Big House.'

'There's a job for you at Chancellor's. I'd find you good lodgings and you could send money home.'

'I couldn. Mum would die. Her idn very well as it is. My little sister Maude's got croup and Mum is up all hours of the night. If only I had a different job but there's nort round here except domestic service. When the wind's blowin' and the rain shuts that awful house off from everywhere else I want to die.'

He shook his head, mutely. Feeling as he did and finding it impossible to put his emotions into words was almost as painful as absorbing some of her misery.

'To make things worse,' she suddenly announced. 'I've got toothache – in one of me back ones.'

'You really are in the wars, love.'

They left the bicycle leaning against the wall and walked the sands which they had to themselves. Crab boats were lying, keels upward, above the high-water mark. Start Bay was the colour of steel under an ash grey sky. The beach curved gently into distance.

The love had to be proclaimed and the kisses were sweeter than he had imagined. Kitty was still small but her body had lost some of its angularity.

'Are you walkin' out with any other maids?' she asked, half-serious despite the cajoling tone.

'Only about five or six and Hazel Cundy.'

'Don't joke, please. That terrible Hazel Cundy!'

'Lacey's sweetheart.'

'Anybody's sweetheart. How's your real lady friend? You did look in on her this morning before you set off to see me?'

'I did. I brushed her mane and put a sheen on her feather and gave her a kiss.'

She giggled. 'You and that 'orse!'

'Our horse. One day we'll put all our belongings in the cart and Beth will take us away somewhere where you won't have to black ranges and polish fish knives for flinty-hearted toffs. We'll have a fine hoolie and take to the road.'

'A fine what?' she laughed.

'Hoolie, shindig, celebration. I'll show you how to dance with a horse.'

Abruptly the beach shelved to deep water. Waves stood up and collapsed with a roar. Again Jack seemed to drift on forces beyond his control: the ebb and flow of light and noise, the shift of pain as her words opened new areas of unhappiness. But it was necessary for her to talk about her work like a sick person incanting the minutiae of an ailment. He could not conceive anything more horrific than being imprisoned in a house doing chores from dawn to dark.

'Fourteen pounds a year,' she concluded. 'And this is what scares me: some women do it all their lives.'

'Not you,' he said, tossing a pebble far out into the water. 'Sir Jack will come riding up on his charger to carry you off to the castle.'

'In Angarrick Terrace?' she sighed.

'Forget the terrace, Kitty. I want a home with some land to stable the horse and grow some veg.'

'My dad don't believe in private ownership.'

'He has his ideas, I got mine. Is he still up on that soapbox?'

'Not at work. Mum stopped that. Her woan have un sacrificing us to his principles ever again. Her doan want to be married to another Tolpuddle martyr.'

'Tallpiddle what?'

'You'm so dumb, Jack,' she laughed.

'Bog Irish.'

'Lovely Irish. All you need is a horse and a dream and you'm happy. My dad's bleeding inside for the whole working class and most of them doan care if he lives or dies. It's breaking his heart.'

The beach and the road remained deserted, and Jack and Kitty felt loneliness creep off the sea.

'The future scares me,' she continued. 'So many honest people have a bad ending. At night sometimes I lie in bed thinking of all those poor, sick old people who die without a candle to light their darkness or a hand to catch hold of.'

'Gloom and doom,' he groaned, breaking away from her and stalking to the wave-brek, a hand raised theatrically to his brow. 'All is gloom and doom. Cruel sea, take me to thy bosom. I can face this life no more. Doomed, doomed I tell you.'

And he fell backwards onto the shingle, clutching his heart. 'You idiot,' she laughed but there was tenderness in her voice and her kiss was warm.

They sat on the pebble bank and watched the waves break and fall apart. Kitty took the leaf from her purse and held it to the sky.

'What are you going to do with it?' he asked. The breeze spread strands of dull, blonde hair across her face.

'Press it in our bible. Keep it always.'

'On psalm twenty-three,' he said.

'"The Lord is my shepherd, I shall not want",' she said and waited for him to complete it.

'"He maketh me to lie down in green pastures, he leadeth me beside the still waters, he restoreth my soul". Beth and me will have our green pastures one day, Kitty. You'll be happy when you see us there and know we're waiting for you to join us after the work day.'

Then the wind coming off the sea had a foretaste of winter in its chill, and her fingers closing round his hands were like ice.

17

They met half a dozen times after Christmas but the days of separation dragged. Bethlehem seemed acutely conscious of his unhappiness. He was up at the farm working and could not get Sundays off. This might have been intolerable if Kitty had continued taking her half-day on Sunday to suit her mistress. But the lady of the house had been told of her between-maid's liaison with the bicycling farmboy and had disapproved. So Kitty's time off fell on Thursday afternoons, once a month, to the satisfaction of her employers. 'No followers,' Kitty was told by the housekeeper, 'means precisely that.'

The Troubles in Ireland rarely carried over the sea to touch the McKennas although Jack and Michael had the occasional brush with loudmouths at work. Dublin was as far off in most people's minds as New York or Berlin, and Mrs Vosper summed it all up when she said every part of the Empire had its troublemakers. Her youngest brother had served with Paddies in India and they had 'got on like a house on fire'.

Mary McKenna rode the condescending remarks gracefully, believing them to be well-intentioned. Her new-found prosperity stood her in good stead with her neighbours. Sean had started work on a crabber so there was meat three times a week now on her table. The gauntness had gone from her face and she appeared to have shed the extra years which poverty and worry had bequeathed.

Married to Christ, Jack thought, shaking the sawdust vigorously out of Bethlehem's feather. The filly's eyes were on him, measuring his actions, harvesting confidence from the touch of his hands. He had walked her in the stream to wash the mud off her legs. When her fetlocks were dry he ran a comb through the long hair and laid it in silky shagginess over her hooves.

Bethlehem gazed through the sun-flushed cobwebs masking the linhay window. The boy's words blurred to a long croon of affection. Bathsheba, standing under Arthur Maddock's brush, passed from her knowing. The world around her faded. But why was he always ahead of her in that countryside behind her eyes? Why was he waiting to open the gate to let her into that green light? Who was the shire gelding cropping the grass with Bathsheba? There were other horses and other men each going their separate ways. A wave of horses broke from the sun and spread across the prairie. Iona, Melody, Princess, others, too, whom she knew yet were nameless. Then she stared through her breath at the ceiling and heard the spring rain tapping through the roof fade to a whisper as it turned to snow.

She lifted a leg and brought it down hard to dislodge the flies. The boy opened the door and she walked into the paddock where the cuckoo snow and hawthorn blossom lay in drifts under the hedges. The shower faded and the snow on the linhay roof began to steam. The curlews were calling as he put her in harness and led her up and down the field. Her power vibrated down the lead and met another force. Bethlehem's nostrils rounded and took in the morning's coldness and scents. The shire geldings and a couple of mares were being led off Cider Mill Hill. They paced unhurriedly to the day's work. Sun gold dappled the chestnut mares as they turned their heads and greeted the fillies with that low snuffling which for Jack was the finest sound of the morning.

'Well,' said Maddock. 'The old King's daid.'

He folded the newspaper carefully and had one last glance at the headlines.

King Porker VII, Jack thought, so close to laughter he had to pretend to blow his nose. The carters were solemn and dejected, and their grief baffled Jack who had a lot to learn about the

139

English character. Some of them had been stood off during the bad weather.

'He wadn much different from us,' Maddock went on. "'Cepting he had a bob or two and could twist the ladies round his little finger.'

'Old Ted with his cigars, booze and race horses,' Pike said, almost reverently as if the King's vices had won the love and admiration of his subjects.

'He went at midnight,' said Maddock. 'Bloody bad chest like the illness that saw off my father.'

'It'll be some funeral,' said Trant. 'They'll all be there, all your kings and queens. I'm buggered but England won't be the same without 'un.'

The horses worked unaware that anything momentous had disturbed the human world. Spring's succulence oozed between their teeth as they tugged mouthfuls of new grass. Calm, moth-haunted nights added a new dimension to the outdoor living, but the fillies were two years old, approaching the time when they would be initiated fully into the worklife.

To begin with there was the shoeing. It would happen the morning after Empire Day at the St Michael's Road forge. Bethlehem and Bathsheba were carted along the Mary's Haven Road to Tweenaway and on to the smithy. The shire gelding pulling them was to have his back teeth filed and stood placidly in line with the other horses while the fillies stamped and shifted apprehensively. The ring of metal on metal was an exciting if disturbing sound.

'Hush now,' Jack said, tightening his grip on the halters.

Trant turned and frowned at the youngsters and said: 'They've got a whiff of the scorched horn.'

'A funny old smell,' said Jack.

'Tidn painful, though. Archie Diamond knows his job.'

Jack chatted with the grooms and farmboys who were holding a variety of animals from hacks and hunters to work heavies. The clanging of the hammer and anvil, and the acrid stink of horn burning to the kiss of hot new shoes gave the smithy an atmosphere of its own. Sparks streamed through the half dark where the fire glowed and the bellows sucked and roared.

'I'll take the roan first,' said Diamond. He was a dark,

140

well-built man carrying no spare flesh.

'She's no trouble, mister,' Jack said.

'Good,' said the smith, lifting one of Bethlehem's hind feet to clean the hoof. Then he trimmed and pared the horn and the filly blew quietly through her nose.

'You'll get used to it, maid,' Diamond said, plucking the shoe out of the forge. He used the shoe-tongs to work it on the anvil, beating it into shape with a turning hammer. Before placing the metal to the hoof he tapped it on the anvil to knock off the cinders and scale. Smoke lofted in a smelly puff.

The scorch marks served as a pattern for the fitting, and the shoe was thrust into the fire again and hammered into something that pleased the blacksmith's eye. He applied the metal expertly, nailed it home and rasped down the clenches. The small boys standing in a tight half-circle around the anvil watched the performance with admiration. Diamond worked from foot to foot, cleaning, trimming and banging home the shoes, making the anvil sing.

'Us'll have a drink before you walk 'em back to the farm,' said Trant when the job was done. 'I want 'em to get the feel of the road.'

Most of Chancellor's draught horses were shod twice a week but farmwork was kinder on the feet and the Tor Barton animals made less visits to the smithie. Afterwards it was customary for Palfrey, Trant and Old Bob to meet for a noonday pint at the King William in Fisher Street. Jack hung on their every word for there was over a century of horsecraft between them.

The stable gossip was rich and varied, and Jack loved everything about the occasion – the pub fire, the muddy gaiters, dogs and boots steaming before the blaze. The chat was his life blood and if every once in a while the horsemen addressed him he felt ten feet tall. He loved the argot, the exclusiveness of it all. He saw himself in the years to come, filling Palfrey's pewter mug, swapping news on equal terms. And Beth would be tethered outside as she was then, the cold spring rain fading round her and blue sky showing in the puddles at her feet.

'Him down Cider Mill as got a couple of real jibbers,' Trant chuckled. 'What old Higgs knows about horses could be writ on a sparrow's eyelid with a fence post.'

141

'You woan make a jibber out of Beth will 'ee boy?' said Old Bob, slyly probing at Jack's knowledge.

'No mister. I'll not start her off in a cart that's too heavy. I'm not stupid.'

The men laughed. Behind the rain they knew warm weather was creeping in from the sea.

Things were going smoothly, but Kitty's letter brought the chill back to Jack's heart.

'Dad', she wrote, 'has the chance of a job at Lansworthy Mill. One of the men is leaving after Christmas. It's owned by Quakers and his boss will put in a good word for him. I hope he gets it because I'll be able to see you again. I do miss you, Jack. I hate it here and I couldn't face another winter under this roof working for these dreadful people. I'm afraid you'll stop loving me if I'm away too long. Sometimes I wish I was dead. Anyway, fingers crossed. Hope us will all be back soon. Lots of love, Kitty.'

He read the letter for the tenth time and was sticking it back in his pocket when Helen and Edward Daubeny rode into the bullock yard with Rupert Chancellor. Jack recalled it was Saturday and his visitors were probably home from school on some sort of weekend holiday.

'Good Lord!' Rupert exclaimed, eyeing Bethlehem. 'Hasn't young watsername grown?'

'Beth,' said Jack and he tied the halter line to the ring in the wall.

'If only she were a pony I'd have her,' Helen said. 'Those eyes and that mane! She makes poor Pru look quite dowdy.'

Pru was not only cock-throttled, Jack noted; she was also a 'star gazer'. Every so often she pulled and pointed her nose straight at the sky. The young lady was not good with horses, he decided. By the looks of it the pony had a hard mouth as well as a mournful gaze.

Young Chancellor helped Helen dismount and the three of them stood admiring the roan filly. Jack sat on the farmhouse steps and watched them.

'What's so special about Clydesdales, McKenna?' Rupert asked. 'Grandfather has a soft spot for shires.'

God, if you aren't the spittin' image of your dad! Jack thought – with your girlish face and chubby little white hands.

'Beth's a sort of Clydesdale cross,' he said. 'Shires are heavy-legged and as big as churches. But for my money these crosses are regular work machines. Beth's mother has enough weight and stamina. Her behaviour in her gears is all you could ask for. Her legs are strong and she's got tough feet. Beth will have all them things come autumn when we start breakin' her proper. Also, she has the sweetest temper. The only thing lacking is the pure Clydesdale's bulk. If it wasn't for the feather you could saddle her and ride her to hounds.'

'I wonder if Father would buy her for me?' Helen said, turning from Jack. 'She's too beautiful for farmwork and carting and awful things like that.'

'Mr Sidney won't sell her to you,' Jack said softly. 'I'm having her. It's promised. Jesus, you'd spoil her to death.'

'Watch your tongue, McKenna,' Rupert said.

'And will you make me?'

'Leave it, Rupert,' said Edward, and he smiled at Jack. 'Don't upset yourself; Helen's only teasing. She's too fond of it.'

'But that doesn't excuse your insolence, McKenna,' Rupert said. 'Apologise to Miss Daubeny.'

'For what?'

'Grandfather shall hear of this. You won't be able to buy the damned horse if you haven't a job.'

'You won't say a word if you're my friend,' Edward said. 'Helen asked for it. Come on, Rupert, be a good fellow and promise you'll keep mum.'

'Very well. But next time . . .'

'She's a fine animal,' Edward said. The other two were clattering down the lane. They had left the gate open and were calling back to him.

'Will Mr Chancellor part with her?'

Jack shrugged. 'He says I can buy her come Christmas 1915. I'll have the money them – but she's already mine in her heart. No one can take her from me.'

'Filthy little gyppo,' Helen declared viciously when her brother caught her up. 'How can you bear to talk to him, Edward, as if he's an equal?'

'Because I like him.'

'He's dirty and impudent.'

143

'But he has spirit.'

'Father will knock that out of him,' said Rupert.

'Why on earth should he want to? By all accounts McKenna is conscientious, totally trustworthy and highly skilled. Why does your father want to break him?'

'Because he has ideas above his station,' Rupert said, colouring.

'He isn't servile,' Edward admitted. 'But I don't find that offensive.'

'Rubbish,' Helen scoffed. 'He's conceited and Rupert's grandfather encourages it.'

'The roan is probably the only thing he wants in life – his one real ambition. We've no right to take that from him.'

'But these people aren't like us,' Rupert said. 'They are dumb, sullen brutes.'

'I don't agree,' Edward smiled.

'Why do the Irish bring ducks, chickens and donkeys into the living room at night?' Rupert chuckled, glad to be off the hook.

Edward shook his head.

'It improves the conversation.'

'You ass!' and Edward laughed despite his rancour.

The trees stood poised, waiting for the wind to shake them into life. Figures hammered out of sunlight called across the farm silence. Bethlehem's lashes fell and her heart slowed. Warmth sheathed her. He was singing the words from a whisper as he brushed the flies off her body. She lifted a foreleg and stamped.

'Beth, Beth,' imposed on the music of doves and all the scents. And there was something which stood aside from the seasons. The shadow of God? His teeth trapped his lower lip. Father Tynan would be incapable of supplying an answer or even a clue. The horse vanished. Helen's breasts heaved when the colour suffused her cheeks. An extravagant wilfulness revealed itself in the way she set her mouth. And she had long fingernails.

'Jack – please, Jack.' His name darted from her furnace breath to pop the lights behind his eyes. All the ecstasy and health of youth was in her sumptuousness. 'Yes,' she said, climbing from his fantasy onto the horse. Tears of sweat swamped the image but he juggled it back to clarity – the sulky mouth, the flesh that was hot to touch and so exciting it turned his knees to mush. Then it was Kitty riding Beth through the sunlight, all golden and unclothed, hair of gold swinging across her face, her breasts as sweet as apples.

'Father I have sinned.'

Confession did not help. It did not leave him with that 'glow of inner well-being' as his mother put it. He got more from his silent conversation with the White Lady than the priest seemed capable of giving him. Tynan's loose, wrinkled face was a mask not so much of indifference as absence from the Now of life. It sagged behind the grille and the dead words of response baffled Jack. The priest was absorbed in something else, like Kitty with her toothache and despair.

He wandered past the Gerston Hotel and Hazel Cundy smiled over her shoulder at him. The breeze brought her musk to his nostrils. Even Lacey curling an arm possessively round her waist sensed the wantonness he would never be able to control but he put on a brave front. Skilly and a couple of boys from the GWR stables were hanging on his words and Lacey was doing his best to shock the passers-by. Christ, Jack thought, weren't the Hail Marys enough? There was a limit to penance. He pushed his cap onto the back of his head and sank his hands in his pockets. The evening heat had a greenhouse stickiness and the jacket draped over his arm was heavy. Again the Cundy girl flashed him a smiling glance and Lacey pressed his lips to her ear and said something which amused her. Then he broke into song:

'Would you like to sin
With Elinor Glyn
On a tiger skin?
Or would you prefer
To err with her
On some other fur?'

Skilly's hee-hawing made Jack wince. But Kitty is coming home, he thought. God, she is! She is! In the New Year she would be walking down the street with him. His fingers closed round her letter. A motor car rattled by and the mare pulling the empty coal cart shook her head. 'Steady, girl,' the coalman said, but the horse stopped and whinnied and shook her head again.

145

She was blinkered.

'Bloody motor cars,' the coalman snarled. 'Steady now, Rosie. That contraption woan hurt 'ee. Steady girl.'

The mare would not be calmed. She jerked sideways and kicked and almost had the cart over.

'Hold still, Rosie,' the coalman cried, giving her a crack with the whip.

Jack caught her head and clicked his tongue. The mare shuffled and tried to break from his grip. Then he understood. Trapped behind one of the blinkers the wasp clung to her eyelid. When she brought her head down once more he flicked off the insect and stroked her muzzle. The coalman joined him. Already the eye was swelling but Rosie no longer danced in the shafts.

'She'll be all right now, mister.'

'Thanks to you, son.'

'She's a good-looking animal,' Jack grinned.

'I wouldn part with her – no sir. You're Irish Jack, idn you? Old Bob Sherwill's always speakin' of 'ee down the pub. Well, I'd let you take Rosie out anytime.'

It was a great compliment and Jack's self-dislike had diminished when the pavilion was reached and he joined the flow of people taking the air along the promenade. Three South African war veterans were busking on the green. 'Goodbye Dolly I must leave you, though it breaks my heart to go'. Always partings, he thought. Foals from mares, lambs and calves from their mothers, old from young, lover from lover. The Blue Hungarian Concert Band swung awkwardly into their opening medley of operetta tunes and the buskers trailed away to find a fresh pitch. Low over Hollicombe drifted the yellow and scarlet striped hot air balloon showering leaflets. Hanging from the basket was a banner bearing the legend 'Shop at Chancellor's'. Everyone was pointing at it except the buskers who stared straight ahead as they marched.

18

The September moon shone on Cider Mill Tor and the stream winding down the valley was a thread of silver fire. Bethlehem faced into the wind lifting off the bay. Her forelocks curled round her ears and coolness swept along her flanks. Iona and Bathsheba scattered the dew as they sauntered down the hillside. Behind them the farm mares and geldings raised their voices in barely audible enquiry. Up from the lowlands floated the piping of water birds. A star fell and vanished, but the large bright star beside the moon shone in Iona's eyes.

The animals pressed together. Other stars shared the sky dance, shifting within their own glow and bringing the horses to the threshold of trance. Iona lowered her head to munch the grass, for the dark world of hedges and trees was losing to dream and she had seen *him* again. The past broke over the present and she was content. He had come to the orchard gate at dusk but trotting down to answer his call she had encountered only the things which had gone: the smell of his clothes, the warmth of his voice which remained when the words had flown, glimpses of events she had formerly inhabited. Everything was dimmed by moonlight but the lane ran over the tor and there the promise waited as surely as sunrise. Her nose came up and her eyes closed. For a long while she stood hardly breathing, waiting for him to speak her name.

Bethlehem nudged the old horse and rubbed her muzzle repeatedly on Iona's cheek. Side by side they walked around the tor and met the mares and geldings who were preparing to sleep on their feet. Above them the sky dance continued but a dog yelping pushed Bethlehem's ears forward.

'Farmer's mazed fleabag got caught in a badger gin last night,' Mrs Trant said, addressing the stable door and her husband but directing the news at Jack. 'Pike found un when he called the cows.'

Trant blew his nose. 'Daid?'

'A broke leg. All that twistin' and turnin' in the gin – all night,' she said smugly. 'I heard un round three or four, whining away. It was one of his hind legs, broke in two. Pike shot un.' Her jaws snapped shut, like a trap, but her eyes never left the stable door.

'Dad reckons a fox made old Sam break his rope and take off,' Arthur said. He blew little bubbles of saliva through the gap in his front teeth.

'The bliddy dog wadn all there. Serves un right. All he could do was bark.'

'Sure, he never had much of a life,' said Jack, shouldering the harness. He recalled the desperate collie with its one dead, blue-glazed eye, leaping at the end of the rope.

'Dogs' lives idn supposed to be fun.'

'My dog's life will be.'

'You habn got a dog, Jack.'

'I will have, one day.'

Arthur smiled. 'And a horse.'

The hens strutted around them and wasps cruised through the pale sunlight between the cider orchards. An east wind was lifting the bay in swells close to the shore. In a bloody gin trap all night after spending its last years tied up! Jesus! There was something awful about the business, something that left him feeling cold and dirty inside. Then Jack wondered if he was in the right frame of mind to begin the breaking.

Trant walked a little behind them up to the paddock. He had a gum abcess and the last of his back teeth was loose and ready to come out. Working at it all day with the tip of his tongue he knew a visit to the dentist was unavoidable. But he watched the boys put the bridles on Bethlehem and Bathsheba, and checked

148

to make sure the bits sat firm against the corners of their mouths.

'Don't jerk they lines,' he said. 'Do what I learned 'ee, nice and smooth. Have Beth walk about a bit, boy, and don't be afraid to call her by name. Arthur will stay quiet. Her's got to know that he at the end of the lines is boss. The rope in your hand is to hold her. The lines and Jack do all the talking for her must get used to being driven like her's in the shafts.'

Jack flicked the lines and said, 'Walk on, Beth,' and the filly strode across the paddock with the boy keeping pace at the rear.

'Don't jerk.' Trant's expressive gesture emphasised the point. 'Now, turn her to the right. Good. And the left. Slack right line, tight left. Stop her now.'

Jack leaned back and pulled gently on both lines, crying, 'Whoa Beth. Whoa girl.'

Bethlehem champed on the bit and turned her head to quizz him.

'Good girl. Beautiful girl.'

Pike had patiently undertaken much of the schooling. He showed the boys how to shorten the lines using half-hitches, for the breaking of the fillies was also an exercise in controlling them safely. Horsemanship involving the driving of carts, wagons and farm implements was fraught with danger. Pike's limp, he ruefully admitted, was a 'present' from a three-year-old shire who had stamped on his foot.

'I got too close as 'ee turned and I was daydreaming. Next minute – smack! The bugger must've smashed every bone from heel to toe.'

Letting the fillies get the feel of things was important. The boys took turns holding and driving, and the horses, who wished to please them, played the game for an hour or so each day. The weight of the leather was now part of a daily ritual that ended in good food and grooming. At sunset they stood under the linhay roof and the human voices crooned their praise. Curry combs and brushes brought them to the edge of drowsiness. Then Bathsheba's chestnut coat gleamed in the moonlight which was sometimes wild with scatterd leaves. The moon over the bay was the colour of the evening sun and very big.

*　　*　　*

149

Jack was at Tor Barton for a week each month and spent the rest of the time down the yard. Here he found Lacey concentrating on a new victim, possibly because Moony had less sense than Skilly and no father to curtail the baiting. The horsemaster had thought the two simpletons would take to each other but they rarely spoke or made any sort of contact as if they were aware that the one conspicuously mirrored the other's oddness. In the uncompromising environment they competed for kindness but the dice was loaded in Skilly's favour. Even Fred Luscombe seemed relieved to discover a creature dafter than his son.

So Moony was sent on impossible errands and became the butt of the cruel mindless humour flying about the yard. But he was happy earning enough money to put meat on the table and a smile on his mother's face.

One foggy morning Jack asked Lacey why he took such delight in 'bullying cuckoos'. The carters were breakfasting under the awning outside the grain stores and Moony had been trotting about trying to borrow a magic hammer for knocking nails into glass.

'You know your trouble, Irish – apart from being Irish?' Lacey said. 'You haven't got a sense of humour.'

Melody had cast a shoe and needed a swift visit to the forge. The fog swirled around her but she stood patiently untethered.

'Come on, Arthur,' Jack grinned. 'You make me laugh. Me and Moony fell about when you pitched off the cart the other day and landed on your ass – bruising your brains.'

'Better a brown ass than a brown nose,' Luscombe said, bringing a sneering smile to Lacey's face.

'Don't you two ever give up?' Ernie Cooksley asked.

Moony clasped his great swollen hands together and murmured, 'Please, please. It idn right. Tidn proper.'

'You idn proper,' Luscombe snorted.

The fog brewed sepia shadows, full of sepia figures and sepia horses. The wagon lamps were muzzed and finely spoked gleaming in the murk like giant dandelions.

'Why idn I proper, Jack?' Moony whispered as the vehicles rumbled out of the yard.

Jack humped the sack of oats onto his shoulders and grunted. 'Your mum thinks you're proper, don't she? And she knows best.'

'McKenna,' Luscombe boomed from the fog. 'Have you

150

heard the latest? Iona's copped it. She'll be catmeat by tomorrow. Catmeat and glue.'

Old Bob was waiting at the stable door. Jack pushed past him and let the sack drop.

'Is it true, mister?'

'About the horse? Yes boy. Her was put down last night. Palfrey was goin' to tell 'ee but Mr Chancellor wanted him up the store.'

'Down the bloody knackers just like that,' Jack said, digging the toe of his boot into the sack. 'A lifetime of service and chop! All over, finished, all bloody forgotten.'

'The knackers is part of the business of caring for horses, boy. Most animals end up there. But Iona didn get the poleaxe. She slipped in the lane coming down to the stables and the vet shot her. The fall broke her back.'

Jack nodded and closed his eyes. Some of the day's greyness had crept into his face.

'Iona is going to be buried like a real Christian,' Sherwill continued. 'Chancellor will make sure of that. Maddock don't like it but . . .' The old man lifted his shoulders and let them fall with a sigh. 'The boss had a soft spot for the mare, or at least his late wife did.'

But he wouldn't give Kitty's dad a job, Jack thought. He was surprised he could be so uncharitable.

'Tidn good for horse or pocket to put it out to grass till it drops,' said Old Bob and Jack swallowed his unease. 'You can't afford to have deep feelings for an animal unless you've more money than sense or you want to starve.'

'Mrs Endacott is close to doing that.'

'Right. Right,' blustered the old man, 'but Iona idn to blame and in any case, if it wadn for sentimental fools like Chancellor us wouldn have so many horses in the stables. When he dies that Ormond will make changes. Mark my words, it'll be all motor vans.'

Jack thought of asking the White Lady to tell St Francis to intercede on Iona's behalf.

'Saints start off like you and me,' Michael said. He blew on the tip of his cigarette to make it glow in the darkness. 'St Francis was a bit of a boozer and gambler with an eye for the ladies.'

151

'Of this world, as Mother would say,' Jack smiled.

The brothers were in no hurry to get home.

'Do you suppose the other horses are sad about Iona?' Jack continued.

'How the hell should I know?'

'It happened so quickly. I didn't think it would end like this – a hoof slipping, her leg giving out and bang! Gone.'

'Like Dad caught between the trucks.'

'In plays the dying takes forever. You have a chance to get used to it.'

'Dick Turpin's horse,' Michael said, 'Black Bess took twenty minutes to pass away down the Bijou. There were enough tears to flood the theatre.'

His cigarette flared. They skirted the roadworks marking the end of the tramline that was nearing completion.

'If Mum catches you doin' that she'll wring your neck,' said Jack. 'You know how she feels about smokin' and boozing.'

'I'm sixteen not six. If I can do a man's job I can do the other things.'

'Like sniffin' round Hazel Cundy.'

'And isn't she full of you? Forever gawpin' and rollin' her cow eyes and swinging her udders.'

'Our Lady's taking note of this for future reference.'

'Our Lady doesn't listen to talk like this. It wouldn't be decent.'

'Father Tynan says animals haven't got souls.'

'He's an idiot. They've got everything else. Is St Francis unemployed, sittin' round heaven all day doing nothing? Priests don't know it all. If Arthur Lacey has a soul then Iona must have a bigger one.'

Before long a headstone appeared on the mound marking Iona's grave but Maddock and Trant were far from impressed. The inscription read: 'Iona, a true friend of man'.

'A lot of folk round here can't afford to put a stone on a loved one's grave,' said the farmer. 'Dang me! The wife wondered if he was goin' to bury all the 'orses when they died. Us would have a regular cemetery on Cider Mill Hill. Then where would us put the live animals?'

'They rich buggers think more of their pets than they do of the likes of us,' Trant agreed.

Iona was a work horse, Jack wanted to say but he bit his tongue.

As winter set in and the breaking followed its course he was often comforted by the thought of the old mare lying in the hill she had once walked over. At least she hadn't known the stink of the knacker's yard. Pike had buried the collie, Sam, so why shouldn't Chancellor bury his favourite horse? Putting Bethlehem in her gears the boy considered how he loved her and valued her life more than that of humans like Fred Luscombe. On the one hand was the innocence of the horse; on the other a mess of inner ugliness. Moony possessed some of that spiritual purity which Time could never touch, and the midden was full of wide-eyed innocents. It was there, too, in Kitty's eyes – something fine left over from childhood.

Then Bethlehem was playing the stop-and-start game, going through her paces in the lane with stones under her hooves. Jack put her in and out of the stream and trotted her through the deep puddles.

'Us can't have her afraid of water,' Trant said. 'You can always tell a horse broken by a fool. The beast will pull up hard at a ford and has to be dragged across. You try it, boy. On a winter's day it idn no joke.'

Jack's chilblains jumped and the pain swelled to a hot, prickly ache but he still came home at night to cook his feet on the fender. He spoke of the breaking with a passion Mary McKenna reserved for prayer. She slid the potato cakes out of the oven and closed the door. Jack sprang up and pushed the supper plates to one side. Mother of God, she thought, he's taller than me without his boots on! And he was filling out. Pride was swamped by anxiety. He was growing and she was ageing. Soon he would go his own way and she could see herself turning desperately to the little girls to salvage the last pieces of family life.

Mooney knocked and stayed long enough to borrow half a pound of dripping.

'He's so polite,' said Mary Mckenna. 'You lot could learn from him. He may be touched but his manners are those of a bishop.'

'Jack ought to be the politest lad in town then,' said Michael. 'He's got two idiots teaching him – Moony and Skilly.'

'Skilly's a funny name,' giggled Blanche.

'Loony Moony and Silly Skilly,' said Sean.

'Skilly is paupers' soup,' said their mother. 'A handful of oatmeal chucked in a bucket of hot water. A lot of nothing.'

Michael laughed. 'That's Skilly.'

And you are the dead ringer of your father, thought Mary. His pug nose, screwed-up eyes and dark curly hair belonged to Kevan McKenna, who might have been a boxer if he had not taken to the bottle.

'Skilly's harmless enough,' said Jack. 'So's Moony.'

'Moony is beautiful,' Blanche said. 'A big monkey.'

If the horses were fashioned from the wind, Jack thought, why did they have to be broken to work for man? And if he loved them shouldn't he be considering their return to some wild place where they could be kings? But it wasn't like that, no more than the world was the Old Testament world. People didn't sacrifice animals and Jehovah was dead, killed by Jesus Christ.

Then the winter sun was paler than a sparrow hawk's eye and frost rimed the valley. Bethlehem and Bathsheba emerged from the linhay adding the whiteness of new breath to the morning's whiteness. Their shaggy coats kept out the cold.

'Us always get what Pike calls 'ansome weather after Christmas,' Arthur Maddock said, blowing on his fingers before withdrawing them into his mittens.

Obediently the fillies stood while they were harnessed and taken through the disciplines. Some mornings they wore the farm gears and on others they were fitted for the streets. The collar brought only a mild protest from Bathsheba but when Trant decided the horses were ready to experience the hauling they disapproved. The heavy log attached to the whipple tree behind Bethlehem surprised her as she tried to walk forward. Suddenly something very heavy was pressing against her shoulders and she staggered and tried to bolt sideways. But again she checked.

'Steady girl,' Jack said. 'Walk forward.' But she was attempting to retreat and escape it.

'Beth,' Jack said, gritting his teeth. 'Walk forward.'

And she knew despite the squirt of panic that if he wanted her to walk everything would be all right. She stamped her forefeet

154

and the pressure registered. For a moment the weight restrained her then yielded and she paced on.

Down in the bottom of her paddock Bathsheba bucked and reared and kicked out her hind legs. The raw desperation and anger in Arthur's commands fed the animal's fear.

'For Christ's sake steady yourself, Sheba,' he croaked.

Bathsheba danced broadside and whinnied.

'Hold to, hold to,' the boy cried, and he tugged at the lines. One of the plough traces snapped and Trant intervened before mishap turned to tragedy.

'Don't fret, boy,' he said. 'Her'll get used to it. They all gyp a bit at first. As soon as you've changed that trace put her at it again. Keep 'em moving, and make sure your tack is in good order. Check the harness and spare harness before you go home. Broke leather can cost 'ee half a day's work – or a horse. Now praise 'em and ease 'em through it. I told you to start 'em off on a rope as well as the lines, but seems you know best. Put Beth back in the shed, Jack, and get Sheba on a bridle rope. There's no short cuts in this business.'

'I didn ask to be a horsekeeper,' Arthur grumbled as Trant departed. The cold sores on his lips were open and bleeding.

'Come on,' Jack said. 'It'll warm us up.'

'So would the fireside,' came the despondent reply.

But Trant was correct. Bathsheba did settle to the job although she never accepted the collar after that without some token carping. By the time the blossom was on the blackthorn both fillies knew what it was like to be yoked to farm implements. Apart from the hauling they were also held back after the loads were removed to sample the strange new lightness. Melody provided steadiness when the fillies graduated to team work.

Pulling the harrow across the five-acre field with her mother presented difficulties which Bethlehem soon overcame. She was far brighter than her stablemate in learning inside and outside speed. The lines relayed Jack's wishes and she lengthened or shortened her stride according to her position at the turn – inside, short; outside, long.

Kitty watched the team's progress over the hillside. The metal teeth of the harrow rattled through the stony soil, raking up the dust. The roan filly matched the mare step for step

155

although she lacked her fleshiness. Some of the field's redness had discoloured her mane and shanks. Out of the wind the sun was warm. It was a good day to come home even if the Widdicombe's new house in Winner Street was more cramped than the cottage they had vacated at dawn.

Standing hunched under the wayside elms Kitty recalled the first time she had seen Bethlehem. That spring seemed as far away as her early childhood. Mrs McKenna's cool greeting had not helped. She blushed at the memory of the little Irish woman measuring her with her eye, like a poulterer appraising a Christmas duck. She drew her chin down into her scarf and felt the wind tug at her hat.

'Jack,' she called as the team jingled by and he came running through the dust cloud in his shirt sleeves and braces, a huge smile on his face. Silently she opened her arms. Her lips quivered. The horses stood and regarded the boy and girl.

Holding her at arms' length he said, 'Why didn't you let me know? God, I was thinking about you, wondering what you were doing.'

She was a little figure in grey and black, with a cold, runny nose.

'I wanted to surprise you,' she gasped. 'Careful, you'll break me.'

The kiss left her breathless. She blew her nose and sniffed.

'Kitten,' he whispered, hugging her with more care. 'My little blonde kitten.'

'I'm going to cry, my heart's that big,' she said. The tears were gathering under her lashes.

'I'd rather you laughed,' he said and his fingers dug into her ribs.

'Beth is watchin' us, Jack McKenna,' she squealed.

'Sure, she's old enough. I'll have her walkin' the streets for me in the spring.'

His eyes sparkled.

'Jack!'

He was serious now. 'Are you home for good, Kitty? No more parting or pining?'

She nodded and cupped his face in her hands.

'No more partings, Jack. I love you. I love you.'

The tension had left her face and her cheeks were hot and red.

156

19

Larks sang and catkins danced in the wind along the edge of the water meadows. The hills of Clennon gleamed. Daffodils had sprung up in the orchard above the paddock and Bethlehem could smell sunlight on the air. The rooks shuttling between field and treetop were patching the nests that swayed whenever the wind hit the hedgerow elms.

The fillies had reached the final stages of the breaking. They were accustomed to the feel of bit, bridle and belly band, and much of their daily life was governed by the lines. Trant watched their progress with quiet satisfaction. The Irish boy was totally absorbed in the work and when he rode Bethlehem from the paddock a window opened on the carter's past. He recalled spring mornings buried under years of hard graft. He had ridden the shire gelding at the farm he hated and let the animal take him far from the sharp tongues and grasping natures. Why hadn't Mabel given him children? The pain corkscrewing suddenly at the base of his spine brought him up sharply with a little cry and a gasp. The prospect of old age was chilling. Yes boy, he thought, as the roan came clattering down the lane, it could easy happen to you. You'm bright and active now but buggers like Ormond Chancellor will put 'ee on the scrap heap when you'm too old and wore out. We see horses bred and trained for farm or street; us feeds 'em and grooms 'em and

157

cares for 'em when they'm sick. Then we send 'em down the knackers or put a bullet in their heads. Then, then tis all over and us have got nothing. Nothing except a few bob a week pension and a handful of sovereigns under the mattress.

'Tell 'em they'm beautiful,' he said, taking the afternoon warmth on the back and hoping it would provide a miraculous cure for his lumbago. The sun twinkled on Arthur's buck teeth.

'Sheba isn goin' to come along at Beth's speed,' Trant continued. 'But her's obedient enough.'

Two long fence posts had been cocked up on the gate, one end of each resting on the third bar, the other on the cobbles like the shafts of a cart. Then the fillies were backed in and led out again, repeatedly, until they could be relied on to negotiate real shafts without breaking them.

The bullock yard was ideal for tip-cart work. The wheels rattled and sang over the cobbles and Bethlehem was forced to execute some tight turns while Jack reduced or increased the load. Rain drifted down the valley bringing with it the blackbird's song and the scent of blossom. Jack and Bethlehem were happy. The filly gazed at him as he wiped her eyes and nostrils. Raindrops hung from the peak of his cap. Gently she snuffled, soliciting attention.

'Yes, yes,' he murmured. 'You are still the lovely lady.'

She was trotted and walked from the yard to Cider Mill Farm and back. En route Arthur Maddock supplied the sort of noises and situations she could expect to meet on the streets. He would stand in the hedge and whirl his crow clapper or swing a dead rook on a piece of cord past her eyes. All the Maddock children were brought into the drama. They ran about in front of the horses, shouting and banging tins while the dogs pranced and barked. Then Beth and Solomon were hitched to a variety of vehicles until Trant finally had them between the shafts of the heavy wagon. The filly's performance convinced the horseman she was ready for the road, although he had a sneaking doubt she would save her best behaviour for Jack. He voiced his suspicions to Palfrey the day Beth and Bathsheba were walked down to the yard.

'I swear there's something bloody odd about that filly and Irish. You don't know where animal ends and human begins.'

Palfrey held his pipe by the bole. 'If you say her's ready to work her's ready to work. I'm retiring Boxer and Maggie. They'll be able to do light stuff up the farm but there's no place for them in the stud no more. Tez always a sad to-do.'

'Can us expect a couple more burials?' Trant said with the ghost of a smile.

Palfrey shook his head. 'Iona was part of the boss's past, Mrs C's pet. The rest is just business.'

Trant attempted to straighten his back but failed. 'That's what we are, Tom,' he groaned '– part of the business. When us breaks down we'll be replaced.'

'It's the way things are,' Palfrey remarked philosophically, wondering how many more winters Trant would negotiate before he was paid off.

Beth's beauty attracted comment the first time she took to the streets drawing one of Chancellor's blue vans. Her hooves were oiled, her tail plaited and her harness gleamed. Easing her through the light Lansworthy traffic Jack felt she was his in every sense save the most important. And he had begun to doubt Chancellor's promise. She and Melody were the best behaved animals in the stud and good brood mares were the life blood of the trade.

'You have his word,' said Mary McKenna. 'And if he's the Christian you think he is there's no need for all this worry.'

'People have a change of heart.'

His mother looked at him. 'You're not growing a moustache, are you?'

'I was considering it.'

'Well don't. A moustache won't make a man of you.'

He grinned and coloured, and Mary's tone mellowed.

'Beth won't recognise you,' she said. 'Does Kitty like it?'

'No.'

'Shave it off, please Jack.'

She chopped up the potato peelings, carrots, onions and turnips and added them to the rabbit bone stock.

'A moustache on a boy is a comical thing – like a beard on an egg or caterpillar on a beach.'

'I suppose you agree with her,' Jack said as he led Kitty up the hill to the tor where the primroses were thickest.

'Monkeys have hairy faces,' she said mysteriously, stooping

to pick the little yellow flowers. Lansworthy church bells flooded the Sabbath morning with their harmonies.

'The bells make me sad,' Kitty added. 'Funny old Sunday. When us used to go primrosing back at Churston the bells were always ringing away.'

'I like them,' he said, unable to think clearly about anything except her face holding the primrose light whenever she bent over the flowers. The straw hat with the black ribbon was faded and the catkin dust on her new brown jersey was darker than the weak sun which clothed the hillside.

They sat on the tor, arms around each other, and Kitty took off her hat. The breeze rising from the sea smoothed back her hair to reveal her ears.

'Like little pink shells,' he murmured, kissing one then searching for her mouth. The fair lashes ascended and revealed the golden green eyes. The skin each side of her nose was delicately freckled and her lips were parted. From a husky whisper she called his name and drew his head down and pressed half a dozen butterfly kisses to his face. When their lips met again he was sucked into the hot quicksand but her fingers closed over his own as he fumbled the buttons on her jersey.

'No, Jack. I idn Hazel Cundy.'

'And I'm no priest,' he grinned, pressing his face into the primroses they had bunched and tied with blue wool. 'Surely to Christ it's natural.'

'Yes, and that's what marriage is for – to make it right.'

'But you've got to have a bit of practice, Kitty.'

She pushed her fingers through her curls and blushed. 'If you really love me you'll wait.'

'Of course I will, but it's not easy and it's no fun.'

'You'd best go primrosin' with Hazel Cundy, then.'

'I'd have to join the queue.'

'You idiot,' she laughed, but now his face was serious.

'Listen,' he said, taking her by the shoulders. 'Always remember this. There's no one but you and there never will be. No matter what happens you'll always have my love. All we have to do is think of each other.'

Then the tenderness made words unnecessary. They sat together on the rock above Iona's grave and the farm horses

160

broke the hush as they came over the brow of the hill, stepping, so it seemed, from the sky.

Central to the activity in Chancellor's yard was the power and simplicity of the animals. They woke to the stable routine and waited to be put in the gears which included warm, dry collars. The ring of familiar voices, the laughter and all the other sounds crowding the morning set them at ease.

Beth was sharing a stall with Melody and mother and daughter had rekindled the blood bond. The mute communion of the animals really began as soon as Palfrey locked them up at night. They were at peace. Horse smell and horse sounds rippled around them and quietude provided the rest.

Whenever possible Palfrey made sure the mare and her filly worked together but he could not guarantee Jack would be at the reins. Ormond Chancellor was having a greater say in the running of the stables, although he still stood in awe of the horsemaster. But the fleet continued to leave the yard each day despite the disturbances. Beth and Melody walked over the shine left by the water cart on a morning of blurred light and cloud that disguised the heat to come. About the old sandstone warehouses and stables the house martins stuttered to a halt in mid-air and turned to speed back over courtyard and vacant lot. Then the smell of the washed streets met the scores of other smells issuing from the shambles where the horses lived.

Jack was subdued and pensive, and Wotton misread the boy's mood.

'Doan let Luscombe vex 'ee, boy,' he said. 'You know what they say about empty vessels.'

Jack nodded and retied his apron. The roans stepped together down the street which was barred with shadow. Loitering tramps stared after them while the awnings came down in front of the commercial buildings and the shop assistants' brooms licked over the pavements. Jack's heart turned to ice. A kind of self-loving, human grubbiness was reaching out and touching the horses but they walked through it. Not like the first horses, he thought. On that first morning the wind would not have carried the smell of the butcher's shop, the baker's, Chancellor's ground coffee and the stink of the abattoir.

161

They stopped at the wheelright and picked up three new cart wheels for a farm at Preston. Cattle were on the Abbot's Quay Road, plodding beside the tramway. The wagon ploughed slowly through a sea of horns and bulging eyes. The midden smell rose with the bullocks' body heat and their scrummaging raised the dust in a white cloud. But Beth and her mother walked into the noise holding their faces to the sun which was laying most of its gold on the bay.

20

Something small and light fell from the gap between the stable wall and the roof into the straw at Beth's feet. She sniffed at it but the ossified sparrow gave nothing back except the breath of dust. Swift, whispering footfalls betrayed the coming and going of rats in the loft overhead. An owl cried from the yard and another white bird answered from the roof of Lansworthy Mill.

Throughout the early hours she was wakened by goods trains although the hooting was part of the darkness now. A sea mist blanketed the bay and the colliers coming to anchor off Abbot's Quay were sounding their horns.

In the next stall Bathsheba was climbing awkwardly to her feet. Lifting a hind leg she pushed it forward and set her teeth chattering along the feather to tug out the grit tangled in the hair. She had come late off the streets, too tired to be groomed. Then the stable door creaked and Mullah ran in, wagging his tail and slavering. The aroma of Palfrey's pipe tobacco heralded the start of a new work day, and Beth waited for the boy's footsteps on the gangway.

'Hazel Cundy is in the pudding club,' said Harold Dunsford. The oats hissed through the sieve and gleamed as they caught the lantern light. 'They'll be holdin' a lottery to find the father.'

'Get home,' said his brother. 'It's that ornament from the

chip shop. He's botched everything he's done.'

'How's Hazel?' Jack said.

'Big,' Harold laughed. 'They found out up the store and Ormond sacked her.'

'God! If he isn't a saint of a man,' said Jack.

'St Arsehole,' Harold observed. 'But her asked for it, Irish.'

'Asked for what?'

'A bellyfull of arms and legs.'

'And what about him who put them there? Did he get the sack?'

'Irish is courtin' a suffragette's sister,' Harold explained apologetically to the horse. 'That Dora's a proper Amazon.'

Jack shook his head. 'Bury an animal, sack a girl carrying a baby.'

'Well, tidn right, Irish,' Harold said gently. 'And her couldn be expected to work in that condition. Wouldn be Christian.'

Jack pressed his forehead against the filly's side. She was warm with life and he remembered as a child on Cider Mill Tor, gripping the long grass like it was a horse's mane, as if he could ride the world bareback through summer. Sprawled among the stems under the poppy heads which the wind had swung in red arcs, forward and back, he had seen a vision. Silver horses cut through the darkness beyond the poppies, ploughing their furrow of light. The quicksilver animals cast drops of heavy liquid which had their own separate life. Star horses bursting from nebulae. The conversation and other noises of the stud faded. Rising in the saddle the hero touched his mount with his heels and urged her out of the coombe into the field. The roan was dappled and marbled, white-maned, white of tail, white of feather. A corncrake spoke as she passed. Grass quaked. The sabre swung, snick-snack, and the poppy heads flew and bled and vanished. Diamond's forge, he thought, snapping his fingers. Sparks showering the darkness. Then Beth's gaze held him and her muscles twitched beneath her coat, jerking off the flies which had risen from the straw. The scent of stale sunshine escaped from her mane beneath the comb. Her muzzle pressed cool against his hand but behind everything she did was a melancholy that pierced him to the soul. And it was like walking towards the hills which were forever retreating to reassemble on the unreachable horizon. A protracted journey littered with events designed to delay arrival. He sucked in a breath and held it for a second or two before expelling it through his teeth. Beth's eyes housed no falsehood.

The fly buzzing and beating on the window became enmeshed in the spider's web. It vanished under something swift and dark and the buzzing stopped. Jack looked up. Moony was standing at the entrance to the stall, crushing his cap in his fists and wearing that sickly look of terror which rabbits display when the stoat closes.

'I habn done nothing,' he whispered. 'Why do 'em keep on at me, Jack? Idn I a good boy?'

Boots clattered on the gangway and Moony groaned and pushed past him to crouch in the corner.

'Moo-oo-nee,' Lacey's voice was an ululation of self-indulgent cruelty tinged with boredom.

'Come out, come out, wherever you are, you girt cake. Uncle Arthur's got a present for 'ee.'

'For Christ's sake,' Jack hissed, grabbing the pitchfork.

Lacey poked his head in the stall and suddenly found himself on the business end of two muck-encrusted prongs.

They pressed hard against his chest and he stepped quickly on his heels until he banged against the woodwork of the opposite stall. Jack leaned on the fork only vaguely aware through his anger that Skilly and some of the other lads were shouting at him.

'Stay back,' he growled over his shoulder. 'Uncle Arthur is going to get a present from me.'

'You mazed bastard, McKenna,' Lacey gasped. 'Put that down before you land yourself in trouble.'

The tips of the prongs penetrated his shirt and pressed into his vest. A lock of brown hair fell over his forehead and the tip of his tongue curled up and slid across the beginnings of a moustache which contributed something bizarre to his look of dismay.

'McKenna.'

'Shut your gob and listen to me. If you ever give Moony or Skilly or anyone a hard time again I'll plant this fork in you – God as my witness. Tell me you understand, Uncle Arthur. Go on, spell it out.'

'I understand,' Lacey yelped. 'I understand. Now take the

bloody thing away.'

'Take the bloody thing away,' brayed Skilly.

'McKenna,' from a sob now. 'For the love of God.'

'What are you going to do about Hazel?'

'Nothing – why the hell should I?'

'Come on, come on, Uncle Arthur – no games. This is the confessional.'

'I didn put her in the family way. She's any bugger's. Twadn my fault. Why blame me?'

'She's your sweetheart.'

'Is she hell! She's a whore.'

'That's uncharitable, Arthur.' The prongs punctured Lacey's flesh and he screamed. Tiny beads of blood marked the twin pinpricks below his nipples.

'You led her up the garden path. I bet the devil's got something really nasty up his sleeve waiting for you when you croak. Anyway, from now on you watch your step or I'll nail you to the stable door.'

The carters were breakfasting when Old Bob met Jack leaving the harness room.

'Stay away from Lacey,' the boy was told. 'Get on with your work and let un be. If he's giving folk a hard time that's Mr Palfrey's business. No more forks or threats. Things have got to be done right, all down the line.'

Jack grinned. There was a moment's awkward silence.

'Have you seen Ormond's contraption?' Sherwill said. Steering clear of trouble was never easy for an old man who had not learned how to mince words.

'Go and have a look boy. It's parked over by the grain sheds.'

He found Ormond Chancellor and his father ambling round a royal blue motor van while the store manager stood smiling his approval. Large gilt capitals on the sides proclaimed 'Chancellor's for Quality'.

'Solid tyres,' Ormond was saying. 'And the latest acetylene headlamps.'

'And you know how to keep it going?' said Mr Sidney.

'Piece of cake. They're easier and cheaper to run than horses.'

'But so ugly and noisy and dangerous.'

'Like steam engines,' Ormond said. 'Without steam the Empire would be in a mess. In a few years we'll have a fleet of

166

motor vehicles, Father. Move with the times – change, adapt and progress.'

'What about my animals?'

Ormond shrugged. 'The motor van will do the town deliveries and we'll use the horses for the out-of-the-way jobs.'

'First of all you'll have to convince me that that thing is reliable.'

'You'll give it a chance though, Father? It's enormously prestigious.'

'One motor van, one chance.'

Ormond sighed. 'Isn't it time you moved into the twentieth century?'

'Why? I'm not fond of it. Horses have dignity.'

'But dignity's not necessarily profitable. Still,' he added placatingly, 'she's my pigeon.'

'Your toy,' his father said, yawning.

'In five years' time we'll see who's right.'

'What do you think, McKenna?' Mr Sidney said, catching sight of the boy.

'I want to be a horseman, mister, and to me that thing's just a heap of rubbish.'

Ormond was nettled. 'Your future may depend on how quickly you learn to handle that expensive heap of rubbish, McKenna – always assuming you have a future with Chancellor's.'

'Mr Sidney asked me a question, mister.'

'Yes, well, get back to work and concentrate on the things you are paid to do.'

'Looking after the horses,' Jack grinned.

'Off you go,' Sidney Chancellor said, reading his son's mood and disliking it.

So the motor van became part of yard life despite the carters' resentment. Cooksley was taught to drive it and gloom prevailed when the men learnt Ormond had orderd two more.

'Us'll not have room for the horses,' Old Bob complained. 'They contraptions will take over.'

But the van's first trip into town was disastrous. It broke down with all the horses busy elsewhere. Palfrey had it towed back to the yard by a shire at dusk to the cheers of the departing carters. The following day produced three more breakdowns and Ormond was heard bellowing into the telephone. The order for the other vans was cancelled and Sidney Chancellor's smile was something the Cheshire cat would have envied.

The following Saturday Jack put the shires in their show brasses and hitched them to one of the heavy wagons. The vehicle was planked over and three hampers loaded in the rear. Then he took it to Morning House to collect young Chancellor's party for their hayride. It was Rupert's idea.

'McKenna should be wearing a cap,' Ormond remarked.

'Grandfather's regard for him is absurd,' said Rupert. 'After the pitchfork incident he should be out of a job and in a cell – Palfrey or no Palfrey.'

'NCO's work, Rupert. And Lacey's name is linked with the Cundy girl.'

So is practically every other lout's name south of the Parish Church, Rupert thought. Yet there was a violent streak in McKenna. It blazed in his eyes – that Irish thing wavering between anarchy and arrogant contempt for the Establishment.

'I'll ride with the driver,' Edward Daubeny said, using the wagon wheel as a ladder.

'Palfrey would have chewed off your ears if you'd mounted a vehicle that way down the yard,' Jack said. 'The horses only had to step forward and you'd be on your way to hospital.'

'Put it down to ignorance, Jack.'

'The undertaker's friend.'

Edward Daubeny bowed. He had a smooth face, untouched by care, large brown eyes and a neat head of chestnut hair. A square chin cancelled out any suggestion of effeminacy.

The horses walked under the jingle of their harness into the haze that was firming into an unsteady wall of heat. Edward was afraid one of the noisy youngsters behind would snare him in small-talk.

'How is Beth?' he said.

'Out on the streets earning her keep.'

Daubeny wondered if it was a jibe. People like McKenna led such odd lives. He could not imagine a childhood without books or nice things; but perhaps the McKennas of the world didn't have childhoods.

'What you goin' to be when your schooling's finished?' Jack said, and the boldness of the question surprised Edward. No

168

'sir' or 'Master Edward'. But I have created this situation, he thought and now it really has become man to man I'm retreating into class and convention. One either remained aloof or became involved. Lord! It was so difficult.

'I'm keen on geography,' he said. 'I suppose I'll come down from Cambridge and traipse off to some corner of the world exploring and mapping.'

'That sounds fine.'

'And you?'

'Me and Beth will traipse off to some corner of Devon, doing anything to earn a bob or two. It'll be nothing to make the Empire stop and stare.'

He laughed and flicked the reins.

'But it's what you want.'

'Of course. Fame and fortune is for the likes of you. We had one famous man in our family on my mother's side but we don't talk about him.'

'Really? What did he do?'

'He was a bosun on a tea clipper and after the ship lost her masts and half the crew in a storm, him and the other survivors ate the cabin boy.'

'That's awful,' Edward said, aghast but laughing.

'By Our Lady it's true.'

'And did he regret it?'

'Yes. The boy wasn't very well cooked and they all got indigestion.'

The party was to picnic on Churston Point, close to the sea, but Rupert told Jack to take the team to the marsh first so they could cool off and drink.

'The Widdicombes lived near here, didn't they?' Edward asked, a little too casually to be convincing.

Jack answered the real question. 'Dora and her family have a house in Winner Street now.'

'She probably has dozens of admirers.'

'Loads,' Jack laughed and gave his companion a long, sideways look.

The picknickers went paddling in the sea, but the two boys remained with the horses. The mist which had covered the marsh throughout the night was thinning to ghost across the flood-lake. Jack gazed into the smoking glass and saw the shires'

169

facsimiles separating his face and Edward's. Helen's high peal of laughter pierced the hush. Her brother's fingers gently tugged at the horse's mane.

Three miles away Beth was hauling the light canvas-covered van up the hill out of Lansworthy when the nail penetrated the frog of her left forefoot. Instantly she reared but the belly band kept the shafts down and sent her tottering to the side.

'Crazy bastard,' Lacey roared. He tugged savagely on the reins so that the bit cut into the corners of Beth's mouth.

'Hold still. Whoa. Whoa.'

She never behaved like this for the Mick. The bloody stupid Mick had turned even the animals against him. He stood up to use the whip with maximum effect. Four blows stung Beth's neck and she whinnied, pulling hard to the right. The tram rattling down the hill added to her confusion. Her hooves scrabbled on the lines and she slipped and fell on her side, snapping a shaft. As the van tipped and the tram braked Lacey jumped clear, glimpsing the broken shaft raking Beth's flanks. Then he was on his knees and the van smashed down, narrowly missing him. Beth struggled to rise but the weight of the vehicle held her down. Blood puddled under her and she was throwing her head about in bewilderment.

'Get up, you crazy bastard,' Lacey hissed. He snatched the reins and jerked them viciously. 'Crazy,' jerk, 'bastard,' jerk.

Shock left Beth numb. She lay on her side, flanks heaving, feeling the pain but expecting the boy to stop it and free her.

'Up,' Lacey roared.

'How can she with all that holding her down?' said the tram driver. The passengers crowded round him.

'Unhitch her,' he went on. 'Unhitch her, empty the van and we'll right it. Get in touch with Chancellor's and they'll send for the vet.'

'What about me?' said Lacey. He held up his grazed fingers. 'It wadn my fault.'

'You'll live,' the tram driver sneered. 'Let's have the animal on her feet.'

'Stupid brute,' grunted Lacey.

'She's bleeding badly,' said a gentleman bending over Beth.

'I don't know what got into her, sir. She's seen trams before.'

'Maybe it was the whipping you gave her,' a woman

remarked. 'You really laid into the poor creature.'

'You've got to learn them discipline. That horse is too high-spirited. Her could have killed someone.'

'Then she shouldn't be on the streets.'

The tears sprang to Lacey's eyes. 'It idn my fault,' he wavered, and it occurred to him that it was one of his most used expressions.

It was on his tongue again back at the yard but this time Palfrey gave him the benefit of the doubt. The electric trams had been responsible for several accidents and Beth's large 'S'–shaped gash was not deep. Josephs soon stitched it up and she was standing placidly when Jack visited her that evening.

'Lacey's fed and groomed her,' said Old Bob. 'But her's still poorly. Nothing's broke but her took a hell of a tumble.'

Jack ran his hands over her and found two horizontal cuts a little below her right ear.

'Those were made by a whip,' he said. 'And the corners of her mouth are sore.'

'Us can't be certain,' said Sherwill.

'A whip,' Jack said emphatically, murderously.

'If Beth was playing up and got onto the tram lines Lacey was right to use the whip.'

'Beth doesn't play up unless she's scared.'

He lifted her feet one at a time and saw the swollen frog.

'A bloody rusty nail, mister. I'll need the iodine.'

'He said he looked at her.' And Sherwill's head bobbed. 'Can't that ornament do nothing right?'

'He can lie,' said Jack.

21

'But why does he hate you?' asked Kitty. She stood on tip-toe to peer at the red admiral butterfly that had settled on the buddleia near the yard gates.

'Because Jack is everything he wants to be and can't be,' said her sister.

The butterfly zig-zagged to another flower and spread its wings.

'Jack idn special,' Kitty smiled. 'Only to me.'

'And the horse,' said Dora. Her hands flew up to tug at the brim of her hat and straighten it. Jack's arm encircled her waist, playfully, but Kitty blushed.

'Are you coming back to our place for tea, Dora?' he said. 'Mum wouldn't mind. There's plenty of room at the table and plenty of grub.'

'I'm going for a walk.'

'Oh yes,' Kitty said and her eyebrows arched.

'Why must every walk a young woman takes end in a rendezvous with a man? I'm simply strolling down to the harbour and back. When I'm alone I think clearer.'

'Think about what?' said Jack.

Although Dora's dark grey coat was clean and well pressed there was evidence on the sleeves of some anxious repair work. He removed his arm and smiled.

'How to help me dad and his friends change the world.'

Dora was tall and her features lacked the coarseness typical of even the most beautiful working-class woman. If it hadn't been for her soft Devon accent, Jack reflected, she could have fitted quite easily into the Chancellors' hayride party.

'You ought to meet Dad,' she went on.

'Kitty won't take me home. She's too shy.'

Again the colour rose in Kitty's cheeks. 'You doan know my sisters. And Mum would make fun of me.'

'Dad wouldn.'

'But he'd jaw about the Labour Party and bore Jack to death. Dad's always preachin'.'

'Preaching the truth. You should be proud of him.'

'I am,' Kitty cried. 'But there's things just as important as politics and votes for women.'

'When you've got the other things what then?'

'I doan know. Tomorrow can look after itself.' Her voice dropped to a whisper. 'I idn askin' for much, Dora.'

'Don't worry,' Dora said, kissing her sister. 'You'll get what you want. I suppose the secret is not aiming too high. A husband, babies, and a horse should come fairly easy.'

'I want to be happy.'

'You will be. Meanwhile I'll try to help Dad sort out society so tomorrow will come as a pleasant surprise.'

'You're too young to be the the the fairy godmother,' Jack laughed.

Dora took a pace back and waved an imaginary wand. 'Forget the beanstalk, my brave Jack – you shall go to the ball.'

'Dreams sometimes do come true, doan 'em Jack?' said Kitty

'Yes,' he said softly.

His mother was an expert when it came to absenting herself from reality. Dreaming was her ticket out of misery—dreaming and prayer. The daily chores had the power to transport her to some area of the past bathed in the light of ecclesiastical stained glass. The White Lady of Landsworthy walked Dingle's storm beaches, her robes brighter than the foam. From the kitchen of Number Eight Angarrick Terrace, Ireland had become the Holy Land for it had that distance only thought could visit.

She allowed Kitty to boil the kettle and fill the teapot.

Really the girl was nice – thoughtful and caring. What a pity

173

she was a Protestant. Mary McKenna sighed. Bacon fat joined the mashed potato on the scrubbed deal. She added the seasoning and used the top of a glass to shape the potato cakes. Had Mary ever made little savouries for Our Lord? The notion brought a smile to her face and Jack knew she was elsewhere, probably Slea Head or Galilee.

Blanche dusted the cakes in flour and put them to fry in a pan of dripping.

'Does your mum make potato cakes, Kitty?' asked Sean.

'Sometimes,' she smiled.

'Jack loves them,' said Mrs McKenna.

'But they make him purp,' Lily giggled and blew a raspberry.

'Lily!' exclaimed her mother but everyone was laughing and she had to join in.

'You know Jack would have his horse to supper if Mum would let him,' said Michael.

Kitty nodded.

'The Germans would have his horse for supper,' Mary McKenna said.

Jack gazed up at the ceiling. 'Mr Chancellor told me the Celts – that's us – used to eat horses in olden times because they were magic.'

'That was different,' said Mary McKenna, smoothing down her apron. 'You won't find pony pasties on sale in Dublin now.'

'Maybe the Germans are so poor they eat anything they can get, like Gran and Grandad did in the bad times.'

Her lips pressed together and whitened.

'Don't,' she gasped, fighting to hold the nightmare at bay. But she opened the door for them when Kitty had to go. Autumn's scents and smells spiced the crisp night air. A train hooted, and the mist which had captured some of the chimney smoke was coiling round the lamp. Jack and Kitty walked towards the light and into it and disappeared. Mary clutched her shawl tightly to her breast.

'Oh Kevan,' she whispered. 'Why did you have to kill it? Why?'

It was his turn to sweep out the Ladies' Fashion Wear Department and Ernie Drew soon set about entertaining the stable boys. He got out some of the tailor's dummies which were wasp-waisted and flaunted generous bosoms. Then he waltzed one of them between the counters, eyes closed, a rapturous expression on his face. The boys collapsed in a giggling heap.

'Can't 'ee get the real thing?' Fred Luscombe said.

'To be bliddy honest I can't,' Ernie laughed. 'I gave up chasin' women long ago for serious boozin'. I bet your pal Lacey wishes he'd stuck to scrumpy instead of all that park work with the Cundy maid.

'Me and a hundred others,' said Lacey, glancing nervously about him.

'But it'll be you her dad points the shotgun at.'

'Let un try,' Lacey snorted. He was conscious of Jack's eyes boring into his back and by the time he had reached the yard he was seething. His mood was carried onto the streets. Normally half a load on a tip-cart pulled by the old shire Gabriel would have seemed a soft number but Lacey was conscious only of the hostility closing in. The whip was laid on Gabriel's rump and the horse jumped.

'Get a move on, you old bugger,' Lacey barked.

Again the whip cracked and Gabriel winced. Rain and leaves gusted round the cart. The villas of Midvale Road could not dispel the air of melancholy with their stucco and bedraggled shrubberies. Although the weather was bad it was too warm for the oilskin and Lacey was sweating. He made the first delivery at a house whose steps were slippery. Twice he nearly fell carrying the heavy roll of netting. Then he had to wait a long time at the back door, white with temper.

The lash chewing into Gabriel's hide got rid of some of Lacey's spite but he felt like whipping the world and continued to vent his spleen on the old horse all the way up the road. Cart and animal were now travelling at such a speed it was impossible to take the bend at the junction. Lacey clawed the brake but his wet hand failed to find purchase. Instinctively Gabriel swung to the left as the pavement and garden wall raced to meet them.

It was happening again like the tramway mishap. Gabriel mounted the pavement and made a desperate attempt to avoid the wall. But he struck it with his right knee and keeled over. The weight of the cart thrown by the kerb pushed him over a low stone balustrade into the rockery, breaking his hind legs. The cart came to rest at a drunken angle, its wheels spinning

175

and goods crashing down on the stricken animal.

Lacey had landed unhurt in the road but when Gabriel began to whinny the horror of the situation filtered through the shattered jig-saw of the morning. He looked around for help and saw people emerging from nearby houses.

'Send for the vet,' he bawled, but Gabriel's high snuffling was louder and shriller.

'Help me, please. Someone help me,' Lacey cried.

He covered his ears with his hands and tottered away; and Gabriel continued to thrash about until the vet came and put a bullet in the animal's brain.

'What happened?' Old Bob said as Lacey crept into the yard. The other vehicles were on the streets and the stables were deserted. 'Where's your cart?'

'Crashed – back there, up Midvale Road.'

Lacey looked as if he had passed through a threshing machine.

'And Gabriel?'

'The vet's comin' and – and . . .'

'He's hurt and you left un?' Sherwill said with more disbelief than disgust in his voice.

'There wadn nothing I could do. He went over the wall. It wadn my fault.'

'Jesus Christ! Where exactly? Come on, you snivelling bloody coward. Show me. Two accidents in as many months and all you can think of is yourself.'

'I can't show you. Up the end of the road. You'll find it. They've sent for the vet. I idn goin' back.'

'What about Gabriel?' the old man shouted and he gripped the front of Lacey's oilskin.

'The bugger bolted. Twadn my fault.'

'It never is.' Sherwill was shaking him. 'Never your fault. By Christ I'll beat the shit out of you if that horse has to be destroyed.'

The blood hammered at the base of Lacey's skull. He looked down at the white, blue-veined fists clenched on the oilskin.

'You and the soddin' horses and whole soddin' yard can go to hell,' he roared.

His knee came up and Sherwill jack-knifed. 'Come on, you old bugger, come on. You've had it in for me ever since I came here. You' – Lacey's fist crunched into Sherwill's face – 'and Palfrey' – punctuated by another blow – 'and that Irish bastard.'

Something hard thudded against the side of his head and sent him reeling. The silent explosion of stars behind his eyes faded but the yard was spinning.

Jack spat on his fists. 'It's the Irish bastard, Arthur. Aren't you the bucko when it comes to knockin' old men about?'

Sherwill was sitting in a puddle of rain and horses' urine.

'Leave un be, Jack,' he gasped. 'He's finished here. Go and see what's happened to Gabriel, there's a good lad.'

'What me and Arthur have to do won't take a moment,' Jack said and he stooped to take the old man under the arms.

'There's a good lad,' Lacey snarled.

Standing against a heap of barrels was a long-handled shovel. He snatched it and swung it as Jack turned. Metal rang on bone and the force of the blow numbed Lacey's arm to the elbow. Jack fell like a tree and lay motionless.

'Now you've done it,' Sherwill whispered.

'Twadn my fault,' Lacey cried. 'For Christ's sake – it wadn my fault. He would've had me. He's been waitin' for the chance. Oh yes, you'm all against me.'

He walked from the yard with the dawdling steps of a man for whom the future has ceased to exist. It was raining heavily and yellow sycamore leaves were glued to the surface of the lane. A row of starlings on the wall sang as if nothing had happened to transform the morning into trauma. Lacey lurched to a halt, placed his hands on his knees and vomited. The rain hammered down but the starlings would not be silenced.

The lump on Jack's brow swelled to close his eye. Beth gazed at him and laid back her ears.

'You'm like one of they Hallowe'en masks,' chuckled Old Bob. 'Her doan recognise 'ee.'

The bristle brush lifted the dirt from her coat and she was at ease. Only the occasional shift of the feet betrayed her pleasure. The lantern light gilded her flanks and emphasised the marbling around her thighs. A faint sienna tint had crept into her mane and the shaggy ends of her feather. Her tail, too, was brown streaked and the redness of her haunches had deepened. The chestnut of Bathsheba, who was sharing the stall, set off the

177

beauty of her companion.

Blood things, dimly felt between heartbeats, united the animals. Jack was conscious of the bond although it remained elusive when he tried to label it. The reek of urine-soaked straw prickled his nostrils, and the chomp and snuffle of feeding animals gave the evening its texture. Rain falling across the moon did the rest.

Beth stood over fifteen hands high. Her flat-profiled head against the light was so still it might have been carved from marble. Jack massaged her neck, pressing hard with his palms. Human voices blurred for it was the time of day that inspired men to speak softly.

Walking home with Kitty he tried to shrug off his confusion. The church had got it wrong and he attempted to work it out, but could not. There was the gut reaction but no intellectual scaffolding. The wet streets were empty but they led to the cheerfulness of the fireside. He kissed her goodnight and quickened his pace so that his body was glowing by the time he reached the terrace. Blanche and Lily yodelled his name and ran alongside him clutching his hands. The faint sooty smell of the chimneys met the fragrance of suppers roasting or frying.

'Are those boots wet?' said Mrs McKenna.

'They are not,' said Jack, and he pulled them off and angled them on the fender.

'But your coat and pullover are. Take off that woolly before you catch your death. Has your face seen the flannel today?'

'I'm not a child, Mother. Stop naggin'.'

'A lick and a promise is not a wash,' she said. 'See to it before you eat. Cleanliness is next to godliness.'

'Didn't Jesus ever get his hands dirty? I mean, did he carry a bit of carbolic everywhere wrapped up in a flannel? He's always so damned neat and tidy in the pictures – lovely blond hair, nice white nightshirt, blue eyes. Do Jews from the dusty old desert really look like that? I thought they were dark with noses like hawks' beaks.'

'Jesus is Jesus. The Son of God is bound to be different.'

'But why so Engish, so well-fed and wet looking?'

'Right,' his mother said in a hard flat tone. 'I can see what you're up to. Michael loves it. Don't worry, you won't get me going. Tell me, Mr Know-it-all, why should the Son of God be ugly? Why shouldn't he be handsome?'

'Handsome and wet,' said Michael.

'You can't have him lookin' like a common workin' man.'

Jack grinned. 'Why not? Wouldn't the toffs go to church if he looked like a carpenter not a wealthy gent who read poetry and did a bit of shooting?'

'This will stop,' his mother said without a trace of humour in her voice. 'I don't want to hear no more. Go and scrub your face and wash out your mouth. I've got you a bit of fish. God knows why I bother.'

'Because you know I'm destined for the priesthood,' Jack said, grabbing her and whirling her round until she was giddy.

'I wish it was true,' she gasped.

'Father McKenna. Jesus! How could I listen to all the lovelies confessin' their sins without taking advantage of them?'

'Sin has a way of gettin' back at you,' said his mother. 'That dreadful Cundy girl has found that out.'

'Sure, lots of girls get into trouble,' said Michael. 'It takes two to –'

'Don't say it,' snapped Mary McKenna. 'Hazel Cundy's baby was stillborn this morning and she nearly died in the process. There's judgement for you.'

'Poor Hazel,' Jack said. His low, dark voice lent pathos to the words and the woman was moved despite her irritation.

'Poor infant,' she rasped. 'Poor Mrs Cundy who has to carry her daughter's shame.'

'The only one to get off scot-free is the father,' Michael said.

'And who would he be?' Their mother's sneer surprised the boys. It made her ugly.

'What do we do now?' said Jack. 'Stone her out of town?'

'If the child had lived she would have gone to the madhouse.'

'Why, for Christ's sake?'

'You've got to be unbalanced to do what she done.'

'Or off-balance,' Michael grinned. 'Or maybe she over-balanced and Lacey pounced.'

'Was Lacey mad too?' Jack said. 'I mean, would they have banged him away as well?'

'Go and wash or I'll give your fish to next door's cat.'

Parts of the terrace pig hung in the scullery, but the butcher's knives, he decided, weren't as sharp as the gossips' tongues.

He considered the injustice of it all on the way to Deller's Café. Kitty asked him what he was brooding about but he kept his thoughts to himself. What would happen if Dora became pregnant? Would the authorities stick her away in the asylum and put the child in a workhouse orphanage? He straightened his tie and pulled the peak of his cap down over the corner of his right eyebrow. Kitty clung to his arm wondering what was wrong.

The dance hall was packed and Frank Carter's Mandolin Band was plucking a confident route through 'Dolly Grey'.

'How do you dance to that?' Jack said. 'What the hell is it – a waltz, a polka, a bloody jig?'

'Something's upset you,' said Kitty and he caught hold of her hands and kissed her.   'The world is crazy, sweetheart.'

'Have you been talking to Dora?'

'No. Mother told me about Hazel Cundy.'

'Isn't it awful?' Kitty sighed. 'I don't feel sorry for her, though – only the babby. Hazel has been askin' for it since her left school. Dora went to see her but Mr Cundy wouldn't let her in. He called her a bliddy Socialist and said Dad's lot was responsible for what was happening to young people. Then he slammed the door in her face.'

'Come on, let's dance,' he whispered. 'Standin' here jawing and fretting won't change things.'

He slid an arm round her waist and nuzzled her hair.

'One Saturday I'd like to do something different for a change,' she said.

'Like what?'

'Us could go to the Burlington over Abbot's Quay. Dad says it idn bad.'

'I've never been to a cinema or a variety show,' Jack said. They swung around together and she smiled and closed her eyes, loving the music and his confident hold on her body.

'Your mum and dad get about a bit don't they?' he smiled. 'I think our mum's afraid of moving pictures. And Abbot's Quay is a bit out of the way.'

'Get home do,' Kitty laughed. ''Tis just a tram ride up the road. My little sisters go over Abbot's Quay nearly every Saturday afternoon. They say it's really exciting. When the lights go out everythin' comes alive on the screen. It's like being

180

in another world.'

'But you finish too late for us to do anything except walk down here or go down the Bijou.'

'I know, but it's what I'd like to do, Jack.'

The music had stopped and couples were leaving the dance floor. He led her slowly back to the table.

'They'll have a cinema in Lansworthy one day and we'll go every Wednesday night.'

'With the children,' Kitty said

'After we've got round to making them – if ever,' and he sighed in that theatrical way she found so amusing.

22

Beth enjoyed leaving the yard in the grey first light, her hooves scuffing drifts of fallen leaves and her senses taking all the morning had to offer. The collar sat comfortably on her shoulders and the shaft was perfectly hitched to her harness. Neither she nor Bathsheba showed any nervousness even amongst the growing number of motor vehicles. When old Chancellor commented on this Palfrey told him rather smugly that both fillies had been correctly schooled. And the horsemaster forecast unparalleled success at next summer's Cart Horse Parade which Chancellor's had chosen to ignore in the past.

'Why did Lacey get the push?' Moony asked Jack.

They were riding Beth and Bathsheba to the smithy. A white horse stood in the shafts of the coal cart at the roadside. The animals glanced at each other but exchanged no greetings. One of autumn's golden mists veiled the town, softening the formal geometry of the villa gardens.

'He got a horse killed,' said Jack.

'I didn like un, no sir. I didn. I didn.'

He scratched the stubble on his chin and drew down the corners of his mouth. Chancellor's peak caps had been issued and Moony's was too large. It sat on his ears, throwing them out. Like jug handles, Jack thought, grinning to himself and wondering if his own cap looked daft.

Their turn came. Sweat beaded the farrier's brow and dripped off his nose and chin. His face had the leathery sheen of his apron. The stink of scorched horn spread. The shoe was nailed and clenched home.

A carter from the GWR gave Jack a 'good morning'.

'Seen your mate Arthur gettin' on the early train,' he said. 'He had a suitcase with un. Goin' to London, to some fancy job he reckoned.'

'Not with horses, I hope,' said Jack.

The carter lit a Woodbine. 'That was a bad do, boy. Anyone who ill-treats a horse idn fit to live.'

He squinted at the young Irishman and liked what he saw. Jack was of medium height, well-muscled and slightly bow-legged. His greatcoat was slung across his arm and his cap tipped back. The shock of black hair and the crooked nose were things he could have borrowed from any street urchin.

'I saw Hazel Cundy up Winner Street,' Skilly said apropos of nothing at all.

'The Sherlock Holmes of Lansworthy,' Jack laughed.

'Her was shoppin' as if nort had happened.'

'What should she be doin'? Standing in the stocks for you to biff rotten veg at her?'

Fred Luscombe kneaded his paunch. 'I doan know how her's got the gall to show her face after droppin' a dead bastard.'

'She's got more pluck than your pal, Arthur,' Jack said.

'He idn no mate of mine. Anyway, us idn certain it was him who got her in trouble.'

'God, your're right Fred. It could have been Skilly or Mr Sidney or Father Tynan.'

Luscombe grinned. 'Not my Skilly. He still thinks it's just to pee out of.'

The carters laughed but Mary McKenna did not find Hazel's behaviour amusing.

'She's the shameless one.'

'And we won't let her forget it, will we Mother?'

'God won't.'

The draught horses carried themselves effortlessly. They ambled among the pigeons and sparrows and sent them back to the rooftops for a moment or two. Melody and her daughter were almost the same size. They worked in unison, pulling the wagon or standing at the kerbside while things were unloaded. Dusted with hoar frost under the evening lamps they assumed the biblical splendour Jack was never surprised to rediscover.

The town round was best. Off the main roads Lansworthy was full of old shops and hidden corners which had escaped the Victorians' compulsion to rebuild. Cobbled pavements followed streets hardly wide enough for a cart to thread through. The clamour of geese and chickens rose from backyards and gardens, and rooks cawed from the churchyard trees. Smoke wreathed the rickety chimney stacks which attempted to stand upright above a jumble of rooftops.

At dusk all the architectural eccentricities were mantled in mist. Sleet would whisper through the hush as, slack of mind, the horses became shadows. Then melancholy would follow Jack up the steps of the Globe Inn after the stabling and fade as he sat drinking beer by the fire. The tiny bar was the colour of an old violin and the landlady who liked to gossip would rise whenever a customer entered, drop her cat to the floor and brush its hairs off her apron. She was alert and birdlike with round eyes and sharp features. Left to its own devices the cat would strut up and down on the hearth, growling and hissing at the hands that presumed to stroke it. The landlady loved to tell obscure stories which only she found amusing. Half listening, Jack knew her mind was elsewhere and her words were just noises to keep loneliness at arm's length.

The westering sun was touching the hills so that the frost sparkled as red as the berries on the holly the children brought home from the fields. The front room and kitchen were decorated and the Christmas spirit was caught in the laughter of the guttersnipes playing their street games while they said silent prayers for snow. Then Father Tynan went away to London, to die, Mary McKenna said, at the Marist hospice. The old man had some terrible disease, which had probably accounted for his increasing aloofness over the past year, Jack thought. But he took an instant liking to the new priest.

Father O'Driscoll had been trained in Dublin. He smoked cigarettes and was older than Tynan, with a limp and a watery eye. The Irish brogue and cheerful smile made Mass less of a

184

penance. Although he sensed Jack's doubt he bided his time and waited for the young man to come in search of Christ. Some you drove, he mused, some you coaxed, others were best left to tread through their confusion at their own pace.

On Christmas Eve he settled comfortably in the kitchen of Number Eight and allowed Mary to pour him a large scotch. Kitty, who was helping the girls at the table, was bubbling over and the priest noted the look that sparked between her and Jack. Eating cake alone with Mary McKenna in the front room he said, 'And they are to be wed?'

The woman blushed. 'She is a lovely girl, Father, but she's not a Catholic.'

'I thought I hadn't seen her at Mass,' he smiled.

'It's hard work getting Jack to walk up the road,' Mary McKenna said apologetically. 'If you'll forgive me, Father, he couldn't take to Father Tynan. It was the English accent.'

'And the horses,' said the priest. 'From what I hear the horses kept him from Mass. He has a way with them, so they say.'

'Like St Francis. There's no wickedness in Jack, Father. He thinks too much, that's his trouble.'

O'Driscoll nodded. 'He and the girl seem very close.'

'They've been walking out together for over three years.'

'She intends coming into the church?'

'I honestly don't know, Father. But she has promised to bring up the children as good Catholics.'

Again the priest nodded and smiled, and lifted his glass for a refill.

Mary regretted there were no grandparents to grace the family Christmas. She decided she would write to the church in Dingle and try to trace her relatives. Old age could be a barren place. Sons and daughters went off into the world to make their own lives and the stillness of a home without a husband or children would be too much like the tomb. But now the little terrace house was the heart of Christmas. Mary McKenna and the girls darted about the kitchen in a cloud of spicy steam. The low-ceilinged, lamplit room was full of jars, basins, pots, pans, bowls and plates; pickled cabbage, pickled onions and piccalilli, hams, herbs, sausages, loaves and tarts had been assembled like treasure trove. Mincemeat nestled in cradles of dough; pies lay ready for the oven; potatoes were being peeled and baptised in

185

the great saucepan while Blanche skilfully operated on a white cabbage. The cake had to be iced and the hams boiled and the goose plucked. The bird had come from Tor Barton. Farmyard dung braided its plumage. It lay across Michael's lap leaking blood and feathers into the bowl.

Sean and the girls reached a point around which excitement whirlpooled. They went to bed late, tipsy on the ruby wine, and fought sleep until it took them by surprise. Then, suddenly, their room was glorious with the light of Christmas morning and they were tearing open their parcels as the bells began to ring from the parish church.

The occasion reached its zenith at lunchtime. The family sat at the best table in the living room, under the huge, gloomy print of the play scene from Hamlet. The fire smoked and light sparkled on the glassware. Mary KcKenna said grace and set the carving knife to the bird. A plume of steam saluted the first cut, followed by a gasp of delight from the children. Blanche sat picking at her meal because she did not want to finish it. For her the last mouthful of goose and roast potato meant the beginning of the end. Beyond Boxing Day stretched a desert of weeks which she would have to cross before another Christmas loomed on the horizon.

Jack and Michael toasted their mother in the best port – the stuff that made them cough as it hit the back of their throats.

'Go and fetch the pudding, you pair of idiots,' she said, the tears twinkling in her eyes.

So they went to the kitchen and blacked their faces with a burnt cork. Michael had drunk a lot of port and was loose-kneed. He could not take three steps without colliding with the furniture.

'Ready?' said Jack, and Michael nodded. From his neck, on a piece of string, hung an empty biscuit tin which he banged with a couple of wooden spoons. Jack lifted the pudding on its holly-trimmed plate and they marched noisily back to the living room that smelt of cigar smoke. Mrs McKenna and the youngsters cheered and clapped as the pudding was set down in its place of honour. The ruins of the feast dismayed everyone but the wine kept them cheerful. Christmas was slipping away as it did every year. There would be games of Blind Man's Buff and Hunt the Slipper; ghost stories would be told by firelight, chestnuts roasted, and the pickles and cold meat would provide a memorable supper. But there was no way of reliving the rapture of Christmas Eve with all its nuances of excitement.

Boxing Day was a drowsy anti-climax. Moony and his mother called and after they had gone Kitty came to supper. Then Jack wanted the gluttony and goodwill to last forever. He had something special to celebrate and at the appropriate moment called for silence. Kitty and Mrs McKenna were seated facing each other across the fire with the rest of the McKennas squatting on the hearth waiting for the final ghost story. The fire shifted and gold danced on the walls and ceiling.

'Kitty and me are engaged,' he said stiffly. 'She got the ring as a Christmas present. Her mother and father are happy for us. I hope you lot are.'

Kitty raised the hand she had kept tucked in her lap and the firelight flashed on the tiny stone set in the band of gold. The face she swung from Jack to his mother was radiant.

'Oh my dear girl,' Mrs McKenna whispered, opening her arms. 'Let me kiss you – quick, before I start bawlin' like a baby.'

A cat loped across the pavement before them and clawed at someone's front door. The frost of early evening was vanishing as the south westerly ushered moist air in from the Atlantic. The fog that had threatened had already sealed off half the sky, and one by one the stars were going out. As if they're being turned off, Jack thought. His grip tightened on Kitty's hand.

'Does being engaged make you feel different?' he said in the deep pleasant voice he had inherited from his mother.

'Grown up,' she murmured, pressing her cheek against his shoulder. 'I can't wait to show the girls at Chancellor's. They'll be so jealous when they see the ring on me finger.'

'And the one in my nose,' he laughed.

'But you really do love me, don't you Jack?' she said and the anxiety in her voice surprised him.

'God, yes,' he said, lowering his face and negotiating the brim of her hat to kiss her. 'And love's the only thing, kitten. It's bigger and brighter than them stars. If it's true it's in your heart till you die, like a light nothing can put out.'

187

23

Beth's hooves crunched through the cat ice on the puddles when she walked from the yard. Mullah scurried behind the van to wolf the balls of manure left steaming in the road.

'It's the oats,' grinned the new stable boy. 'Our dog eats horse conkers as well if us let him.'

Jack's eyes twinkled. 'I suppose it's cheaper than a bit of meat.'

'He doan eat 'em all the time,' the boy laughed.

They were carting furniture to a farm at Waddeton. The boy had a thin white face and a red nose. Every so often he sniffled and a bubble swelled from one of his nostrils and burst. The residue was sucked back up his nose again, noisily. The beat of Beth's hooves rang across the hush that was rose-tinted now. The sun stood above the bay, flushing the surrounding hills and the robes of the White Lady. Birds filled the mist rising from Clennon Valley. The boy stopped gibbering and the bird calls drifted into Jack's solitude. Where the mist was dense the horses of Cider Mill Farm stood with only their heads and necks visible. They called to Beth. She was a mare now but her vision of life had not changed since the first summer.

The valley was climbing into sunlight and beyond its mists Iona walked free of infirmity. The mare, who was no longer old, would wander out of the Summer Field into the thoughts of the sleeping horses or suddenly appear to stand between them and the sun.

It was difficult to separate what had been from what was, and Beth was never sure of any clear division. The life behind her eyes was often more vivid than anything the living world could offer. At times she could see and smell Iona so sharply she emerged from a dream to find the mare beside her. Even as the image faded and the valley or street returned she heard the gate open and then the great herds moved down the hillside. Her sleep was a parade of dreams. In the grass she would stretch out and soak up the summer's warmth. Again the muffled whinnying burst from the mist. She tasted coldness on her lips. The birth and death of days flickered on the edge of something her emotions could not unravel, something intensely exciting, a place that had filled her being while she lay within her mother.

Leaving the outskirts of Lansworthy the lane ran high-hedged over the hills to the old Mary's Haven Road. Buzzards skirled but looking up Jack saw none although rabbits ran in front of Beth. Then sheep were cropping the wayside grass and the boy who was Albert Wotton's nephew, Charlie, swore at them.

'Why did you say that?' Jack asked, taking the cart carefully around the animals.

'Bliddy stupid old mutton-heads,' Charlie grinned. 'Everyone knows sheep are mazed.'

Jack nodded. What, he thought, if horses really had been fashioned from the wind? God could conjure up great trees from a handful of seeds, and Jesus walked on the water. God could do anything. The wind was everywhere. It was as difficult to understand as lightning.

He glanced back at the sheep. They followed him with a frozen stare. He clicked his tongue at Beth and suddenly felt small and lost.

'Mazed,' Charlie said again. He cocked his head and grinned sideways at Jack.

Sheep and cattle massing at the abattoir gates. Bulging eyes, silence mistaken for passive acceptance. Then, then, the muffled trilling of horses' hooves along the road to Calvary. Mares and stallions swarming over Golgotha in answer to a wordless plea. Another sacrifice. But why were sacrifices necessary?

189

All day the notion haunted him but the sunset was too magnificent to ignore. They had collected half a load of barley from Aish and rattled and rumbled back through the lanes with the side lamps lit. The wind was shaking chimney soot into the dusk and the street lights were on. A skyline of roofs and chimneys climbed to the White Lady who also stood in silhouette. Grey, gleaming streets rang to the hoofbeats of horses and the grating crunch of wagon- and cartwheels.

After the faded colours of the winter countryside Lansworthy had life flowing along its thoroughfares. The lamps glowed in a warm, inviting way but the stars were blurred by the smoke which spread. A carriage horse shied and came under the whip before settling to its task. Urchins ran beside the van or hung on the tailboards. At the corner of Winner Street and Palace Avenue was a brazier of hot coals and workmen labouring in a pit. Around the fire were the silhouettes of children and tramps. A pauper family in drab, patched clothes trailed past the park in the middle of the avenue. Their heads were bowed but a girl with a little pinched face glanced up and looked at Jack. Her misery reached out to him and he wanted to speak but let Beth pace on because words were never enough. Then the sight of Chancellor's store, all lit up, with customers still coming and going, irked him.

In the road outside half a dozen carriages and motor cars were assembled, and a gang of guttersnipes and down-and-outs had collected before a barrel organ. The monkey holding the tin mug was underfed and shivering. Its eyes reminded Jack of the pauper girl he had passed near the park. How do you fight the suffering, he thought, when you can only put your hand in your pocket and come up with a bit of loose change? Maybe Dora Widdicombe had the answers.

A train left the station under the hiss and bellow of steam. Darkness closed behind it but the piercing wail continued to haunt the night for a long time.

'They've got a Salvation Army lantern slide at Palace Avenue Theatre tonight,' Charlie said. He blew on his fingers before stuffing them back in his pockets.

'I'll probably give it a miss,' Jack smiled.

'It idn too special,' said the boy. 'Scenes from the bliddy Holy Land. My sisters only go for the tea and buns. The buns are

190

always good,' he added wistfully.

Mullah waddled out of the yard to greet them.

'You got a dog, Jack?' Charlie said.

'No. I keep meaning to get one but . . .' he shrugged.

'Us've got Laddie and two cats. They'm handsome. Mum lets 'em sleep on my bed. Animals make good pals, doan 'em Jack? Dad says you'm magic with 'orses and you'll learn me everything about 'em.'

'You really want to be a horseman?'

'Crikey, yes! Beth's bliddy lovely.'

Charlie's eyes blazed and Jack smiled.

'How old are you, Charlie?'

'Just fifteen.' He coloured. 'I idn very big for me age.'

'You'll grow, don't worry,' said Jack. 'Take Beth. A few years ago she was no more than a pony, a toy. Look,' he added, putting on the brake. 'Why don't you run up to the theatre? I can manage here.'

The other carters were gone but Palfrey and Old Bob were busy in the harness room when Jack came in with Beth's gears.

'Plant your behind on that stool and have a drop of rum, boy,' said the horsemaster. 'Will 'ee be takin' the young mares up forge tomorrow?'

'I thought I'd let Charlie and Moony have a go at it by themselves.'

'Charlie's all right then?' said Old Bob.

'The horses like him and he likes them. He's a good lad.'

There was a moment's silence as the men drank.

'Mr Sidney wants you to go out with the vet in the mornin'.' Palfrey frowned at his pipe and got out the matches. 'He'll be up round Tor Barton and all over, tendin' horses. The old man reckons you'll pick up a thing or two, things I can't learn 'ee.'

The rum and the prospect of doing something different brought the colour to Jack's face. Palfrey smiled and went across to the peg on the wall where his coat was hanging.

'Go home and read this,' he said, pushing a small book into Jack's hands. 'The old man wants 'ee to be top dog. What you've done with Beth has pleased un no end.'

'Most of it was Mr Trant's doing.'

Palfrey blew smoke and plucked the pipe from his mouth.

'Trant's a farm horseman. I keep a town stud. But you could

191

be the best all-rounder I've ever knowed. Listen to Josephs and study that book.'

Jack read the title, *Animal Management*, and the smaller print on the cover – 'Prepared by the War Office'. He flicked through the pages and had a longer look at the chapter headings. There were a lot of long words and puzzling phrases: 'Animal structure and function', 'The points of the horse, colours, markings and age', 'Stable construction and fittings', 'Stable Management'.

'I'll need a dictionary to get through this,' he grinned.

'Then buy a dictionary,' said Palfrey. 'That's a complete manual of horesemanship for soldiers but most of the principles can be applied to a town stud. Take it all in Jack. Mr Sherwill is retirin' soon and I suggested to Chancellor that you take his place. More responsibility and more money.'

'I'm sorry Mr Sherwill's goin',' Jack said, and the old man was touched by his sincerity.

'Pensioned off, boy,' he sniffed. 'I idn up to this caper no more but I'll be happy if I know you'm filling the gap.'

'I can't break my promise to Beth,' the boy grinned. 'One day I'll have her and my own round.'

'Maybe you'll change your mind,' said Palfrey.

'I won't, mister.'

'We'll see. Anyway, the job's yours. I'll tell Mr Sidney you'll take it.'

'Whain I'm gone, of course,' Old Bob chuckled.

The wind had died and fog was bringing the smoke down from the chimneys into the streets. A drunken soldier came reeling along Midvale Road singing a ditty that was both dreary and obscene. From the nursery window of one of the villas a music box tinkled and a child laughed. Jack looked down Palace Avenue for the little girl but she and her family were gone and the street was empty. After dropping into the Globe for a Guinness he strode home and was glad to see the small, familiar figures circling the lamp post. The Vosper's front door was open and Mr Vosper stood on the step smoking his pipe. Behind him, from the kitchen, came the bleak song of the caged greenfinch.

The mangle was creaking in a scullery full of steam when he hung up his coat on the hallstand of Number Eight.

'Couldn't get the washing done this morning,' Mary

McKenna explained, blowing hard. 'Lily's home ill with a bad chest – poor lamb. Will you go up and see her, Jack, while I get your supper on the table?'

He did not speak about his new prospects that evening. Sean had had a hard day at sea and the drink had left Michael quarrelsome. Sitting by the fire he recalled the skinny little monkey whose eyes held nothing but despair.

The day spent with Josephs was rewarding. Until then he had not realised how many horses in poor condition were scattered around Lansworthy. Their ailments varied from injuries to the ridge of the spine, girth galls, cracked heels and strangles as well as colic and staggers. The practical experience added a new dimension to the evening's study and Kitty was impressed by his new knowledge.

'Head carter at your age!' she exclaimed. 'Us've got a fine start in life, Jack. Dad wants 'ee to come to tea on Sunday. He've been badgerin' me for months but now I think you'm ready to sit down with the family.'

'I hadn't realised what a dreadful snob you are, Kitty Widdicombe.'

'I only want 'em to like 'ee,' and she blushed. 'They do leg-pull something awful. It would have been so humiliating if they didn take us serious. Tez all Dora in our house. You'd think her was a saint.'

'She's such an intelligent young lady,' said Jack, and he pretended to sigh.

'Oh she'd jump at the chance of grabbin' you and convertin' you,' Kitty declared fiercely. 'Now you've got prospects all the maids will be flauntin' themselves.'

'They already do,' but his lips smothered her reply before pain could turn to vitriol.

Later that week he carted palings to the Daubeny residence. Helen was exercising a couple of retriever pups on the back lawn but he did not expect her to acknowledge him. Her coat was trimmed with silver-flecked fur and she looked like a Russian princess. Ferrying the hurdles up to the garden shed Jack saw the high colour in her cheeks and interpreted it to suit his fancy. Of course it wasn't wantoness, he concluded reluctantly as the situation failed to develop except in his imagination. Most of the men's bragging about conquests and their talent for getting married women into bed on the rounds was wishful thinking.

He made the job last, though, carrying smaller loads and hoping she would follow him into the shed. Then what? The fantasy fed on his own hunger but as it developed it was Kitty stepping out of her clothes among the sacks, chests and garden equipment. Returning to the cart for the last armful of palings his eyes were on Helen and he failed to notice Ormond Chancellor approaching with Rupert.

'Look where you're damn well going,' Ormond barked when a collision seemed inevitable. 'Keep your eyes on the path and your mind on the job.'

Jack grinned, glad yet again his cap was in his pocket.

'Have you finished here?' Ormond added and received a nod.

'Don't nod your head at me, McKenna,' the man roared.

His face was red to the rim of his bowler and his body quivered. Mother of God! Jack thought, the silly bugger's going to blow up.

'I'm sorry, mister,' he said. 'My mind was elsewhere.'

'I know exactly where your mind was. Now get back to your cart before I sack you.'

'For what, mister?'

'What for, *Sir*.'

'What for, sir,' Jack repeated woodenly.

'I don't need a reason.'

Ormond realised the conversation should not be taking place. Rupert was wincing with embarrassment.

'Idleness, impudence,' he blustered on as anger fizzled into petulance.

'I do my job, sir, but my thoughts are my own.'

'We pay you to work not daydream. Now get out of my way.'

Jack did not pursue the matter. He knew he had gone as far as he could go and stepped aside to let father and son pass. Ormond's stiff-legged gait reminded him of a bad-tempered tom cat. He whipped out his handkerchief and let the laughter go in a cross between a cough and a sneeze.

The sequel to this skirmish did little for Ormond Chancellor's vanity. The motor van broke down at Tweenaway and no one could restart it. As the expert, Ormond was expected to perform miracles but his tinkering was more speculative than successful and the van remained lifeless at the roadside. Wilfully, Ormond thought.

'Damned shoddy workmanship,' he bleated.

Jack was crowing when he was sent out with Beth and the van to off-load the chinaware destined for the vicarage at Berry Pomeroy.

'You can't trust them motor things, mister,' he said. 'Put a horse in front of that and it'll go all day – no trouble.'

Ormond glared at his chauffeur and Cooksley but they managed to hold their countenances stiff. Snow fell from an east wind. Gritty particles bounced off the road, swirled and settled. Confrontation was again souring to defeat. Ormond sensed it as helplessness flooded his anger. Surely the Daubeny girl hadn't encouraged McKenna. It was inconceivable. Those trollops at the store had their bully-boy heroes but Helen! She had such exquisite shoulders and neck, and a voluptuous mouth. He tried to concentrate on the sensitive soul housed in that firm, unblemished flesh. The Cundy girl was all bosom and buttocks. Quite a different kettle of fish.

He cleared his throat. 'McKenna.'

'Yes, mister?'

'Yes, *sir*. Sir.' He spat out the monosyllable.

'Yes, sir.'

'Come down. I want a word with you.'

'Yes sir?'

The businessman's breath smelt faintly of dental decay and cigar smoke.

'You are under the illusion that you have some claim on the horse. No – don't interrupt. Just listen. She is part of the Chancellor stud and I will make sure she remains in it until she's ready for the knackers. My father is an old man who indulges his whims but I want you to understand clearly: Beth will never be yours. You will never own that horse.'

Looking him straight in the eye Jack said: 'And your father's promise, mister?'

'Have you got it in writing, McKenna?'

'He gave his word.'

The cold got into Jack and he shivered.

Ormond smiled. 'Off you go and make sure none of the crockery gets broken or you'll pay for it. The roan can manage

195

without you but can you manage without the roan?'

Beth swung her head to look at Jack. The snow which was lying on her coat had begun to melt and steam.

Oh Beth, Beth. He repeated her name constantly to himself, exorcising the misery. Then he said: 'Walk on, girl.'

Anger hardened to an ache in his chest.

24

Jack was tempted to ask Sidney Chancellor direct if their bargain would be kept but the more he thought about it the less he doubted the old man's integrity. Ormond was a windbag, like Lacey, and Michael laughed at the prospect of him ever doing anything to thwart his father.

'All wind and pee,' he said, grabbing their empty glasses and bringing them to the counter for refills. They had the Globe to themselves. 'He's fine when his wife's not lookin' and he can pinch the girls' bums in Daddy's store.'

'Language,' the landlady chuckled. She laid her forearms on the bar and drummed quietly with her fingers.

'Aren't I right, Lucy?' Michael said and he planted a kiss on the woman's cheek. 'He's a forgery of a fella.'

'Ask Hazel Cundy,' came the provocative reply.

'Now why should I do that?' said Michael.

'That Ormond is a sly bugger. He knows what he's about.'

'Will you have a drink Lucy?'

'I got me tay.' But she brought her cup and her cat to the fire.

'Hazel's friend's mother often drops in for a chinwag – her that chars for the solicitor in Palace Avenue. Do 'ee know Mrs Hannaford – Sybil Hannaford's mother? Her husband worked at Lansworthy Mill till 'ee died of a bad chest. Any rate, Hazel told Sybil twadn the Lacey boy who got her in trouble. Her

197

swore, hand on heart, twas Ormond Chancellor. He got her at it after hours in the store.'

'God, he hasn't the nerve,' Michael snorted.

'A lot you know, boy. All sorts of fun and games goes on whain that store closes. How do'ee think her got the money to go to London? Who found her a job and pays the rent for her digs – Lacey? He habn got a farthing to scratch his ass with. If that babby hadn come into the world daid Ormond would have problems. Why be 'ee lookin' so surprised? There's more than one gennelman round ere supportin' a whole parcel of bastards.'

'Well, well,' Michael grinned. 'The old ram. And him like a barrel of butter.'

Part of the creamy collar on the Guinness had transferred itself to his moustache. 'The bloody ram.'

Jack brooded on his own lust for Helen and said nothing.

'Spiders, boy,' Lucy said from a pale smile. 'That's what 'em be, spiders.'

Particles of spring were assembling—sounds, colours, scents, and, while the warmth of the sun was partly imagined, winter's chill had some green in it. Beth's eyes were brimming with that mysterious response to the living world which the blackbird carries in its voice. Returned to Cider Mill Tor with Bathsheba for a rest she pranced on her hind legs. Light lay on the hillside and the sunrise drew her thoughts. The mud smelt of life and movement was a slow-motion waltz. Bathsheba's lumbering gait brushed the raindrops off the cow parsley leaves under the hedge. Thrushes bounced across the field, stabbing the grass with their beaks. But the intense sexuality of the dawn chorus failed to silence other noises caught in her blood. Rooks cawed and then the curlews began to release the cries she had heard at birth.

Leaving the terrace on his bicycle Jack let the old desire knot his innards. It was still the animal thing spilling out of childhood, like the morning he had come to Melody and seen the foal slide into the world. Sunlight twinkled on the blackbird's beak. The faint stink of farm animals clung to the air and the horses were on the hill. They arched their necks and tossed their heads, light streaming off their flanks. Always the placid gaze and the slow rise and fall of their hooves.

'Beth.'

But there were sensations whose beauty defied interpretation. When the horses first gathered under the stars their language shared kinship with the song of the leaves and grass.

He drew his hand down her nose. The bond could never be broken. He leapt onto her back and clutched her mane and she cantered round the tor. Then he felt he was the morning, so breathless was his passion for life.

Skilly's accident harvested the usual crop of 'ifs'. If Wotton had not left the wagon to urinate things would have turned out differently. If the cat had not chosen to crouch under Solomon as he stood with Boxer in the shafts Mullah would not have gone crazy. The cat was a stray tom whom Mullah hated. The bull terrier hit him like a thunderbolt and Solomon bolted, taking Boxer with him. At that moment Skilly was mounting the wagon wheel and the jolt dislodged his feet from the spokes. The first revolution of the wheel wedged his legs and shattered them. For a horrifying moment he was dragged thrashing across the yard until Old Bob caught Solomon's bridle and calmed the horse. When they pulled Skilly clear he was unconscious and Palfrey who had seen similar injuries in the Transvaal said it was lucky he had passed out. The blood and splinters of bone were too much for some of the boys and they took their greenish-white faces behind the shed to throw up.

'They had to chop his left leg off at the knee,' said Mrs McKenna. 'And he may lose the other one. The poor devil. Perhaps that father of his will stop knockin' him about now. Mrs Luscombe's a hard-working woman. It don't seem fair at her time of life.'

Jack and Kitty walked to the beach.

'It makes you wonder what God's up to,' he said.

Easter sunlight was tinting Kitty's hair as the breeze curled it across her face.

'As if having an idiot son in the first place isn't a big enough cross without crippling him when his parents are getting old.'

They sat on the sea wall by the pavilion. A gentleman in top hat and morning coat sauntered along the promenade with his wife on his arm and his free hand enfolding the silver knob of his cane. From the carefully trimmed beard to the polished leather of his boots he was a study in prosperity. She was school-girlish, a little faded. The man's small talk evoked no response. Boredom had perhaps conditioned her to burrow deeply into herself, but better, Jack thought, that claustrophobic cosseting than the plight of Mrs Luscombe or Mrs Endacott.

Skilly had been transferred from Lansworthy Cottage Hospital to the asylum infirmary. His father did not appear too upset although cider made him lachrymose and sentimental.

'Mrs Luscombe walks round like death warmed up,' said Mary McKenna. 'There are many ways of committing suicide. God! I hope you lot won't see me buried by the Parish.'

'You'll outlive us all, Mum,' said Michael.

Her face blanched. 'Don't say that. Never say that again. What sort of life would it be – outliving my children?'

The clock behind the crucifix chimed. Lily yawned and coughed. The curtains lifted on a breeze loaded with the warmth of early summer and the scents of Grosvenor Road's gardens.

Another of Lazewell's even-tempered stallions was brought to the farm to cover Beth and Bathsheba. Palfrey approved the match because Mr Sidney was running the stables on similar lines to a thoroughbred stud and Lazewell's animals rarely failed to sire good foals.

The dark, terrible strength of the stallion passed to Beth and became part of her in a coupling that awed Jack. Afterwards when the stallion was led away and the mares stood together Jack sat on the outcrop looking across the trees at the White Lady. Mother of God, Mother Earth, so why God the Father? It was difficult to puzzle out. Mother of God. How was that possible? How could someone like Father Tynan or Father O'Driscoll guide young people who were in love? What did they know about lust and passion and tenderness? You couldn't read up on those things any more than you could read up on the pain of toothache. If the feeling was so good why was it wrong? And there was O'Driscoll worrying away at them to get Kitty converted and the unborn children promised to the Faith.

He drew the grass stem through his fingers and nibbled it. The Church was like the workhouse. You had to conform and obey as if the rules were everything. He let his confusion settle. I

200

love Kitty. I love nature and the horses who live in nature. The horse's life was like a prayer because it never broke faith with creation. If God is truth for me than he's also truth for the animals. He's not a person. Each animal has its vision of God and if we live in truth and beauty there are no roads to the centre of the mystery. We are at the centre, now.

He heard the drumming of the mares' hooves below the tor and the cries of the geldings answered in kind. Those first horses had not stepped out of the Book of Genesis but from somewhere more pure and distant than anything organised religion could imagine. Children and animals had a naked awareness of the wonder which existed beyond the walls of dogma. To enjoy truth and beauty all you needed was freedom. Leaders, prophets and priests were unnecessary. The bond with the living world was a birthright. You explored it in your own way or you rejected it. What O'Driscoll and his kind offered was rigidity and fear of retribution; ritual and incense to blur the beauty of what lay outside the church.

Beth gazed up at him and Jack sighed. He could push his mind no further across the problem. The things he intuitively felt supplied no facts but the White Lady of Lansworthy was a symbol of something more potent that the bible stories. It was inseparable from spring and the birth of animals and the re-emergence of life from the soil. Then the sunlight was a parable.

201

25

He ran a critical eye over Charlie's performance and said 'Make sure none of her mane's stuck under the collar.'

The boy worked confidently and quickly until he came to the belly band.

'That's too loose,' said Jack. 'Buckle it snug or she'll lift a hoof one day to scat off a blowfly, get hooked up and you'll have a three-legged banshee dancing in the shafts.'

Although the normal yard work continued the stable staff had been preparing for weeks for the Lansworthy Cart Horse Show and Parade. Ormond had persuaded his father to enter the In-hand, Harness and Wagon classes which the GWR stud had previously dominated. The prizes were to be presented by the High Sheriff of Devonshire's wife and the show promised to attract a large section of county society.

Saturday broke fine and warm from the haze over the bay and by breakfast-time the Council labourers had erected the tents and marquees on the green in front of the Palace Hotel. Then the Show Secretary arrived to organise all the celebrity wagons and to push back the surrounding side shows, swings and roundabouts. Now the sun stood high over Thatcher Rock.

In the Station Lane yards the carters were putting their best horses in the specials. The narrow leathers were decorated with star-shaped brass studs and the brasses clipped to the broader harness.

'Show-off stuff,' Old Bob called it as he fastened a brass-mounted buckle. But Palfrey would not entertain false martingales or face-pieces hanging from brow bands. It was, he insisted, a question of taste and balance, just enough brass and shining leather to set off the beauty of the animals.

'Some of 'em get tarted up like bliddy gypsy caravans,' he said. 'Especially the Co-op horses. They got capes like garden gates.'

Capes were stiff pieces of upright leather festooned in brass and tassels, set behind the harness.

Excitement filtered through the morning chores. Jack took Beth into the yard which the boys had scrubbed clean, and worked on her coat, brushing out the scurf and the detritus deposited among the hairs by her sweat glands. The vigorous action of the bristles stimulated the oil glands and turned her shagginess to dull gloss. He washed her legs, and soaped, rinsed and dusted her feather before oiling her hooves which had been freshly shod the evening before. Then the horn comb was applied to fetlock and mane and Old Bob said the mare already looked a winner. He and Jack watched Palfrey plait Beth's mane with green ribbon, starting behind the ears and working down the arch of her neck. Her tail was plaited at the top leaving the bulk hanging like a great, silken tassel. She was put in a white halter and Charlie held her while Jack changed into the clothes Mr Sidney had bought for the occasion.

'What a toff!' Harold Dunsford whistled as Jack emerged self-consciously into the brightness.

'Little Lord Muck,' laughed Cooksley and the stable boys gathered round doffing their caps and bowing.

'Show a bit of respect,' Jack said, straightening his bowler and screwing a penny into his eye like a monocle.

His gaiters and boots, breeches and Prussian blue jacket, the white shirt, black tie and tan waistcoat were regarded with more admiration than envy by the other carters. If anyone could bring a championship rosette back to the yard it was Jack and Beth. The mare was well-fleshed and lustrous. The white of her legs had turned to ivory and she possessed the alertness and controlled urgency of a thoroughbred.

203

'My God,' Old Bob whispered. 'Her has the bone and feather, if not the size. Dang me – if her idn good enough to race at Ascot!'

Melody was also competing in the In-hand class, Bathsheba in the Harness and four shire geldings had been hitched to a decorated wagon for the heavy horse turnouts. Led by Beth they clattered along Station Lane to the jeers of the other studs and processed down Lansworthy Road which was already crowded with people heading for the show. The deep piping of steam organs gusted between the buildings and the cries of children down on the beach were slightly less shrill than the screams of the swifts.

Palfrey assembled his contingent in front of the pier and supervised last minute preparations. The dust was brushed off the horses' hooves and oil applied again. Then the carters lightly buffed the shires' coats with paraffin-dampened cloths to fetch their shine into brilliance.

'Let's have those animals in the collecting ring,' the steward said. He was a puffy-faced little man who kept consulting his fob watch.

'This is more of a circus than a show, boy,' Palfrey observed.

'Just get them into line,' the steward snapped.

The crowd parted and let Beth and Melody through. It was a boisterous, tightly packed crowd, a mixture of blazers, best suits and summer dresses. Beady-eyed locals poured out a babble of Devonshire, burring the 'r's and broadening the vowel sounds. The tanned sinewy faces of carters and farm workers set them apart from the shopkeepers, shop assistants and hotel staff. Union Jacks fluttered over the main marquees. The sun shone and the first small white clouds sailed in from the sea.

People had gathered from all over the Three Towns – farmers and their families, clerks, fisherfolk, a scattering of the well-off from the villas of Abbot's Quay. Rows of carriages and motor cars blocked the promenade with carriers' carts and hawkers' handcarts. Life was spilling from the stands and tradesmen's stalls to the ringside. Swarthy Mary's Haven women with baskets on their hips offered soused mackerel or pasties, cakes and fruit, while their daughters sold cut flowers.

'Where do 'em come from?' Kitty said, linking arms with Dora. She was serious and watchful despite her excitement.

Some of the season's colour was in her hair and eyes. Her straw hat, too, displaying a new, ice-blue band and a large cloth moon daisy, belonged to the summer. Dora gazed at her, smiling. It was like taking a child to the zoo.

They walked among ladies whose parasols and expensive gowns set them apart from the rowdier locals. Behind the marquees the organs continued to hoot and the roundabouts whirled.

'Tez better than the fair,' Dora said. 'Doan the horses look handsome?'

'And Jack,' Kitty grinned.

'Dapper.'

'He's not!'

'Spruce, then – except for his face. That has a nice honest outdoor look about it. Compare it with Ormond's. That's a face to set off the ample waistline of the unearnt income.'

'You'm a bit harsh on un, Dora,' Kitty giggled. 'You'm gettin' like that funny old French woman in *A Tale of Two Cities* who kept on knittin' shrouds for toffs.'

Dora lifted her eyebrows. 'Madame Défarge. Lord, I hope not!'

'Just because they got a bob or two doan mean they'm bad.'

'You and Jack are a real pair of innocents,' her sister said, kissing her. 'You're dazzled by the glitter of things – Empire Day parades, the smiles of those stupid young ladies who come round ladling out soup and sympathy whenever there's an epidemic in the poor districts. You get taken in by the soapbox windbagging of Tory politicians, a tanner and a pat on the back from old man Chancellor.'

'I idn bright like you, Dora. Me and Jack have our own plans. And doan imagine he's stupid. He thinks about things that would never enter your head.'

'A dreamer not a doer.'

'Doers cause all the trouble.'

Dora nodded. 'That's true. So what's the answer? Do us sit back starving and dream we're well fed? If we dream long enough will the social injustice sort itself out?'

'Please, Dora,' Kitty pleaded. 'Can't us just enjoy ourselves without putting the world to rights? Can't us leave the revolution till after tea?'

'You silly empty-headed little rabbit,' Dora laughed. 'But

I'm sorry Kit. Me and Dad are always on the soapbox, idn us?'

She turned unexpectedly and confronted a couple of youths who had been trailing them and barked 'Go away' loud enough for everyone close at hand to hear. The boys beat a hasty and embarrassed retreat.

'Weedy and Pimples,' Dora smiled. 'Those two get around.'

'Don't you ever want a boyfriend?'

'Yes – when I'm ready. But I don't want to be harrassed by something foolish in a pair of trousers who fancies himself.'

'You'll end up an old maid.'

'Only if I choose to. Perhaps I'll settle for a lot of lovers.'

'Like Hazel Cundy.'

'I said lovers. Love – not playin' around. With Hazel it was a habit, like smokin' or eating chocolate.'

'Mother says tidn that wonderful, what you do in bed with a man.'

'Depends how you feel and how the man behaves. A lot of people do it as often as possible so it can't be that bad.'

Kitty laughed and coloured. 'I won't let Jack do it till we'm wed.'

'Why not?'

'Cos it idn right. Anycase, he might hate me once he's had it. Some of the maids at work say men go off you afterwards.'

'But they don't if you're married? Human nature changes after you've been to the altar?'

'Going there proves they respect you.'

Seeing the hurt spring into Kitty's eyes Dora squeezed her arm and said: ''Course it do. I'm just jealous. No one wants me. Don't let me upset you, Kit.'

The judging of the In-hand class was not to take place for a little while and Jack seemed absorbed fussing over Beth. The girls strolled between the tradesmen's stands where the saddlemakers, wheelwrights, farriers and ropemakers were displaying their wares and expertise. The heat thickened. Sandwiched between the canvas walls it held the stink of sour perfume. Lilac shadows stirred as the breeze shifted tent flaps or crumpled the profile of a canvas roof. Inside the refreshment marquee the pale, underwater gloom was tainted with the smell of sweating grass and cigarette smoke. Middle-aged men had contrived to stand in a mass as close as possible to the bar.

'Awful place,' Dora shuddered. 'All those beer-loosened bodies.' She brushed the predatory glances off the front of her blouse. Then they bumped into Moony. His billy cock hat emphasized the oddness of his head which was long-skulled.

'Mornin' Miss Dora, Miss Kitty,' he beamed. 'Look – I gotta dog.'

The tan mongrel swiftly encircled him, wrapping the string attached to its collar around its master's knees.

'I found un half-starved over Clennon. Mum doan mind – long as I feeds un.'

He tripped and sat down, and the girls left him to untangle himself from his new pet.

'Jack's mum is here with the rest of the family,' Kitty said.

'Do you want to try and find her?' Dora said, detecting the contrary in her sister's tone.

'I suppose we'd better. She gets a bit funny sometimes.'

'She's afraid Protestantism or socialism is contagious.'

They pushed through the throng at the ringside knowing Mrs McKenna would be near the front. The Chancellors, Daubenys and other important visitors were already seated on the planked-out hay wagons. The pastel shades of their clothes added to the illusion of coolness, of persons detached from the masses and the heat. Helen Daubeny was shielding her face with a white-gloved hand and laughing. She rocked forward and back and Rupert Chancellor leaned over to whisper in her ear. Dora's auburn-tinted blondeness suddenly caught the sun and flashed as she tugged off her hat. Both Helen and her brother looked across at her and were held by the wonder ful eyes. Edward continued to stare secretly from under his lashes until Rupert recaptured him with a question. Dora smiled.

'Mrs McKenna is right over the other side,' said Kitty and she waved.

'Then we've an excuse for not joining her,' Dora said. Her straw hat, when she replaced it, Edward noted, was encircled with a band of artificial dog roses.

'I wish they'd start,' Kitty sighed. 'The horses have been waiting ages in this terrible heat.'

But the animals continued to stand patiently in the collecting ring. Every so often they twitched their skins or lifted a leg and slammed it down to dislodge the flies. The G W R shire gelding was first off the mark.

'Walk in and around,' said the steward.

Jack did not like the look of the animal's hind legs, but Beth made a beautifully paced entrance when her turn came. The spontaneous applause brought a smile to Ormond's face.

'McKenna's sorrel,' said Rupert. 'Lord! She's perfect!'

'Our sorrel,' his father corrected him irritably. 'Chancellor's is a microcosm of the Empire. Excellence achieved by team effort under astute management. We'll sweep the board here.'

Light gleamed on the faces crowding Beth but she never faltered in her progress round the ring. Her ears pricked forward whenever a child squealed but neither the noise nor the movement alarmed her. The breeze freshened. Flags snapped, dropped and flapped again. Jack was asked to make her trot and on his command she complied. Then she was halted and stood four square, and an old gentleman in a bowler hat ran his hands over her legs, gazed intently at her head and body.

'Does she bite?' he asked.

'No, sir,' Jack said.

The plaited mane made it impossible to ignore the arch of Bethlehem's neck. Her alertness communicated itself to the crowd. Here, said the ripple of muscles and the brightness of her eye, is a fine animal. Everything about her proclaimed health and strength. The judge continued patting and stroking her. Then he examined her ears, teeth and eyes, and noted the shape of her head.

'Look at that stance,' Old Bob said, and Palfrey smiled.

'Like her's waiting to carry St George against the dragon.'

The beauty of her limbs ending in the splendid white feather brought a favourable grunt from the G W R horsemaster who was not a generous competitor. Like Palfrey he never blinkered his animals, and it was the basis of a mutual, if carefully hidden, respect between the rivals.

Obediently Beth lifted her feet while Jack flicked the flies off her face.

'Diamond is quite the artist,' the judge murmured, nodding appreciatively at the shoes. Then, with his eyes elsewhere, 'How did she get the big S-shaped scar on her side?'

Jack explained and let the bitterness wing out of his heart.

The bloody scar! Bloody Lacey's signature! All that beauty marred by a few moments of neglect. Now she wouldn't get the winner's rosette.

The judge went behind Beth and told Jack to step her back. 'Now trot her round once more.'

In the collecting ring Jack was downcast.

'The scar don't matter, boy,' Palfrey consoled him. 'Us get branded animals being showed. Brigadier Dearson knows what it's all about. Beth's got plenty of flesh on her and her moved sweetly when her was trotting. Us had a champion before her left the yard.'

'When Melody dropped her,' Jack grinned.

She was acutely aware of the other horses. A shire's gentle bulk cast its shadow across her. Whenever the mares and geldings moved there was a ripple under sungloss and the jingle of harness. Flies tormented them and the snorting and snuffling was part of the summer's fabric – a comforting part.

The High Sheriff's wife clipped the rosette to Beth's bridle and turned, smiling, to shake Jack's hand. 'Such a divine creature,' she said, from the heart.

Melody took the runner's-up ribbon and Bathsheba won the In-harness class, but the Starkey, Knight and Ford four-horse dray team and the GWR heavy horse turn-out beat Chancellor's geldings into third place. Moony did not care. He gave Beth a great wet kiss on the nose before the parade set off along the Esplanade to the Redcliffe Hotel and back behind Totnes Town Brass Band.

'A magnificent spectacle,' old Chancellor said. He and the Brigadier stood a little apart from the rest of the company. 'It easily rivals the purebred shows – despite the animals being all shapes and sizes.'

'We won't see many more,' sighed the brigadier. 'The world's changing, Chancellor – and not for the better. Germany's sabre rattling, motor carriages are running the horse off the road, traditional values are being scorned by all sections of society.'

'I'm determined to keep my fleet on the streets for as long as I live.'

The brigadier nodded. 'Does your son share your enthusiasm?'

'No,' Chancellor said ruefully. 'More's the pity because I have someone special in McKenna – the Irish boy walking Bethlehem.' He smiled, pinched the end of his nose and sniffed. 'The ruffian wants to buy the roan and start his own business but I hope to persuade him to abandon the idea. His real future is down the yard.'

'Real future,' the brigadier mused. 'There is definitely a rapport between that boy and the roan. Can't remember seeing a finer mare. She would be better saddled than between the shafts.'

'A labour of love,' said Chancellor. 'McKenna's dealings with her are legendary. The natives believe he can talk to horses.'

'Really? I must confess to finding the animals rather lacking in grey matter.'

Lansworthy Carnival Queen and her attendants sat in the GWR heavy wagon at the front of the parade, drawn by four uniformly dark shires in their show gears. Then came the In-hand class, the Harness animals and the winning dray followed by the heavy horse turn-outs and the Shand Mason steam fire engine. Various horsedrawn omnibuses, council and other commercial vehicles brought up the rear.

'Did you see our Jack?' Mrs McKenna said. She drew her best shawl round her shoulders wearing a dull flush of pride. Instinctively she reached for Kitty's hand, excluding Dora. They found a space at the far end of the green and sat down. Other families were picnicking on the grass which was littered with nannies, prams and lovers. Dora regarded Mrs McKenna and Kitty sardonically. They were transfigured by happiness. All around them the dilapidated faces of the poor seemed to have picked up the glow. The horses had awoken something in them, something fine that transcended drudgery and the monotony of existence. Looking about her Dora knew what united and uplifted them. It was the need for change and escape, not singly but as an entire community. None of them desired a lone journey. The most unacceptable thing in their lives was uncertainty. Maybe Jack's love of horses stemmed from this knowledge.

Things jostled for attention yet the vision of the patient animals remained when the sky darkened and rain fell. Big

210

drops beat into the crowd, and people fled back to the tents.

'Dora,' Kitty cried, running with the McKennas. But her sister remained on the green.

'Dora.'

Her name shouted aloud and the smell of drenched grass nudged other summer afternoons into clarity. Pieces of childhood floated back: a long-dead cat curled up on the doorstep of a vaguely remembered cottage; Granny rinsing out the clothes in a small backyard; pavements hot under bare feet; the water cart hissing. Episodes like lantern slides with nothing in between.

'Come on, Dora.'

Hunching her shoulders against the rain she walked back to the show.

26

Then the year had to take a downward swing. Beth walked and trotted through the summer while the buddleia behind the GWR sidings bloomed and died and the cider apples ripened on Tor Barton's trees. Her pregnancy confirmed, she continued to draw on Jack's devotion. The clanking, whistling start to the morning assumed reality when he came to her stall to begin the ritual. The crowing of cockerels and the clamour of hens and ducks spilled from gardens over the way. Mornings became mistier and the days shorter. And Mr Sidney would sometimes stand at the top of Station Lane to watch the fleets leaving the yards. Scores of carts and wagons took to the streets within minutes of each other, testifying to the pride of the rival horsemasters. Raising their whips the carters saluted the old man who had come to admire not pry. Usually he would make Jack draw rein so he could make a fuss of Beth.

'No tit-bits, hey Jack?' he smiled. 'We mustn't spoil her.'

'No sir,' said Jack, thinking of the sovereigns in the tin in his bedroom and the day Beth would be his.

'It's not so much owning an animal that's difficult,' Palfrey said when they had occasion to speak of the future. 'A lot of didikais and riff-raff have ponies and carts but the animals always look like they need a good meal and a good brush down. Tis the stablin' and feedin' that hits your pocket, boy. Where would you keep Beth, and could 'ee feed her and bed her down like us do here? Then there's the gears, the cart and the vet's bills, harness repair, wheelrights, farriers. Tis all money.'

'Has the old man been speakin' to you?' Jack grinned.

'Yes,' Palfrey admitted. 'He doan want to lose you or the horse. But he won't go back on his word. That idn his style. But have 'ee really thought about what's best for Beth? Her's got a good life and so have you. Go it alone and your troubles will start. Stay on and you'll have my job one day.'

'What if I get the sack? Ormond can't wait to get rid of me.'

'He's no fool, though. He won't cut off his nose to spite his face.'

'Ormond would, mister. He's a mean little bugger.'

'You can handle him.' Palfrey drew on his pipe and his words came out wreathed in smoke. 'The money you've saved could go into the home you and Kitty will be setting up. Business is for the big boys with the big money. You can't compete. Don't try unless you want to burn your fingers.'

'I'll think about it, Mr Palfrey.'

'And keep readin' the book. Old Mr Sidney rates you, son. Chancellor's is growing – grow with it.'

'The Chancellor Empire,' said Jack quietly.

Alone with Beth it was enough to listen to her regular breathing as he brushed the day's grime out of her coat. The mare pricked her ears to catch the cries of the barn owls hunting the coal dump in Queen's Park. She was tired and ready for sleep. Bathsheba had nodded off during the grooming. The stables were hushed. Soon Beth's eyes closed and she slept on her feet.

In the mornings and evenings the stalls were redolent of horse living. The roan caught the lamplight and her marbling took on a warmth which sunlight could never bequeath. Her displays of affection began with a prolonged whickering as soon as the stable door clicked open and she caught the sound of his footsteps. Her indoor smell filled the stall as she read his mood. If he came to her preoccupied she pushed an inquisitive nose into his face although contact was unnecessary. His presence was enough but whenever he gave Bathsheba too much attention she became jealous and showed it in her demeanour.

The autumn gales frightened the younger animals.

Throughout the hours of darkness the wind would howl around the yard, rattling the rain against the windows. The thunder of a downpour on the roof was amplified by the half empty loft. Then the sky would clear for moonlight to shaft through the window, and she would puzzle over the flutter of the small, white moths which were caught up in the spiders' webs above her. When dawn broke they were always motionless.

The outside world intrigued her and each journey made with cart or wagon was a walk into mystery. The streets were as full of excitement as the morning skies were full of birds. She loved the smell of the sea rising on a storm, and the warm smells pouring from the shops. But the bustle of stable life at the beginning and end of day was necessary to her peace of mind. She let human laughter and the cries and whistles of the stable boys wash over her as Jack attended to her welfare. Faintly through the morning din cocks could be heard crowing all over Lansworthy. The horses drank and fed to the muted snuffling of stallmates while the yard cats charged around and Mullah toured his territory. The old back alley ruffian was heavier and fleshier but still capable of maiming most of his rivals. In Jack he recognised affection that was not bogus. When he said 'Good Mullah, good old boy,' he meant it. The veracity was there beneath his gaze.

Jack often came early to the stables and went from stall to stall speaking the animals' names as he had done during his boyhood. He valued their trust and regard, for he had divined in them a magnanimity of spirit. They accepted whatever life offered. They never destroyed anything, never questioned their state or carped about their lot. He considered the casual brutality that was never absent from terrace life or Tor Barton; the ritual slaughter of the pig, the careless treatment of sheep, the drunkenness and violence, and the myriad fears which attended human old age. Confronted daily by the gentle horses he promised himself that Beth would have all he could give her.

Nuzzling the bran mash her eyes rebuked him for she preferred hay, and after the first joyful utterances she felt she could take small liberties. He had never raised his voice to her in anger. Only Luscombe resented the way the other horses came to him and followed him. For a while the fat man tried Jack's calm approach but the animals were not fooled and did not

214

respond, so he resorted to the bawling and bullying which they disliked but obeyed.

One horse remained unimpressed by Jack's authority. He was the gelding cross-bred shire, Captain, who had been broken hurriedly elsewhere and brought into the stud. Despite everything he remained unruly and his temperament made him a penance to groom. Palfrey, out of sheer devilment, would put him in Luscombe's charge and the rest of the staff made no attempt to conceal their glee when Captain kicked out and shook the wooden partition of his stall. Then Luscombe would rant and storm up and down the gangway cursing everything on four legs from Mullah to Melody.

'Serves the bugger right,' Old Bob would chuckle. 'Captain's his cross.'

Like he was Skilly's, Jack thought, wondering if life consciously provided rewards and punishments. But if there was a basic morality operating in the world why was Skilly crippled and the workhouse full of old people whose poverty was regarded as despicable?

The day was cold. It made his eyes water and the tip of his nose ache. Melody coughed. Captain whinnied and rolled his eyes. In the nearest stalls the geldings were showing an eagerness to take to the streets. Their huge hooves skidded and grated across the flags as they trampled the bedding.

'You're up bright and early Jack,' said Mr Sidney.

Jack had not heard the old gentleman's approach. All around them the animals were stirring.

'One of the mare's had a bellyful of red worm, sir. Mr Palfrey asked me to come in and see to her.'

'And how is Beth?'

'Fine. She'll give us a good foal, sir. So will Sheba.'

Chancellor smiled. There were bird droppings on his bowler. He stood tall and upright, looking down, Jack thought, from the dignity of his social position.

'Having a horse's loyalty is a great privilege. I didn't bury Iona simply because I'm a rich, sentimental old fool. My wife and I knew that animal from the very beginning and we loved her. The thought of her ending up as glue and pet food and what have you was too much. So I put her in the hill, close at hand, part of what's going on. Do you understand, Jack?'

215

'Yes, sir. If they aren't suffering all workhorses should be turned out to pasture. Beth will be – I've promised her that.'

'Will you stay with the firm, Jack?'

'I may, sir, I'm happy here.'

'I hope you do,' Chancellor said warmly. 'You know why I've come to see you, don't you?'

'I can guess sir.'

'Bob Sherwill left us yesterday and I wanted to confirm that you are now head carter.'

'Assistant horsemaster, sir,' Jack grinned.

'Ah yes! I forgot how touchy the fraternity is when it comes to correct titles and things. What will you do with the extra money?'

'Get married sir. Me and Kitty Widdicombe are engaged.'

'Good show! Marry, settle down; stay with Chancellor's.'

'Yes sir, I'll think about it.'

'Stay with us and I'll guarantee Beth has her green pastures when her working life is over.'

He followed Jack along the gangway to Beth's stall.

'A healthy horse is a happy horse, sir,' Jack said. 'If the animal is old and sick and you keep him alive you're not doing him any favours. When I was a boy I swore no horse of mine would ever be put down. I was wrong. Health is the key. Mr Trant told me once that you've got to give them death as you help give them life. If it's done calmly the horse don't know. You help him pass from life into death as if you're bringing him back to the yard and stripping him of his gears.'

Chancellor sighed. 'But it's such a wretched business.'

'It's part of your duty to the animal. Anything else is a betrayal of the trust he's given you from the beginning. When it comes to the crunch I suppose I'd ask myself if I'm just postponing her death by having her stand miserbly in some field too sick to care about anything. Putting her down is the last great act of love. Knowing the moment is the difficult part.'

Beth watched the men from under her lashes.

'What do you like most about horses, McKenna?'

'Their peacefulness, sir.' And their beauty and innocence, he thought as the old man extended an arm and smoothed Beth's nose.

Behind her eyes the gate swung open and the field lay

waiting. Who had opened it? Who were the horses striding out of the sun to join Iona? Water splashed from the pail into her trough. She lowered her head to her wobbling image and drank it.

'Skilly's home, sir,' Jack said, suddenly. 'Can he come back to work?'

'With a wooden leg!'

'The horses don't know he's got a wooden leg.'

'You think he's up to it?'

'It's all he knows. He loves it here. They shouldn't have sent him to the loony bin. He's just a toddler inside his head. Something just stopped him growing up, that's all. He's not crazy.'

'Lucky perhaps – despite his mishaps. Tell Palfrey to start him back tomorrow.'

'You're a good man, mister,' Jack said.

'Think about your own future too, McKenna,' Chancellor said gruffly. But he was touched by Jack's sincerity. In business and society one opted for the conventional deceits. Honesty was refreshing. Walking to the store he was aware of having shed important things on the way to prosperity.

Mrs Endacott could not cope with Moony's rowdy pup that was part lurcher and part collie. One suppertime Moony appeared at the McKenna's front door in tears, saying his mother was prepared to leave home if the mongrel stayed. So Jack got his dog and the simpleton went away happy because the creature would always be close at hand.

'Our lives are ruled by animals,' Mary McKenna pretended to complain. The dog leapt onto her lap and washed her face with its kisses.

'Get the silly mutt off me,' she laughed but Jack could see she was flattered by the attention she had received.

'What'll we call it?' said Sean.

'Rover,' said Blanche.

'Pal,' said Lily. 'Or – or – Georgie.'

'Why Georgie?' Mary laughed.

'Any old name won't do,' said Jack. 'And the animal isn't an it; he's a he. The table is an it.'

'Let mum name him,' Sean said.

Mrs McKenna thought a moment and said 'We'll call him Dando.'

'After your old dog,' Lily said, and she knelt to cuddle the dog who squirmed away and went from person to person in an orgy of affection.

'Dando,' Mary McKenna said softly. Then everyone was repeating the dog's name, and it sat on the hearth rug thumping out the rhythm of ecstasy with its tail.

'Another mouth to feed,' Mary McKenna sighed. 'Sure, but he's a fine little chap.'

'Little!' Jack grinned.

'Well, little enough.'

'All we need now is a cat and everthing will be just right,' said Blanche.

'Dando would eat it,' Michael observed.

'Poor pussy,' said Lily and she began to cry.

'It's a joke, silly,' said her mother, glaring at Michael. 'Jack will bring home one of those stable kittens won't you Jack? You keep promising.'

'When they're a bit bigger and ready to leave the old she.'

'A tabby one?' Lily sniffed.

'We'll see.'

The Widdicombes had a couple of cats and both were sleek, private creatures that gave their affections sparingly. Mr Widdicombe would sit with the orange and black female on his lap, smoothing her as he spoke. The little house in Winner Street was full of books and pamphlets. Like the McKenna household it had that indefinable, lived-in atmosphere and was never really silent. But Jack and Kitty craved solitude and the long dark evenings after Christmas provided few opportunities for them to be alone unless it was in a shivering embrace somewhere cold and uncomfortable. They could eat fish and chips together at Dimeo's and dance at Deller's Café but passion was difficult to foster on a draughty doorstep with Mrs Widdicombe calling her daughter from inside.

'Is it hard for 'ee Jack?' Kitty whispered. 'I know how you feel.'

'You feel it?'

'Yes. Tidn easy to fight – but we must.'

'Why?'

'I want to go to church in white and I doan want it to be a lie.'

'Bloody church.' Jack grated.

'Don't make me feel bad. I've made up my mind; I'm going to become a Catholic.'

Jesus, he wanted to roar, as if that's important. Having Father O'Driscoll beaming and hauling in the net full of souls. Yet he saw the felicity in her eyes and her devotion humbled him. Then tenderness eclipsed desire and left them clinging together like children. But society made sure you stumbled through a labyrinth of tests before it left you alone. To love was to be part of the goodness embracing all life. It was their birthright, and no dogmas or taboos could impair its beauty or dictate its course.

27

The morning was frosty but the sun was creeping over the mist. The horses stared at each other through the silence. A hoof banged down, breath lofted grey and dense.

'I'm freezing,' said Charlie Wotton. His teeth chattered and he pushed his hands inside his coat and up under his armpits.

'Run beside the cart for a while,' Jack said.

'Are you serious?'

'Get your circulation going. This is brass monkey weather and it'll get worse. We're going to Kingswear and that's a long way. I never push Beth, especially on icy roads and her carrying a foal. If you don't get warmed up now you'll be half dead by the time we're there.'

The boy running on the spot reminded him of his own starveling days.

'Take my scarf,' he said, tugging it off. 'And come prepared tomorrow. Bring a blanket to wrap round your legs.'

'S-sod this for a lark,' Charlie groaned. 'My mum said 1913 would be an unlucky year.'

'It'll be just like any other year,' said Jack. 'We can make our own luck. If you had wrapped up well you wouldn't be freezing. If Skilly hadn't climbed the wheel he wouldn't need a wooden leg.'

'It goes with his wooden head,' Charlie laughed.

They stopped outside the post office as Father O'Driscoll emerged frowning up at the sky.

'Can I give you a lift, Father?' Jack said, mischievously.

The priest declined with a smile and said, 'Are we in for snow?'

'You're the one who's got the important contacts up there, Father. I should be asking you things like that.'

'You over-estimate my powers, Jack. How is Lily?'

'Still poorly. We thought it was pneumonia but it's pleurisy. She got soaked going to school and sat in her wet clothes.'

'I'll pray for her.'

'Thank you, Father.'

Prayer was the cornerstone of Mary McKenna's belief but Jack was convinced an awareness of truth and beauty came from beyond self. It went with the certainty that life did not end in emptiness. Frost lay on the field where the plough had worked its will. The great horses of Tor Barton shook the whiteness off their coats and came quietly down from the hill. Sunday broke grey.

He loathed the prospect of church. Participating in the ritual and offering up the dreary Latin chants left his skull numb. 'Hail Mary full of grace' had a barrenness which the winter countryside, laundered by extremes of cold, somehow set in true perspective. It went beyond people and the affairs of people. The oak trees clothed now in hoar frost; Beth and Bathsheba with foal; the flocks of starlings and foreign thrushes rushing overhead; the cattle – everything that drew breath was part of the truth and beauty the Church called the Love of God.

He let the mares out into the paddock and smiled at their slow canter. Their manes smoked on the biting air as weightlessly as their breath. Frost crumbled from the hedgerow twigs and drifted white into whiteness. Crows and songbirds sat silently in the trees but the buzzard was aloft and mewling. Its cry followed him home. He walked briskly up Fisher Street, past the King William and Mrs Duke's run-down corner shop which his mother used only in emergencies. The Salvation Army Band had assembled at the lamp, and a solo cornet was playing the opening bars of 'Abide with Me'. In the clear, cold air the sound was strangely sad and uplifting. Even Moony's capering could not impair its beauty. Then the entire brass took up the melody, bringing the Sabbath hush to life. Smoke rose and hazed over the roofs and Jack was happy. The wonderful coarse vitality of the terrace was generating its own warmth. Sunday never curtailed the noisy exchanges and laughter the front doors muffled. Pigeons scattered among the chimneys, leaving their noise to fade back to stillness. Moony raised his voice: 'Fast falls the eventide. The darkness deepens, Lord with me abide.'

The bandmaster smiled at the overgrown child. Pushing open the door of Number Eight Jack wondered why the vicar was never seen in Angarrick Terrace. The Vospers were regular churchgoers and staunch Anglicans but the vicar never strayed beyond Grosvenor Road's privet. Maybe, Jack thought, the Church of England heaven was a bit like the Empire – posh and exclusive at the top.

'Kitty's here,' Mrs McKenna called.

Her scent was in the passage like the breath of flowers. Watching them enter their happiness the woman tried to see the girl through her son's eyes. She was such a pale little thing with those big green eyes and hair the colour of a chicken's foot. Her expression when she was not smiling was one of startled frailty. The awkwardness of girlhood had gone and she had filled out a bit but she looked half-starved on a cold day. There was nothing wonderful about her so what was it that had turned Jack's head? God! The average man wouldn't spare her a second glance.

Mary McKenna sighed. Everyone was growing away from her – Michael, Sean, Jack. Dando laid his chin on her knees and whined. Pets remain faithful, she reflected, trailing her fingernails down the dog's nose.

'Dando, you old softy,' she said loudly enough to catch the attention of Kitty and Jack.

'He's really taken to you, Mum,' said Jack, joining her at the table.

'So he should, with you out all day and me talkin' to the walls. We stop each other going stark, starin' mad.'

But she was flattered by his remarks and the dog's devotion. Calling him Dando had done the trick. She blinked on a tear, remembering the other Dando in the other place and herself younger than the girl who was stealing Jack.

Stars trembled in the dark sky which was cloudless. The rowdy gang of youths whooped and launched a bench into

222

Victoria Park duck pond.

'Noisy tikes,' Jack murmured. He drew Kitty under his greatcoat but she still shivered and her lips lifted to his own were stiff and cold.

'Courtin' on a seat in the park in winter idn very romantic,' she said.

'Where else can we go without being watched all the time? You won't come down the yard. The hayloft is warmer than this place. It would be like going to bed together.'

'Yes – and you know what happens in bed. Come on, let's walk,' she added, jumping up before he could pursue the subject.

'I need new boots,' he groaned. 'The cold's coming through the soles of these.'

The yelling and laughter were spreading across the darkness.

'Mike's among that bunch of mad young buggers,' he continued, enfolding her once more in his coat. 'They drink cider in the shelter and go runnin' about Bunnyland like devils. Bumfluff affects some boys like that. God, it's a frightening thing. No one's safe at night with the dreaded Bumfluffies about – least of all young ladies who prefer haylofts.'

They walked over grass which the frost had turned into penknife blades. Somewhere behind them glass was broken and a police whistle piped. Boots rang on the paths and the laughter dispersed although the shouting continued.

'Look up there,' Jack said.

The town had borrowed some of the moon's brilliance and frost sparkled on hedges, trees and lawns. The rooftops climbed into the sky and Our Lady of the Bay stood white and serene among the stars.

'Idn her beautiful?' Kitty whispered.

The parish church clock struck ten. Arms wrapped round each other they walked up Church Street past the cottage hospital into the lamplight and human warmth spilling from the pubs. Later, lying alone staring up at the moonlit bedroom ceiling Jack could see the horse's head amongst the other patterns formed by winter's dampness. Then he thought of Beth and Bathsheba in the linhay and Iona lying under the hillside beyond the night's beauty.

'But it can't end in emptiness,' he murmured. A train wailed, coming from somewhere and going somewhere. And the wind did not die. After the last breath the horses went to it and became part of it to know the world as it was before there were houses and streets.

'Yes,' he whispered, letting the images crowd his mind. Then Dando was scratching and whining in Mrs McKenna's bedroom. There was an angry 'Mother of God!' and the thump of feet as she leapt out of bed. The bedroom door opened, Dando yelped, his paws scrabbling on the stairs. Seconds later the front door bolts rasped followed by an angry grunt. Again Dando yelped.

'Out and piddle, you bloody nuisance. That's the last time you sleep on my bed.'

But the pup's charm won. After a noisy night in the scullery he was returned to his place of privilege, a wiser animal, less inclined to worry about cocking his leg once he had settled on the foot of her bed.

Winter was nearly over and the discarded blackthorn blossom was dancing along the gutters of King's Ash. Jack had been out with Josephs to a farm at Longcombe. The visit had left him depressed and tired. Putting down an animal rarely saddened the vet for he had a clear unsentimental grasp of his responsibilities. But to find an old horse so full of worms and so badly neglected it could hardly lift its head from the mud where it had fallen in harness made him shake with rage. He had ranted at the farmer and the man had stood sullen and unmoved, asking how much it would cost to get the animal back on its feet.

'Damned callous ignorance,' Josephs fumed after putting the horse out of its misery. 'Working it like a machine. How can you win?' It all boils down to lack of education and poverty. And that's society's fault. The man back there really believes a horse has less feelings than a human. He couldn't imagine it suffering from toothache or thrush or pneumonia any more than he'd credit a wheelbarrow with sensitivity to pain. We've got too much power over dumb beasts, McKenna. The worst moral bankrupt can do as he pleases to a noble, four-legged creature. We cage songbirds, make bears dance on chains, bait badgers and work horses to death, yet we continue to claim nobility of spirit and insist all other creatures lack souls.'

224

His cold, dry laugh summed up the situation.

'Do you believe in God, Mr Josephs?'

'No,' came the blunt reply. 'I believe in the here and now, and getting on with it.'

Jack was waiting to collect a load of sewing machines at the station when the Paddington train steamed in. The usual bunch of old men and layabouts were hanging round the platform waiting for the pubs to open. They stood back eyeing the passengers and crossing words with the porters. Doors slammed and the warm damp smell of upholstery and steam mingled. Then Lacey stepped down from the third class compartment and set his bowler at a jaunty angle. Jack had forgotten how tall he was. The dark grey suit and patent leather shoes proclaimed an elegance that was London commercial. His tie was silk and on his suitcases were several stickers, the momentoes, it seemed, of foreign travel: Cairo, Venice, Baden-Baden. The cane and well-groomed moustache contributed to the image of man about town, the rakish young entrepreneur the Empire fostered and admired.

Michael McKenna regarded him with disbelief.

'The bags,' Lacey said. A little cockney had been injected into the Devon accent but no one was fooled. 'Carry them bags to a cab for me. You're paid to do it.'

'Go to hell,' Michael grated. 'The only thin' I'll carry for you, Lacey, is your coffin — so long as you're in it.'

'I'll carry 'em, sir,' one of the layabouts said, touching his cap.

'Carefully,' Lacey said. His eyes settled briefly on Jack and he sneered. 'Still playing Ben Hur with Chancellor's bone bags, Irish?'

'Don't bite, Jack,' Michael cried, but he was too late.

Lacey used his cane like a sword only to find Jack coming in a rush under the first wild swing. They grappled and slammed against the side of the carriage. Blind with rage Jack clawed at Lacey's throat but his brother and some of the other men overpowered him and dragged him off.

Lacey straightened his tie and pointed a trembling finger

'Next time,' he panted, 'I'll go to the police. Stay away from me, you mad Irish bastard.'

'If you watched your mouth you wouldn't be in the shit every time you opened it,' said Michael. 'I'd get in your cab if I was you before Jack ruins your suit.'

'One day, McKenna,' Lacey said, 'I'll be in a position to make you crawl.'

Jack stared at him through that snarling grin, unable to speak. Michael held onto his brother's arm and wondered how long he could restrain the hard, muscular body.

'I looked at him,' Jack said as the brothers walked together to the van, 'but all I saw was Gabriel lying broken and dead in someone's bloody front garden.'

'Let it drop, now, or you'll end up in jug.'

'I don't care.'

'What about Kitty? If they put you away what will happen to her and Beth? Let Lacey alone.'

'I don't think I'll be able to keep my hands off him, Mike.'

'When you get punchy try me for size,' Michael grinned.

'You're just a child,' said Jack and their boxing had all the elements of love and comradeship.

Lacey's new occupation soon became known. He was a commercial traveller for a famous brand of whisky. Over the next few weeks Jack sometimes met him on his rounds but he rapidly became a background figure, no more disturbing than Ormond Chancellor. The men used different pubs and even when their paths crossed at Deller's Café dances Jack found it easy to maintain a stony indifference.

'He looks every inch the gent till he opens his mouth,' said Dora. 'And the romance loses its gloss when you learn he's living' above the chip shop in St Michael's Road. Tidn all that dashing. Keep ignoring him, Jack. Kickin' his behind won't bring Gabriel back to life.'

'But it makes me feel good.'

'That should impress the magistrate!'

Greenness came back to the countryside. Showers fell and rainbows arched over the valley to dim again and appear elsewhere. A little cuckoo snow lay as it always did among the daffodils and primroses but the curlews were crying in courtship flight. Then the swifts returned to Station Lane and the bluebells under Clennon's oaks took on their deep radiance. The days lengthened and when the blossom had firmed in the cider orchards of Tor Barton Beth had her foal.

The event took everyone by surprise. Since they had been let out of the shafts the mares had done the normal light farmwork. As the time approached Trant studied them with increasing interest. Bathsheba's walk became heavier, her udder swelled and the tell-tale wax formed on her teats. But Beth's body offered none of these clues. Jack, who had often felt the unborn creature stirring inside her during the grooming, was deceived and told old Mr Chancellor she would probably foal in a week or so.

The weather was mild but Bathsheba had a cold and was confined to the linhay while Beth was given the run of the paddock. At Jack's suggestion the top ditch had been fenced off that winter so the roan could be safely left to herself as her companion's time approached.

Then Bathsheba went into long, disastrous labour and Josephs extracted the dead foal from her body. Throughout the small hours of the new day he and Jack worked to save the mare's life. Bathsheba, who was too ill to sniff the lifeless package the men had removed, was none the wiser. Something strange had happened to her but they would make her well. The voices were kind and the pain gradually subsided. Laying her head back on the straw she was unaware of the birdsong and light creeping over the hill.

Mrs Trant brought them a jug of tea but did not speak as she filled the mugs. Her husband took the dead foal outside and placed it on the grass. Jack and the vet watched him silently. Dew and the first flush of sunlight added to the pathos. Eleven months inside Sheba only to come dead into the world. Jack grimaced. It was one of those nasty ironies spring could produce from its plenitude.

He gazed across the paddock. Beth was standing against the far hedge and a small creature was wobbling around her hind quarters.

'Christ!' Jack cried. 'She's done it!'

He dropped the mug and began to run, but nearing the roan he brought his excitement under control and called her name. She glanced up at him and her ears twitched forward.

'You crafty old girl,' he grinned. Trant and Josephs joined him.

The chestnut foal thrust hard against Beth's udder and

guzzled the colostrum. It was a sturdy little colt with a large head and long legs. The birth wetness still clung to its coat.

'He's steady enough on his pins,' said Josephs. 'Beth must have waited till we were all shut up in the linhay last night and dropped him under the hedge, privately.'

'Win some, lose some,' Trant smiled.

Jack approached dam and foal crooning the familiar endearments as he came. At first she lowered her head and nudged him away with a whicker of irritation. Then his smell and voice penetrated emotions clouded by motherhood and he was permitted to touch the creature the night had magicked out of her body.

PART THREE

ALL THE KING'S HORSES

28

The wood was green and full of rooks whose cawing spread over the summer afternoon. Cattle stood beside the stream in the bottom of Clennon Valley. Every so often one would lift a hind leg and rake the flies off a flank. Around them spread the water meadows beneath the heat that brought verticals to life and made them dance: fence posts, Scots pines, boys pulling ragwort.

Gazing down the valley from the shade of the hawthorns on Cider Mill Hill Beth shared the calm of the foal sleeping beside her. Birds sailed through far-off silences and the sea was so hazy it was difficult to tell where it began and the sky ended. Elms stood motionless, insects zithered and hummed, a lark sang and grass laid its scent on the sunlight. But the outside world only brushed her thoughts. The fullness of the season echoed her contentment; then she had to touch the foal with her muzzle and the little animal stiffened its legs in a luxurious stretch of well-being.

The lark climbed higher, spinning its melodies across the cawing of the rooks. Warmth crept through Beth's body. She shook the flies from her head but they returned almost immediately to crowd the corners of her eyes. The fox trotting down off the tor paused and watered the thistle close to her, and their glances met for a moment before he loped away. Pigeons shattered the hush as they left the farmhouse roof and exercised their wings. Then stillness poured back leaving the afternoon to the rooks and the lark. Beth lay on her side and slept.

There were currents of life which refused to relate to substantial things. Night world brought her close to the vastness of the universe. Stars flashed around her and in the foal's eyes. The dim light of the sky held whirlpools of silence which captured thought. The milk pricked Beth's udder and she wanted no more than the rapture of loving the small creature bunting against her haunches. But the feeling of completeness always faded. Her heart lurched. Beauty sheathed the foal but what it had borrowed from elsewhere the night sky lacked.

Beth lowered her head and snuffled. A quaking of shapes became the farmhorses grazing the skyline. The foal, whose name was Mischief, called to them and was answered. Now the smell of cattle lifted off the valley and bats hawked the field. Mare and foal climbed the hillside to greet the geldings.

Less than a week later, on Derby Day, Emily Wilding Davison, a young suffragette, threw herself in front of the King's horse killing herself and the animal.

'Poor horse,' said Mary McKenna. 'What on earth was that idiot thinking of? They ought to bang them women in gaol and throw away the key.'

Jack glanced up from his Friday mackerel. Her face was hard and pale. Michael drew the side of his hand across his nose, hiding the grin he had brought home from the pub.

'Just imagine that happening to your precious Beth,' Mary McKenna continued, sawing viciously through the loaf.

'Jack loves her,' said Blanche.

'Worships her,' said the mother scornfully. 'He's like a priest when it comes to horses – a pagan priest, down on his knees to a horse god.'

'Godess,' Jack grinned.

'If God was a horse,' slurred Michael, 'Jesus would've been called Dobbin. Dobbin Christ.'

Mary McKenna's knuckles rattled against his head.

'You're treading your father's slippery road. He had a mouth.'

The lamplight could not soften her expression and Michael

was too drunk to care. All the sense had gone from his face. He sat there in his grubby GWR uniform like a replica of Kevan McKenna. The tousled head wobbled, his eyes closed and he nodded stupefied at his plate.

Dando growled a hatred of violence, and when his apprehension had died, ran from Michael to Mrs McKenna and back, time after time, whining for a reconciliation. Jack ate the fish and new potatoes and pushed the plate to one side. Then with exaggerated care he poured condensed milk from the tin onto the bowl of rice pudding. Iron hoops rattled and clanked along the pavement outside, skipping ropes whirred and clacked, children laughed, a dog barked, and later, as dusk became darkness, the hooting of goods trains rekindled emotions he thought time had dulled.

'They've nearly finished the Picture House down by the level crossing,' Sean said, disliking the quiet that filled the house after dark.

'You'll never get me in that place,' said Mary McKenna. She folded her hands on her knitting and frowned at Dando. The dog yawned and laid its chin on its front paws. The lamplight's gold climbed the walls and flushed the samplers which bore hand-stitched legends: 'God made the Country, Man made the Town'; 'The King's carriage must stop for the sheep'. Jack grinned. Then he thought of the horses on Cider Mill Tor. Beth and her son, Mischief, standing in the starshine.

Michael slept at the table and Blanche and Lily were singing one of the sentimental Irish songs their mother had taught them. Dark curls picked up the lamplight in gleams. They were perched on the edge of the Joseph chair swinging their bare feet – Blanche with her black piggy eyes and enormous smile, Lily with the snub McKenna nose and dirty pinafore, an ugly little thing. Jack closed his eyes and the horses appeared. On the silver landscape they floundered like creatures fighting the undertow of surf. Light trembled along the horizon and the thunderstorm broke.

'No!' he cried, leaping suddenly to his feet. 'No!'

'Mother of God!' exclaimed Mary McKenna. 'You've shaved five years off my life startling me like that.'

'He's got cramp,' said Sean.

'I was dreaming,' Jack said.

233

'But you weren't asleep,' said Lily.

'Daydreaming,' he smiled.

'As usual,' said Mary McKenna. 'Your mind's always somewhere else.'

Handing out the brooms at the store the following morning Jack deliberately shaped another dream where he could withdraw from the small talk which sometimes irritated him. Beth was a foal again rolling in the water of Broadsands Marsh and the breeze sweeping off the sea was whitening the willow leaves. The dream faded on the walk to the yard. The water cart passed, drawn by an old mare in her council-issue straw hat.

Striding along the street Jack felt he was on the edge of something only the senses could identify.

A sparrow hawk crouched by the cornbins defleshing a chaffinch. It flew off leaving a puddle of small, blood-spattered feathers. Jack went about the grooming only half aware of the bustle. The shire geldings – Tacker, Rook, Janner and Goosie – were led out and hitched to the heavy wagons, and he spoke their names more to reassure himself than to soothe the horses. Then he hitched Melody to the light van and took her into Lansworthy.

The sunshine, quiet streets and clop of hooves conspired to brew an atmosphere that was peculiarly hometown. Motor cars and vans, mingling with horse transport in Station Square, created the first traffic jams of the day but Jack was content to sit and wait for things to start moving again. A couple of butcher's boys swaggered along the pavement with their trays and Mr Heinlen, the German chimney sweep, came whistling up Lansworthy Road, his brushes on his shoulder. Over the railway line the workmen were laying tiles on the new cinema building. The railway crossing gates closed and an engine steamed into the station. Traffic began to flow again but he could not shake off a mood that bordered on unease.

'Us all get like it,' said Kitty when he told her. 'Try to think about the good things going on in the world. Beth's happy enough and so's her foal. You and Dad have a lot in common. As your mother says, your mind's always elsewhere.

'Elsewhere's a good place,' he grinned, slipping an arm round her waist. Her hip bumping against his own was no longer bony.

'We'll get you a bicycle,' he added. 'Then we can go up on

234

Dartmoor and see the ponies.'

'I'd like that,' Kitty said. The taste of the strawberry ice cream she had just eaten clung to her breath, giving the kiss a fine summer flavour.

Although there was less than an hour of sunlight left the evening was warm and people were still in the sea. The bathing machines followed the ebbing tide but girls with cotton costumes glued to their curves ran squealing along the shallows.

'Making a spectacle of themselves,' Kitty snorted. 'That Mabel Freathy and Alice Gross from the store are following in Hazel Cundy's footsteps.'

'It's like "What the Butler Saw",' said Jack.

'How do you know?'

'Mike's always on about the peep shows.'

'Says you! Boys are all the same.'

'So are girls.'

'I idn no Hazel Cundy,' she said hotly.

'God! And would I be here with you now if you were?'

'Oh I'm sorry, Jack – I really am. Only, only I know I idn no belle.'

'But you bloody well are. You're perfect – bloody perfect.'

He kissed her fiercely on the cheek. Away to the left on the promenade next to the pier the Salvation Army Band began to play 'Jerusalem'.

And did those feet in ancient times . . .

'I love that hymn,' Kitty whispered. She pronounced it 'hem' and Jack hid his smile. Out to sea the Mary's Haven fishing fleet with sails flapping came slowly round the head.

'Growin' up with someone you love is beautiful,' Kitty went on, and he let the vision of Melody and Bethlehem racing through the surf steal the moment. The Irish warriors of long ago would have ridden them bareback, naked to be as vulnerable as the animals.

During the summer a public-school scout camp was assembled at Clennon. It was Ormond's brainchild and met the approval of the Daubenys. Every morning the flag ceremony was watched by a curious herd of Devon Rubies and farm workers; but the boys were considerate and polite, and Maddock

Maddock had no complaints. Yet he could not help thinking almost everything the privileged did was part of some exclusive game.

When the scouts departed there was no litter and the yellow patterns left by the tents soon vanished. Shuttling between the beanfields and the farm Beth saw the canvas come down and the summer pass. Cockchafers whirred round the horses' heads as they gathered under the tor. The deepening dusk was an extension of their silence. It walled in the play of mare and gelding, the slow shift of posture, the arching of necks and stamp of hooves. Mischief aped them, flinging himself about until night turned all the animals inward upon themselves.

A little before the foal was weaned Jack cycled along the Old Mary's Haven Road at cock crow. The October moon still shone over the South Hams although sunrise was catching the peaks of the waves from Hope's Nose to St Mary's Head. Leaves scattered in the wind that set the beech trees roaring and Jack whooped with the excitement of it all – the wind punching his body, the Sunday morning full of flying leaves and the smell of damp farmland. The air was cold and the sky cloudless, but the clarity threatened rain.

Then he came down the cart-track past Cider Mill Tor and the horses pursued him. The shires slithering across the pastures were massive under their aura of gentleness. So by the time he reached the paddock and caught sight of the roan she seemed quite small and elegant. Mischief galloped around her, kicking out his hind legs. His shrill whinny of joy had the mares calling from the hill but Beth remained silent. Her watchfulness was reassuring. The trees thrashing in the sky, the birds darting in and out of shadows, the constant shift of light, were regarded from brown, untroubled eyes. She stood under the comb, suckling the foal while the dizzy fall of leaves continued as the sun climbed off the horizon and the first clouds drove in from the west.

'Why do we have to clip 'em?' young Charlie asked later that autumn.

Jack snipped away at the hair on Janner's belly. The shire gelding stood perfectly still in the yard where the brazier glowed, ringed by stable boys.

'Their heavy winter coats make them uncomfortable. If we

work them hard they sweat and get grumpy. So we clip out, trace high, belly between front and back legs and round the lower thighs.'

'Doan 'em get cold?'

'Not in the shafts, and the stables are warm at night. Everything the horsemaster tells you to do is for the animals' own good.'

'Does Mr Palfrey know more about horses than you, Jack?'

'God yes! I'm still learnin'.'

'What about me?'

Jack grinned. 'You're on the bottom rung of the ladder but you'll get to the top quick if your heart's in the job.'

'Dad says I'd be better of learnin' to drive a motor van.'

'If everyone thought like that who'd look after the horses?'

The boy smiled and nodded. 'Anyway, they'm alive, like us. They idn things. They got hearts. Do you think they talk to each other, at night when us idn here?'

'Not with words,' Jack said.

'I doan understand.'

'They share something.' But he did not elaborate.

Rain fell. Large drops hit the brazier and hissed among the red-hot coals.

'I hate winter,' Kitty said one Friday night with a shiver. 'Everything's so grey and dark.'

The wind gusted along the pavement and they stepped into a shop doorway to finish their chips. The puddles vibrated and became flat and still once more until a station rank cab rattled by.

'I finish early on Wednesday,' said Jack. 'Do you want to go to the cinema?'

'The Picture House?' she exclaimed. 'Dora went last Saturday and her said tis much posher than the Burlington. What are they showing?'

'I don't know,' he smiled, amused by her enthusiasm. 'Michael took Mum a couple of days after the place opened. He told her there was a religious motion picture on and the place was full of Catholics. For all her squawkin' she allowed herself to be hauled into the building. Now wild horses wouldn't keep her away. She's like that – against everything till she's tried it.'

'Mrs Butt from Palace Avenue plays the piano down there,'

said Kitty. 'Our mum went to school with her and reckons her was the cleverest girl in class.'

She chattered all the way home, clinging to his arm and thowing back her head to laugh at his jokes. The night was no longer gloomy. Everything takes its colour from the way we feel, Jack thought.

29

It was Mischief's destiny to be sold to a farm at Yalberton but the colt occupied a corner of Beth's being which the passing of time could not touch. Sometimes dream met dream there in confusion but the outside world never let go.

Three of the farm geldings were rested so she and Bathsheba plodded between Tor Barton and the yard. The hushed countryside was a direct contrast to the noise and excitement of Station Lane and the work was harder. On icy mornings the bit was so cold it burnt the corners of her lips, and if one of the carters neglected to warm her collar it made her tense up and tread irritably into the day.

For the labourers the winter work was the usual penance. Frozen fingers stammered over broken chains and knotted lines. Curses came out in white puffs. The hush of snow on the fields had the texture of nightmare and men and animals responded silently, miserably.

Walking through the rain behind the plough team Arthur Maddock could hardly lift his feet so heavy with mud were his boots. At the end of the day he was exhausted and would fall asleep in the armchair, his damp clothes drying on his body.

Standing at the front door one evening Mary McKenna noted for the first time that the spring had gone out of Jack's step, and the realisation chilled her. She saw Kevan and her father and the young men of her past. The cold hours spent perched on cart and wagon were taking their toll. He stooped a little and groaned as he bent to unlace his boots. Then the fireside would claim him and he could not be moved from the glow.

It was the way of things, she thought. The sadness of loss made it difficult to hold back the tears. The boy had gone and the man raised so many sorrows sitting there toasting the winter out of his bones. She took the teapot off the hob and filled his mug.

'What did you do today, son?'

'Moved a couple of tons of oats, took Melody to Totnes, froze to death.'

Michael came in half drunk and boisterous and gave her a great wet kiss on the forehead.

'Why don't you get lodgings at the Globe?' Mary McKenna smiled, but he was too merry to be brought down and his warmth engulfed the household. The wind buffeted the terrace, shaking the windows and spilling smoke down the chimeny into the kitchen. It was blowing strong enough the next morning to lift the corpses on the keeper's gibbet at Cider Mill Farm. Small birds sat in the trees round the frozen pond but the New Year was less than a week old before the lambing began. Then the smell of sheep swept from the pens on the South Devon hills across the farmland. Sheep bells tinkled in the darkness when wind and temperature dropped, and Chancellor's vehicles came back to the yard behind panting horses. The drivers were too miserable to speak until the warmth of the stables thawed out mind and body. Charlie Wotton and his mates laughed as they forked hay through the hatches, and Skilly banged his wooden leg on the cobbles while Moony got down on all fours to bark at Mullah.

'Girt cake,' sniffed Fred Luscombe. A stomach ulcer brought on by cider drinking and lack of regular meals had taken the sting out of his tongue. He was gross and had difficulty getting on and off the vehicles.

Stepping out of the stud Jack felt the night swell cold around him. He turned up his coat collar and buried his hands in his pockets. Cart wheels had left knife-edged ruts in the lane. The hoofprints were indigo and vaguely luminous. He stood a moment and took the coldness through his nostrils letting excitement climb. It was not loving God that mattered but loving what God is. The thought astonished him. Loving Christ was not enough, despite Father O'Driscoll's insistence or church doctrine. God was everything, so what did the crucifixion mean? How could that very human sacrifice affect the rest of creation – the horses, wild creatures, the heathens who had never heard of Christ? The death of God's son hadn't made people behave better towards each other or towards the animals. Why did everything revolve round Christian man and his needs? Did God think that was right? Somehow it cheapened the rest of what he'd done and it didn't ring true of the mind that had filled the universe with such a variety of living things. Everthing hadn't been created just for human beings to use. The horses were free long before man broke them to the saddle and the shafts. He recalled the Bedouin story. The horses were beautiful in themselves and deserved regard and respect. They were God just as Kitty was God and Clennon Valley was God and the sky was God.

But it was impossible to voice his thoughts. Mary McKenna was deaf to anything even vaguely heretical, and Kitty's vision of truth, if it could be called a vision, was a kind of vague hangover from Sunday-school days. He considered talking with Dora but her agnosticism disturbed him. Maybe Edward Daubeny would understand and his education might provide some of the answers. On the other hand, knowing with the heart was sufficient and clever words would only create more bewilderment.

'Frank Emmet, in Number Three passed away this morning,' said his mother. 'He had that terrible chest for months and was coughing blood. God rest his soul. Elsie will be going back to her relatives in Abbot's Quay as soon as possible. She never liked it here since her boy Charlie went off to be a gamekeeper in North Devon. If you want the place she'll put in a good word for you with the landlord. Old Vickery isn't a bad fellah. The Vospers get on all right with him.'

Jack whistled as he buttoned his shirt. The material was crisp and warm from the iron.

'Well?' Mary McKenna persisted.

'Me and Kitty wanted somewhere in the country.'

'The terrace isn't good enough for you, I suppose – you being

241

the assistant horsemaster?'

Her sarcasm brought a smile to his lips. He ran the comb through his hair and said, 'We'd like a bit of garden and a place to stable the horse – somewhere Beth would feel free to run about.'

'Sure, and won't that come later? There's good grazing up behind St Michael's Road and Old Man Pottinger has a couple of sheds in his field.'

'I'll think about it.'

'A lot of young people start married life with their in-laws.'

'You didn't.'

'No. Give Kevan his due, in them days he had bags of pluck and he was a worker. I would have followed him to hell and back. The way he talked you'd have thought England was just down the road. The crock of gold was waitin' for us, only he never delivered it.'

'I'll find it for you, Mum,' Jack grinned, taking her in his arms. 'Then we'll get you a white gown and a parasol and you'll ride along the prom in a carriage like the Queen.'

She pressed her face to his shirtfront while the past which grew more distant every winter reassembled and the kitchen vanished. The tinker children were walking their ponies along the great storm beach. Slea Head was veiled in spray and the mountains beyond were rain-blurred.

'You'll take the Emmet house, won't you Jack?' she choked, lifting her face now.

Gently he brushed away her tears and kissed her.

'I'll ask Kitty.'

'You could do it up nice, the pair of you.'

'And you could help.'

'Oh yes – I'd like that, Jack. My son, my life.'

Kitty's reaction surprised him for he had expected disappointment, recalling her scornful remarks about 'Sir Jack' and the 'castle' in Angarrick Terrace. But she was enthusiastic and hung round his neck kissing his lips as he spoke. Then he realised how much marriage meant to her. She would have settled for a hovel providing they could be united in the eyes of God. Dreams get humbler as we get older, he thought, understanding his mother's possessiveness and the look she gave him across the firelight.

242

'We can get married in April,' he said. 'I'll start paying the rent as soon as Mrs Emmet moves out. That'll stop old Vickery lettin' it to someone else.'

'Mum can start makin' me wedding gown,' Kitty whispered, her eyes bright and moist.

'And Beth can be a bridesmaid,' said Jack.

'Lily and Blanche and my little sisters Maude and Vicky.'

'You've got it all planned.'

'Well, us've only got a few weeks to arrange things,' she said, pushing him away. 'Oh God! Maybe us should wait till June.'

'I may go off you by then.'

'Tidn no joke. Is April too early?'

'Not the end of April.'

'Idn it romantic?' she exclaimed, laughing with her eyes closed, like a child at the Christmas tree.

The aroma of horse living filled the stables at Tor Barton. It was a dark sleet-scribbled morning and the mares and geldings were kept in their stalls. Half the workforce had been laid off and the remaining labourers were busy doing the jobs they loathed – repairing machinery, humping hundredweight sacks of meal, ditching. The older hands were laying hedges but there was little for the horses to do. Arthur Maddock let them out for exercise and smoked a cigarette as they galloped round the field. His moustache partly concealed the rabbit teeth but not his boredom. Beth and Bathsheba ran together, kicking up the mushy snow, their hooves flailing from the centre of great leaps and bounds. The sky broke into small pieces which fluttered down, white and hypnotic. And Jack was suddenly calling her to the gate.

'Beth. Come on girl.'

She snorted and stamped and paced over the whiteness to rest her head in his hands.

A plane of light spread to the horizon, and they walked together, the boy and the horse, casting no shadows and leaving no footprints. The sun and moon rose and took their stations low in the sky. It was a place of total silence, a landscape spilling from anxiety into untroubled distances.

He turned the key in the padlock and shook the yard gates to make sure they were secure. Tom Palfrey and his dog had departed a little earlier and for the first time that winter Jack thought of Clubfoot Charlie Emmet and his family whose house he would soon occupy. Winter brought the finality of death into focus. Frank Emmet was dead. The warmth his loved ones had accumulated at Number Three Angarrick Terrace was turning to dust. Yet the Vospers' finch kept singing and the gulls would not be silenced above the rooftops.

He whistled as he marched along Station Lane towards Lansworthy Mill and the Congregational Church. But turning into Dartmouth road he met several large dark shapes.

'McKenna?' said a cold voice, and Jack covered his genitals as the boots and fists flew.

'Naughty Irish,' the voice purred, but Jack evaded the kick and delivered a flurry of punches before he was brought down. Someone shouted, heavy footfalls crunched through the snow, the evening whirlpooled and became shrill with roosting starlings.

'Go back to the bog, Irish. Go back or we'll cripple the horse.' Jack grinned. The toecap of the boot crushed back the fingers shielding his face.

'You have a go, mate,' said the voice. 'He's helpless enough.'

'That wasn't the agreement,' snarled another faintly familiar voice. 'Kick his head in. Go on—do it.'

'No, that's enough. You'd better hurry, mate, if you want to complete the job. Your little Irish terrier is coming round.'

'Shit on you, Cairns.'

Jack clawed at a trouser leg.

'Cairns.'

'slip us half a sovereign and we'll put him on crutches.'

'You've been paid.'

'But that was back in the pub. Isn't the bastard worth a bit extra?'

'Apparently I wasn't,' Jack said, joining Michael at the pub fire and dabbing the lumps on his face with whisky.

'Lucky they only aimed at your head,' Michael said cheerfully. 'Whenever you're in a scrap your nose always cops one. Is it broke again?'

Jack pinched the end between forefinger and thumb and gingerly wiggled it.

'Bruised I think,' he said.

'And swollen. Kitty's going to give you some stick. For God's sake don't waste all that whisky on your dial.'

He swiftly downed his own double and reached for his tankard of beer.

'When do we kick hell out of Lacey?'

'We don't. Jack said. 'One dark night I'll catch up with him but we're not turning this into a feud.'

'I didn't realise marriage prospects could do this to a bloke,' Michael laughed. 'What about the others — the cockney rubbish?'

Jack shrugged and scuffed the sawdust with his boots. 'What's the point of goin' round pubs lookin' for them? I wouldn't know them from Adam if they walked in here now.'

'But it'd be fun lookin''

'Dora was right. Go looking for trouble and it grabs you by the nuts. Arthur and me will meet up again one day, somewhere quiet.'

'And that's the McKenna way of squaring things?' with contempt in his voice.

'It's my way,' said Jack.

The cold strengthened. East winds brought snow from the Continent and falls of thrushes from north of the Baltic. Beth and Bathsheba were back at Station Lane where work had come to a halt. The carters had been laid off and the horses left in the care of Jack and Palfrey. Whenever there was a lull in the blizzard animals were led out and walked round the yard. At first they lifted their legs high but soon discovered they could comfortably push through the drift. Steam rose from their coats and breath wreathed their heads. Sparrows chirped in the loft and the song of the starlings had the horses pricking their ears.

Beth liked the snow beneath her hooves and the flakes whispering down. The sky was dancing. Pieces of it settled on her nostrils and vanished. She arched her neck and whinnied to be answered by Bathsheba and Melody. The whiteness had no scent but the shire geldings could not resist rolling on it, snuffling with joy and kicking out their legs. Soon the yard was full of animals churning up the snow under the mist of their body heat.

If they can feel happy they can also feel sad, Jack thought. They suffer as we suffer. And his heart went out to the great noisy children in their rapture, dark and glistening under the grey light and the snow driving hard again off the sea.

It was not long before the snow had gone even from the hilltops but the rain was cold and the sun cheerless. Maddock and Ormond Chancellor shot wildfowl on the salt marsh. Curlew, snipe and mallard lay side by side in the canvas bags and the evening flights continued despite the noise of the guns. Then Jack would come home and join Kitty, Dora and his mother in the empty house whitewashing the kitchen and wall-papering the bedrooms.

'Best paper in the front room,' said Mrs McKenna.

'For the Co-op insurance man to see,' Jack grinned. 'Why do front rooms have to be bloody showpieces for visitors? Sure, it would be better if ours was used as a bedroom instead of us all crowdin' together upstairs.'

'Wouldn be proper,' said Kitty. 'If anyone called where would us put 'em – in the kitchen?'

'Why not? For heaven's sake! Why not?'

'Because it's a game, Jack,' said Dora. 'Ape your betters.'

'Betters!' he snorted. 'Ormond Chancellor better than me!'

'Society thinks so,' she laughed.

'Bugger society.'

'Your language,' said Mary McKenna but she had dismissed it as male nonsense and was running an approving eye over the wallpaper. 'Now that looks splendid, Kitty.'

'Of course it does,' said Jack, 'You chose it, Mother.'

'Chancellor's. Ten per cent discount,' Kitty smiled.

He returned to the kitchen and the whitewashing.

'Is this what it's all about, Jack?' said Dora. She folded her arms and leaned against the door. 'Wallpaper and furniture and lino and a bit in the bank?'

'I honestly don't know.'

'Don't let it take over completely.'

By candlelight her beauty was ethereal. She was so calm and relaxed.

'Dreams are no good unless you do something about them, Jack.'

'What if I'm dreaming about you?' he said laughingly; but Mrs McKenna called Dora and broke the spell.

He walked to work under the morning stars and joined some

246

of the carters on their way up Fisher Street. Dora's words cut into his thoughts. He was nineteen years old and already in a rut. Nothing could be more futile than grafting for wages until old age shouldered you onto the scrap heap. He glanced at his companions. Albert Wotton had spent his entire life in Lansworthy working for Chancellor's. He went from house to yard to pub to house day after day, and most of Sunday was spent in bed. By the time Jack had joined Palfrey, and the men were busy grooming, he was on the edge of desperation.

Beth was to be harnessed for the town van and the Lansworthy round. I've enough to buy her now, Jack thought. Surely the old man would take the gold and let the horse go? Excitement welled and left his mouth dry. He would ride her bareback out of town and over the hills to Dartmoor and on through Wales to catch the Irish ferry. There were places facing the sunset where horses were still regarded as fabulous creatures. He would take her along the storm beaches on the journey that had no ending. People held you down, crushed the dreams out of you and left you as barren as themselves. Did it have to end in a stale relationship and a betrayal of all the heart saw and the living world promised?

A dead crow lay in Station Lane, the wind ruffling its feathers. Gulls circled high and noisily. Lifting her head Beth was aware of small shapes flickering on the morning's greyness. The weight on her shoulders was not troublesome. Motor cars stopped to let her pass but she laid back her ears and trod warily over the tram lines.

Jack clicked his tongue; the familiar streets unfolded, other horses crossed her path or trotted briefly beside her. A short wait at the billiard hall in Totnes Road was followed by a longer halt outside the ironmongers. Then she trotted along Winner Street to the Oldenburgh and listened to the parrot squawking from the public bar.

Jack came and went, leaving with a parcel or a roll of material and returning empty-handed. Evans the saddlers, Butleys the butchers, builders like Langley and Sons, the umbrella shop opposite the Baptist chapel, Jefferies the tailor and Poole's Panorama – the van became lighter until at noon Station Square was reached and she was turned towards the yard again. Other vehicles were queuing up to enter their own particular yards, and the carters sat blowing on their fingernails, glad half the winter's day was behind them.

Often he walked home with Moony, his mood changed and his entire being crying out for the fireside and hot food. The smack of skipping ropes, the chanted rhymes and the laughter filled dusk with friendliness. The sight of the small figures circling the lamp usually produced an inner glow and Jack came to the hearth pursued by his sisters. Thick slices of home-cured bacon crisped in the pan with just a suggestion of smoke rising from the bristles.

Preparations for the wedding kept Mary McKenna occupied but as she was putting the finishing touches to Kitty's curtains she knew there would be an empty place at the fireside next winter. Voices cried from the street and brought alive memories of other evenings when he was a child. Dando gobbled up the remains of his meal. Lamplight and firelight met and created the rosy glow which she loved. It lit his face and her spirit cowered. The moment she had dreaded for years was approaching. Dando came and sat beside her and whined. He would be there after Jack's departure. The thought galled Mary McKenna.

'Go away, you stupid, greedy animal,' she cried and the vehemence of her tone made everyone look up.

'Forever on the scrounge. Stupid dog.'

But she regretted the outburst instantly and knelt to fondle the animal. Then she blessed herself and whispered, 'This winter is going to last forever. When Jesus died why didn't the seas freeze over and the mountains fall?'

A week passed, darker and colder than anything else the New Year had managed. Yet the days were imperceptibly lengthening, and bringing Beth and Melody up Kings Ash Hill at the end of a visit to Rattery, Jack was relieved to see blossom on the blackthorn.

He stopped the wagon beneath the branches for a closer look. The tiny white florets stirred against a sky the colour of pewter. The horses turned their heads and stared at him.

'Spring, my lovelies,' he murmured. 'For me it always begins here, on these trees.'

'Get home, Jack,' Charlie smiled. He was embarrassed by his hero's behaviour. 'A bit of bullen blossom doan make a spring.'

'Beginnings, Charlie – it's the beginnings that count. The horses know.'

'How do 'em know, Jack?'

'They feel things in the blood, like we used to when we lived in caves and understood the magic we've forgotten now.'

But Jack knew spring had really come the morning his mother opened the bedroom window to shake her duster and let the scent of rain-soaked flowers flood the house.

The Kings Ash blackthorns were in tiny leaf when he and Kitty were married.

30

The morning was showery. Blossom from the ornamental cherry trees floated on the puddles all down the path to the chapel. Guests caught in the rain ran under their umbrellas with the women gathering up their skirts and squealing. Throughout the ceremony sunlight illumined the stain glass windows and faded and swelled as clouds passed; but nothing could take the glow from Kitty's face.

They walked down the hill together to the reception in the Co-op hall, and Jack wondered uneasily if it really was a beginning. He glanced at Dora. She was talking to his mother and radiating charm. The remark she had made back in the winter drowned Kitty's bright chatter: 'Dreams are no good unless you do something about them.'

He refused the gateau but accepted a glass of sparkling white wine. The reception was a small affair. Michael and Sean acted the fool, Mary McKenna cried, his new in-laws and their relatives danced to the music of a hired gramophone, and when Kitty turned to kiss him she had pastry crumbs round her mouth. He laughed and brushed them away with a fingertip.

'Tidn much of a do is it?' she blushed.

'Sausage rolls, light ale and your dad crankin' the gramophone? It's everything I imagined and more. Legless Mike and witless Sean doin' the jig; Mother weepin' buckets;

Father O'Driscoll half blotto; and you and me sittin' here jawing when we should be in bed.'

'Oh Jack.'

'I'm only joking. For God's sake! I like pantomimes.'

'The presents are nice, aren't they? Especially old Mr Chancellor's. Fancy him thinking of you!'

'He was thinking of the horses.'

Bed then, and no embarrassment or hesitation except in the undressing.

'Put the candle out,' she whispered, wriggling free of the flannel nightshirt and settling beside him.

Beyond touch were unimaginable sensations and sleep and waking that had little to do with opening the eyes. The doubts vanished and morning brought nothing but happiness. They were up early and walking the beach, barefoot, kicking through the shallows on one of those windless calms when everything appears to have been sculpted from light. The black-headed gulls in their summer hoods cried along the wavebreak, swooping every so often on the ridge of seaweed and dead shellfish that traced the high tide mark. The faintly rotten, faintly antiseptic smell registered between kisses.

'The Kaiser's daughter got married in May,' said Mary McKenna.

'I hope she didn't have her reception at the Co-op hall,' Jack smiled.

'Sure, it wasn't that bad,' she said, yawning and running a critical eye over Kitty's kitchen. The tiny room was clean and sparsely furnished. Kitty was out but Mary had come to speak to him before she went on with the family to Mass. She was puzzled by the troubles in Ireland. How could the Ulster men under that devil Carson prevent the unity of North and South?

But he was tired of her growing involvement with a cause and place which had no emotional pull.

He thought about it a day or so later as he walked Beth from the yard. The cart rumbled over the cobbles past the hoarding opposite the stonemason's yard. The top of the Colman's Mustard poster had ripped loose and was flapping in the wind. Why was his mother so afraid of being alone? Everything worthwhile came from self. You had to go your own way, look at

251

the stars, make your own life.

The breeze sweeping up off the sea carried the musk of gorse. He dropped the first load at Cider Mill Farm and watered Beth at the pond where the local work horses stood hock deep. Watching her drink he wanted her to know she was loved. All around them the elms whispered and the horses swallowed the water. Jack gazed over the countryside. You green valley, hills and trees and fields. Who will look at you and love you when I am dead? But the wonder would remain. Yes, he smiled and patted Beth's neck. When the White Lady was gone the swifts would fly through the gap she had left in the sky.

Beth walked up the lane to Tor Barton, in and out of lateral bars of sunlight. Birds sang and the cartwheels bounced and rattled over the stones all the way to the bullock yard. Here Jack unloaded the rest of the sacks of bran onto Arthur's shoulders, unwilling to chat.

'He's gettin' a moody bugger,' Trant observed, watching the cart disappear between the hedges. 'Typical Irish – up one minute, down the next.'

'He do's a lot of thinking,' said Arthur.

'About what?' Trant said scornfully. 'It don't make any odds what us thinks, boy. Us idn going to change the world.'

Bacon frying, piles of washing on the scullery floor, suds, steam, and Kitty at the tub.

'Your mum called with a bit of cod.'

'Again?' he said from a kiss. 'She practically lives here now.'

'I doan mind, her's company.'

But when evening blued to dusk company was not desired. They drew the curtains and Kitty sat on his lap in the armchair, aching to drag him upstairs but unwilling to advertise her appetite for what went on between the sheets. Her kisses soon became impatient yet she would not undress on the hearth rug.

'Your mum might walk in,' she whispered, and he laughed and led her up the short flight of stairs to the bedroom. The honeysuckle in the backyard shook its fragrance through the open window.

'Tez so hot,' Kitty said in a husky voice while he stripped.

'Flaming June,' he smiled.

'You look funny,' she said. 'White body, brown arms and face.'

252

'Skewbald.'

'Jack,' from another soft whisper.

Maybe the news from Sarajevo cast its shadow over Dora's mind. In another summer in another place she was to recall laying down the *Daily Mail* after reading about the assassination of the Archduke Franz Ferdinand and going to the front door. The first shoppers came clumping down Winner Street then Jack passed, upright on the cart with Beth in the shafts. He turned, waved and smiled, ignoring the motor car and motor vans crawling along behind him, eager to overtake.

It occurred to Dora in a flash that the man and horse had one thing in common: no future. The motor car would see to that, the motor car and progress. It registered more as a shudder than a thought.   The early editions of the *Illustrated London News* were full of scenes from Sarajevo.

'There will be war,' said Mr Widdicombe and he sighed. 'Everyone's talking about it down the mill. The mazed buggers want it to happen. The working class are their own worst enemy. Mazed buggers.'

Dora related his words to her sister when the supper things had been cleared away and Jack had opened all the windows. He sat on the sill in his shirt sleeves listening to the women while day faded among the backyards.

Dora's voice rose. 'Dad idn going to fight no capitalist war. He says we shouldn't get all upset because some royal drone was shot in some foreign place.'

'Him and his wife,' said Kitty. 'Poor lady.'

'At least she won't know what it's like to apply for pauper relief.'

'I hope we won't either.'

'But do you know what we are?'

Kitty shook her head and glanced apprehensively at Jack.

'We're the invisible servants of a huge, posh household called the Empire. The family – the upper class – get all the good grub, the fun, the rooms with views, respect, security, the lot. Britain owns a quarter of the world and we don't own an inch of this town. But without us it would all collapse.'

'If it was left to clowns like Luscombe, Lacey and co., would it be any better?' said Jack.

253

'Why pick on them? There are plenty of decent, intelligent working-class people who could run the country better than Asquith and his lot.'

'You're probably right,' he grinned. 'Only, why should our class have more good people than their class?'

Dora came to his side, eager to press home her argument. Her scent was more cryptic than the honeysuckle.

'The wall, Jack,' she said. 'There, at the back of your coal shed. It's not only to keep us out of Grosvenor Road's gardens but to hide their private lives. We're the threat they fear most.'

'Dora hates Ormond Chancellor,' said Kitty.

'You're wrong,' Dora swung round and returned to the hearth. 'That's fool's no problem. He has less of an inner life than Moony.'

'Do you think only bright people have inner lives?' said Jack, thinking of the horses.

'No,' she smiled. 'In Ormond Chancellor's case having a soft centre makes him less dangerous.'

'All wind and pee?' Jack frowned. 'I'm not sure you're correct. Ormond's sort can really put the boot in. If you want to be a bastard bad enough one day you'll succeed.'

'You are married to a philosopher, Kit,' Dora laughed.

She stood up and stretched. Her light calico dress was creased but she seemed unconcerned.

'There won't be no war,' Kitty said when her sister had departed and the love-making was over. She lay in Jack's arms staring at the bedroom wall. Moonlight gleamed on the jug and washbasin.

'Our royal family and the German royal family are related. They wouldn't want to hurt each other. Dad and Dora doan know it all do they? Do they?'

It was a plea for comfort.

'Course they don't.'

'Politics is just a load of trouble. Why did they foreigners shoot that duke and his missus? It couldn happen here.'

'Someone always has a reason for doing something, Kitty.'

'Makes you think,' she said.

'Makes you think what?'

'I doan know. I just feel it's wicked killing people no matter

254

how bad they'm supposed to be. Loving you like I do makes me want everyone in the world to feel the same.'

'But there would be a bloody great queue outside our back door. All them ladies after my services.'

He could not imagine Fred Luscombe loving anyone except himself. The fat man had trod warily in the yard since Jack's promotion and the ulcer had censored his bullying although Skilly still came under fire. The wooden leg had ceased to inspire pity. It was a clown's stage prop which the idiot used to his advantage.

'He's more stool than fool,' Luscombe observed, tapping the celebrated leg; and Drew choked on his bacon sandwich.

The horses had been groomed and watered and the yard staff were breakfasting in the sun. Mullah and the cats sat at their feet cadging the odd crust or rind.

Jack led Beth and Melody across the cobbles to the wagon.

''Ere Irish,' Luscombe called. 'Have you seen the paper? Your cousins over in Dublin have been kickin' up hell again. But they haven't had it all their own way.'

'What happened?' said Albert Wotton.

'The Fenians landed arms in broad daylight but our boys soon put paid to that little lark. We sent in the Jocks and they shot three of the buggers.'

Jack backed Melody into the shafts to join Beth, and adjusted the harness.

'The King's Own Scottish Borderers shot into the crowd,' said Walter Cooksley. 'That don't sound very brave to me.'

'Bloody Micks,' Luscombe said under his breath. Then the stomach pains had him groaning, and Skilly limped behind the grain store to laugh.

'Get back to your animals,' Jack shouted and Charlie Wotton came running from the stables with the nosebags.

The heatwave made everyone edgy but the animals lumbered obediently through the soaring temperatures and the dust churned up by motor transport. The old open-top horse omnibuses were fighting a losing battle with the faster and bigger motor vehicles, and summer brought a flood of cars to the Three Towns. Ormond smiled.

'Times are changing, Rupert. Lansworthy is actually

catching up with the rest of England.'

They sat in the 'Prince Henry' Austro-Daimler cruising along the Esplanade. Parasols and white summer dresses were dotted here and there on the green, and the villas of Abbot's Quay struck their Mediterranean chord under a hazy blue sky. The Three Towns had an air of quiet prosperity and the battle cruisers anchored in the bay were somehow a gesture of defiance as well as a confirmation of British muscle power. Ormond's smile broadened. It was an ideal age for a man of his capabilities. A man of the age! Yes, he thought, the age produces the man. The business gentleman as hero. A more modern ideal was difficult to conceive.

'She goes like a dream,' he said breezily, tapping the wheel of the Austro-Daimler.

'And I'd let her continue that way without your help, Father,' said Rupert.

Ormond Chancellor glanced at him.

'A gentleman does not tinker with his motor car,' Rupert continued. 'No more than a gentleman would hitch a horse to his carriage. It's servants' work. The motor car is no longer the gentleman's hobby. It is a fact of life.'

'Point taken,' Ormond said. 'Have there been comments?'

'Of course not, but the Daubenys don't miss much.'

'How are you getting on with Helen?'

'I'm not. She spends her happiest hours before the mirror.'

Ormond laughed. 'Keep plugging away. She'd be a feather in your cap if you could walk her to the altar.'

'And it wouldn't do the family any harm,' Rupert observed languidly.

The motor car rattled over the railway crossing. Outside the Gerston Hotel the newspaper placard proclaimed 'Austria Threatens Serbia', in giant black capitals.

Yet beyond Lansworthy summer took its normal course. The wagon sailed down lanes of red dust, dislodging the last petals of the dog roses and scattering butterflies.

It bumped and juddered behind Beth and Melody, the load threatening to tip at every jolt. The horses' ears pricked forward as the green woodpecker undulated away, yaffling from a blur of tropical colour.

'Like a bliddy parrot,' Charlie said. 'Why did God make so

many different animals and birds, Jack?'

'Because he loves life.'

'Then why do things die?'

'They'd just get older and older and tireder and tireder till the world was full of grey creeping things. When your coat wears out you get a new one. It's a question of repairing, replacing and replanting.'

'I don't want to die, Jack.'

'Maybe you won't mind too much when you're older. Think how glad you are to get your head down when you're tired after a hard day's work.'

'When I'm a hundred but not now. I'd miss all this – the trees and fields, summer, the horses.'

'You're not going to die. You're as healthy as them young oaks in the hedge. Everything has its season, Charlie, and ours is spring.'

They had reached a hilltop and at their feet the whole of South Devon melted into something more mysterious than haze. A curlew passed overhead on its way to the River Dart, crying the clear double notes Jack loved. He and Beth looked up. The smell of horses spiced the air. Everything was perfectly still and the light around them was soft and vibrant. The far-off places held humans and animals spellbound.

'Tidn like nowhere else,' Charlie whispered and Jack smiled.

Kitty was singing when he crept in the front door late that evening. The clamour of swifts flying high above the terrace brought summer right into the house.

Jack took off his boots quietly and came to the kitchen on tiptoe.

'You are an angel, Mrs McKenna,' he breathed, folding his arms around Kitty from behind.

'My clean apron!' she squealed, wriggling free. 'And don't come up on me like that again. I nearly passed out. Stop it! Don't you want your supper? Wash your hands and I'll bring it in.'

He was sitting at the table when she called: 'Have you seen today's paper?'

Jack leaned over and plucked the *Mail* off the arm of the easy chair.

'"Austria declares war on Serbia",' he read. '"Powder keg of

257

Balkans ready to go up".' The small print elaborated on Europe's gloomy prospects.

Kitty set down the steak and kidney pie and poured the tea.

'Dad reckons it's really serious now. It's to do with who backs who and what they'll make of it. The Germans are dying to get at our throats.'

'Not before supper, I hope. If they've got any decency they'll invade us in the boss's time.'

'Jack,' she laughed.

'Brooding about what might happen won't help.'

She was the pretty, wide-eyed child, fearing her happiness was under attack.

'Life scares me, Jack,' she said, and her voice shook.

He lit the lamp against the darkness but outside the swifts continued to scream.

All Europe was arming while the corn ripened and the skies remained blue above parched landscapes. Beth, Melody and Bathsheba were loaned to Tor Barton again to replace some animals who had eaten horsetail ferns down in the valley. The sick were confined to the stables and Trant's irascible nursing; but for the yard mares those nights loose upon the tor were precious interludes. They swished through the long grass, glad of the comradeship and content to be there. Standing on the rock with the moon behind them their silhouettes were silver-edged. They could smell the valley and the sea but late one night another, a more pungent smell stung their nostrils: the stink of fox.

Kennelling in the reed beds at the top of the valley the old dog ranged far over the countryside every evening, returning to his couch around dawn. On this occasion his luck had run out. Trotting between the pheasant coverts at Litstone he had been shot by the gamekeeper who was lying in wait for human poachers.

Dragging useless hindlegs he had crossed several fields and the Old Mary's Haven Road, following the fox trails and badger paths east, driven by an instinct he could not comprehend. Coming off the brow of Cider Mill Tor his strength failed and he sat back panting as giddiness mounted and died. He was disorientated, frightened and puzzled. Slowly the horses walked down the hillside and gathered around him, their heads lowered. The fox whimpered and crouched in the grass. Beth gently placed her muzzle against him but he lay on his side and his tongue flopped out. The numbness in his limbs hit his mind but fear had gone. Beth's long white face became a blur. Then he was at the vortex of the whirlpool although there was no giddiness or anguish. The horses stared across the dark countryside to the sea without knowing the life had gone out of the animal lying motionless before them.

'Why would 'em stand round a daid old fox?' Arthur Maddock said.

'Curiosity,' Jack offered, unwilling to share his real conclusions.

'Like they'm upset,' Arthur said.

Or mourning, thought Jack, meeting Beth's gaze. He picked up the fox's carcass.

'I'm going to put him in the blackthorns on top of the hill behind the tor so that he can look down the valley.'

'Mazed,' Arthur murmured, and he called the mares to be watered and fed.

That Saturday was memorable for another reason. Germany declared war on Russia as a consequence of an inevitable chain reaction of alliances and counter alliances. The next day the Kaiser's armies invaded Belgium en route to France, and Lansworthy, like the rest of Britain, was gripped by war fever.

'I don't believe it,' Widdicombe said. 'Down the Crown and Anchor last night they were baying for German blood. Your mate Lacey led the chorus. The Kaiser would quake in his boots if he knew what the lads had in store for un. Lacey talks one hell of a war.'

'But it'll be all right, Dad – won't it?' said Kitty.

She was black-leading the kitchen range.

'No. It will get worse. The whole world has a sudden appetite for slaughter.'

'I haven't,' Jack said.

Widdicombe shrugged. 'You'll do what you'm told boy.'

'Will I?' Jack grinned.

The Regatta Fair drew the crowds to Lansworthy seafront and few people were aware of the khaki figures boarding the noon train. Mr Heinlen, the German chimney sweep, and his family were booed and jostled outside the pier until the police escorted them away. Mob violence went with the panic buying and the hoarding.

'God, if that isn't typical of the bloody English!' said Mary McKenna. 'Old Heinlen has been here twenty years and he married a local girl. What the hell do they think he is – a spy? The damn fools.'

'I'd keep quiet if I were you, Mum' said Michael. 'The accent is a dead give away. Shout like that and the mob will think we're all Sinn Fein or Fenians.'

'A dose of The Troubles wouldn't hurt this lot,' Mary McKenna huffed, elbowing a path through the crowd.

But when the laughter and shouting blurred it was not unlike the snarl of some beast of prey, Dora thought. Wrapping a protective arm round Kitty she glanced at Jack but his face was impassive. He was a bit like a horse himself, she decided, suppressing a giggle: noble, hard-working, rather dense and dreamy. Unless he was simply bored by run-of-the-mill events like the fair. He was an enigma, she decided.

Michael and Sean deserted the party to find the beer tent and Kitty persuaded Jack to join them. By the time the women had eaten a shrimp tea and yawned their way through the Pierrot performance the brothers were drunk.

'Isn't that Arthur Lacey?' said Dora pointing at a young man who was lurching off between the stalls clutching a handkerchief to his face.

'Oh Jack,' Kitty sighed.

'I couldn't help it,' he admitted on the unsteady walk home. 'He was telling everyone what he would do to the Germans and all of a sudden I looked over his shoulder and saw Gabriel standing at the bar.'

'The archangel?' Dora frowned.

'The horse,' said Sean. 'The horse Lacey got killed.'

'So I hit him a few times to make Gabriel disappear.'

'Did it work?' asked Dora.

Jack winked and raised a thumb.

'They'll put you away for a long time if you keep hammering that poor bugger.'

'Talk to a brick wall,' Michael said.

'Christ man!' said Sean. 'You belted him as well.'

'Only when Jack was done.'

Mary McKenna blanched. 'Were the police called?'

'They were not,' crowed Michael. 'Lacey is well hated wherever he goes. Men were queuing up to sock him. We had a rare old donnybrook.'

'You great liar,' said Mary.

Next morning Jack brought his hangover to work and time dragged. The Three Towns smouldered until evening once more released the masses and they flocked to Lansworthy Green. The government had given the Germans an ultimatum to withdraw from Belgium, and it was due to expire at midnight—eleven o'clock British time. As the hour approached a crowd gathered outside the town hall singing 'Land of Hope and Glory'. The minutes ticked away and the night seemed to hold its breath but the multitude broke into the national anthem then fell silent. The parish church clock struck eleven times and after a long pause the town clerk raised his voice and said, 'The German government has not replied. We are at war.'

'War,' the crowd echoed. Fists and hats were held aloft and shaken. A roar of joy and defiance rang across the bay and was answered by the cheers of the ratings on the dreadnoughts and cruisers off Abbot's Quay. 'War,' Lacey cried and Rupert Chancellor flung the word back into the cauldron of noise.

'By George!' his father sobbed, 'I hope Kitchener's got room for an old un.'

War was on the lips of the young men dashing down the streets to crowd the bars. Like the Klondike, Dora thought, and everyone had struck gold. They were singing the national anthem again as she turned and walked along Totnes Road into Victoria Street. Chancellor's windows were lit up and a huge Union Jack hung over the entrance.

'Why aren't you cheering?' said a voice in her ear.

'Cheering what?' she said.

Edward Daubeny was unsmiling. His arm encircled her waist and met no resistance. Dora did not offer the usual platitudes or coy defence. She closed her eyes, parted her lips and returned his kiss. Then she went with him towards the seafront knowing it was right and glad she was true to herself. Now the crowd assembling at the pier sang 'Dolly Gray' but Edward and Dora

261

did not join in. They walked on the beach and the firework display, which had been put back an hour, banged and crackled into life.

Starlight quivered on the bay but the sudden arc of rockets was brighter. The hills ran black to horizons where the light was full of noise. Beth picked her way cautiously off the tor, her eyes alert. One by one the other horses came and stood baffled by what was going on below.

31

The police were going from door to door delivering wires to the reservists. War meant adventure but even so Jack was surprised at the number of boys and carters who failed to show for the morning work. The Dunsford brothers made a brief apologetic appearance.

'We'm joining up,' Harold said, his eyes blazing. 'Lord Kitchener wants a hundred thousand men, and me and Will want to show the Hun we mean business.'

Palfrey took his pipe from his lips and tapped it on the stable door. Then he looked at Jack.

'Who else has enlisted?'

'Practically everyone – Moony, little Charlie Wotton, Rupert Chancellor, bliddy Lacey, Arthur Maddock, the Daubeny boy, hundreds of 'em. They've opened a recruiting office below the billiards emporium in Station Square. Your brother Mike was there, Jack.'

Jack nodded but said nothing.

'There's this Royal Artillery sergeant in his dress uniform,' said Will. 'Christ he could charm the birds off the trees! Lacey's going to an infantry regiment but all the lads from the yard and Tor Barton have joined the Gunners. So've Rupert and his pal. The sergeant said they were looking for real horsemen. We hope we'll all be together. Can you manage without us, Mr Palfrey?'

'I'll try,' smiled the horsemaster and they shook hands.

'Idn you coming, Jack?' Harold said.

'No,' said Jack.

'Someone's got to look after the horses,' Albert Wotton interjected.

'You'll find enough old fellas to help 'ee,' Harold mumbled.

'And they reckon it'll be over by Christmas.'

Jack went into the stables.

'What's up with Irish?' Harold asked. 'I never thought I'd see un turn his back on a fight.'

'Perhaps he don't feel it's his fight,' said Palfrey.

'Bugger it, Mr Palfrey,' Harold cried. 'Tez everyone's fight. The bliddy Hun's in Belgium givin' folk a roasting. If us doan help out he'll be over here. Anyway, what's it like?'

'What's what like?'

'Action. Fighting.'

Palfrey thought for a moment. 'Tidn all it's cracked up to be. Let's hope Kaiser Bill will back off now we're showing the flag. Maybe it'll end with the politicians chinwagging round the table.'

'Spoil sport,' Harold laughed.

Towards noon when half the fleet was out on the streets some of the younger boys mooched in looking despondent.

'So they turned 'ee down,' Palfrey chuckled. 'Doan worry, you'll get your chance.'

'Not if it's over by Christmas,' said 'Ginger' Yeoman who was nearly fifteen.

'Meanwhile you can help the men in Flanders by seeing things go smoothly here. Begin by mucking out.'

'Aw, Mr Palfrey!'

'Monday was your holiday. This is a work day, so set to.'

'Tidn fair. They took Charlie Wotton. They're going to give him a uniform and a gun.'

'A rifle,' Palfrey corrected him.

'He joined the artillery like everyone else,' said another boy. 'So he'll get a big gun.'

'And you'll all be carters till him and the others come home.'

'You mean that, Mr Palfrey?' said Ginger. 'I get a whip and me own cart?'

'Some of you may. Us'll ask a few of the old hands back to show 'ee the ropes.'

264

'Did Jack join the gunners, Mr Palfrey?'

'What he does is his own business. Jack's a horseman before anything else.'

'Before King and country?' Ginger whispered.

'There's a lot of ways you can serve King and country,' said Palfrey. 'Now muck out and exercise the animals that idn working. No more yap.'

Mary McKenna could not disguise her pride over Michael's enlistment. Half a dozen other young men from the terrace had taken the King's shilling but for a while Jack's refusal to run with the herd was hardly noticed. The numbing acceleration of events fed on enthusiasm and hysteria. German 'atrocities' in Belgium united the classes in a resolve to put things right. Then as the crusade gathered momentum some of the new army came home on leave before their training began and Luscombe opened up.

'Did you fail your medical, Irish?' he enquired innocently at breakfast time.

Jack grinned.

'You just didn bother then? – to enlist, I mean?'

'That's right.'

The note of sarcasm deepened in Luscombe's voice. 'Maybe it don't seem worth the fuss, not with them other lads willing to do your share. Maybe you'm more interested in Dublin than Flanders. On the other hand you may have no stomach for that sort of work. Doan worry, boy – little Charlie Wotton will do it for 'ee.'

Lifting a forefinger Jack gently tapped the side of his nose and winked.

Luscombe coloured. 'If you were English you'd be pullin' your weight instead of loafing in the sun like a bliddy – bliddy –'

'Bloody what?'

'Coward,' the fat man barked, and everyone stared at Jack.

'Even mazed Moony enlisted. Every fit lad in the Three Towns has taken the shilling – excepting them Quakers up the mill and blokes like you. Arthur Lacey was first in line.'

'Jack's worried about the horses,' said Ginger who was unwilling to see his idol pulled down by someone he despised.

'Jack's worried about Fritz,' Luscombe sneered.

'Tell un,' Ginger appealed to Jack.

265

'There's nothing to tell.'

'But my brother enlisted and he's knock-kneed.'

'Lord Kitchener's secret weapon,' another boy chuckled. 'The Hun will look at him and die laughin'.'

Luscombe's sneering smile followed Jack out of the yard but before the fat man could build on his victory Palfrey cornered him.

'Any more shit stirring,' he said waving his pipe stem in Luscombe's face, 'and you are out on your arse. You know McKenna isn a coward. If he doan want to fight that's his business. Wars are usually fought by professionals, not hare-brained rabble. So just keep your mouth shut.'

Jack's growing isolation became apparent when he brought the carrier's van to the store. Roadworks at the rear of the building meant loading up at the front where a knot of figures in blue serge tunics were receiving free cigarettes from Ormond Chancellor. Among them was Lacey.

'Where's your shilling, Irish?' he crowed.

'Bloody laggard,' came a shout.

'Bloody Irish.'

'Us won't let Fritz hurt 'ee, boy. You stay home by the fire with the maids.'

Jack's Irishness was proposed as a reason for him shrinking his duty. Michael was 'a different animal altogether', to quote Ormond. 'We have the fighting Irish and creatures like McKenna.' His father was astonished but Helen Daubeny merely thought Jack was reverting to type.

'The back street bully boy would always show his scut in a crisis.'

Driving Beth along the road to Churston Jack was aware of a changed landscape. The young men had vanished from the fields and the old questioned him with their eyes as he passed. Damn you God, he thought, clenching his teeth. Damn you and your tricks. But behind the human muddle was the solace Beth offered. She enjoyed the country rounds. She could smell fields and woods and farm animals. Birds fluttering from hedge to hedge were bright blurs of noise. An elm was a waterfall of leaf-glitter, a pond a small sky-coloured circle of coolness. She blew the flies off her nostrils. The sea showed between swells of downland to her left. Swallows and house martins flickered high on haze. Again a shake of the head set the flies dancing. Now the trees were fewer and the sea constantly in sight. A crab boat lay off Churston Point, the fishermen motionless in the stern. A bell began to toll and entering the village Jack halted the cart to let the bereaved pass into the churchyard. The coffin was very small and the mourners were weeping but around the tower the jackdaws whirled and jangled. Then three white ducks waddled across the road to the stream. Beth laid back her ears as the wings flapped and beat the water.

'Walk on,' Jack said, blotting out the memory of her thrashing about in the mud at Aish.

The last of the recruits had gone to the training camps and the sergeant swaggered up and down in front of his empty office glaring at the small boys who paraded before him, broom handles sloped on shoulders. The holidaymakers had departed early and the first Belgian refugees arrived by fishing boat at Mary's Haven. Their grey faces loomed large on the cinema screen – women staring from dark-ringed eyes, thin children, men cowed by helplessness. War fever was stoked by patriotic films and the refugees looked nobler in the picture house than they did on the fish quay.

'Poor souls,' said Mary McKenna.

They had sung the national anthem and were buttoning their coats against the chill night air outside the cinema.

'I wonder what Mike's up to?' she added absently.

'He'll be half blotto by now,' said Jack.

Kitty squeezed his arm and snuggled into him. 'I'm glad you didn join up. I'd die if you went.'

'Jack goes his own way,' said Mary McKenna. 'Like the cat.'

Rain fell, at first lightly then in a downpour.

'You two go on,' he said. 'I want to make sure the horses are all right.'

'Jack,' Kitty sighed.

'Leave him, love,' Mary said. 'Thank your lucky stars it's a horse and not another woman or the pub.'

Behind the privet, wet gardens were filling the darkness with scent. The rain hammered down and died leaving the sky clear again. Now the stars had the hard brilliance of winter and the night was transformed. He fumbled the padlock and opened the gates. One of the yard she-cats bounded across the cobbles but refused to be stroked. He went inside the stables and lit the lantern. The horses were all on their feet facing inwards as though they were expecting him. Jack walked slowly up the gangway calling their names and lingering at each stall to stroke the face lowered to his light.

'Maggie, Goosie, Janner, Rook, Tacker, Solomon, Melody, Bathsheba, Rosie, my Beth, Major, Zion, David, Joseph, Captain, Prince' – and back again between the silent ranks of animals while the rats rustled along the floor of the loft above and raindrops pattered into the darkness.

'Goodnight, my beauties.'

He returned to the terrace via the King Bill. The half-mumbled remarks intended to be heard, and the glances of the elderly left him unruffled. Kitty had stepped from the bath in front of the fire when he came home. She towelled herself with a bashfulness she never displayed upstairs, as though nudity and sex were improper in the living room. Her body gleamed pink and gold, and water beaded and fell from her breasts. The firelight threw her shadow on the far wall but his mind was elsewhere.

'What's wrong?' she whispered.

'I remembered something that struck me the night war was declared. In the big children's room at school they had this picture of the Charge of the Light Brigade. Grey horses were galloping into the cannon fire and dying horribly. It was a corner of horse hell and when the fireworks were banging to celebrate the start of this all I could see was those animls flying into death. And I knew it would happen again.'

'To Beth?'

'Perhaps. She's a horse.'

'Old Chancellor wouldn't sell her, never. He loves her almost as much as you do.'

'What if he hasn't any choice? Palfrey says the army is short of horses.'

'It won't happen, Jack.' She wriggled into her nightshirt and began drying her hair. 'They've got motor cars and lorries and things these days. Beth's a draught animal. No self-respecting gent would want to chuck a saddle on her.'

'She's built like a carriage horse. They'd find a use for her. A use!' He shut his eyes and grimaced. 'All that comradeship and trust and loyalty betrayed. They never get considered.'

He rested a foot on the fender, trying to fight the misery.

'All them horses in all the wars, killed or maimed or buggered up in battle. Heroes ridin' the real heroes – no, not heroes, innocents. Like they were riding dumb children to their deaths.'

'Stop it, Jack. Please.'

'That's the trouble. I can't tell anyone. I can't make Mum understand or you understand. I'm walking down a road in the rain by myself. It's always been that way. Always.'

'You idn alone, dear. I love you and I'm here with you.'

'They never know what we've got in store for them. They never suspect us or doubt us, and they can't question us. They just go on giving all the time right to the end. And we've used them.'

'The army have got their own horses.'

'Yes,' he grinned mirthlessly. 'Ready to trot into the jaws of death again. A touch of the spurs, gee-up and off you go.'

'But not Beth.'

'Beth's kind. And the lads from the yard who went off waving bloody flags and singing "Rule Britannia" are part of the damned awful deceit.'

His eyes glistened and she touched them with her fingertips, astonished. 'Jack, you'm crying!'

'Must be the booze.'

'Let's go to bed, sweetheart.'

'Yes.'

Then the sharp blaze of passion and her bare white arms held up to the ceiling.

32

The war was in possession of the national consciousness and the minds fluttering over the newspaper headlines measured the passing weeks in battles: 23 August, The Battle of Mons and the retreat; 6 September, the opening of the Battle of the Marne and the German retreat to the Aisne where the Battle of the Aisne commenced on 13 September. But swift victory was no nearer as the chestnut leaves yellowed and the plough teams opened the earth. The stubble fires smoked, mist and dew lay longer in the valley and the sun set the thatch steaming behind showers.

Albert Wotton lit a cigarette despite the asthma which the yard staff took for granted and were apt to mock. His willingness to please by simply not offending no longer rankled. He was a considerate, somewhat baffled old man with a nephew who was preparing to do a hero's job in Flanders.

'Little Charlie,' he would smile. 'Just a tacker and can't wait to be over there giving the Hun hell. His mother had a letter from him Friday. He asked after you Jack. "Do you know what outfit Jack McKenna is with?" Them's the boy's own words.'

'"The Slackers Brigade",' Luscombe grunted and ambled off to collect his horse. No one commented but for the first time since the outbreak of war backs were turned on Jack and someone hissed when he hitched Beth and Bathsheba to the wagon. His mother spoke often of a pilgrimage to Mount Brandon, the holy mountain. In the winter rain she would say to the very top. Not Cider Mill Tor or one of Dartmoor's outcrops that tugged at the guts. He closed his mind and dragged a sleeve across his mouth. The horses stood waiting for instructions. Then more than ever he felt a need to share their simplicity.

The first weekend after Michaelmas some of the yard animals were taken to Tor Barton and set loose. They galloped together, loving the sunshine and the company of their own kind. Back and forth across the hills they ran as dusk thickened to darkness. A sheep coughed, the wind came whispering up from the orchards and a badger sneezed. Then the night rang to the hollow trilling of hooves before the horses gathered silently at Iona's burial mound.

'Why did they take Moony?' said Kitty. 'He's more trouble than he's worth.'

'But he's also big and strong,' her mother-in-law smiled. 'And he does what he's told. Michael, on the other hand, will have them officers hoppin'.'

It's still a game, Dora thought, laying down her book. Toy soldiers charging around and banging drums and marching up and down hills. Mrs McKenna actually believed the story of the Angels of Mons whom the newspapers claimed had helped the British troops. The boys had all gone off to play, only this time when they were shot there would be no counting to twenty and swift smiling resurrection.

Dora sighed. Jack had become more of an enigma. The reluctance of the Lansworthy Mill Quakers to kill fellow Christians was understandable but who would have credited him with strong principles? The three women sat before the fire drinking tea from Kitty's best china.

'Jack will be home latish tonight,' Kitty said, smiling, and Dora saw the warmth cloud Mrs McKenna's eyes. Unconsciously she began rocking and humming like a mother clutching a baby to her bosom. Then Dora understood. Michael was the necessary sacrifice to be tossed in the neighbour's faces if they dared to criticise Jack. The realisation was chilling.

'Anyone home?' called Jack's voice.

Mrs McKenna and her daughter-in-law grinned at each other like children sharing a secret.

'Are you going to tell him, Kitty?' said the older woman.

'Shouldn't I wait till he's had his supper?'

'Lord, no! Tell him this instant.'

So when Jack padded to the fireside in his socks he learnt he was to be a father. Watching husband and wife embrace Dora felt a pang of jealousy and was conscious of Mary McKenna's surprised stare.

Dead leaves drifted across the euphoria and the dark, persistent rains of November brought with them rumours of another Allied offensive. 'Wipers' Mr Widdicombe called it. He took off his cap and the sweat gleamed on his bald head.

'I looked it up in the atlas. It's a town in Flanders. Apparently we're doing fine. Doing fine! That's a joke. Kitchener's pals pretended we didn't exist a few months ago. Now the lads are khaki heroes. Our betters have let us out of the slums and ghettoes to fight their war. That's nice of them. But when it's over they'll make sure everything's back to normal.'

'It's our country, too, Dad,' said Kitty.

'Don't be bloody daft. We rent a few rooms and keep out of the way. It's their country.'

'You and Dora never let up,' she said.

'Dora's applied for a job down Chancellor's yard.'

'Doing what?'

'Carting. They're short of men.'

'Tidn proper,' Kitty said, the colour rising in her face. 'All them boys gawpin' at her.'

'She'll cope.'

'She'll enjoy it!'

Lansworthy lay in the silence of an autumn morning. Mist hid the bay and the wind slept. Another small fleet of Belgian fishing boats crept to the quayside at Mary's Haven, but the battle on foreign soil remained impossibly remote and romantic. The 'bestial Hun' who 'bayoneted babies' and 'raped nuns' was tasting 'British cold steel'. Charlie Widdicombe crumpled the newspaper in his fists. Kitty was hooking the bath up in the yard. No matter what happened, Widdicombe thought, trivia had the final say because terrible things always happened elsewhere to other people.

Long shadows were spreading over the countryside.

272

Lapwings tumbled above Clennon's wetlands. The moisture on the spiders' webs caught the sun in a broad tension of light.

Jack sat on the empty cart partly aware of Dora following every flick of his wrists with comical intensity. Beth walked up the lane jerking her head whenever the raindrops falling off the trees struck an eyelid or an ear. That morning she had been clipped trace high and had visited the farrier. Now the pleasant smell of the farmland rose around her. The sky was blue between boughs and the woodpigeons' song woke memories of spring. Beth felt alive in a thrilling sort of way. Her muscles glowed and she lifted her legs high and set down her hooves with a crunch. Like a filly, Jack smiled. The past would flicker and flare up, borrowing from autumn's sadness. The mare entered the bullock yard and Jack took her to the barn and forked hay down from the loft. Maddock regarded him sullenly although he was at pains to ignore Dora.

'There's more important work over in Flanders, Irish.'

Jack stared through him.

'Doan it bother you?' the farmer continued. 'Ridin' around all day with a maid when you should be doin' your duty like the rest of them?'

'What's his duty?' Dora asked.

'I idn speakin' to you,' Maddock said. 'If I was boss down the yard he'd get the sack.'

'But you're not the boss,' said Dora.

The man turned and glared at her. 'Out here I am and I want him up there to know he's not welcome. My boy's doin' his dirty work.'

'Don't be so damn childish,' Dora snapped.

'Bloody Socialist no-good,' Maddock roared and Jack laughed.

The trip back to the yard was less cheerful.

'You won't give in, Jack?' she said.

'No chance,' he grinned. 'In another year I'll own Beth. Then I'm away.'

'Where to?'

He shrugged. 'A place where I'm not Irish Jack. I promised Beth. I'll put Kitty and the furniture in my cart and just set off.'

Dora's serious face surprised him.

'What's wrong?' he said.

'You look like a soldier in that cap and top coat. They always dress us up in uniforms – maids, chaffeurs, railway workers, carters, shop assistants. They're scared stiff of individuals.'

'Who are "they"?'

'Lord French, Sir Douglas Haig, Chancellor, the GWR.'

'Edward Daubeny and Rupert Chancellor are both in uniform doing their bit as Luscombe calls it.'

'Of course they are! They have to set an example if the herd is to follow.'

'Is it that simple, Dora? Them and us?'

'Yes,' she said.

'Bugger politics and wars and people hating each other,' he declaimed, so loudly she jumped. 'I like Edward Daubeny. Why can't we just get on with living?'

It proved a cruel month. Arthur Maddock and Moony were killed when their gun exploded on the firing range, and Rupert Chancellor and Charlie Wotton fell at Ypres.

'Died instantly,' said Albert Wotton through his tears. 'Didn feel a thing. Well, I suppose us should be grateful – poor l'il tacker.'

Sidney Chancellor visited the yard to console the carter and share the grief.

'They died doing their duty.'

Jack ran the horn comb through Beth's mane, waiting for a chance to speak, but the old man turned abruptly and walked away.

'Mr Chancellor,' Jack called but the tall figure squared its shoulders and was gone.

'He's seen through your brown-nosing,' Luscombe said, and Jack grabbed him by the lapels of his greatcoat.

'Not another word, you tub of lard. Not a word – now or ever again. Understand?'

Luscombe choked and nodded.

'Fine. So you keep your mouth shut and get out on the streets or one of Dora Widdicombe's mates can have your job.'

'He isn't to blame,' said Dora. She stood hands on hips, the hem of her skirt wet and muddy and her face flushed by the wind. 'He's forced to work like an ox for a pittance. No wonder he's surly.'

'You've got too much lip. From now on leave your bloody

274

soapbox at home.'

'I didn't realise you were so pig-headed,' Dora fumed.

'Finish mucking out,' Jack said. 'Grab a barrow and fork and show us you're worth your wages.'

The Three Towns rang their bells for the dead soldiers. As if they care, he thought, ramming his fists into the trouser pockets of his best suit. A thrush sang from one of Grosvenor Road's plane trees. The melody washed over his recollection of Mrs Endacott's wan face of ill health and grief. Moony was lying alone in the French soil, alone forever. 'Forever.' He closed his eyes and clenched his teeth but the bird continued its song.

By the time he had reached the harbour misgivings loomed large. Maybe it would have been easier on a dull morning. The Sunday was bright enough for spring. He walked up the drive flanked by Portuguese laurel and knocked at the door. The maid hesitated before letting him in.

He stood in a lofty hall hung with oils of landscapes and highland cattle. A woman's voice said, 'McKenna? Do we know a McKenna, Ormond?'

'Good lord!' Ormond exclaimed, stepping out of the drawing room. 'The stupid girl has actually let him in.'

Mrs Chancellor's face appeared at his shoulder.

'Well, McKenna, what does this mean?' Ormond prompted.

'I came to tell you how sorry me and the missus are about Master Rupert,' Jack said.

The woman's heavy eyes were still unwilling to accept the reality of her son's death. Oh Christ, Jack thought, I shouldn't have bothered. I'm only making things worse.

The Chancellors continued to stare from the doorway, half hidden by big, leafy pot plants and making no effort to close the gap between themselves and their unwelcome visitor. The colour rose in Jack's cheeks. Of course! I should have used the back door because working-class condolences don't amount to much when the father of the dead subaltern is a shit.

'It's a terrible business,' he mumbled. 'Master Rupert being so young.'

'He died instantly and did not suffer,' Ormond said.

'Did McKenna serve under him?' Mrs Chancellor frowned.

'McKenna works at the yard,' said Ormond. 'I believe his brother is at the Front.'

275

The woman nodded dismissively. Tributes had been paid and accepted. Then the maid was ushering him out to reflect on the folly that had nudged him towards Roundham when he should have been at Mass. He came off the headland onto Goodrington Sands. 'Died instantly.' 'Did not suffer.' Jesus! As if the words made everything acceptable.

An off-shore breeze was stiffening the waves into walls which dumped down on the beach and scattered the dunlin and turnstones. Small waders thronged the shore, running with a blur of legs whenever a wave broke.

More than ever Jack was conscious of the dignity of horses. He would loose Beth from her gears and attend to her needs reluctant to speak to anyone. At the end of the grooming after a hard round he found Palfrey waiting for him in the gang way.

'Ormond's keen to sell some of the animals to the army,' said the horsemaster.

'Including Beth?' Jack said stonily.

Palfrey lit his pipe. 'His motives are good enough. We've a surplus of horses and the army is crying out for them.'

'And Beth will have to go.'

'Not necessarily. You know how the old man feels about her. We'll probably lose half the animals.'

'That bastard Ormond.'

'He's given a lot to the war effort – including a son. It's about time you started to think of something other than horseflesh.'

'It's our war, not their's. No one's asked them if they want to take the King's shilling.'

'Do you think that when you work them? No one asks them if they enjoy hauling carts in the rain from dawn to dusk. Don't be bloody daft, boy. It's never that simple.'

Jack brushed him aside, speechless with rage.

'You can't alter the way things are,' Palfrey called into the darkness.

She knew he had come home angry. The slamming door pressed the kitchen curtains to the window for an instant.

Throughout the meal she waited for his mood to change.

'Is it the boys?' she said when the silence had become unbearable. 'Is it Moony and Arthur and little Charlie Wotton?'

'Come and sit on my lap, Kitty.'

'Tell us, Jack.' She kissed his broken fingernails.

'There's nothing to tell. The job just sickens me sometimes.'

'Is Beth ill?'

'No, but I will be if you keep nagging.'

Happiness was fragmentary. Kitty shaking and folding the tablecloth. Kitty yawning on the edge of the bed, pulling on a stocking, her shoulders clothed only in the shadow of his caresses. From the bedroom window the vision of her hanging out the clothes, pegs clamped in her teeth, and a cat watching the shirt flap on the line. Her painstaking progress through a newspaper.

Oddly enough it was the trivia of married life and not the moments of grand passion which retained their clarity.

'The German bakery over Abbot's Quay was looted and burnt the other night. They say old Braun was signalling to German warships out on the bay.'

'They?' he sighed, staring at the ceiling.

'Everyone.'

'The lynch mob.'

'Why are you so awkward?'

'Why are you so lovely? I swear I could eat you.'

She pressed her lips to his chest and whispered; 'Do you know what I dread more'n anything? Being a widow.'

Before he could reply she raised herself on her elbows.

'I saw some today. Oh God, Jack. One wadn much older than me. She was all in black. Poor little lady. My heart bled for her. And Mrs Endacott! Your mum says it won't be long before they put her in the union. Her's going ga-ga.'

With Christmas approaching the band was out again in Station Square; so were the flags and girls from Helen Daubeny's set dispensing patriotism and cigarettes. The widows stayed at home as late that afternoon the train steamed into Lansworthy Station full of soldiers who had once been merely brothers, husbands or sons. Among them were a handful of what the press called 'Our glorious wounded'. The cheering was hushed when the badly injured were carried to the ambulances, but the noise swelled as the walking wounded emerged. The crowd sang 'Tipperary' and saw off the setting sun with 'Land of Hope and Glory'.

277

'Edward Daubeny has a bandaged head,' said Dora, standing on tiptoe.

'Officers get the best wounds,' Mary McKenna smiled.

'The lieutenant picked up a bit of shrapnel at the Front,' said Old Bob.

'And Mike picked up a bit of shrapnel in the arse,' Jack grinned. 'Look Mum,' he added, 'the lad will want to have a wet before he comes home for the hero treatment. Give him a kiss and go on back with Kitty. I'll try to keep him sober.'

The shuffling gait he put down to the buttock wound.

'How did you manage to cop one in the bum if you were pointing in the right direction?' Jack said, shouldering his brother's kit bag.

'Arse first. Old Gunner drill,' from the look of smiling despair.

They shook hands. Michael's greatcoat smelt of stale cigarette smoke and trench mud. His cap was perched on the back of his head but he was a pasty-faced, hollow-cheeked stranger whose unstedy movements belonged to old age.

'Why do they keep singin' and shoutin'?'

'They're glad to see you.'

'Well, I'm not glad to see those dozy buggers,' he said on an impassioned outburst. Then he giggled. 'Good old Jack, you always know what's best. You guessed from the very beginning it was just a dirty bloody trick, didn't you?'

He groaned and wiped his forehead. 'Why don't them noisy buggers shut up. You shout at the guns but they never stop.'

'It'll be quiet up the Globe.'

'Lucy's lovely lies,' Michael laughed. 'Ormond banging one off in Hazel Cundy. You don't believe that, do you Jack?'

'No. Ormond's a watcher not a doer. Lucy would talk the pope into a noose.'

'Everything happens in Lansworthy. Nothing happens in Flanders, except blokes get killed.'

'You haven't,' said Jack.

'Not yet. Give Jerry a chance and he'll soon put that straight.'

'Mum would give you hell if you got killed.'

The noise faded behind them and they had Palace Avenue to themselves. Michael laid a hand on his brother's arm. 'She's a sham. All she cares about is you. So stay home – keep her happy.'

278

He laughed and coughed and staggered like an uncertain child play-acting. On the corner of the avenue and Winner Street five or six young ladies had formed a half circle to sing patriotic songs. Another of their group was waiting to hand a rose to anyone in uniform who passed. Christmas shoppers stood close by, applauding and cheering whenever she made a successful pounce. A few servicemen, an elderly shop assistant noted, had acted churlishly, turning their backs and stalking off. Jack glanced at his brother. The manic, fixed grin had turned his face into a Hallow'een mask, but he took the rose and the crowd which was growing by the minute voiced its approval. The young ladies sang on, and reached the 'God who made ye mighty' part of 'Land of Hope and Glory'.

'Sing up, tommy,' laughed the girl with the flowers. 'Sing up, sing up – it's your song.'

'Bloody sing? Bloody sing that shit?' Michael shouted. Savagely he plucked the red petals off the rose and scattered them at his feet. Most of the choir fell silent, sensing something unpleasant developing.

'You stupid bloody cow. There's no glory. There's nothing.' His chin jutted and his eyes were tightly shut. 'There's just cold bloody awful nothing. Fear so bad your shit runs free. You leak shit every time a five-nine explodes. Sing about that.'

He dredged up a great sob and the rest of the choir faltered into silence.

'Stick a rose in the shit. Give it a medal. Save this – this puke for the poor stupid bastards about to go out there.'

His shoulders shook and the tears came in a gush. A long worm of mucus slipped free of one nostril and slid into the corner of his mouth. Then the young lady dropped her roses and recoiled aghast, lifting her hands to her face.

'Bloody go,' he sobbed, 'you and your soddin' lie. Go.'

Jack wrapped an arm round his shoulders and led him up Winner Street. Dusk was creeping over the far buildings and the lamps were on. Shop windows laid rectangles of light on the pavements.

'Blow your nose and we'll grab a pint,' said Jack.

'Sorry about that. Sorry,' Michael said in a broken voice. '"Land of Hope and bloody Glory!" Out there it's just so much shit. Christ! I wanted to come home. When I copped a Blighty

279

wound I could hardly stop myself dancin' with joy. Now I'm here I wish I was back with the lads.'

He shuddered and the church bells began to peal again.

'Merry Christmas, Jack,' Michael smiled, unlatching the pub door and struggling out of his big pack.

They brought their drinks to a corner table, glad the bar was nearly empty. A whippet sprawled before the fire.

'As long as there's no "Rule Britannia",' Michael said and he took off his cap.

The curls Jack remembered had been cropped to sweat-greased stubble which exaggerated the size and darkness of his eyes. He lifted the pint pot to his lips and gulped.

'Nectar of the gods after that foreign gnats' piss – Christ! What a bloody hole it is over there. Shit, mud, bits of dead blokes and animals. Your horses are taking a pounding but the rats don't mind. You've never seen rats that size. Christ, it's quiet here. Get us a double rum, there's a good chap.'

They drank steadily while other customers trickled in and the hum of conversation grew.

'D'you know what the war is, Jack? It's cold, wet, noisy fear. You crouch in your hole by the gun and they shell you. Then you give it back. Holes and sweat and cold and noise. But you can't run because you're shit scared, paralysed.'

'The papers speak of a stalemate,' Jack said.

Michael paused, blinked and let the alcohol coin a response.

'Don't let them trick you into khaki. Stay home. The war will never end. The generals don't want it to because they're mad. Now another rum. The stuff the battery gets is no more than coloured water. The CO is a teetotal bastard.'

Then he sang softly:

> I don't want to join the bloody army.
> I don't want to go into the war.
> I want no more to roam,
> I'd rather stay at home,
> Living on the earnings of a whore.

His left eyelid closed and twitched, and he giggled. Jack turned away afraid to speak.

33

Winter provided the stage props for pessimism – the carcass of a sheep hollowed out by foxes, the wind moaning in a badger's skull, withered leaves in the hedge bottom, water lying dead under ice. Yet the horses galloping over the fields were as alive as the stream gliding down the valley.

Beth did not like the cold but a spell at Tor Barton with a minor eye infection meant the chance to kick her heels and run free of the shafts. The farm horses welcomed her and because the weather was fine shared the pasture beneath the tor on the rest day. At the end of a bright afternoon sunset would fade to dusk and stillness. Then Trant would call them to the gate and lead them to the stables. It was comforting, the old man thought, to hear them stamping in their stalls as he hobbled through the lamplight. Despite his crippling ailment he was still susceptible to their serenity. When Jack wheeled his bicycle into the yard he heard the carter talking to them.

'Get your haids down, ma boodies, or come morning you won't be fit for ort.'

He would never forget the lantern glowing in the winter night and the smell of urine-soaked straw, and the purring Devon accent. Arthur Maddock had once been part of the scene, wobbling under the weight of two full pails and weaving a wet trail from the pump to the stables. But no more. The farmer fed rabbits' entrails to his sons' ferrets and cut Jack dead before the night swallowed him and his malice.

'He's got nothing to say,' Trant grunted. His loose front teeth came together in the hope they would take fresh root in his gums. 'Clicketty clicketty clack', they went, like mating turtles.

'Some hurt goes too deep for prayers and bible stuff. Words don't cure toothache or heartache.'

The doves massing in the sunlight on the barn roof were silent but the starlings sang loudly. Old men and boys gathered at the farmhouse steps to be given jobs. The manure heaps steamed and the frost failed to mask the reek of swedes. A score of pregnant ewes were penned under their warm, damp stink between the milking shed and the barn. Trant broke the ice on the big granite trough, quibbling his jaws and forcing the boys to hide their grins in handkerchiefs.

Jack arrived before breakfast time to look at Beth's eyes, and Trant accompanied him to the stall.

'Her's a lot better, boy,' and Jack waited for him to chatter his teeth. 'When be 'ee gwain to buy her?'

'Before the year's out.'

'Do it quick. That sod Ormond will sell off the stables if he has his way. Two of our geldings are joining Kitchener's Army next week. Palfrey tells me some of the bus companies are selling all their horses. Tez a wicked shame. They buggers will regret it. You can't rely on machines, no sir.'

'Old Chancellor is reluctant to let me have her.'

Trant shrugged. 'Things can only get worse now Master Rupert's dead. What's a few horses compared to a grandson? The old man will be thinking like that. He'll be thinking he owes it to the dead boy – just like Maddock pretends you idn alive. In his heart he reckons he owes it to Arthur and all the others like un who idn around to pamper horses and such.'

'I understand,' Jack said quietly.

'So do I,' Trant said and he clacked his teeth. 'You can't leave they animals, can 'ee boy?'

'No – I can't.'

'When I was a tacker the only mates I had was the old shires. Maister used to bawl at 'em but I didn. They were fine creatures, better'n humans.'

'Better than a lot of humans.'

282

'I'm glad I habn got a son,' Trant said. 'Christ knows I used to think I was hard done by havin' a barren wife. Now I can see it was God's will. This war has just begun if you read between the lines of what they tell 'ee in the papers.'

It was an opinion Palfrey shared. The bond between the horsemaster and his assistant was strong enough to heal any minor rifts. As far as Palfrey was concerned Jack's character was unblemished, and he was at pains to point out to Old Bob Sherwill, who had been recalled to the yard, the difference between conscience and cowardice. The sermon was delivered for Luscombe's benefit but the fat man's determination to hate had flared up again.

They were rubbing mutton fat onto the horses' hooves and discussing paper money. Back in January gold sovereigns had been called in and bank notes issued. It was still difficult to take the new currency seriously.

'A bit of bum paper!' Old Bob snorted. 'Worth ten shillings? They'm pullin' our legs.'

'Some say tis a government swindle,' said Luscombe.

'Who says?' Palfrey wanted to know.

'The lads up the Victoria and Albert.'

'The experts!' Palfrey said contemptuously. 'The lads up the V and A! You really are a bloody stupid old maid. I bet you think the world's flat and the moon's made of cheese.'

'All I know is,' Luscombe gulped, 'they boys out there should be home now. It's gone wrong, Mr Palfrey.'

The horsemaster's face softened and he stared down at his boots.

'Yes, it's gone wrong, Fred.'

But Ormond Chancellor's loss had not curtailed his bumptiousness. He breezed into the yard, tugging off his gloves and loosening his scarf. The morning mucking out and grooming was still under way and Palfrey resented the intrusion. Jesus wept, thought the horsemaster, he's going to give us one of they patriotic speeches!

The portly figure in black top coat and bowler marched to the middle of the yard, the gruel of mud and manure oozing over his boots. When the staff were assembled he cleared his throat and holding his gloves in one hand slapped them against his thigh. Like the army officer he isn't, Palfrey observed. Mullah ambled around the massed ankles placing his nose to interesting smells. Then Ormond began.

What the master wanted was more men from the yard to enlist. Apparently there was a sort of recruiting league in Station Lane and the G W R had a slight lead over Chancellor's, with the Co-op and Lansworthy Mill stables trailing badly.

'They've too many men near retirement age, and a fair sprinkling of conshies,' Ormond brayed. 'But the G W R put another three fellows in khaki this week. So you men in your thirties and forties take note. Lord Kitchener can use you and the country expects you to do your duty. Come on now – who's game?'

The cheer brought a growl rumbling off Mullah's chest. Old Bob watched Jack disappear into the stables as men and boys crowded round Ormond.

'My grandson went down with the *Bulwark*,' he murmured. 'I'm buggered if Irish don't puzzle me. What's he playing at?'

Palfrey puffed out his cheeks and sighed smoke. There was nothing to be said. Mullah squatted, slung out a hind leg and began to clean his slack, magenta scrotum. The wind moaned among the slates on the stable roof. Sherwill climbed the ladder and said, 'Be 'ee up there, boy?'

He was sitting on a pile of hay pretending to tie a bootlace. The clank of wagons crept over from the goods yard. Then recollection of his parents quarrelling rose from unhappiness. His mother was forever going to leave Father, never the reverse. Kevan McKenna had been content. Yes, the lodger by the fireside, aware of his good fortune and getting the best of both worlds.

'Do you want a chat?' Old Bob said awkwardly.

'No. Words aren't much cop. In the end it's just wind. My brother Mike got it right.'

'But what the lads are doing out in France idn bullshit.'

Jack got to his feet. 'All I know is I don't want to be part of the hating. The horses don't hate.'

'Horses don't run the world,' said Old Bob, impatience creeping into his voice.

'I wish to Christ no one did. I wish it was like it was in the beginning.'

'Well, it idn.' Sherwill kicked open the loft shutter and the explosion of light startled Jack. 'You can't turn back the clock, boy. You just have to do the best you can – get on with the job. The rest is up to God.'

'I'd like to know what God's up to.'

'If you knew that he wouldn be God,' Sherwill smiled. 'When I was your age I used to puzzle over things. Ridin' behind a horse gives 'ee too much time for chewing things over. Every once in a while the doubts get the better of me – even now. Why did my grandson have to die? and Moony and the little Wotton boy? Do you know I still think of the dog I had as a tacker. Her just disappeared one day and I never saw her agin. Why, I asked God, and he didn answer. I still ask.'

He hawked phlegm and spat. 'You see, I idn old in here,' tapping a fist on his chest. 'My heart idn old.'

They forked hay through the hatches into the cribs below. The wind fretted along the yard and Jack saw his brother swaying on the street corner, his face white and taut.

'There's nothing, nothing. Cold bloody awful nothing.'

Then the horses came galloping through the silver light, the hayloft vanished and he was standing on a great beach. The wave broke and rolled over the past leaving it as clean as new snow.

Lacey came home on leave with Hazel Cundy hanging on his arm. The couple were married in a ceremony that most folk agreed wiped the slate clean. Arthur was in uniform and he had done 'the proper thing' by walking Hazel to the altar.

'A bright pair of bliddy ornaments,' Old Bob scoffed. 'Some people have short memories but that sod don't pull the wool over my eyes.'

The horsemen parted company at the yard gates and on the way home Jack called at the King Bill for a pint. He found the Friday night bar crowded. The lamps were lit and the curtains drawn but there was room at the fireside and he stood resting an elbow on the mantelpiece. Flames swarmed up the chimney and again Michael came to mind. The boy had loved fires. Their father would have been proud of his replica, the happy-go-lucky beer-swilling soldier. Jack smiled and tilted his glass, unaware that the bar had fallen silent.

'Enjoy your ale,' said a sharp, female voice behind him.

285

'While you are pouring it down your gullet my brother and thousands like him are doing their duty.'

Jack set down his glass and turned to face her. Helen Daubeny's look of contempt was more theatrical than the expressions worn by her companions. The young ladies were wrapped up against the cold, for their mission meant a lot of walking and Lansworthy had a lot of pubs.

'Workers and fighters defending the shirkers,' Helen continued. 'Aren't you ashamed – or is the word unknown to cowards?'

Jack blushed, but he was trapped and the woman knew it.

'Why are you here,' she said, 'when you should be over there?'

The hand she withdrew from her muff held a white feather. Deftly she planted it in his buttonhole and some of the older men grunted their approval. Jack nodded, unable to react beyond a pretence of coolness.

When the women had departed he drank his beer without haste while the blood hammered at the base of his skull. His humiliation was indelibly printed on the evening. Men would talk about it for years. Words, he thought bitterly. 'You're not going to die, for God's sake.' Sunlight flooded the mental picture he had of Charlie Wotton on the cart at Churston. The spring of his life! Then the foal taken dead from Bathsheba's body. Standing among the winter stars the White Lady of Lansworthy was a symbol of God's remoteness. Or were the tears of the mothers and widows his tears? Did he find comfort in the horses who had kept their bargain with life in the tradition of all voiceless creatures?

The feather, he noticed, had come from a dove.

34

I saw Esau sawing wood,
And Esau saw I saw him;
Though Esau saw I saw him saw
Still Esau kept on sawing.

Blanche and Lily swung the heavy sash cord and little Betty Vosper chanted the rhyme as she skipped. The light clatter of her feet and the smack of the rope on the cobbles fetched Jack out of himself. Charlie Vosper was smoking at his front door.

'Have 'ee heard about old mother Endacott?' the dark bearded man said after they had exchanged 'good evenings'. 'Her fell down in the scullery and they've taken her to the workhouse, poor dab. Still tis for the best. Her can't look after herself.'

They, Jack thought. It's always They.

'We lost Melody and Punch this morning,' he said, easing his stiffness into the armchair and tugging at his bootlaces. 'When I got back from the round Palfrey told me the horses had been shipped off to some army camp. *They* took the horses. They – bloody They. Then They went and put Mrs Endacott in the grubber.'

'Let me do that for you,' Kitty said softly as the blackness of his mood reached out to her.

'None of it's right. None of it. The whole of life is just a shoddy damned trick. But I thought Old Chancellor would take care of the horses.'

'The war has done a lot of bad things to people.'

He held his hands to the blaze. 'I'm not Palfrey's assistant anymore. Old Bob's got his job back and I'm just a carter again. Ormond had to tell me himself. The little shit loved it. So did Luscombe.'

'But that's not fair!' Kitty cried.

'Sending Mrs Endacott to the workhouse isn't fair. Sending Melody to the war isn't fair. The boys' deaths weren't fair.'

'I hate Ormond Chancellor,' Kitty said in a trembling voice.

'But he believes he's right. He's a real patriot.'

'Rotton, dirty little snob.'

'A snob's heart can break just like yours, Kit. It's stupid to think the death of his son hasn't hurt him. Selling horses to the army probably makes him feel better.'

'But why take away your job?'

'I'm still alive. I'm safe at home, safe and sound as though nothing's happened or nothing's changed.'

'Bliddy war,' she whispered, wrapping her arms round his legs. 'Haven't they had enough? Can't they just call it a day and come home now?'

'That's too sane,' he smiled and stroked her hair. 'Mike was convinced the generals were all crazy.'

'Buy Beth tomorrow and we'll go to Ireland.'

'Do you think Ormond would let me have her? And the old man has changed. I can see it in his face. Loving and caring don't count anymore. It's all duty and honour and sacrifice.'

'I'm scared Jack. If they take that horse you'll be off after her. You will. You will.'

'"They" again,' he laughed. 'They won't take Beth. She's magic. How can they catch the wind?'

'Whatever happens let's move to a place where we're not known. I can't bear the stares and the talk.'

'And the white feathers?'

'Yes, that was horrible. Have you seen the notice in your mum's front room window? "A man from this house is serving in the forces". They're all over town.'

'Sure and isn't it a charm against evil spirits?' he grinned.

'Everyone wants to sweeten God. Ormond has sacrificed a couple of horses in memory of his son just like the stupid bloody Israelites who were always killing goats or cutting lambs' throats, as though God needed that sort of shit to put things right.'

Kitty and Mary McKenna were knitting for the men at the Front – comforters, mittens, waistcoats, scarves. The clicking needles brought them closer to Michael and his comrades. The crusade had frozen to a halt in the mud and squalor of trench warfare but the newspapers continued to drum up enthusiasm at home. Letters from serving soldiers were printed in the *Lansworthy Observer*. Reading them Jack kept seeing Michael's shuffling dance of bitterness among the rose petals. He lay in the candlelight and kissed the blue-shadowed curve of his wife's belly knowing the child was there.

As always the first intimations of spring and an inauspicius St Patrick's Day. The sparrows had nested in the yard and celandines gleamed down the valley. A drying wind lifted the dust off the fields but the hedges were still bare except for the blackthorn blossom. Then, with March less than two weeks old, Michael was killed at Neuve Chapelle. The official letter coincided with the official first day of spring, an irony which Jack was alone in noticing.

> Madam,
>   It is my painful duty to inform you that a report has this day been received from the War Office notifying the death of [Michael's serial number, rank, name, regiment and the date of his demise], and I am to express to you the sympathy and regret of the Army Council at your loss. The cause of death was [and a firm hand had written in the appropriate space]'killed in action'.

Mary McKenna's face said everything. She sat in the Joseph chair, the rest of the world excluded by her grief. Kitty's company was enough. The women held hands, the one pregnant and close to having her child, the other barren and full of loss. Wisps of grey hair lay across her brow and she looked old and ill and defeated.

'Mother of God,' she groaned. 'Mother of God help me.'

Her grip on Kitty's hand tightened. Then she swallowed half a dozen times, like a scared dog.

'Help me. Help me. Help me.' Tears gushed from a prolonged wail of grief. She was shivering although the room was uncomfortably warm. Clearly then Jack saw Michael coming through the door from work, the fog grey on his railway uniform.

'Oh Mike,' Jack whispered. 'Poor old lad.'

The ice water was churning in his bowels. Never coming home. Never. Long shadows played as the flames leapt and the coals crumbled red. Again his mother choked on misery and offered a plea to the empty air. Father O'Driscoll's arrival was a necessary intrusion. Mary returned to herself while her fingers plucked at the beads.

'He is at peace with God.'

No he's not, Jack thought. He's not up there playing the harp. Looking at the Truth was like staring into the sun. Michael was part of that blinding brightness.

Shrugging off his thoughts Jack smiled across the room at Kitty.

Dreamily she traced the curve of her pregnancy with a double set of fingertips and he was puzzled why the action should annoy him.

Day after day she continued the slow, downward sweep until the labour pains began and the baby was delivered.

Mary McKenna placed his supper on the table.

'A boy,' she said. 'And I know what you'll call him.'

'I'm going up to see Kit,' said Jack.

'She's all right, son – strong as a horse. Eat your supper.'

'No. Put it back in the oven. I want to see Kitty.'

She nodded and smiled on the brink of sarcasm.

'Don't say anything bad,' Jack said.

His mother thought a moment behind closed eyes.

'Sean wants to join up,' she murmured. 'When you're a mother there's no winning this war.'

'Please,' Jack said, fixing her with his pale gaze.

Spring sunlight dappled the bedroom walls and ceiling, and the blackbird sang from the garden wall.

'It doesn't matter.'

'What doesn't?' Kitty murmured.

290

'Nothing – except you and the baby.'

'And we'll call him Michael?'

'You don't mind?'

She smiled from the pillow and shook her head. In her arms was something very small.

The next day Sean joined the Devons and left another space at the McKenna fireside but the plaited jute continued to smack the cobbles of Angarrick Terrace.

> The wind and the rain and the wind blew high,
> The rain comes blattering from the sky,
> Blanche McKenna says she'll die
> If she don't get a bucko with a rolling eye.

Blackness was no longer inky. Gulls were on the wing and raindrops scattered from the trees. But the scent of spring flowers behind rain was an obscenity, for Michael had gone from it all. Michael, Moony, Arthur Maddock, Charlie and Rupert, the Vospers' eldest, gone and the blackbird sang in the darkness. Then O'Driscoll's words seemed incredibly stupid. The new Michael did not fill the gap left by the other. A birth could not cancel out a grief or lend meaning to a death. And if there was life after death why should it be like this one? Was all this so bloody perfect?

Sunday's curious enervation touched the Three Towns. He watered and fed Beth and threw a rug over her back. Riding her through the deserted streets was like going backwards in time. Horse-boy and filly and the dawn chorus crescendoing. They came off Roundham to Goodrington and galloped through the shallows. He was with her so everything was satisfactory. Her mane flowed loose and her hooves smashed into the small waves. She loved the coolness and the light and the way the world flowed around her legs. The spray rose and masked them while the gulls flashed in and out of her thoughts. She was alive in all her senses.

Returning along the shore she saw the sun blood red on the horizon and the bay running at her. The gleam beneath her hooves was delightful and his weight on her back reassuring. She flung herself forward to become part of the brightness. Horse and rider was transformed to light by the light of the new day whose scent was sharp as a knife. Her nostrils flared. Waves no higher than spring grass broke and melted back into the bay.

Jack was rubbing her down when old Mr Chancellor entered the stall. Rupert's death had deepened the lines in his face.

'I thought you'd be here, McKenna. Some things never change.'

'How are you keeping, sir?'

'Well enough. And you?'

'A bit under the weather. My brother Mike got killed in Flanders.'

'Yes, I know. I'm sorry. So many brave boys have – have . . .'

Their eyes met across the silence of the unfinished remark. Beth tugged hay through the bars of her crib and champed a mouthful.

'Pity we're not like her,' Chancellor said. 'The world would be a splendid place if we were.'

He leaned forward on his cane and watched the mare feed.

'I gave Sherwill his job back hoping you would decide to enlist. What on earth's kept you out of uniform, McKenna? You're not like the Quakers up the road or the rest of the pacifists.'

'I've got my reasons, sir.'

'And you don't mind people thinking you're a shirker?'

Jack picked up some fresh straw and continued the whisping of Beth's flanks. 'Folk can think what they like.'

'It's everyone's fight, lad, and you owe it to your pals not to stand back and watch. We're talking about the highest form of duty.'

'The highest form of duty, sir?'

'Defending your country and the Empire.'

'My brother said it was a bloody great trick and a mess.'

'A mess someone has to clear up,' Chancellor said, squaring his shoulders.

'Maybe they ought to put it to the soldiers on both sides. Ask them what they think.'

'That wouldn't do at all, McKenna. There are areas of life best left in the hands of those who know the ropes – our betters.'

'Then maybe they ought to fight it out among themselves, sir – general against general.'

'An Irish solution,' Chancellor said with the faintest of smiles, but his disapproval was obvious. Working away at

292

Beth's legs Jack knew an episode of his life had come to an end.

'What about Beth, sir? Can I still buy her? I've got the cash.'

Chancellor's brow furrowed. 'We'll have to see. The war has altered things, McKenna. We must all pull together for King and country.'

'She hasn't got a king or an empire.'

'But I have and so have you,' said Chancellor, his tone sharpening.

'Is that all that counts, sir – someone almost as invisible and distant as God, and the red bits on the map?'

'Get on with the grooming. Stick to what you understand and do as you're told, McKenna. In the end life is all about pulling your weight.'

The films at the picture house continued to fan the emotions of those stranded at the Home Front. 'England's Call' produced spontaneous applause as the national heroes – Raleigh, Nelson and Wellington – stepped from their portraits to demand more recruits. 'Britain Prepared' revealed Kitchener's Army in training. But some of the soldiers on leave spoilt the show. Captions like 'Away he went with throbbing heart' produced a barrage of ribald comments from the back stalls.

'Away he went shittin' himself,' a voice bawled.

'Bloody louts,' Mary McKenna fumed. 'They should know better.'

'They do know better,' said Jack when her account of the evening was delivered at the fireside of Number Eight. '"Throbbing hearts"! Was that our Mike for Christ's sake?'

'Michael was his father's son.'

'Good. No one cares what the ordinary tommy has to say. No one wants to spoil the jamboree. The waves have to be ruled by Britannia and bugger the price.'

'What about the babies?' said his mother. 'The ones the Germans bayoneted in Belgium? Father O'Driscoll says we're fightin' Satan's army.'

'And blokes like Lacey are saints and crusaders?'

'The officers know how to knock him into shape. But the Germans are all the same – pillaging and looting and raping.'

'What's that?' Blanche whispered.

'Murderin' hostages, robbing folk and doing foul things to

women including nuns,' said Mary McKenna. 'It's all in the papers.'

'Sean will stop them coming here,' said Blanche from a shudder. Jack smiled and roughed up her hair.

'Shelling cathedrals,' Mary McKenna went on. 'Blowing up the house of the Lord!'

'He's got plenty of others,' said Jack.

'They crucified a Canadian soldier on a church door,' said Kitty, her eyes wide and round. The baby slept in her arms.

'Edward Daubeny will tell you things like that are rubbish,' Dora said. 'There are no crucifixions and babies aren't skewered on bayonets. But some of our lads are bound to gun wheels and flogged to within an inch of their lives for stepping out of line.'

They looked at her but no one put the question into words.

'I met him on the sea front,' she said, colouring. 'He's a very level-headed young man and he's got a lot of time for Jack.'

Mary McKenna's eyelids lowered and she nodded regally, reminding Jack of Ormond Chancellor's wife.

The spring night was silent but a little after dawn the curlews began to cry in the valley. Out of the mist winged the long-nebbed birds. Their calls pricked Beth's ears and she snorted and pawed the grass. Solomon and Bathsheba glanced at their companions. The moon was behind them, partly concealed by the tor. Primrose scent ghosted off the dew. Up on the skyline the farmhorses slept, some standing, others on their sides. And the curlews flew overhead to the feeding grounds on the Dart, delivering the clear double notes which gave them their name.

By the time the first of their chicks had emerged from the nests in the reeds the Cunard liner, *Lusitania*, had been torpedoed with the loss of over a thousand lives.

'So many children,' Kitty sobbed. She dropped the paper and buried her face in her hands. 'Why did 'em have to take those pictures of the poor little dead mites all lined up on the beach? Oh God, it's terrible.'

The baby's distress was rising to a shrill, prolonged bleat.

'For Christ's sake,' Jack breathed.

'At least he's alive,' Kitty snarled, and she lifted a face he had never seen before. 'He's your boy and he's here, safe and sound.

294

Why's the world gone mad? Why? Why?'

'Kitty,' he said, but she went to the cradle and comforted their son.

'I'm sorry, Kit – really I am. Maybe it's time I followed Sean into uniform.'

The baby was sobbing now in that bitter apparently inconsolable way which mothers take in their stride. Kitty crouched over the crade, rocking it and weeping.

'That's it. Run away and leave us. Go on, Jack. It's what you want to do.'

'He cries a lot, doesn't he,' Jack grinned.

'Because the poor little bugger's swimming in pee.' And she laughed.

> Johnny Morgan played the organ,
> Jimmy played the drum,
> His sister played the tambourine
> Till Father smacked her bum.

The skipping ropes ticked off the lengthening evenings and summer was passing at the jerky, unreal pace of a Charlie Chaplin film. Events leapt together and blurred.

'Irish doan hand out the brooms no more,' Luscombe chuckled. 'Little Paddy Brown Nose has run out of arses to creep around.'

'And he'll run out of brothers before he do's his bit.'

Mary McKenna laid aside her knitting and yawned. 'Of course we won't get any air raids. Why would the Hun want to bomb Lansworthy?'

'No zepp attacks,' Blanche said, a note of disappointment in her voice.

Heat bounced off the cobbles and the plaited jute cracked and the little figure rose and fell hypnotically. Dusk spread from the sea and lamplight bloomed. Then the noise of the sash cords was heard less often as the skipping craze died and hoops came back into favour. Helen Daubeny, wearing a khaki dress, condemned the Welsh miners' strike from a podium on the green, and after her patriotic speech the band played 'Dolly Gray' and 'Rule Britannia'. A large crowd waved flags and sang 'Keep the home fires burning'. Slogans were taking over. 'Remember the *Lusitania*', and a catalogue of German atrocities loaded with the foe's imagined vices. 'Hun frightfulness in Flanders'. War Office telegrams announcing the death of loved ones. The cry of anguish, the sobbing, the emptiness nothing but time could heal. Jack's head drooped and he clenched his fists on the reins. Beth stood patiently in the shafts wearing the flies and the grime like a penance. Four abreast the ranks of khaki figures marched along the road over Galmpton Common. Their boots crunched and the soldiers whistled until they were a smudge in the haze. Then the larks sang on and on, and the doves leaving Lord Warborough's columbarium showered the afternoon with small white feathers.

'Walk on Beth.' Out of the town into the South Hams while the last of summer bent the apple trees and swallows filled the spaces left behind by the swifts. A lane climbing to a high ridge. Memories of Charlie Wotton chirping at his side. Maybe it went on forever, in and out of dusk until the last horizon wrapped him in greyness. A young widow eyeing him from a mixture of resentment and lust. The lip of the cider jug cool. Tristford, Belsford, Hazard, Avonwick – the war had touched village and hamlet. The occasional black armband. Rooks sailing off the stubble in a cawing mass.

Beth's tail curled around her haunches and her head jerked up. The sky was dizzy with black, flapping birds, but he spoke to her and she settled again. There was little weight on her shoulders as she hauled the cart up the rise under the hedgerow beeches. In Totnes the torn placard proclaimed The Battle of Loos. Hearts faltered to ice at the sound of the telegraph boy's boots outside the door.

Rain slanted through the yellowing sycamores, turning the lanes to streams of mud and washing the smell of summer off the landscape.

'Do you know what requisitioning means?' Dora said. He lifted his head out of the sink and shook the water from his eyes.

'The army can take people's horses when they want to, Jack. There's a Remount Commission doing its best to fill that bottomless pit out in France with Beths and Bathshebas by the thousand.'

'Chancellor won't let her go,' said Kitty. 'He couldn.'

'It's out of his hands. What Edward has to say about conditions at the Front and the plight of the animals is not pleasant. Can't you cripple her or something?'

'Dora!' Kitty cried.

'Just enough to make her walk with a limp.'

'I couldn't harm her,' Jack said. 'And I bet this is just another rumour. If we listened to all the rumours we'd go mad.'

Dora shrugged. 'The military need horses so they'll take them off the streets and farms. The army will get what it wants, Jack – men and animals.'

'Not Beth,' said Kitty. 'There's stronger horses than her in Chancellor's stud.'

She clutched the baby to her breast and crooned.

'Sitting back and wishing don't make things happen,' Dora said showing her irritation. 'Sometimes you have to get out and turn the world upside down.'

35

That autumn the British came to the River Somme and faced
the German line from Hébuterne to Thiepval on the Ancre, and
from Thiepval to the banks of the Somme itself. Sean's letters
were catalogues of boredom, all marches, exercises and
fatigues, and visits to French villages. At home the lovely quiet
days left their mark on the Devon countryside. Light departing
in silence had the horses standing motionless and the yard staff
were reluctant to speak.

Jack worked with the bristle brush, putting his weight
behind each downward stroke and removing the dirt of the
day's round from Beth's coat. The mud caked on her legs
crumbled away under the curry comb. Then he picked out her
hooves and washed and dried her feather, and combed her mane.
Finally, after a brisk hand massage, she was wisped down.

Every so often the roan swung her head to look at him and he
made the noises she would carry into sleep. They stood in the
lantern light ringed with shadows, and Beth held her silence
between breaths. She had drunk fresh water, and eaten oats and
hay. Her bedding was clean. Everything was as it should be and
he was the source of her contentment. He brought nothing but
joy and kindness into her life. She was never put into a cold
collar or carelessly hitched to a shaft. Whenever he came up the
gangway at dawn her heart quickened and she snuffled a

greeting and laid her muzzle eagerly in his hands.

Leaving the yard on a crisp morning and peering at the lighted shop windows through her breath she would sometimes glimpse another place. Then the wind raked the beech leaves from the gutters and bore them upwards. The air had the bite of woodsmoke and soot. Her left rein tightened and she turned the corner. Mud gleamed on the street. Women gathered up their skirts to cross from one side to the other. A dog walked beside her before slipping into an alley. Motor cars overtook her, sounding their horns and when Jack flicked the reins she began to trot.

'You're still with us, then, McKenna,' old Mr Chancellor said ironically.

Jack lowered the tea chest to the pavement and grinned.

'But my young brother Sean is in France, mister.'

'Good show. When are you joining him?'

'I'm not.'

The old man turned crimson. His cane rattled on the cart wheel before it was pointed at Jack.

'I credited you with bags of pluck, McKenna, and thought you'd be good for the firm. Now I can see I was wrong.'

'I give you a fair day's work but I don't belong to Chancellor's. My life's my own.'

'Lucky the lads at the Front don't think that way. Lucky for England there are enough Charlie Wottons and Ruperts to cover up for the laggards. Lucky we have ladies like Nurse Cavell who are prepared to die for their country.'

Chancellor's outburst came to a breathless halt.

'What about your promise, mister?' Jack said. 'I'm to get Beth before Christmas. You gave your word.'

'My word?' Chancellor said harshly. 'My one and only obligation is to my country. I am offering as much as I can give to the war effort. Even my son is joining up. So do not speak to me about that animal, or what went on between us in peace time. Damn it all, man! Your own brother is pointing the finger at you.'

The ice water shifted in Jack's guts but he would not be silenced.

'Then the army will get the horses?'

'Not all of them. Obviously with the petrol shortage we'll

299

have to keep some.'

'Will you keep Beth, sir?'

'I'm leaving it to Mr Ormond. He's organising things for the Remount Commission. It really is a question of duty, McKenna. And if my horses can help bring a swift end to the war then the army shall have them, and Rupert won't have died in vain.'

Listening to the old man Jack knew he would have to take Beth off somewhere and hide her. There were plenty of coombes on Dartmoor where they could live rough. They would travel the back lanes in the dark and he would get her to Ireland. Maybe her green pastures lay over the water in the land his mother had created from fireside stories.

The following day he was told his services would no longer be required from the end of the week. It was a cold, misty morning with rumours of the requisitioning flying round the yard.

'They'm taking folk's pets as well as draught animals, hacks and hunters,' said Albert Wotton. 'Any horse above fifteen and a half hands is on the list. Stan Mugford up the GWR stud reckons something's happening today at Newton Abbot. Exeter's already copped it.'

'You know I've got the sack, Albert.'

'Yes, boy, and I'm bliddy sorry.'

Old Bob was also unhappy when he came into Beth's stall.

'Leave her, Jack,' he said, lowering his glance. 'Perce Hancock habn showed for work so Tom wants 'ee to hitch Rosie and Zion to the heavy wagon and take some stuff to the big house in Harbertonford – a new kitchen range, pianola, a couple of mangles; it's on your sheet.'

'Beth has to go to the farrier,' said Jack.

'One of the boys can take care of her. You'd best get on your way. Tis a long trip, and Jack,' he cleared his throat with his eyes still on the ground. 'You know how us feels about you having to leave. Move sharpish, son. Ormond will be buzzin' round the yard after breakfast and I doan suppose he's your favourite human being.'

The Clydesdale and the shire-cross gelding were a good pair. They paced amiably out of the mist into the sunshine. Well, Jack thought, this is it, Mike. Soon he would be excluded from Beth's life with the Remount Commission breathing down her neck, unless he acted quickly. On Saturday when he finished he would steal one of Palfrey's stable keys and come back for her around midnight. Then they would move across country to the moors. He had the Horse Fund and once he was clear of the country he would be just another farm labourer travelling the road to market. He might even get work in Wales and send for Kitty before going to Ireland.

At Berry Pomeroy he met an old man and boy mounted on cart horses, and leading another four. Jack was stopped and asked for a light but could not oblige. The man had a nervous shift of the eyes. They were the eyes of a watcher who was never required to pass an opinion or make a decision.

'Where you off?' Jack said.

'Newton Abbot and the muster.'

'What muster?'

'The Remount. They'm paying good prices for draught animals.'

Jack's heart sank as he watched the horses walk up the hill. More heavies passed, heading for the same destination. Most of them had the confident, rolling gait of creatures about to start a day's work.

The country road ran over high ground until it looped down to the South Hams village of Harbertonford. Jack braked and as the wagon began its long descent he suddenly realised why Sherwill had given him that particular job. Chancellor's would be sending horses to the muster. Beth, Bathsheba and Solomon would be there now with the other registered animals on the first stage of their journey to France.

'Christ,' he cried, throwing back his head. 'Christ.'

The old horses started at the sound of his voice. He sifted through panic and anger, letting in all sorts of absurd hopes. Maybe Chancellor had relented. Maybe the war was over. Maybe Beth was out on a safe country round.

'Don't let it happen, God.'

The road ran into nightmare now and cold, fluttering sickness curdled to despair.

The shire geldings Tacker, Janner, Rook and Goosie vanished never to be seen again. They were selected to haul heavy guns at the Somme where their dying was full of bewilderment. But they were loyal and trusting to the end in the tradition of their kind.

The break-up of the stables began shortly after the morning parade. Instead of being hitched to carts or wagons half the stud were led to the goods yard where the cattle trucks waited. Yet even the darkness and unsteady journey left them placid. Emerging at Newton Abbot Beth walked between Solomon and Bathsheba to the muster in the market place. Here several hundred horses had already been assembled – hunters, hacks and cobs as well as draught animals. They stood in a nervous mass while the soldiers strode among them checking their condition. Those who were accepted after the veterinary inspection were given the broad arrow brand on the quarter and had their tails and manes hogged.

Playfully Beth leaned forward to snip a button off the subaltern's tunic.

'The sorrel has spirit, anyway,' he said.

'Gun team material,' said his companion. 'There's some Clydesdale in her but we can't be too fussy. She carries herself like a good 'un.'

The young subaltern nodded sadly. 'Too good for the mess out there.'

'Chin up, old lad,' said the captain. 'The war will probably be over by the time these animals are ready for the Front.'

'Do you believe that, Frank?'

'No, but if I keep saying it it may come true.'

'Three blue flares at midnight,' the subaltern smiled.

The remounts were herded down the street to the station and Beth and her companions were once again driven into a cattle truck. The door slammed and the animals stood anxiously wondering what was happening. Each of them expected to hear the special human voice that controlled their work day. Their senses were alert to catch familiar smells and sounds, but they were not dismayed by the darkness and the company of strangers.

The train moved off. Trucks clanked and jerked forward, throwing some of the horses off balance. The younger, more excitable animals whinnied until the peace of their elders silenced them. Sunlight fanned through the slats. Beth,

Solomon and Bathsheba stood together, breathing each other's smell and drawing strength from their fellowship. It was just another night, however strange and unexpected; but it would end. Then Jack would come whistling to open the door and splash water into her trough.

The stables were half empty and the staff had gone home but Palfrey sat reading his newspaper in the tack room. Beth's stall was dark and silent, and Jack could think of nothing else as he loosed the horses from their gears and watered them. They were too tired to be groomed. Then he had to bring the lantern to Beth's stall and stand there making no effort to fight the misery. Palfrey's boots rang on the gangway.

'Old Bob did you a kindness boy. Ormond came round just after you got on the road. If the bugger had had his way you would have been told to walk Beth to the station yourself. Bob couldn hold back the tears when the animals were led into the trucks and the train pulled out.'

'Where has she gone?' Jack said quietly.

Palfrey took the pipe from his mouth and tapped the stem on the side of his nose.

'The Artillery, more'n likely. She's not too bulky and is light enough for the eighteen pounders. They'll trim the feather off her fetlocks and stick her in a gun team. Failing that it'll be a water cart or general service wagon. In a few months' time she'll be over there.'

'Christ! I should have listened to Dora.'

'Dora Widdicombe got the sack. Her gave Ormond a few home truths and us thought her was going to stick one on him.'

'Beth, Bathsheba, Solomon, Janner, Tacker, Rook and Goosie,' Jack whispered.

'And Major and Prince,' Palfrey said. 'They've half stripped the G W R stud and the Co-op. Folk will just have to come and get most of the stuff themselves.'

'It's like takin' children and setting them up for lunatics to shoot at.'

Palfrey nodded and placed the pipe back between his teeth.

'The magic never lasts, never has a chance,' Jack went on. 'We bugger it up every time. Do you know what I see whenever some priest like Father O'Driscoll talks about Jehovah God the

303

Father? An altar the size of Dartmoor standing in the middle of sod all and running with the blood of slaughtered innocents.' He fetched up a sigh. 'I love that horse and I swear she'll have her green pastures. I swear it.'

'What green pastures, Jack?'

'Just something I promised her when she was a foal.' His face darkened and he grinned. 'The old bugger goes and buries Iona then sends that living beauty off to war. Isn't that fine and Christian!'

'Go home and rest, boy. Don't do anything stupid. Sleep on it.'

By lantern light Jack's grin was jaundiced. He turned and set off along the gangway but before he reached the stable doors he stopped and said, 'They've sent my horse to the knackers.'

'Go home, Jack,' Tom Palfrey urged gently, hating the emptiness of the stalls at either hand; hating, too, his own helplessness.

Drugged with misery and lack of sleep Kitty said, 'I suppose you'll abandon us now.'

She blew into her cocoa and lifted her eyelashes a fraction.

'Abandon you?' he frowned, kicking off his boots and holding his feet to the blaze.

'You'll go after that horse – go and get killed. It's always been Beth, Beth, bloody Beth, above everything else.'

The baby began to cry.

'You will go, won't you Jack? Won't you? Damn you.'

'Kitty.'

'Don't go, darling. Please. Please. What would us do if anything happened to 'ee?'

She came across the hearth rug on her knees and raised her face to him. Reaching out he stroked her hair.

'Promise me, Jack.'

He shook his head and cupped her face in his hands. They've betrayed us like they've betrayed the horses, he thought. Don't you understand? We are the horses.

She had gone to bed and he was raking the embers to keep the fire alive for morning, recalling his Irish West Coast ancestry.

> I preserve the fire as Christ preserves all.
> Brigid at each end of the house,

Jesus in the centre.
The three angels
And the three apostles
Who are highest in the Kingdom of Grace,
Protect this house
And all in it, until dawn.

36

'Sit in Michael's chair,' said Mary McKenna, moving Dando. 'I had a letter from Sean this morning. He's doing well.'

Like it's a boy scout spree, Jack thought. But Michael's death had occurred in a far-off elsewhere so it lacked reality. He wondered then if his mother thought of the boy as just being away for good – an absentee time would never touch. Licking his lips and trying to swallow the misery, he imagined Beth in a strange place waiting for him to come and put things right. Dando thrust his muzzle into his hands and whined.

'Why aren't you at work?' Mary asked suddenly.

'I got the sack. Anyway, it's dead there now.'

'And how do you intend to live and keep your family?'

'Chancellor's isn't the only stud around here.'

'I'm surprised you didn't put two and two together about the muster.'

'I thought Ormond would wait for the Commission to come to Lansworthy. Then he could make a big thing of parting with the horses. Palfrey didn't let on. He's got a heart. So has Old Bob.'

'Kitty's right. You'll go now just like your brothers. You won't won't till you're lying next to Michael.'

'Don't cry,' he said gently.

Her head rocked from side to side as the tears flowed.

'Why do you keep crying?' Blanche said in a whisper. Is it because of Mike and Jack's horse?'

'For how it was. For what might have been. God Jesus! The pity of it all.' She choked and her nose ran. 'And Kevan gone so unprepared.'

Her eyes rounded. 'Do you suppose Michael has flowers on his grave?'

'Of course,' said Jack. 'France is a Christian country.'

He had to escape from the terrace, nagged by the memory of her galloping off Cider Mill Hill to greet him at the gate. Her mane would blow across his face and her eyes would speak to him, so eager was she for attention. The pain corkscrewed as he pushed the bicycle from the front door and pulled the cap down tight on his head.

'You idn goin' far, Jack,' Kitty cried.

'Just down the road. I've got something to do but I'll be home for supper.'

'Wrap up warm, love; tez goin' to snow.'

The rope cracked on the cobbles and the treble voice piped:

> Good King Wenceslaus
> Knocked a bobby senseless
> Right in the middle of
> Marks and Spencers.

It would be Christmas in a couple of weeks but there was nothing festive about the year's end. The ache for Beth returned again. The dark browns, blacks and greys of the season had come together to create a landscape which was an extension of his grief. He pedalled aimlessly into it and from the high ground above Totnes saw the hills of Dartmoor dusted with the first snows of winter. Hay Tor reminded him of the White Lady of Lansworthy who was deaf to prayer and indifferent to human suffering. The great granite tower was as remote and mysterious as the Swiss mountains he had seen in lantern slides. It stood waiting for him like all the nameless sensations of childhood made concrete and placed within reach.

He cycled across the afternoon and into the in-country of small fields and narrow abrupt lanes. A final uphill walk brought him to Cold East Cross and the moors. Lapwings scattered, crying on the wind, and Jack rested a moment.

307

Looking back he was aware of the great vistas smoking below where South Devon ran to the sea. The slow, far-off flocking of birds signalled the approach of night. Coombes were vanishing and lights were coming on.

He pedalled into starkness which was spread here and there with snow. Ponies in poor condition stood about breathing heavily. Again he saw and heard Beth. His fingers were freezing but he almost welcomed the pain because it was easier to bear than the heartache.

The road brought him to Hay Tor and he left his bicycle and crunched up through the snow to the rock. All about him he could feel winter preparing to launch itself on the lowlands. The whine of the wind in bracken and gorse held phantom horses. She is waiting for me in a strange place, he thought, climbing onto the snowy tor. Greyness spread on all sides and he felt he had reached the centre of something. Despair gave way to elation. He knew he would go and find her and keep the promise he had made during the first summer of her life. He knew also he was saying goodbye to the countryside he loved, but walking towards death was unbelievably exciting. Then he wanted Kitty and the baby and all the things the future might hold. Yet nothing could break the covenant. We are all on our way to somewhere else. Jack shivered, and the powder snow lifted and danced, and dusk cut into him.

The horses were unhappy in transit, and none more so than the sensitive Clydesdales and Clydesdale crosses. Throughout the long, slow journey Bathsheba fretted, and most of the animals in the cattle trucks who came from happy homes were distressed; but they waited patiently for release.

It was late afternoon when the train arrived at the marshalling yard and the horses were driven out of the city to the Remount Depot. Beth, Bathsheba and Solomon, and a few of the other light draught animals that were trim enough to be ridden, were allotted to the Royal Field Artillery. The friends' good fortune persisted and they were kept together while others suffered the anguish of being separated from lifelong companions.

Printed on haze the Norman cathedral dominated what had once been the capital of Saxon England. The smell and feel of the place perplexed Beth and some of the horses around her.

Their heads caught the last daylight as they jerked skyward. Light draught-crosses and hacks poured out of the suburbs and along the road into dark unknown countryside. But Beth knew Jack would be there at the end to feed and groom her. No matter how strange the day it would close in comfort and friendship.

Rain fell and turned to sleet as the blackness became inky. The lanterns swung and she expected at any moment to find herself in the stony lane leading to Tor Barton. Sleet wobbled down through the shifting light. On every side horses' eyes flashed and coats gleamed. At times she thought she saw Iona among the mares and geldings. Memories swelled her bewilderment. She gazed about her but neither nose nor eyes could decode the darkness. Bathsheba whinnied a cry full of alarm and enquiry. A cob bumped against her and flung her off balance. The men were shouting and whistling, and the cob rose on her back legs and pawed the air. A ripple of tension passed through the herd but the human voices were kind and the animals calmed down.

'You got to treat 'em like ladies,' said the sergeant major. 'You can't bawl out a horse or she'll bugger things up when you need her most.'

The horses were brought into stables with a single line of open stalls. Here they were tethered to the bars which served as gates and allowed to cool down. Then they were watered, fed and groomed.

Again Beth's heart lifted. Men in khaki jodhpurs and puttees came whistling along the gangway, but he was not among them and her head drooped. The building was too clean. There were none of the pleasant, layered smells she had encountered in the yard or up at the farm. Left alone for the night the horses stood tuned to the past waiting for their surroundings to take the shape of the home-dream. Outside, the darkness was shaken by the wind and squalls of sleet. No trucks clanked, no owls cried and there was no Mullah to run barking after stray cats.

The rest period passed, homesickness faded and the animals began to come to terms with their new life. They had good food and exercise and were well-treated. Those who had been neglected were clipped trace-high. The vet and farrier paid regular visits and Beth lost her feather. Like the other horses she gave her best according to the ethic of obedience governing all work horses.

The chalk downs beyond the park where the camp was situated brought the sky and winter dramatically into the lives of mares and geldings. The landscape was huge. Little space was left now for memories but Beth continued to look for him on the horizon. All things were made tolerable by the certainty of his coming. She galloped in the company of the fine, intelligent hacks and a carriage mare called Grace. Khaki figures stood watching them.

'Wouldn't wear roans like that in the Brigade if things was normal,' the sergeant said. 'But they ain't here for ceremonial duties. Once they get the mud of the Front on 'em they'll all look the same – poor buggers.'

Snow fell. With little puffs of breath the hares scampered over the fields, leaving their prints on the whiteness. Rooks cawed but were rarely seen. Routine stamped itself on the stables and those images of the past which had once been so vivid faded although a few animals were forever expecting the old life to return and take over.

Work at the camp was not hard. The light draught horses had to be broken to the saddle in preparation for pulling guns and ammunition limbers. They did not object to the weight of men on their backs and were in and out of the riding school in a fortnight. Beth and Bathsheba became the lead pair of a six-horse gun team, followed by Solomon and Grace and a couple of hacks called Chance and Liza. Their gears were fitted with quick-release buckles and when they were hitched to the limber pole their positions never varied. Each pair had its own driver who held two sets of crossed reins in his left hand and a short-handled whip in the other. Most of the men were as new to the business as the four-legged recruits and there were some comical mishaps.

But training in snow or freezing rain left little time for cheerfulness. The open countryside with its clumps of Scots pines had a doleful air and while the wind blew across the plain the batteries wheeled and swung through their exercises. The teams galloped the eighteen pounders into position, learning to think and act as one.

The weeks passed, and each drill was practised and mastered.

310

Then Beth's battery was moved closer to Winchester where, despite her allegiance to Jack, she began to respond to the kindness of her driver.

Stan Milburn was a middle-aged Geordie who had come to horses late in life, first as a Co-op coalman and now as an Artillery Driver. Tall, ungainly and short-sighted he would stare at the red roan through his glasses and keep his voice low recalling how he used to speak to his dog back in Durham. The smell of his pipe tobacco put Beth in mind of Palfrey and how things were before the world changed.

37

When morning broke there was stormlight in the sky and the hills were white. The drivers led their pairs out for the exercise with the wind flattening to a whisper and sparrows massing at the grain shed doors.

'Come on, my girls,' Stan grunted.

The pole bar was supported on neck, hip and withers and the team pulled the gun back and forth over the meadow. Soon the horses were steaming but the drill continued. The ammunition in the light wagon called a limber was attached to the gun trail and hauled at speed to the emplacements on the range. Here the eighteen pounder was unhitched and brought into position while Beth and her companions were returned to the picket lines.

The barking of the quick-fire guns disturbed the horses but the majority had been broken to town work and did not kick up a fuss. Those that became unmanageable were discharged as 'casters'.

The lucky ones, Stan thought, feeding shells into the baskets which were stacked horizontally on the limbers. A whiff of cordite carried to the lines and the teams shifted nervously. Then the battery commander galloped up, shouting orders. Men and animals relaxed, and the firing stopped. Once again the shock of the winter world rushed in upon Beth. Number

Seven Battery was sent across the plain with all its guns, general service wagons and limbers, and the men dug fresh pits. The grey sky had separated into small, sun-flushed clouds. Loneliness rose from the landscape and Beth wondered why he did not come. Light was undecided on the hills in a place that held no friendly smells. Then the guns were firing again and Chance was laying back her ears.

Being herd animals the horses felt secure in their own company although memories of past life would tug at them, especially after dark. The drivers were moved by their trust and willingness to serve; indeed, the number of tough Artillery men who doted on the animals surprised many subalterns.

As the weeks passed a rapport developed between driver and pair and each member of the team. The horses were hauling pieces and limbers or standing at the lines behind the action. They were out in all weathers but every evening the stables were waiting and the grooming was thorough. With the animals getting plenty of exercise it was easy to keep their coats clean but for Milburn the use of curry comb, body brushes and sponge was the pleasant part of horse management. He was shown how to twist straw into a rope and double it to make a pad or wisp. The wisping was good for an animal's skin and coat, but his awkwardness set Beth longing for winter evenings at the yard.

Horizons blurred. Over the dark land the gun teams raced and the drivers whooped all the way back to the tents. Then the animals were left to cool down in the lantern-lit stalls and the noise of stable life filtered through their fatigue.

Always on the brink of sleep Beth thought of him, never doubting he would be there one morning or evening. A man laughed, a young voice cried out and her ears pricked, but it was not Jack, and the hands laid on her neck, although kind, had no magic in them.

She snorted and shook her head. Deceived, Milburn stepped back a pace.

'There, there, lass,' he said, and she turned and looked at him. The question in her eyes went unobserved.

'Rest easy. No one's going to hurt thee.'

The gun drill had all the elements of ritual. Sometimes they worked to a lather and Bathsheba's body smell mingled with her own in the steam of effort. Grace was unused to hauling for long

313

periods but the exercise rapidly built up her stamina and if she flagged the other horses slowed to accommodate her. So between the five mares and the gelding a bond was born; yet Jack remained behind Beth's thoughts.

Often she woke hearing his footsteps only for them to fade into the thunder of rain on the roof. Her stablemates stirred, the windows rattled, and the squall left the moonlight wet and alive. Again she closed her eyes and became part of the brightness. The field was quivering. Light spilt off it like the glare off a knife blade. The brightness spread and thinned to reveal the horses coming out of it at a gallop.

One day Number Seven Battery passed a circle of huge, upright stones set in the downs. The grass powdered around the horses' hocks. It was very cold but winter was nearly spent and the rookeries close to camp were noisy with nesting birds. A clear sharp morning dawned unlike any other. The men went about their stable chores chattering and laughing. There was an air of excitement which gripped the entire battery. Then they left the camp – teams, guns, general service wagons and carts, officers mounted on their own horses. Soon the road to Southampton rang to the crunch and grate of wheels and the jingle of harness. Gradually the noise died as the column vanished beneath the valley mist. Dust settled and a wood pigeon crooned.

O'Driscoll shared Sidney Chancellor's angry dismay. He prided himself on the willingness of the young men in his flock to join the fight against the anti-Christ and Jack baffled him. Laying his forearms on the pulpit the priest incanted lines from Job 39:

Canst thou bind the sweet influence of the Pleiades or loose the bands of Orion? Canst thou bring forth Mazzaroth in his season? Or canst thou guide Arcturus with his sons? Canst thou set the dominion thereof in the earth?

Jack returned the old man's gaze, wondering if the words had special significance.

'Father O'Driscoll is coming round to talk to you this afternoon,' said Mary McKenna.

'He is not,' said Jack.

'Jack,' Kitty pleaded.

314

'He is not.' Then in a quieter voice. 'Are you making ends meet, Mum?'

'I'm managing. I've got some savings and Blanche is working full time. She says I could get a job charring at the store.'

Kitty caught her arm. 'Me and Jack have talked it over. We'd like to move in with you – if you'll have us. It'd be cheaper and easier for us all.'

'He hasn't been badgerin' you?' Mary McKenna said.

Kitty shook her head. 'It was my idea.'

'He'll go after that horse one day. Then we'll have a house full of women. A convent.'

'Jack won't leave me.' But her voice shook.

'Conscription will grab him love, if he doesn't decide to volunteer. They're taking single men now and it's just a question of time before the married ones are called up.'

'Tis all talk,' Kitty said. 'Jack wouldn leave us. Me and babby are more important that a bliddy horse.'

Mary McKenna lidded her eyes and peered through her lashes at her daughter-in-law, but she did not say what she thought.

'Don't be rude to the Father, Jack.'

'I won't be anything except absent when he calls. Jesus – it's my life!'

Edward Daubeny came home on leave and to his parents' chagrin took Dora out to the theatre in Abbot's Quay and to local restaurants. Charlie Widdicombe also disapproved.

'Edward would like to meet you again, Jack,' Dora said, holding Dando off her best coat. 'Sunday morning at Goodrington Beach if you can manage it.'

'What on earth have he and Jack in common?' Mary McKenna asked derisively.

Dora shrugged. 'Integrity, compassion.'

'But the Daubeny boy is in uniform and an officer.'

'They get on, Mrs McKenna,' said Dora.

'Is he a socialist?'

'Unfortunately no – just a nice human being.'

Kitty giggled. 'Dora's sweet on him.'

'No, Kit – I'm in love with him. When he's away I can hardly breathe with the worrying.'

They stared at her, too moved and surprised to speak.

315

'Old level-headed, votes-for-women Dora in love with an officer and a gentleman.' She sighed and gazed up at the ceiling.

'Are you goin' to marry un?' Kitty said.

'Of course not. Apart from anything else he doesn't want me to join the ranks of widows.'

'You sound as if you expect him to get killed.'

'He expects to get killed. All his friends are dead.'

'Oh this bloody awful war,' Mary McKenna whispered. 'So many good boys turned to corpses.'

'But his sister gave Jack a white feather,' said Lily.

'She's an empty-headed little so-and-so,' Dora smiled.

'And Edward's a good lad,' said Jack. 'I like him.'

'You thought old man Chancellor was the cat's whiskers, too,' said his mother.

'The war has got to him. Doesn't Father O'Driscoll blame everything on the Kaiser?'

Rain fell, light and warm and good for the crops. Jack walked the beach which the ebbing tide had wrinkled. Melody and her foal ran before him to melt into greyness. His heart lurched.

'Jack? Jack McKenna?'

The collar of Daubeny's waterproof was turned up against the rain that beaded the peak of his service cap. He looked older than his twenty-one years and some of the day's greyness was in his face.

'Like a gasper? No? I smoke all the time now.'

The cigarette was lit between cupped hands and Daubeny chuckled.

'Christ! It's good to be here by the sea knowing the bloody shells can't reach Lansworthy Bay.'

They strolled together along the wave-break.

'Listen, Jack, I hope you aren't contemplating taking the King's shilling.' Daubeny flicked his cigarette into the water. There was none of Michael's nervousness or tension about him. He was tall, slow-moving and rather graceful although he had the habit of hunching his shoulders.

'It would be another victory for the asses at the top who are responsible for this mess. Stay home and the men in the trenches will love you for it. It's a shitty do over there. I suppose when the last poor sod cops the last Blighty wound they'll have to blow the whistle on the business. Every bloody fresh volunteer prolongs it. God knows what conscription will do.'

He lit another cigarette and inhaled or disguised, perhaps, an indrawn sigh of despair. The raindrops on his moustache vanished when he choked and coughed.

'Me and Rupert thought it would be one great cavalry charge into glory. Most of the chaps had that notion. They were decent enough and bloody brave – officers and men. Then they were pitch-forked into hell, all of them, and no one at home seems to know the score.'

'Michael told me.'

'Seeing chaps get killed like that gives you the impression God has played just about the worst kind of trick by keeping you alive. There are no heroes, only victims. The mud out there is full of victims. Did you know Palfrey, Ormond and Josephs have all enlisted? Palfrey's gone to a cavalry regiment – poor stupid bastard. It's not like the Transvaal.'

They had reached the low line of rocks which divided North Sands from South Sands. The rain stopped but the sky remained overcast and oystercatchers were prising open shells. The weather had left the beach deserted.

'I'm sorry about Bethlehem.'

'Where will they have put her, Edward?'

'Probably the Field Artillery at Winchester. There are thousands of horses at the Front. God, man, you'll have a job finding her.'

'But I will,' Jack said softly.

'Is she so important?'

'She is.'

'More important than your wife and child?'

'No. It's a different kind of caring. I can't let her down. If you saw a child drowning in the surf out there you'd try to save her wouldn't you?'

'I suppose so,' Daubeny conceded, '– although I can't raise any enthusiasm for heroics.'

'If she's at Winchester I'll have her out and away with the minimum of heroics.'

'Ah! I see,' Daubeny chuckled. 'Well, that's a perfectly sane scheme, McKenna. The chaps in my battery would approve. Where will you take her?'

'Ireland, I suppose. My mother says horses are understood in

317

Kerry. Horse is a second language over there.'

Daubeny began to laugh. He wrapped an arm round Jack's shoulders and the two of them staggered about howling helplessly, knowing the idea was doomed and idiotic but loving it all the same. Daubeny's hat came off and he groped for it on his knees, still laughing.

'You mad bugger, McKenna. You beautiful mad bugger.'

'People will talk, Edward, if they catch us actin' like this.'

'Soldiers don't bother about people. Living in the death cell has its compensations.'

But the atmosphere at Number Eight was tomb-like. Too many women under one roof perhaps, Jack thought. Everything revolved around the baby until Sean came back for good after being gassed. Mrs McKenna tried to winkle him out of his shell but he would sit by the fire nodding mutely, unwilling or unable to speak about his experiences. When he drew breath he sounded like a sick sheep.

The hour before dawn was a threshold Jack had been unable to resist since childhood. He slid out of bed praying the baby would remain silent. Kitty was dead to the world, her face pressed in the pillow. He kissed her head and took in the fragrance of her hair. Dando growled softly from the foot of Mary McKenna's bed. The darkness breathed. It was warm and comforting and hard to leave.

He lit a candle and opened the Horse Fund box. One bank note would be sufficient for his needs; the remainder would see the family all right for months. He placed the money on top of his letter on the kitchen table. Now the goods trains were hooting and the cockerels crowing. The past spilt around as he opened the front door. But he had finished with the past. Maybe, he thought, closing the door gently behind him, he really wanted to go, Beth or no Beth. Maybe he disliked being on the outside looking in. Maybe we remain strangers to ourselves from the cradle to the grave.

Moony was speaking to the pig and Kevan McKenna was laughing and dancing over the cobbles. The plaited jute cracked out the rhythms of his own spent childhood.

318

38

The carriage window had steamed up. He rubbed a sleeve over the condensation and peered out. The countryside was still dark but dawn had broken and there was a high bank of cloud, grey, the colour of a herring gull's back. Superimposed on it was another lighter layer of grey, open in the centre like a stage and lit by the sun. Like a glimpse of heaven, Jack thought. The conscripts opposite him slept, mouths gaping and heads resting on the nearest shoulder.

The train puffed through wetlands dotted here and there with pollard willow. Its progress was stealthy. Everything has come to an end. Tom Palfrey, Josephs, Ormond Chancellor, the boys, the carters, the horses – they were all gone, and he had sneaked off in the night. France was the only place to go. Everyone he knew, living or dead, was on the other side of the channel. He smiled. Father O'Driscoll said each day a person lived shaped his soul. As a boy he had wanted to live like the horses, drinking stream water, eating grain, partaking of their magic. Now the day was brimming with light and what had been was gone. He dozed and let the ache for Kitty have its way. How had it all come about? All the deaths? So many endings while the seasons passed and young creatures entered the world unaware. No one, not even the Pope, knew why. Maybe they were all mad, God as well.

He stared out of his unhappiness at the cathedral. Pigeons burst silently from the tower and scattered behind the trees and rooftops. It was happening and he was part of it, yet he felt curiously detached, like an onlooker at a mysterious event. Three or four little boys shouldering wooden guns marched by singing 'Tipperary'. Jack hesitated at the barrack gates. The guards and military policemen looked him up and down and he grinned.

'Have you got any horses in there, mister?'

'A few,' said the sergeant.

'Can I have a look at them?'

'Why? Ain't you seen one before?'

'I like horses.'

The sergeant nodded and his companions smiled.

'When you're in uniform you'll get all the horses you want.' Jack's grin broadened.

'Follow me lad. The King can use experts like you. You are an expert aren't you?' The irony amused his companions.

'I was assistant horsemaster at the stud back home.'

'Comfortin' news,' the sergeant observed, shepherding Jack through the gates into the camp. 'Now you go in that 'ut and the nice officer will sort you out. Soon you'll have all the horses you want.'

Again there was a numbing sense of looking from the outside in at his own life. He entered a room where half a dozen men in their thirties or early forties sat with a crowd of boys who were probably eighteen but could have passed for fifteen-year-olds.

After the interviews the medical proved something of a formality and everyone seemed elated when they took the King's shilling and the oath. They collected their kit and were marched to the billets to join the other new recruits. Jack had a bed between a West Countryman who was surly and obsessively neat, and an amiable Scot. Once more the sense of isolation dulled his response. The hut was cold. It smelled of carbolic soap and all sorts of thin alien odours which heightened his discomfort. He was wearing khaki trousers, puttees and a shirt that was too big. His hair was cropped and he was miserably homesick; and as he sat writing to Kitty he knew the last bridge was burning.

★ ★ ★

320

The ferry had been converted to carry horses and mules which, because the journey was short, were stabled on deck. Some of them were unhappy about going abroad and required cruppers.

'Do you think they know?' Milburn remarked but the men next to him shrugged.

Beth led the team onto the ship and took her place in one of the pens that held four animals. The morning was grey and the docks stank of industrial grime. It was an offensive grey smell which persisted after the ferry cast off. Then there was the sky and the noise of the engines hacking into their thoughts. The world tilted under Beth's hooves but like her companions she stood relaxed, facing inwards and tethered to the breast rail. A long row of pens each side of the deck and another in the centre left the horses with plenty of room. They were never sideways to the roll and the coir matting beneath their hooves gave good grip. Immediately before embarkation all of them had been shod. Now they stood placidly, aware of the comings and goings of the men, and the gulls overhead.

When the sky had brightened the pens were mucked-out and the horses were walked around the deck. Some of the sailors watching the morning exercise were moved by the sight of the animals tossing their heads and calling to each other as the ship nosed through the Channel swells. There was an unutterable sadness in the parade of men and horses, and a dignity, too, that all save the meanest spirit could recognise.

The French coast appeared and the sea became choppy. Spray whipped over the bows, upsetting the horses furthest forward but Beth, Bathsheba and Solomon continued pulling hay from their nets. Milburn patted her flanks and she turned expecting to see another figure. The tugs departed, the noise died and the deck no longer tilted. One by one the animals were walked off onto the quay. Without haste the column assembled and while men and horses waited to move to the train the clamour of church bells crept out of the distance. There was then a swift draining of the men's enthusiasm, and morale dropped even lower when the other ranks learnt they were to travel in cattle trucks like the animals.

The faintest suggestion of spring was on the air but it failed to lift the hearts of the Devon horses. Their confusion mounted to anxiety as the train staggered across the French countryside,

321

stopping for long periods, and starting again, jerkily, with blasts of steam. At either hand the snuffling and stamping increased Beth's unease.

Then the railhead was reached and they were coaxed from the trucks into the remains of a fine afternoon. To the East guns could be heard loud enough to prick Bathsheba's ears. The battery paraded amid the chaos of motor wagons, lorries, carts, horses, guns and troops. The sort of inertia peculiar to military depots was setting in but Beth and her companions were watered, fed and walked off along grey, cobbled streets. Half the army seemed to be pouring in and out of Albert, choking the thoroughfares which found their way to the market place. The last sunlight illumined the basilica of the church that had been hit by enemy artillery fire. A shell had toppled the gilded statue of the Virgin and Child from the tower, and it hung face downwards directly above the market, secured by wires as if the church were afraid the Madonna would take flight.

Raising her head at the clatter of wings Beth saw the pigeons leave the great basilica to circle the rooftops and flash in the sun. Mist and shadow half-filled the river valley and other birds were on the wing. Milburn stroked her neck, listening to the guns which lent a sinister edge to the close of day. All about him was the evidence of previous bombardments: the odd ruin, roofless, its stonework blackened; shattered walls, holes in roofs and the sides of buildings; debris which had once been a home.

The column moved up the valley behind the front line with the temperature dropping and the mist thickening. Beyond the River Ancre was gently rolling farmland not unlike East Devon. White patches of chalk showed on the slopes between fields. Now larks were singing each side of the long, straight road that brought them through twilight to the rest camp behind the brigade's wagon lines.

Resting drowsily under the curry comb, Beth heard the curlews pass against the stars on their way to the marshy breeding sites beside the Somme.

39

He was one step behind her although he never knew it. The conscripts had swelled the training camp to twice its normal size and acres of canvas covered the fields under the downs. Whenever he had the chance Jack searched the stables and horse lines but the handful of roans he discovered lacked her refinement and the distinctive 'S'-shaped scar. Once or twice his heart leapt only to sink again. He even considered walking the six miles to the barracks in the city but shelved the idea. Court martial would mean separation from Beth for good. Fortunately the horse management was absorbing despite the fatigues, drilling and parades.

The West Countryman Sercombe came from St Austell and had the most difficult temperament Jack had encountered. Relaxed in a bar he was easy-going but under pressure he could be abrasive. When things went wrong he had the habit of puffing out his cheeks and blowing his frustration through pursed lips in a way that made Jack grit his teeth. He ate too much, fussed too much and was the prisoner of trivia. To quote the Scot on the other side of Jack, Sercombe was just 'a big old lassie and a pain in the arse'.

Tall, lean Wattie Maxwell was a Galloway man, soft spoken and perceptive, and just the wrong side of forty. 'The most ineligible bachelor north of Hadrian's Wall,' he grinned.

323

'Maybe I'm lucky, though,' he added, noting the shadow on Jack's face. 'There's only my mother to grieve for me.'

'You're a cheerful bugger,' Sercombe growled, spitting on the toecap of his boot and applying the cloth savagely.

'You have to be realistic, man. There are better places to go than Flanders if you're hoping to enjoy a ripe old age.'

Sitting by himself in the canteen Jack reread Kitty's letter and the postscript his mother had scribbled.

My own dearest Jack. I cannot tell you how I cried after you went. You must know how I feel but they say conscription would have taken you anyway in the spring. So it's no use going on. God, I do miss you. me and Baby are so lonely and I worry all the time. But everyone here is thinking of you and Mr Chancellor called to say 'well done'. He's a good old man, really. Everyone in the terrace sends their regards, and the girls down the stores and Old Bob. Darling, *please* look after yourself and come back to me and Mike, but whatever happens may God protect you and bring you home safe and sound. All my love and lots of sweet kisses, Kitty.

PS I pray for you every night son. Father O'Driscoll prays for you and we've asked the Holy Virgin to bless you and keep you. I know you'll come back. How else will I get that white gown and the carriage ride? God bless you. Your ever loving mother.'

'Letters are a luxury,' Maxwell said shortly before lights out.

'Don't you get any, Max?' said Jack.

A shake of the head, fingers raking back the gingerish hair and a smile appearing on the dark, moustached face.

'Mither canna read nor write – but God! she can yap.'

'So can you two,' Sercombe said. 'Just my bloody luck to be billeted with an Irishman and a Scotsman who can't stop gassing.'

'You're a bundle of fun, Sercombe,' Jack said.

'Go to sleep or I'll put you to sleep.'

'He means it,' Maxwell chuckled.

'No more chat, Jock, or I'll break your jaw.'

Jack grinned. His eyelids descended and he thought of Beth sleeping in the straw under the same stars. Then he saw Kitty

324

nursing the baby and heard the church bells of the three towns lapping over his sisters' laughter. The boy in the corner bed was sobbing but no one mocked him.

One of the big problems was the conscripts' ignorance. Very few had worked with horses and even Sercombe committed the most elementary errors. Before long everyone in the battery recognised Jack's expertise. The RSPCA staff who gave talks on horsecare would glance in his direction when they made a point, as if seeking his approval. Some NCOs resented this but the majority drew on his knowledge and even the sergeant-major knew where to go if a difficult horse failed to respond to training.

After the evening meal Jack would walk through the stables and say goodnight to the animals. One evening he was joined unexpectedly by the battery's second-in-command, a couple of subalterns and the sergeant-major. They had come to inspect the conditions.

'McKenna,' said Captain Berry. 'I understand from the sergeant-major that you've worked with draught horses all your life.'

'Since I was a nipper, sir,' Jack grinned.

'Stand up straight and take that wet grin off your face, lad,' the sergeant-major roared. 'Don't grin unless you're told to.'

'Sure, and isn't it daft, mister? Grinning's not something you do to order.'

'Stand still, you little Irish clown, and answer the officer's questions.'

Captain Berry coughed into his fist and his eyes twinkled. He was a pleasant young man, passionate about horses and the regiment. His Charlie Chaplin moustache and large, aquiline nose were like a novelty set a child could buy at a joke shop.

'Why did you join the Artillery and not the Cavalry, McKenna?' he said. 'Can you only handle cart horses?'

'No sir. We had carriage horses and crosses of all kinds. Some of our stud were good enough for any gun team. A lot of the light draught crossbreds are built like carriage animals and their temperaments are better.'

'Did you think that by becoming a driver you'd have a cushy number?'

'It never entered my head, sir. They took my horse and I just

325

came after her.'

'Your horse?'

So Jack was compelled to explain.

'But surely a Clydesdale cross-bred roan would end up pulling siege guns?' said Berry.

'She's hardly a cart horse, sir. She's small and elegant with a big 'S'-shaped scar on her right flank. Hauling heavy stuff would break her.'

'Does it ring a bell, Sergeant-Major?' Berry asked.

'Roans aren't common, sir, but we're desperate enough to take anything these days, what with the wastage and the demand elsewhere. Can't say I've seen her, though. A horse is a horse and thousands have passed through this camp.'

'Thousands,' Jack whispered, shaking his head.

'The sergeant-major tells me you are a bit of an expert, McKenna.'

Jack shrugged and the NCO winced.

'I had a good teacher, sir. Our horsemaster was a Boer War veteran. He knew the lot.'

Captain Berry sank his hands in his trench coat pockets. Then he said, 'Come and have a look at this animal and tell me what you think's wrong with her.'

'Don't you know, sir?'

'If I thought that was insolence you would spend all your free time on jankers,' the sergeant-major said from the back of his throat.

The bay mare lifted her head upwards and sideways, twisting her neck and wobbling slightly. Out of habit Jack dug his hands in his pockets.

'McKenna,' the sergeant-major bellowed.

'Jesus, mister,' Jack said, coming to attention. 'No offence intended. I'm new to this soldiering lark.'

'Don't worry lad, we'll soon alter that.'

'In the meantime perhaps you could persuade McKenna to run an eye over the animal, Sergeant-Major.'

'She's a bit loppy on her legs,' Jack said, frowning. 'It could be one of several things, sir.'

'Like an ear infection?' said Lieutenant Callaway.

'Bad ears aren't common, sir. Things can go wrong with the parotid gland and the mastoid process but I doubt if she'd be on

326

her feet if that were the case.'

Captain Berry laughed. 'Mastoid process! D'you know what all the fancy stuff means, McKenna?'

'The local vet used to take me out with him on his rounds, sir, but most of what I've picked up came from an old carter and Mr Palfrey.'

'Your average recruit doesn't know the difference between a hoof and a hock,' Berry said. 'So you aren't diagnosing an ear infection? Come on, lad – I really am in the dark and the vet has a hell of a lot on. He won't come in a hurry unless I give him a good reason.'

Jack took the mare's head in his hands. 'Most likely it's her throat. Her nostrils are a bit raw. What about discharge, sir?'

'I believe her nose has been running. To be honest, I thought it could be linked to the old ears. Bad ears can upset a dog's balance.'

'Horses are different, sir. We had a similar case on the farm. Then it was what I think this is – an infected guttural pouch.'

'A job for the vet?'

'Definitely, sir.'

They went to the harness room.

'As soon as you've done your basic training, McKenna, we shall put your talents to good use,' Berry said. 'The sergeant-major needs help getting these chaps ready for the Front. I'm certain you'll fit into the team.'

'I'm not after any favours, sir,' Jack said, the colour rising in his cheeks.

'Whatever you get you'll earn. Off you go now.'

'Sir,' Jack said. 'Just one thing. Isn't the training of them animals to go out to France and get blown to bits the worst kind of betrayal?'

He was stared at silently for a moment.

'They won't all get killed,' Berry said. 'And it's not up to us, McKenna. We take orders. We do as we're told, and if we stopped to think about everything nothing would get done. Look, isn't it better for the horses to get proper care and training from men like you than a bad show from some ham-fisted chap who doesn't give a damn? The war is going to continue with or without you but if you can make it a little easier for the animals then you've done your bit.'

They watched Jack depart. Then Captain Berry lit a cigarette.

'Well, Sergeant-Major, what do you think?'

'He's a strange little sod, sir, but he's your twenty-four carat horseman and a definite asset to the battery.'

'NCO material?'

'I'd like a longer, closer look at him, sir. He's Irish and I want to be sure that wide-eyed innocence is not insolence in disguise. Couldn't-give-a-damn makes a bad soldier; bad for everyone.'

'Is he Irish Irish?' asked Second Lieutenant Royce. 'You know - come to us from over there?'

'Emigrant family, sir, living in Devon. But he has that challenge about him. You can see it in the eyes. Some of the horses have it.'

He felt the conversation had gone too far. The officers were amusing themselves before dinner, even Berry whom he respected.

'Ireland,' the captain smiled, 'is a state of mind, not a place.'

Once during the gun team drills on the downs Jack's battery passed within a hundred yards of the Seventh. It was the only time that winter he and Beth came close to each other.

Dull days passed. The sunlight flared softly and briefly. Snow powdered down but did not lie for long and the horses walked into mornings which were bloodless. The teams rattled through the flawed sunlight to the emplacements. It was odd, Jack thought, living through the beginnings and endings of days but never truly belonging to them. He ran hard leaving the rest of the section in his wake. The running before breakfast was the best part of the training, that and the horse work. So he sprinted over the crisp turf and his teeth ached at every gulp of air.

Unwillingly he was warming to the power play of horse and man. A kind of low-key euphoria prevailed. The gallop to the gun pits left drivers and teams exhilarated, for what lay over the horizon had no substance. The wagon lines, horse lines, guns, shells with red tips to signify shrapnel, the limbers and the ammunition runs were parts of an exclusively male game that had been played for millennia. The equipment changed but the rules rarely altered.

By the time spring arrived Jack McKenna was very good at it.

The dawn chorus was washed by the wind across wet pastures. The night's drizzle endured as mist down in the valley of the Ancre. Horses were restless at the picket line and life returned to the camp. There was a billow of woodsmoke, khaki figures lit cigarettes and coughed and stamped against the cold. Eastward a light artillery barrage was keeping the enemy on their toes. The flickers in the bottom of the sky were succeeded by a string of thuds which blurred to reverberation, and a muted brilliance that came and passed. Larks rose on their song and fell again yet never settled or so it seemed to the human eyes watching them.

The smell of horse-living and farmland, and the fall of apple blossom in the gun park reminded Beth of Tor Barton springs. The glorious weather kept men and horses happy. Afternoons hazed in heat smouldered away to dusk and clear, starry nights.

Sailing over fields which seemed larger than they were because the hedges were low and generally treeless, the barn owls hunted the gleaming chalk plough while light trembled on the eastern horizon. The birds winged across the blades of wheat to plunder the vole runs and Beth's ears twitched forward whenever they screamed. Then there was a tearing roar in the sky and the shell exploded behind the orchard and house, followed by another until half a dozen had landed and the horses were panicking. Black smoke thinned and was blown away.

'Bloody coal boxes,' the sergeant cried, joining Milburn at the lines. 'Bloody Fritz! Why don't he get his head down like the rest of us? One night his heavies will find our range and we'll be wearing our arseholes for collars.'

Milburn tried to soothe Beth and Bathsheba but it was a long time before they stopped quivering. His own calmness surprised him. The high-explosive shells which the soldiers called coal boxes or five-nines fell elsewhere, further to the south, and some on target. Every ten minutes they passed over the lines until the barrage lifted. In the hush that held the faint scent of apple blossom the owls called and the wind blew and stars twinkled on Milburn's glasses.

The muck-spreading added its own sour spices to the other seasonal smells. Only the men from the towns disliked it, but to the Devon horses it was the breath of the past. Dreams would rise from the most trivial happenings: an Irish voice singing at the morning exercise; apple trees printed on the moon; the barking of a dog at dusk. Then, close to sleep, she was flying through white silence to the beach. The gallop and weightlessness ended in starhaze.

Along the white roads came the men of the Thirty-first Division, either up to the Front or back to the rest camps. They came singing through the sunshine and the peasants on the dung carts waved and shouted greetings. Always, Milburn noted, it was the Yorkshire and Lancashire Regiments with their Pals Battalions; the Barnsley Pals, Sheffield, Hull, York and Bradford Pals — columns of cheerful volunteers whose enthusiasm had not been eroded. Ammunition wagons, London omnibuses full of soldiers, mules, water carts and ambulances lifted the white dust to coat leaf and blossom. Dust also drifted over the fields behind the harrows. House martins were nesting and peasants were planting potatoes. Perhaps more than anything the sound of a cuckoo in the afternoon heat set the battery dreaming of other Aprils in other villages and towns. Then distant female voices calling children in for the evening meal made homesickness difficult to bear.

But the infantry continued their march towards the high ground held by the Germans, although the front line was impossibly remote to the gunners and drivers who worked stripped to the waist. The fine weather held. Teeth flashed white in sunburnt faces and between the trenches wild flowers choked those strips of open ground called No Man's Land. Among the barbed wire entanglements beyond the forward saps where the sentries sweated, small birds had nested. Dawns were sung in by hedge sparrow, lark, yellowhammer and goldfinch as the grasses climbed higher and harebells, white campion and cornflowers swayed in the breeze.

On an afternoon in late spring Corporal Jack McKenna stood under the basilica of Notre Dame des Brebieres and gazed up at the leaning Virgin in amazement. She was the sister of the White Lady, and the hair stiffened on the nape of his neck. Religion was stalking him as it had when he was a child.

'When she falls,' said Sergeant Turnbull, 'the war will end.'

'And who will win?' asked Maxwell.

'Us, of course. The padre says God's on our side.' His broad Somerset accent rendered practically everything he uttered comical.

Jack and Maxwell grinned. Last night's French beer leaked from their pores and beaded their brows. They were glad the journey was nearly over, glad to stand in the shadows on the edge of all the noise and bustle. Birds were blurred by the petrol fumes and heat until they climbed to the blueness above the tower. A rapt expression lit Maxwell's face. The boots of marching men crunched out their regular beat until the clatter of hooves filled the square. The friends turned and saw dozens of Percheron draught horses walking in pairs over the cobbles. Troops paused to watch the great animals go by. The traffic came to a halt and no one spoke or moved until they were gone.

'Them good old boys,' Turnbull muttered.

The battery joined the constant stream of convoys on the road to Hédauville. Images dilated and contracted in the dusty sunlight, an aeroplane droned overhead and heliographs flashed from the high ground to the east. Gulfs of unreality were opening between events. Sweat dribbled into Jack's eyes; his shirt was glued to his back. Flies muzzed the heads of the horses and the dust clogged their nostrils and caked their coats. They plodded into the glare swishing their tails and shaking their heads in an effort to loose manes which had been cut away. The roll of their haunches was hypnotic. Men dozed and woke to the sight of horses' rear ends and the swarming flies.

'Did you want to go back when you heard about them lads in Dublin post office?' Maxwell said.

'The Easter Uprising means nothing to me,' Jack said. 'Devon's my home.' He yawned. 'My brother Mike is buried out here, Max. There's more of me in this place than I could ever find in Ireland.'

'You're sure of that?'

The wagon hit a pot hole and lurched. Jack's pale blue eyes clouded and he took the cigarette from Max's lips. Then he grinned smoke.

'I don't know much about anything anymore.'

Maxwell nodded.

40

It was green tableland dominated by a ridge to the east and running to tall skies in swells which were gentle and occasionally wooded. Towns and villages were linked by white roads, and the approaches to the railhead were often hidden under the steam of locomotives bringing in troop and ammunition trains.

The farm was a pleasant shambles at the end of a track a little to the south of the hamlet. It had been vacated by another battery whose field guns had been brought to emplacements less than a mile behind the Front. A shell had removed the chimney and one of the middens was in ruins but its position in a shallow coombe had saved it from total destruction. The house, barns, cowshed and pigsties stood around the yard. There were no civilians or farmstock although life closer to the village was normal enough despite the shelling and the absence of young men. When the noise of the artillery duels lifted rural sounds crept back. Cattle lowed, swifts screamed and the horses called to each other.

Like everyone else at the Front Jack knew the offensive was a matter of weeks away. The lorries grating through the gears at night on the Hedauville Road were reminders of the build-up that never ceased. But men and animals went about their business optimistically, for different reasons. The Big Push would end the war. The throb and rumble of artillery opening up as night fell was like the voice of authority laying about German ears.

'I never saw so many guns,' said Sergeant Turnbull. 'Hundreds of them, and the whole countryside back there is thick with horses. When we give Fritz his iron rations he'll bugger off back to Germany with his tail between his legs.'

'Aye, what's left of him,' Maxwell grinned.

In the outlying orchard men were cleaning the guns and the thin reek of paraffin was on the air. A kestrel hovered above the vegetable gardens but did not fall.

'I didn't know there was hawks in France,' said Maxwell. 'Hawks and blackbirds and thrushes. I always thought the French had different birds to ours.'

'Is Galloway like this, Max?' Jack said, heaving the harness over a fallen apple tree and checking it for wear.

'Lord no, man. Galloway's got muscle.'

'Like Devon,' Jack grinned.

They worked for half an hour to the chirr and zither of insects. Then Maxwell asked him if he had looked over the horses in the battery up the road.

'Not a roan among them,' came the reply.

'When were you there?' Maxwell said. The burnished leather caught the sunlight.

'The other morning after exercise.'

'For Christ's sake! You'll get shot.'

'Sooner or later,' Jack smiled. 'I just put a saddle on Lady and rode up the coombe like I was on army business. No one challenged me. The wagon lines are one bloody great muddle.

Now the grass in No Man's Land had a purplish sheen and soon the fragrance of fields falling under the scythe drifted through the camp. The commanding officer managed to buy some hay and had it stacked close to the farmhouse that served as an ammunition store. Under the trees were piles of provisions, animal fodder and the horse lines. A stray cat had made this her territory. She was a fierce, thin little creature, as black as ink, who would never come too near the drivers despite their attempts to win her trust. She ate scraps and songbirds and came and went as she pleased. At dusk when the men sat outside, a bright pair of eyes would gleam on the edge of the firelight. They remained even after the heavy guns began to roar and flash and the horses fretted all along the lines. As soon as the barrage lifted bats were flickering around the lines.

'Bloody midges and everything that crawls or flies and has six bloody legs is eatin' me alive,' Sercombe railed. The match flared to reveal his big, morose face.

'Where there's dung there's flies,' commented an anonymous wag from the darkness.

'Who was that?' Sercombe growled, getting to his feet.

'Pipe down and sit down,' said Sergeant Turnbull. 'If you're so keen to sling punches, Sercombe, volunteer for a trench mortar team and get up where you can hear and smell Fritz.'

'Or just go to sleep,' said Maxwell.

The boy Maunder from the Devon village of Chagford had a harmonica. He sat cross-legged by the fire waiting for the tea to brew and gave them 'Roses of Picardy'.

'You been to Dublin, Corporal?' Sercombe asked.

'Once,' Jack replied, warily.

'My brother's regiment was stationed there back in King Edward's days. He said it was the arsehole of the world.'

'He was probably just passing through,' Jack grinned.

Maxwell's guffaw was taken up by Turnbull and some of the more quick-witted drivers. Jack lay down to sleep thinking of Chancellor's yard but he dreamed of Beth pulling the open carriage with his mother in white smiling from beneath her white parasol.

The next day the battery was moved forward a mile to the north of Beth's brigade, and the field guns were hauled to the battle zone close to the eighteen pounders of the Seventh. A period of frantic activity followed with the limber teams racing along the military road to stockpile ammunition at the pits. Back at the horse lines there was no farm and no orchards, just the ruins of some cottages between two deserted hamlets.

'So much for the cushy number,' Maxwell sighed. 'To think some sod is going to eat the fruit off our apple trees! God! There's no justice. There's no . . .'

His eyebrows rose and fell as he searched in vain for the words.

The farrier visited the lines and was succeeded by a general and a couple of less illustrious staff officers whom Sergeant

334

Turnbull referred to as 'red-tabbed bastards with pompous arses'. The inspection was brief, the general's speech embarrassing but the farce inspired Sercombe to new heights of vitriol.

Among the endless fatigues and stand-tos, church parades in the open air proved surprisingly moving experiences. Men knelt bare-headed in the grass, a small group of Catholics encircling the priest, the majority gathered round the Anglican minister taking communion. The sun beat down from a cloudless sky and the breeze set the meadow running in waves of light which the horses at the lines followed with their eyes. Sunshine, lark song and the whisper of grass lent a potency to the scriptures.

Watering the animals at noon Maxwell said, 'Do you ever think of Patrick Pearse and his six mates – the Provisional Government of the Irish Republic?'

'No,' said Jack and the Scotsman found the blank gaze unsettling. 'Ireland's a million miles away.'

'Fifty-eight were killed in the fighting and sixteen were hanged, but Eamon de Valera, a Sinn Fein leader, was reprieved.'

'Why?'

'Because he was born in the USA and the English want the Yanks in the war on their side.'

Jack smiled.

'Och well, on our side then. But what happened last Easter in Dublin has a fine feel to it – not like all this. It's so cold-blooded.'

'Don't you believe in the war, Max?'

'Yes, Christ yes! I want to kick the Boche all the way back to the Rhine and drown him in it.'

'So do I,' Jack said.

He smoothed the hack's nose. Mike, Arthur Maddock, Moony, Little Charlie. The yard was empty. No more laughter. No clatter and whinny and stamping of hooves. All gone and the place lifeless. Just the fireweed and doves and rats.

'We are in love with death, Max.'

'I'm not.'

'The Irish. It's a way of life for us.'

'You crazy sod,' Maxwell laughed. 'Even the horse is

smiling.'

The hack showed her teeth and blew hard through her nose.

'She doesn't like you,' Jack said. 'And horses are shrewd judges of character.'

'You and the bloody four-legged tribe!'

'When I was a boy they thought I was just an empty-headed little bastard who'd do anything for a laugh or a dare. But I was good at working out things with my body: the best way up the quarry wall to the kestrel's nest; timing the dash across the railway lines in front of the express; the jump across the stream that was swollen with flood water. And I could run like hell, forever it seemed.'

The mare lowered her head to drink and he grinned.

'This war isn't about the strength or speed or cunning of men, or the bravery of men. It don't matter how fast you are or how wide awake you are. The shell explodes – bang! and you're gone. Knowing the ways of things and creatures doesn't help. None of it matters out here.'

'What does matter, Jack?'

'When I find Beth I'll know.'

'You and that horse!' And Maxwell added as though he were addressing himself, 'Have you ever seen a German?'

'Only Mr Heinlen the chimney sweep back at home.'

'What was he like?'

'Two legs, two arms, a head . . .'

Maxwell began to whistle gently, his eyes closed.

'He was a nice enough fella.'

'Do you suppose Jerry talks like this to his mate?'

'Sure, when he's not raping and pillaging and nailing nuns to church doors.'

The kestrel quartered the surface of the wheat field that was green and shining. A German plane droned high above the British lines and waggled its wings. Instantly the anti-aircraft guns opened up with horizontal jets of smoke. Small white cloudlets of exploding shells surrounded the Taube and it made a lazy turn to drone back towards Beaumont Hamel. Water dripped from Beth's muzzle and she raised her head from the trough to gaze at the sky. The other horses were also watchful.

For the past month the battery had occupied pits behind a

knoll where the flash of discharge was invisible to enemy observers. The gunners could not see the Germans who occupied the hamlet of Serre less than two thousand yards away. The new wagon and horse lines were a few miles behind the emplacements on the edge of a wood. Every day the teams took up ammunition, provisions and mail for the gunners. Only occasionally were the limbers caught in one of the random strafes as the enemy guns probed the British positions. But the battery's good fortune held and there were no casualties although the shock of artillery warfare took many recruits by surprise. The thunder from their own gun pits and the orange flashes lighting the dusk were awesome enough, but the burst of a five-nine in front of a team would bring the horses to a halt and set them back on their haunches. The deep, droning whine of the heavies was followed by the red flare-away and crash of detonation. Acrid black smoke filled the horses' nostrils. Lights went on and off in the sky, like an approaching thunderstorm. Then peace suddenly returned with the rush of the wind and the sobbing snuffle of animals fighting terror.

After they had come under fire for the first time, Milburn patted Beth's neck and knew in that awful moment that both he and the mare had strayed to the frontiers of something dark and immensely evil. The minister of his Baptist chapel back home would have called it 'The Inferno'.

Yet the sunlight was benign. It glinted on the convoys which continued hurrying war materials up to the front. Wagons full of steel and timber for the dugouts, pit props for mines and tunnels, sandbags, wire netting, tools, planks and beams, poured into Hedauville to halt the omnibuses ferrying troops to the trenches. Rain had fallen and the roads were grey and wet, but the poppies in the cornfields glistened.

Beth rounded her nostrils to read the scents lifting off the farmland, listening for his voice among the babble of other noises. The limber run to the gun pits and back had left her tired. A buzzard mewled up the rising air over the ravines of the Ancre and swung in a great circle back to the British lines. Solomon and Bathsheba waited for the water cart from the shadows of the trees. Packing down tobacco in his pipe Milburn wondered why the sorrel was forever staring out of a daydream.

'She's an odd creature,' he remarked to his sergeant. 'I swear

337

she's waiting for someone.'

'No horse is the same,' the sergeant said. 'Some like work, others don't. Some are bright, others dopey.'

'That mare is a gem,' Milburn said. 'I wish to God she was somewhere else. All this is, well – shameful, bad.'

A pair of cabbage white butterflies settled on the fool's parsley against the wood and flirted their wings.

'I don't understand,' Milburn continued. 'What's God up to?'

The NCO shook his head, unwilling to rake over his own doubts and anxieties.

'Have you been to the village, Milburn—the big one behind the wagon lines?' he said. 'Goss reckons there's a bit of available skirt hanging round the *'staminft. Tres beaus*, Gossy reckons.'

'Goss has a lot of imagination, Sarge. Two old dears and a little lass aren't exactly a harem. Goss tends to come the acid but I suppose we all did at that age.'

'Young and shit scared.'

'The horses get really scared, Sarge.'

'It ain't my fault, mate. None of this is my fault or your's or any other bugger's except Kaiser Bill. I hope to get the chance to have a go at the bastard. He's sent more than one of my mates west.'

'The Big Push will do it.'

'Do what?'

'End all this.'

'Yes, Jerry won't know what's hit him. It can't fail this time. We've enough guns to blow Germany off the map.'

The limber runs kept Milburn from brooding. Riding Beth through the warm nights left him breathless with excitement. Beth and Bathsheba were an accomplished lead pair that could have made the trip blindfold. Leaving the wood the road ran east towards the battle zone, crossing an exposed countryside of fields and isolated farms. Three miles or so beyond a hamlet which the German guns had pounded the road narrowed and was no more than a glorified cart-track pitted with shell holes. Eventually the emplacements, which had been dug in the slopes, were reached and the shells unloaded. At night the only other traffic sharing the route were strings of pack mules carrying ammunition to the entrenched infantry, despatch riders on their motorbikes and the ubiquitous water carts.

Providing the enemy guns were quiet Beth enjoyed the canter back to the picket lines. In the past Jack alone had let her run. At the back of thought was the vivid recollection of the beach and the sea and the foal in full flight. Through the moonlight Beth and Bathsheba flew until the cries of the drivers and the rattle of the empty ammunition cart crept back into their knowing. Then they were unharnessed and left to cool off before the grooming. Behind them the wood rustled.

Of the battery's one hundred and seventy-two animals less than two-thirds stood at the lines, with the remainder resting several miles away. Beth's team fed and slept on the edge of the wood close to the road where the stink of chloride of lime from the latrines was powerful but not overwhelming. The smoke from the deal ammunition boxes used to light the field cookers made their eyes smart but brought a brief reprieve from the flies.

The heatwave persisted and at night when she was not hauling shells Beth stood twitching her ears at the thunder of the guns. Around her the ghost moths danced and once in the hush after gunfire a nightingale sang from the depths of the wood.

Horses of the brigade's three batteries were picketed wherever the farmland offered concealment. East of Hédauville over three hundred animals were tethered ready for the return journey to the gun pits. For them it was another work game played against a background of spasmodic noise which was often terrifying and always puzzling. The presence of men who were kind to them made it tolerable. The street rounds, farm work and limber runs were aspects of a common destiny. In the end they would be led up the well-known street or lane to the home-place that was never forgotten even by those who had been badly treated. One day their real owners would claim them and they would sleep in their stalls. Of this they were certain and their trust in man never faltered. One day Beth would be with Jack again. Each dusk she stood pining for him, reliving the good times they had shared.

The casual shelling, the dust clouds hanging over the main roads, aeroplanes crawling across the sky and the sight of troops on the move were somehow incidental to the real life of summer. Larks went on singing while the yellow mustard flowers at the wayside danced in the draught of passing lorries. Sunlight slanted to warm the horses at the lines and the sentries who had seen dawn creep over the fields. Small incidents drifted down her consciousness: the lisp of nestlings in the wood; stock doves crooning; the song of a thrush; the furtive exodus of rabbits. In the brambles beside the arsenal under the trees a quarter of a mile away a vixen and her cubs were kennelled. Sometimes they ran along the horse lines beneath twilight and Sirius to scavenge the garbage heap.

Different drivers made the runs on Beth's back but generally Milburn claimed her. The battery's second-in-command, Captain Venner, who kept the wagon lines operating, was aware of the doomed relationships between men and animals. He had fought at Ypres and had few illusions about the war.

Towards the end of the third week of June he rode along the pickets when the horses were being fed. Men were stripped to the waist, whistling and laughing and the animals slobbered over their bran mash. It was like some Bank Holiday jaunt, and the cricket match between a combined subalterns' and NCOs' eleven and the drivers curried the carnival atmosphere.

Then up the road to the forward positions went the last of the field ambulances. Captain Venner tapped the end of his cigarette on his thumbnail as the din grew fainter and the vehicles disappeared. Yet before the dust had settled he felt a tightening of the guts. It was not hard to imagine the preparations at the Advanced Dressing Stations, the Casualty Clearing Station and the big hospitals in the rear. North of Hédauville was a mobile veterinary unit complete with horse-drawn ambulances which would collect wounded or sick animals and cart them off for treatment.

The birds might be singing and the home-made deal cricket bat could square cut the tennis ball to an imaginary boundary but the shadows were lengthening. Venner shivered. The shadows had voices and the past was coming alive again to claim its tithes. He sucked at his cigarette and goose pimpled. Someone's eyes were on him. Turning he met Beth's gaze across the rumble of the enemy's guns.

41

Jack sat outside the dugout watching the moon's halo dilate and thin. The fair weather would not last but what endured and what passed no longer mattered. He was tired. The limber runs had been uneventful, the horses were resting at the lines and only the sentries were up and about in the shadows of the copse. Drugged with summer scents Jack let Beth into his thoughts. He and Kitty were on her back, riding her down a lane buried under hawthorn blossom. The baby was laughing in Kitty's arms, birds were singing and the bells gave the Three Towns their Sabbath charm.

They rode towards the sea but never reached the shore. The lane went on forever under the chorus of songbirds, winding and dipping through sun-speckled shadows into a calmness nothing could shatter.

South of Redan Ridge the British front line was being shelled and the light in the sky was unsteady yet persistent. The horses shook their heads while the drivers held them and the ammunition was unloaded. Vocal, highly strung Grace cast about in her traces, deaf to the words breathed by the man clutching her bridle. When the work was done the team came back down the road at the gallop, sniffing something more than tension on the night wind, and voicing their alarm as other horses passed hauling full limbers. Then the bombardment began.

Every gun the British and French had brought to the Somme opened up, and Beth and her companions froze. They were caught beneath an immense dome of noise that set Bathsheba and Grace bucking. Up they jerked on their hind legs with Milburn and the other drivers fighting to hold them. Instinctively the men ducked as hundreds of high explosive shells poured overhead in a torrent to rip into the German defences.

'Jesus Christ!' Milburn's mouth shaped the words.

The shriek of the shells filled the night like the sound of express trains travelling at unimaginable speeds. The sky pulsed. A thunderous dazzle lit the east, broken by the jagged orange flashes of the eighteen pounders and howitzers. Between the field guns and the wagon lines the landscape was bathed in a lurid glow. Westward the sky was torn by the white flash of siege guns. The night boomed, cracked and seemed to gallop after the horses who were running wildly now. A chain of thuds shook the ground close at hand. Limber horses out of control passed in an eye-rolling mass. The noise numbed thought but Beth pounded on surrounded by the shapes of horses and light that shivered and fell apart and roared.

The enemy was retaliating. Five-nines came over with the deep awful drone men and animals dreaded. Towers of fire rose in the fields, scattering shell splinters. Earth lifted and pattered down as the team slithered through the liquid excrement left by other horses.

The horizon behind them was ablaze and cobbled with noise. Flinging a glance over her shoulder Beth's fear became almost ungovernable. The feeling had gone out of her knees and her legs did not belong to her. She moved automatically, half-aware of animals calling above the crash of exploding shells. A team had been hit. Horses lay kicking and writhing. Milburn shut his eyes on the horror. The revelation took his breath away. Horses vented their fear, bled, thrashed about and clung tenaciously to life until it left them in a gasp, a sigh or something resembling a scream. It was a nightmare made landscape and flesh. Shells opened the road before him and he slowed his team to negotiate the wreckage of limbers, men and animals. A human voice called on God. Another shrieked incoherently and a horse with its front legs missing struggled to stand. The air was rank with the intensity of animal suffering.

'Keep them moving,' the subaltern cried.

Jesus, Jesus. Let me get home. Please, please, please. The shout rose to a shriek in Milburn's skull.

Earth splattered Beth's face. Bathsheba flung herself to the side but was held. The noise was unbelievable. It smelled of scorched horse hair and metal. Beth forced herself through it, and the limber immediately ahead became a red blur, disintegrating in a hiatus of blinding white light. Human and animal debris rose, fanned out and scattered on a roar, and Milburn's team was pulling hard to avoid the crater. As they gained the shelter of the woods each side of the road the barrage lifted and the sky was left to the rush and drone of British shells. A gentle breeze ghosted across the landscape from Serre, driving the smoke and fumes towards the picket lines.

Other horses were being hitched to the limbers. The sergeant yelled instructions, ignoring the returning teams. Beth was in a lather and Bathsheba on the point of collapse. Legs buckling she stood and slobbered, her whole body racked by spasms of terror. Milburn slid to the ground and crushed his hands together in an effort to stop them shaking. The noise of the guns had blurred to a high surf sound.

'There, girl, there,' he gasped. 'Bide still, don't fret.'

But his words cast upon the din struck him as absurd. Don't fret! For God's sake, why shouldn't she fret? The scream bottled up in the mare's being registered behind her gaze.

'Load up,' the sergeant said. 'Come on, Milburn, you're slower than the second coming of Christ.'

Milburn groaned.

'Get them bone bags to the ammo dump sharpish, lad.'

Sweat trickled into Milburn's eyes. He swallowed but his throat remained parched. The din crescendoed and pressed down on him. Grace and Solomon were out of control, dancing broadside and threatening to overturn the limber. They flared their nostrils and blew in panic-stricken unison. Another groan escaped from Milburn. His sphincter muscles let him down and he dribbled fear. A revolver had been held to his head, perpetually discharging blanks but like everyone else that night

343

he knew there was a live shell in one of the chambers. Waiting for the explosion he would feel, not hear, fused his nerves.

'Milburn,' Captain Venner said gently from somewhere close by. 'Pull yourself together, man, and get your team to the dump.'

Milburn choked on his reply. The sky was full of stars and flashes which were not stars.

And so it continued, the loading, the runs to the gun pits and the return journey beneath the invisible arcs of shells. The bombardment showed no signs of abating but before dawn the guns of the Seventh Battery were taken to fresh emplacements with a view of the enemy trenches. Right down the Ancre valley the tell-tale orange spurts betrayed field gun positions. Beth gazed across at the great firework display of howitzer shells exploding. Her ears drooped and her head was bowed. Why hadn't he come to ride her out of the agony? Glimmers of the new day were behind the explosions. Milburn's team made their return to the lines and collected another load. Before the gun pits were reached the sun was rising from mist into the promise of a fine morning.

Leading his team back to the pickets Jack deliberately let his mind go slack. The memories could not be held at bay. Them Froggies knew all the bedroom tricks, Michael lied. Boudoir PT he called it. The wind turned the poplars to flames. Things wavered in the heat haze and ignoring the gunfire, swallows hawked the air. A chill gripped his heart. Where was Beth? How could he find her? Maybe he would just get up one night and go from battery to battery, pretending he was a runner. But in the dark there was no chance. Dew and starlight meeting sunlight under the non-stop passage of shells. Thought frozen in the limbo between night and day. Back home a dawn of sleeping rooftops would be printed on the mist and cattle would be ambling out of Clennon Valley to the milking sheds of Tor Barton.

During the brew-up he had a chance to read Kitty's last letter again.

My own dearest Jack, I enclose a photograph of little Mike. God bless him. He's the spitting image of you, and your mum thinks the world of him. I hope you are in the

344

pink as we all are except Lily who is chesty again. All the neighbours send their regards, and the tradesmen up Winner Street. Sad to say Mrs Endacott passed away last week and the Prowses in Number Two lost their eldest boy over where you are. Have you found Beth? Your mum says tis only a matter of time. Listen, idn you due any leave? Come home, Jack, please, as soon as you can.

All my love and kisses, Kitty.

The baby stared solemnly out of the sepia-tinted photograph, and Jack grinned. His mother's letter would have to wait. He eased himself off the empty limber and something small lying in the grass caught his eye. He knelt and cupped his hands round the lark. It had been killed by the concussion of an exploding shell, but was still warm. Warm in bed back there how could his mother and Kitty ever know the meaning of what Michael had endured? Maxwell appeared at his side.

'A wee lark,' he whispered, reading his friend's thoughts. 'Christ! That's sad.'

But it was all sad, Jack reflected – the exhausted and terrified horses, the men light-headed and hallucinating from lack of sleep; what they were doing to the foe.

The Germans occupied a great Babylon of entrenchments and fortress villages just 'over the way'. Tons of shells had rained on them throughout the night. Listening to the field guns barking he considered the plight of the men dug into the ridge; and still the high-explosive and shrapnel shells descended.

Up by the gun pits he saw the barrage striking home. Black smoke from the heavies was mixing with the whitish-grey puffs of detonating shrapnel shells. Here and there the cloud had a yellowish tinge. Giant flames lofted, dimmed and vanished. An aeroplane caught the sunlight on its fuselage. From the pit to Jack's left a Q F howitser was lobbing 35-pound shells over No Man's Land. A gunner crawled out of the communication trench between the occupied emplacement and the reserve pit, his ears bleeding. Maxwell began unloading and stacking the shells. The sink of cordite enveloped the teams but Jack held the horses and spoke to them.

Pacing up and down behind the pits the sergeant-major bawled commands into his megaphone: 'Five degrees left of

345

zero,' then the angle of sight and the order to fire. The horses winced. Fumes wafted from the pits where the gunners were naked to the waist handling red hot eighteen pounders that coughed smoke from the breach.

'Do we have to hang around Corporal?' the lieutenant drawled. His horse had nearly thown him twice, and Jack was reminded of Rupert out hunting. A coal box exploded among the pits a hundred yards to their left. The shell's screw-cap whirred over them and the subaltern inclined his head, more in resignation than concern. He was younger than Jack and immensely popular with the men.

'I'm afraid we're in for a dose of our own medicine, Corporal.'

Jack pressed his lips to the lead horse's ear and tried to calm her. The deep, insistent moaning of wounded animals and men crept over from the mud beside the shell crater.

'Some of ours have copped it,' said Maxwell.

'They'll need a hand sir,' Jack said, and the officer nodded.

Moments later all three men understood the grim implications of the quick-release buckles on the harness. The lead pair had fallen but were trying to stand and rejoin the other survivors. The legs of the grey were shattered and the bones stuck out white and jagged. She lifted herself and craned her neck to stare at them. Jack fumbled the buckles and held her while she was shot. The other horse got up but seemed incapable of lifting its head. It's lower jaw had been blown off and a terrible gurgling noise came from its nostrils.

Pressing his revolver to the creature's head Lieutenant Callaway sobbed and squeezed the trigger. More five-nines fell as they dragged the wounded drivers clear and put them in the limbers.

'Long bracket,' the sergeant-major roared at the gunners.

'Long bracket. Sort yourselves out or I'll soddin' well sort you out.'

A teenage driver was on his knees, clutching the sides of the limber and crying 'Mother, Mother', in awful repetition. His chest was a vast blood stain. 'Mother,' endlessly, a numb bleating for salvation that would never come.

The subaltern's voice faltered. 'I really think we should be getting back Corporal.'

*   *   *

346

East of the woods there were dead mules and horses, wrecked limbers and a few overturned motor vehicles. That day the bombardment was less intense but the British guns and wagon lines were shelled for four hours and the drivers forced underground into the candlelit dugouts. Captain Berry was not surprised, though, to find Jack at the pickets trying to calm the distressed animals. The captain and Callaway stood aloof from the five-nines which were falling short of the copse. Explosions smudged the morning's gold but the larks could not be silenced.

'Do you know what you lose at the Front, Geoffrey?' Berry smiled.

'Reason? Limbs? Life?'

'Self esteem.'

There was an awkward pause.

'Do you suppose McKenna's a bit barmy?' Callaway said.

'Aren't we all? But perhaps he's come to terms with something.'

Of course, he thought, the endlessness of life was an illusion. Was it after all merely a question of drawing breath? The further ahead one looked the more one was aware of existence materialising into oblivion. *'Ou sont les neiges d'antan?'* More five-nines cut across the morning and exploded but the field was dew-drenched, undefiled. Cornflowers and poppies were blurs of blue and red in the wheat across the road. Berry took off his cap and wiped his brow. The lark above him sang with a sort of controlled hysteria. The Fellowship of the Soon-to-be-Dead. The notion brought a smile to his lips again. The match rasped, the cigarette glowed and he drew smoke deep into his lungs. Traffic was building up on the road and the heliographs were flashing. Then the water cart rolled along the edge of the copse and Jack was laying his hands on the shire cross who stood snuffling her anxiety between the shafts. A beautiful illusion, Berry reflected, somehow holding back the tears.

'Good huntin' country this,' he managed. 'A fellow could gallop for miles.'

The bombardment continued. On the third day the weather broke and became showery and cool. The cloud ceiling dropped and aeroplanes could not spot for the gun crews. With the sky so low it was hard for the observer to calculate the range and much

347

of the firing was slapdash. But the bombardment lost none of its ferocity and the limber teams were constantly employed. Heavy rain on the 27 and 28 June covered the road in mud and half-flooded the craters. Soon hooves and wheels had created difficult tracks each side of it where teams could become bogged down. Eventually the deluge turned to drizzle and the gunners were forced to use longer time-fuses to ignite the eighteen-pound shells so that they exploded with maximum effect.

The Friday night before the offensive saw the roads leading to the Front congested as the batallions left the rest billets and moved up. Throughout the half-dozen hours of darkness the guns punched away at the German positions. Slowly the mist thinned and vanished to reveal the low green hills and their white scars. A lull in the cannonade almost theatrically coincided with sunrise. The clouds carried off some of the morning's soft gold, and the horses at the line began to munch the grass at their feet. A heron flapped over the wood towards Gommecourt and the well-head of the Ancre. At ten past seven the Artillery provided a spectacular finale. For twenty minutes the siege guns boomed in an unbroken chorus and the German trenches disappeared under a pall of smoke. The ground shook and the horses were trembling and fighting their ropes. The noise of the eighteen-pounders attempting to cut paths through the barbed wire entanglements drilled into the animal's heads.

One explosion dwarfed all others. The huge mine planted under Hawthorn Redoubt in front of Beaumont Hamel, on the breast of the hill overlooking the British trenches, was detonated at twenty past seven. The column of earth, smoke and shattered bodies was massive. Ten minutes later, at Zero, the bombardment lifted and in the lull before the guns extended their range Beth and her companions could hear the wood whispering, and birdsong gusting off the fields. What they did not hear were the whistles shrilling all along the British forward trenches where men were swarming up the scaling ladders to pace across No Man's Land. Nor did the horses cropping the hush hear the chatter of German machine guns and the cries of the British soldiers being slaughtered on the slopes of Redan Ridge.

Before noon the grass between the wire entanglements was choked with the dead and dying, and the Pals Regiments of the Thirty-First Division had been cut to ribbons.

42

The black wisps of shell smoke were slow to vanish and when they did others replaced them right along the eastern horizon. Day broke to the quiver of gunfire. Serre had been taken and lost again, and things were much as they had been except for the British casualties.

Rain fell and the mud on the road to the gun pits and beside it was churned to a morass. The horses squelched unsteadily through the darkness. It was darkness devoid of hope, shell-holed, roaring; darkness without end. Through it passed the teams of snorting beasts their every nerve tuned to the thunder that arched over the battlefield. The whine of shells became the screams of men and animals but Beth could not voice her despair. She slithered and kicked and fought the mud over the last two or three hundred yards to the gun pits.

Orange flames leapt and fell in a line across the night where the eighteen-pounders were directing their fire over the rising ground at the German trenches. No Man's Land was lit by star shells that trembled around the flash and glow of exploding sixty-pound bombs. From dilated pupils the horses regarded the spectacle. Then the limbers were empty and the teams running again.

At daybreak the mist was full of the wounded coming down the line from the dressing station, most on foot, the rest flopped into ambulances; but Beth saw the mud oozing around her fetlocks and nothing else. She stumbled, expected him to ease up her head and talk her quietly to the hilltop and the company of the farm horses. She was weary. Bathsheba dragged her feet and coughed. The body of a chestnut gelding lay beside the road, half buried in slime. Missing her step Grace plunged a hoof through the splintered rib cage and from the hole issued a cloud of flies. They buzzed around the live animals until the carcass claimed them once more.

The rotting compost stench had the drivers retching. A five-nine burst behind them and something began to keen loudly and shrilly. The smoke uncurled and spread, and the horses stared into it. Ghost men and ghost lorries blocked the road. The rest of the world was fading under the animals' despair.

When his battery was mauled by the enemy Jack's stamina and skill were stretched to the limit. He and three other NCOs were mending wheels and harnesses or helping the veterinary section recover injured animals from the road. They saw horses they knew and loved having wounds dressed before the ambulance journey back to the field stations.

'Jerry abandons his,' the veterinary sergeant said as they eased a bay gelding into the cart. 'He don't shoot 'em or try to heal them. He just gives them the elbow.'

He grimaced and hung the green label on the horse's halter.

'Green for surgical,' he explained. 'White for medical; red for contagious diseases.'

'Then back to this,' said Jack.

The sergeant shrugged. 'It stops another animal being sent out from Blighty.'

Misery shifted in the bay's eyes.

'They know,' Jack whispered. 'They bloody know and they can't tell us.'

'Would it make it any better if they could?' said the sergeant.

'It would make it harder to use them.'

Recollection of the Chancellor shires rolling in the snow tore at his heart. Great, glossy children kicking up the snow, calling to each other and arching their necks under the smoke of their body heat. Great, happy children. A shell descended and the fountain of earth rose, hung for a moment and fell apart. Fumes gusted across the road and the sergeant coughed and drew the corner of his turned-up collar over his mouth.

'Walk on,' the driver said, and the two cart horses, who were tandem-hitched to the ambulance, strode away.

Twilight closed on the fields. Screened by trees to the west of the Front the British heavies opened up. Then a column of limbers came along the road at speed. Jack stepped aside and sat on an overturned water cart. The first team thundered past, the horses bounding through the mud. The right lead animal was familiar. Its face was white and despite the mud the marbling on its flanks and haunches was rich enough to catch the eye. Jack's skin prickled. The horse was surging on filling the air with spray that stank.

'Beth,' he cried. 'Beth.'

And she swung her head and tried to dig in her feet and stop. But Milburn's whip smacked her neck and obedience won. Her stride faltered only to lengthen again.

'Beth.' Jack began to run.

'McKenna,' the sergeant barked. 'Stand still, man, stand still.'

The mud sucked at his legs and brought him to a halt.

'Beth,' he groaned.

The lead driver of the next limber team was roaring at him to get out of the way. Then something hard and heavy struck Jack's shoulder and spun him off the road

'You dingo bugger!' the sergeant grunted, dragging him out of the shell hole. 'Talk about bog Irish! Where were you going, you horrible little Irishman?'

'It was my horse,' Jack gasped. He spat mud and pawed at his eyes. 'My bloody horse. My Beth.'

The sergeant stared at him and nodded.

'A red roan mare. Bethlehem. I helped bring her into the world. She's my horse.'

'No lad,' the sergeant said. 'She's the King's horse. There's nothing you can do about it. Best forget her – if it was her.'

Jack wiped his mouth on his sleeve and spat again. His puttees had uncoiled and were hanging over his boots.

'We don't own anything out here, lad – least of all ourselves.'

'She's mine,' Jack whispered. 'I made her a promise.'

351

'I made my old lady a promise at the altar but it don't mean a lot now.'

'She's mine,' Jack repeated, and there was a raw, manic certainty in his voice that aborted further comment.

Behind the wagon lines were the mass graves where they had buried the men who had died at the field hospital.

'Your padre is a good bloke, Irish,' said Sercombe. 'He don't hee-haw at you like the C of E bugger. That old turkey looks at 'ee like you'm something warm and stinkin' he's picked up on the sole of his boot.'

The wheels spun in the mud as the lorry slewed sideways around a shell hole and struggled to regain the road. It was one of many carrying the battery out of action to refit and rest behind the wagon lines. The horses were also brought to safe fields.

With the exception of Sercombe the drivers were silent.

'Hope us gets a bit of this,' he went on, lifting his right forearm and laying his left fist in the crux. 'I fancy a tasty bit of skirt.'

The Cornish was thick on his tongue.

The great adventure, Maxwell decided, had turned sour. He and Jack swapped glances. Each side of the road were men of the pioneer battalions up to their ankles in mud waiting to continue with the repairs. Beyond them were cornfields and pastures which seemed to have escaped the shelling. Then a wood of bare trees came into view and the illusion was shattered.

'Maybe I'll cop me a dose and get back to Blighty that way,' Sercombe mumbled, puffing out his cheeks to release a sigh of boredom. 'I bloody hope we'll see real active service in Bunkupville.'

No one laughed. The tans had paled, the eyes were deep sunk and lifeless. Like creatures released on parole from the abattoir, Jack thought. There was nothing to laugh at. And I'm no different than the worst of them. I'm trapped in the mess and she's back there with nowhere to hide and nothing to cling to. If I had any guts I'd go and find her. But he was drained and could hardly lift the cigarette to his lips. At that moment all he wanted to do was sleep; sleep and go home.

A Red Cap was directing the traffic at the crossroads and the copse on the right had not lost its leaves to the guns. Here war was rumour rather than reality. Once or twice the convoy slowed to overtake small groups of refugees and their handcarts. The early morning drizzle had not quite cleared and sunlight drifted and crumbled. Then the boy from Chagford raked at his lice and began to sing; other voices joined in.

> The moon shines bright on Charlie Chaplin
> His boots are cracking, for want of blacking,
> And his khaki trousers they want mending
> Before we send him to the Dardanelles.

Jack glanced at him, knowing the whizzbangs and coal boxes were exploding still behind the dazed expression. The rabbit in the snare, the starved monkey on the barrel organ. Everything swept away like a childhood summer – Melody, Beth, Iona, the long grass curling on Cider Mill Tor, laughter as evening closed round the yard. Why had it been? Why all the warmth and happiness and hope? Each of the lives in the back of the lorry was a small, anonymous stream that had run to this place.

He let the smoke drift from his nostrils and took another pull on the cigarette. They were entering a village. The lorry stopped and the sergeant-major began bellowing into a megaphone.

'Don't you lot even dream of mixing it with the infantry. Behave yourselves and report to me at 07.00 hours tomorrow for fatigues. *Comprée?*'

The village was one long broad street with houses on each side and no pavements.

'Bunkupville,' Maxwell said, nudging Sercombe. 'Fight your way through the skirt, man, and get us a beer.'

Kneeling in a tub of hot water Jack sweated out his depression. The *estaminet* was a short walk from the bath house and clean underclothes and brushed khaki. It was a dingy building trying to hide behind faded green shutters and grime. The drivers sat stiffly at a table near a dead stove waiting for the beer to be served.

'It's like gnats' piss,' someone confided.

'I like gnats' piss,' said Sercombe.

'*M'sieur?*' the old lady smiled.

'No *comprée*, *madame*, no *comprée*,' Sercombe said, raising his hands, palms upward.

'*Vous desirez de la bière? du vin blanc? du vin rouge?*'

'Bong joor,' Maxwell giggled. 'Commont allee voo?'

'Bocoo jig-a-jig here?' Sercombe pressed.

'*Ne comprend pas,*' said Madame from the broadest of smiles.

'Hoof and chips,' Maxwell said, gesticulating meaningfully.

The tips of forefinger and thumb of each hand came together to form the outline of an elipse.

'Wee wee – hoof. Hoof and chips. Egg and bloody chips.'

'*Ah bien! Oeuf.* Egg and chips.'

'And an omelette,' said Sercombe.

Madame poured a thin unpalatable beer from a jug and they drank.

'Your bloody French is almost as bad as your English, Jock,' Sercombe smiled.

They were calling for red wine when Jack wandered outside for a breath of fresh air. House martins were swooping to their nests under the eaves of the buildings and two little girls passed holding hands. Laughter spilled from the *estaminet* windows.

'Thinking of Blighty, McKenna?' said Lt Callaway.

'Children make me homesick, sir. Children and women like Madame in there.'

'Those aren't swallows are they?' the subaltern squinted at the sky.

'House martins, sir – like the ones we've got in the yard back in Devon.'

Callaway gave him a lazy smile. 'I'd like to buy you and the section a drink. Is the beer up to scratch?'

Jack laughed. 'If you've a taste for alcoholic cat's piss.'

Dusk crept through the village unobserved. Bats were on the wing, children called, the faint crackle of frying eggs came from the kitchen.

Maxwell and most of the drivers were slumped over the table asleep, and Callaway was sprawled in a chair in the corner, unconscious.

'Lucky buggers,' Sercombe murmured. 'Jesus! I'd have to drink a gallon of this stuff before I was halfway gone.'

He sloshed some more *vin rouge* into Jack's glass and drew the tip of his tongue along his lower lip.

354

'Look, McKenna, I don't mean to be a sour-gutted bastard. I don't mean to get under everyone's skin.'

His glass was raised, tilted and lowered.

'My missus ran off with another bloke five weeks before I joined up. I came home from work one afternoon and her wadn there. Seems they had been playing around for a long time.'

He growled up phlegm and swallowed it.

'I suppose tis that what makes it so hard. Whenever her said, "I love you, John", it was a lie. Twas all lies – everything us did together. Still, I dare say we've all got our problems but I want you to know why I'm always pissed off.'

Jack nodded, unable to care about the drunk.

'They'm probably doin' it now while we're sitting in this hole, swilling this muck.'

'Sure, it slides down well enough after a few.'

Sercombe wrapped his hands round his glass and stared into it.

'I doan want to go home, Irish,' he said quietly. 'This is the end of the line.'

Again Jack nodded and a curious frisson lifted the hair on the back of his neck. Where along the way, he considered, would he find Beth? The boy from Chagford woke up and broke into tears. He just sat there weeping silently while Madame collected the empty glasses.

'*Pauvre garçon*,' she said. '*Ils sont cochons, les Boches, cochons. Sale cochons.*'

'Boche napoo,' the boy slurred. Then he rested his face on his forearms and his shoulders shook.

355

43

Shellfire continued to lay its dizzy spell on the horses, goading them into exhaustion. To the east a weird light flared and descended yet was never extinguished. Westward flickered the radiance of the siege guns pumping 1400-pound shells into the enemy. The ground running from the wagon lines to the gun pits was a purgatory of ravaged woods and wet, pitted fields. Almost all of the wildlife had gone but foxes were sometimes seen slipping in and out of the rubble that had once been the mayor's house on the edge of the village. Elsewhere the rats were busy.

Life at the picket lines had deteriorated. A shortage of grazing and fodder had left the horses irritable especially when the evening breeze brought the breath of clover from pastures forbidden to them. They cowered in the clammy darkness under their blankets. The lines had been moved behind the village but heaps of shattered masonry provided scant shelter and summer rain continued to soften the fields.

Returning from the limber runs they would glimpse yellowing corn in the distance. Small, comforting things had been removed from their lives and they ached for them. The August sun turned the rain to steam on their coats and each interlude between barrages alarmed them with its silence. The larks had stopped singing and the crows had the sky and the countryside to themselves. A pair strutted along the line, gorged on the flesh of dead mules. The crows fluttered up but fell again, laying their wings tight to their bodies. Beth gazed beyond the birds at the man who was running through the grass and poppies towards them. It was him, she was sure. It was the horse-boy who had shared the water by the trees in the first spring of her life. The bad dream was ending. Already she could smell the orchards of home and hear Iona's fluted cry across dusks full of moths and flower scent. She raised her head, her ears pointed forward. The man drew near and with a chilling of the heart she saw it was not him. Bathsheba coughed again and the man came through the horse line to disappear.

Beth and Bathsheba leaned against each other trying to forget the flies. The landscape spawned its humming swarms. Every carcass played host to them, and they grew fat and sluggish.

But anything was preferable to the terror of the limber runs. The animals tensed as they were put into their gears and hitched up. Often, too, the drivers feared for their horses and muttered a string of endearments while the harness went on. Endearments incanted against disaster. Oh Christ, protect us all. Milburn leaned forward and patted Beth's neck.

'Good old lass, lovely girl.' His voice broke. 'How can we sing the Lord's song in a strange land?' They met other teams on the road, ploughing hock deep through the mud; but the shelling was casual and the race to the pits lacked its normal tension. Gunners and drivers joked as the ammunition was unloaded. Then out of the blue afternoon sky something curved down to plop into the mud and explode – almost effetely, Milburn thought. The wind blowing from the north east was gentle, but sufficient to sweep the gas over the guns. It spread in a greenish drift, and panic-stricken fingers fumbled the box respirators.

'Get them horses out of here,' the sergeant-major cried. Milburn struggled to ram the gauze plugs up Beth's nostrils and clip them into place with safety pins pushed through her flesh. She whinnied repeatedly and threw herself about; but Milburn won.

The chlorine gas was wreathing the pits. Men were choking and running, some without protection. Milburn tried to ignore Bathsheba's flailing hooves. Savagely he jerked her head down and planted the gauze. The pins piercing her nostrils set her

357

back on her haunches to deliver a staccato squeal. Then she closed her teeth on his shoulder and he had to smack her on the nose to free himself. The panels of his gas mask were misting up. He looked like some grotesque, round-eyed insect and the horses caught the vibrations of his fear. Beth's body was racked by convulsions. She drooled saliva and it dribbled off her chin. Milburn was on her back now, applying the whip. She started forward but the gas had overtaken them and the other teams. Swifter than a horse it covered the farmland and dispersed before reaching the wagon lines. The animals were frantic. They tossed their heads, attempting to rid themselves of the pain clamping their nostrils. They ran away from the pain, blindly, churning up the mud, breaking through the wall of heat and flies. Her sister's fear was a web on Beth's consciousness that she carried to the picket lines.

'Soddin' nightmare,' Milburn grated, tugging off his gas mask. 'Nightmare.' He fished his spectacles from his tunic pocket and breathed on the lenses before polishing them. Flies were scrummaging around the dry crumbs of blood each side of Beth's nostrils. He dug the curry comb into her coat and raked at the dirt. Flies settled to greedy on his sweat. He blinked, snorted and spat flies, hating God and the whole stinking mess of Creation.

'Go and eat shit, you horrible little bastards. Eat a staff officer.'

He giggled and his knees buckled. Beth gazed at him. Her head ached and each indrawn breath hurt. She was too tired to shake off the flies or note the conflict registering again along the horizon in gasps of smoke and light.

The harmonica glided effortlessly up hills of emotion to those heights only his class could divine. Sitting in the sun Jack thought of other Augusts and harvests brought home from fields above the bay. But time was meaningless. The blurred acceleration of events had slackened to a glacial drift and boredom. He heard Maxwell laugh and saw the group of drivers round the farrier's fire. Sercombe raised his voice and gesticulated. The horses were being watered before the shoeing. Captain Berry and another officer strolled along the line chatting with the men.

The coal boxes rushed out of the afternoon's calm, followed by three enormous explosions. Mud and scraps of flesh showered down on a tide of fumes. The ringing in Jack's ears gradually faded and the screaming and snorted moans spread with the smoke. Upwards of fifty animals and nearly that number of men were dead. A subaltern walked among the maimed and mortally wounded pointing his Webley at a head which might have been horse or human.

It was all so horribly casual, an incident scribbled on the fabric of the summer day like obscene graffiti. Jack got up and walked away trying to fight nausea. Maxwell and Sercombe were gone. Nothing remained as proof of their previous existence. They were the emptiness at the centre of a smoking hole.

The boy from Chagford came out of what had once been a walled garden, followed by half a dozen drivers in shirt sleeves and braces.

'Don't go over there,' Jack said. 'Don't. That's an order.'

'Who bought it, Corp?'

'The bloody lot – Max, Sercombe, Berry, all of them.'

He lit a cigarette, astonished at the steadiness of his hands. Down the road laboured the returning teams, and muffled thunder rolled across the Front. Beyond the wagon lines peasants were cutting the corn.

More rain and cool weather hastened the end of summer. Now the hoof prints at the lines were silvered with the webs of money spiders and dew persisted often to noon. Bathsheba's cough had worsened but she gave of her best on the limber runs, requiring no more than the company of Beth and Solomon.

They were picketed badly in a marshy hollow and sleep did not come easily despite hours of gut-wrenching toil fuelled by nervous energy. Their rugs were wet and heavy and fear was never absent. Another offensive had begun and the field guns were rarely silent. The British Front Line had been pushed forward although the situation north of Beaumont Hamel had altered little since the beginning of July.

During the first week of September the battery's gun emplacements were again changed and the teams sweated on the runs over open ground. While the guns were being

359

unhitched and rolled into position they came under fire from howitzers and four-twos. The barrage lasted nearly a minute and was intense. Three guns caught between the emplacements were destroyed with great loss of life. Major Welling, the battery CO, and a subaltern were killed instantly. Then the pits were strafed and two more guns put out of action by explosions which left a tangle of dying men and animals.

Beth's team took shelter in the furthest pit where the drivers held the horses' heads and tried to soothe them. Gouts of chalk spurted out of the shell smoke, and behind the crash of each detonation there was the keening of animals so badly wounded that the men going to their aid wept.

The pole bar off a limber whirled over the pits followed by shell splinters. The driver next to Milburn was struck in the neck. 'Christ,' he grunted as he died, and it was a cry of disgust, not a plea. Milburn loosened the hands clenched on the reins but Solomon and Grace would have panicked if the sergeant-major had not leapt into the pit. Then the surviving eighteen-pounder opened up a counter strafe and the heavies came to its assistance.

'Think you can get these poor buggers back to the lines, Milburn? We need ammo and the wounded need help.'

Beth fixed her eyes on Bathsheba and saw a reflection of her own terror. The mares were lathered all over in sweat, unable to move. Smoke darkened the sun and filled their nostrils. They could smell the suffering of horses. The smoke billowed black and always behind what the heart felt the prolonged soul-shattering cries of animals struggling through death breathed a bleakness.

'Milburn.'

'I'm shittin' myself, Sergeant-Major.'

'So am I. Get back to the wagons and tell them the CO is dead. Come on, man, before the animals go mad.'

He walked them slowly for the fear had not left them. Twice they made way for horse-drawn ambulances. Bathsheba's body sagged and her wheezing breath distressed her companions and worried Milburn. Listlessly she watched the file of pannier mules stumble by. They were thin, determined creatures, sheathed in mud.

'Poor bastards,' grunted the driver behind Milburn. 'You're

360

a chapel man, Stan. Well, if there is a God he's a cruel bugger.'

The fields glistened and the horses seemed to draw strength from the calm that rose off the landscape. Something profound sang to Beth's senses. It was as if the place and her companions had vanished leaving her becalmed beyond emotion. The movement of mules and horse-drawn vehicles failed to bring the countryside alive. Black skeletons which had once been trees hackled the horizon. Light badgered the flooded shell craters for a response. Southward the land rolled into the Ancre valley and the intense melancholy of dusk held the horses spellbound.

The air was faintly bitter with the reek of mud and what it harboured. Rain glittered across the moon then vanished. Milburn stood among the horses and recognised the goodness which sometimes enters human life through animals. The transgressions of the mediocre might go unpunished but the stars continued to shine and what the horses possessed was a freedom unknown to man.

Once more rain filled the gaps between bombardments, giving the landscape a bloom of cold beauty. The horses waited to be fed. Walking the lines their drivers tried to comfort them. Bathsheba's laboured breath continued to alarm Beth and Solomon but all three animals were conscious of Iona's presence. Then they could forget the strained gut, the knife-cut gasps for air after the gassing, and the homesickness. Despite everything they had not relinquished their love of the living world. No despair touched their lives unless it was introduced by man. Yet as moonlight fanned across the fields Beth continued to search the distances for Jack, unwilling to part with the dream of what had been.

Very few of the men at the pickets were unmoved by the horses' suffering. The subalterns, who were predisposed to compassion, attempted to patch up the tragedy. They were young with high principles and were loved and respected by the drivers; but existence had become a bad dream of lives vanishing in mud and smoke. There was such an inexhaustible store of life to throw into the pit death had created that individual suffering was meaningless. To trade on the innocence of animals, though, struck most men as dishonourable. Some dwelt murderously on the cynicism of a High Command whose judgments filled graves, but the majority were resigned to their fate and remained optimistic about the offensive.

What was going on at the Front did not concern Jack. He would lift a grubby face, sniff the wind and listen to the horses puffing into their nosebags. He cared about Maxwell's death but his eyes stayed dry. The hack looked at him. Morning was spreading over the lines. Men were gathering at the field cookers as the bombardment began with a roar from the British heavy guns which lasted three days and nights.

During mid-September the fighting was hampered by bad weather and the limber teams struggled slowly along the flooded roads to the pits. Returning from one such trip Milburn learnt his battery was to be amalgamated with another whose losses had been similar. Around noon limbers, wagons and animals came briskly out of the rain gloom. The horses were tethered and all the men save one sought the shelter of the dugouts.

Milburn was at the lines making sure his team did not trample their hay, and he regarded the approaching stranger curiously. The man looked at each horse in turn until he reached Beth. The recognition was instant. The roan's head jerked up, her eyes widened and she loosed a whinny of joy.

'Oh Beth,' Jack whispered, the tears streaming down his face. Her soul stared out at him and he placed his hands on her head.

'Bethlehem, my beauty.'

The heavy lashes descended and she sighed. Then she took a step forward to lay her muzzle on his shoulder. His arms encircled her neck and they stood together. For a long while she gathered his smell and the love that came from his touch and the sound of his voice. Bathsheba and Solomon whickered their eagerness to share the reunion but Jack and Beth were lost to the world. He had come to her in the place that was not home. Now everything would be fine. Now he would ride her out of the darkness and misery back to the warm stall and the hilltop above the sea.

'What have they done to you, girl?' He pulled off the sodden rug. Her mane was no more than a crest of muddy tufts and the rain running down her flanks and chest cut rivulets through the mud picked up on the last limber run. Jack's heart swelled. Between him and the animal, elements of the past they had shared swelled to clarity. She was breaking free of the sluice at Aish again – a small leggy creature quivering as they took to the flood water. The wet coldness flowed over his body but she was safe there in the summer the war could not reach.

Suddenly the sorrow was too painful to endure and he began to dredge up great sobs, tapping his forehead gently against Beth's muzzle. The linhay under Aish Farm firmed to silent unreality because he needed somewhere he could run to with his anguish. Straw and meal bags and the moonlight holding nothing that could hurt them. In her warmth and gentle breathing was a force he had imagined was inextinguishable. Then, he clenched his teeth, to find her alone in that place. He swallowed and the sobbing stopped. It was a moment of agony mingling with relief.

Another jab of memory brought him to the zero where emotion was frozen by recollection of former happiness. He wanted her to be safe and away from it all. The valley of the shadow. Yes, and the war had left him famished for things he had taken for granted. To walk through Clennon Valley in the spring would be a kind of resurrection. Now he was standing on the edge of a precipice staring into the void. It was a sickening sensation. Yet they had emerged from the mud by the sluice into another spring, to gallop along the beach towards Kitty. The good times were waiting for them on the hill above the sea, facing the sunrise. Mother of God, he prayed, let me take her home.

Beth watched him carefully. She was happy and her movements were honed by a new alertness. He had come as she had always believed he would. Beyond his voice and touch she could see the familiar places. But the mare's beauty had gone, leaving her thin and dirty. Only her eyes retained some of the splendour she had brought with her out of birth.

44

Autumn sunlight twinkled on beaks and berries, and the
bottoms of the hedges were patched with spiders' webs. Small
birds rocked the hogweed in a noisy flock before flitting over the
women to vanish behind the copse. The sunlight smelt of
woodsmoke. Blanche and Lily ran ahead, stopping to pick the
best button mushrooms. Kitty walked a little apart from the
group, hands behind her back and Dando at her side. Beyond
the yellowing mound of Clennon Wood Our Lady of
Lansworthy stood serene in the sky.

The mushroom was cold in Mary McKenna's fist. On a gush
of emotion she recalled other autumn expeditions to the fields
and his laughter and the way be brought her things as if God had
just made them: ripe blackberries, a handful of hazelnuts; a
chaffinch's tail feather.

'Them bloody conshies,' Kitty said suddenly. 'They ought to
shoot the lot or force 'em to walk in front of our boys when they
go at the Germans. Tidn fair.'

'Jack's all right, darling,' said her mother-in-law. 'Jack
always comes home. I bet him and the other lads are kickin' up
hell with the old Hun.'

Kitty nodded. The wind lifting off the bay swept her hair
across her face, and struggling to push it back under her hat she
remembered how he would part the tresses to kiss her. Life had

become a strange routine of walks, conversations by the fire and sick anticipation of the knock and the telegram. It was easy to believe the whole of Lansworthy had a son or brother or father at the front. Newspaper victories were celebrated in bold headlines: 'Great Day on the Somme'. 'British Advances Shatter the Hun'. The khaki heroes were surging forward to scourge the enemy with bare steel. Haig's crusaders were winning, so all the heroism and sacrifice was reaping its reward.

Yet the hospital trains and ambulances bringing home the wounded shocked even staunch patriots like Sidney Chancellor and the Daubenys. The front page of the *Lansworthy Observer* was one great casualty list decorated with photographs of the dead. Every street had its blinds down and against the lamp post at the top of Angarrick Terrace a little shrine had been erected to the fallen. The names of men and boys killed in action were printed on a white card surrounded by their photographs and bunches of chrysanthemums.

Tending the shrine and similar shrines all over town were bereaved mothers and young wives aged by the loss of a man who had seen less summers than there are hours in a day. The grey of the sky and the grey sea subdued the Three Towns. Greyness seemed to have risen like a fog as if the war required it. Sea mist, rain and the grubby bloom of gaslight presided over the empty, night-time streets; but up on Cider Mill Tor the owls called and the hares waited with the horses for the stars to appear.

Duck passed high and silent across the sunset behind the battle zone. All along the picket lines the drivers were rubbing down their animals and grumbling about the rain which had fallen for days. The clear evening amplified the thunder of gun fire, and the tell-tale glow quaked on the horizon.

Beth's ears pricked but she was content under Jack's hands. All the warmth of the past enfolded her and she stood placidly while he wisped down her flanks. Milburn shook his head and wiped the mist off his glasses. Jack's story had rekindled his belief. He was happy to take over Grace and Solomon and leave the mare to the young Irishman.

The village was occupied by artillery and infantry personnel, but there was no shelter for the horses. They stood at the lines which should have been situated on a gentle, well-drained slope with some sort of protection from the prevailing winds. Nothing was ideal at the Western Front. High on the CO's priorities was the need to conceal his animals from the German spotter planes or, failing this, to keep them static and inconspicuous.

The long rope of the line was drawn taut and knotted to picket posts. It was three and a half feet above the ground to discourage horses from stepping over it and snarling their tethers. Each animal's head rope was attached to the line, giving it room to lie down if it chose but not sufficient to encroach upon its neighbours.

During heavy bombardments heel ropes were fixed to the more nervous horses but the lines themselves were spread on ground that held water and this disturbed Jack. He recalled the quagmire on Lansworthy Green if it rained during the Regatta Fair. So he approached the subaltern in charge of his section and suggested they set up two more lines which the horses could use alternately. This would alleviate the discomfort of standing in deep mud night after night.

Behind all the discussion the tragic absurdity of the affair made him ache to bellow obscenities. If it was a question of life or death there was only one choice. The horses must live. The boys in the trenches must live. Every bugger wanted to jack it in and go home. Come on, come on, he thought, blow off Haig's bollocks and let me take my horse home. It was crystal clear.

Amazingly, back a bit from the horror, Kitty was laundering her frillies and his mother was feeding the dog. Trivia won in the end. It swamped every corner of human existence. Polish those buttons and boots. Can't have you going west in shit order, McKenna. The madness left him grinning at the sky. Who lights candles for the horses? Who sends them off blessed into eternity?

Bathsheba had a cold and was isolated at the end of the line, but Jack and Milburn kept it to themselves for fear she would be slaughtered or sold to the local peasants. The RSPCA hospital was full, the rumours claimed, although their ambulances were still busy.

Bathsheba's case was not unique. All the animls at the picket lines were in bad shape. The cool nights, shortage of fodder, and the continual drain on their nervous systems made them lose weight and the will to do anything other than brood. Jack knew it was important to keep up their body temperature and produce the energy a work day demanded. They needed hay to replace the salt they had sweated out but hay was difficult to acquire. When a third of what was asked for arrived it was yellow and limp and had neither sweetness nor fragrance. Black English oats, split beans, a little linseed cake, sliced carrot and some wheat straw as chafe reached the pickets in small quantities. When bran was available Jack made a mash to build up Beth, and he fed oatmeal gruel to Bathsheba. His presence at the lines impressed his superiors and cheered up the men.

Then late one afternoon Jack turned the teams out to graze and incurred the wrath of his CO, the French farmer and a posse of staff officers who chose to visit the picket lines as the horses ate their way across the neighbouring fields.

'Good Lord!' the Brigadier exclaimed. 'Every Taube this side of Serre will be dropping in on you, Dellow.'

Major Dellow said something to the sergeant-major and he coloured.

Later Jack was sent for but the sergeant-major's ill-humour wilted before his sincerity.

'Sure, it was hellish good for their digestion and general condition. All them fields going to waste.'

'Good for the horses but not for the battery commander, McKenna.'

'Without them we'd be in a mess, sir.'

'Shut up,' the sergeant-major said, wagging a finger. 'When me or the CO or the General Staff want your opinion we'll ask for it. Until then you stay put, do as you are told and keep your mouth shut.'

'And isn't this war being run by fools,' Jack said, standing at the field kitchen with Milburn. He half-turned, expecting to see Maxwell's dark smiling face. Hurriedly reshuffling his thoughts he added, 'If you starve the horses and leave them out in all weathers they won't be able to do the job. It really is that simple.'

'Nothing's that simple to a staff officer.'

'Maybe they ought to starve those buggers and leave them out in all weathers and give their rations to the horses.'

'Would the beasts like all that caviare and curried prawns and stuff?'

'Not if they knew where it came from.'

Jack stuck his thumbs in the breast pockets of his tunic and put on an expression of mock gravity.

'I say, I say, I say, Milburn old thing, "if bread is the staff of life, what is the life of the staff?"'

'"One long loaf"!'

It was a well-worn routine brought out and dusted after visits from red-tabbers. The cooks did not smile. Jack held out his mess tin.

'Ah, the Maconochie special! And there I was praying I'd be getting some of your delightful home-made puke.'

The cook sniffed and ladled the thin, grey, lukewarm gruel. As it slid into Jack's tin a piece of turnip surfaced coyly and submerged again.

'My compliments to the chef.'

Again no response.

Jack and Milburn joined the other drivers sitting with their backs to the wall.

'Soddin' crap,' said a voice and a meal splashed into the grass. 'I'd rather eat horse shit – at least it's hot.'

But many animals had diarrhoea brought on by their duties and nervous excitement. When it was available they were given ground corn, yet the drivers knew their condition could only get worse. Over-exertion, fatigue, life at the picket lines and the awful slog to the gun pits were taking their toll. Fear was debilitating and the horses would sweat as soon as they were taken onto the road with the limbers. The men, too, fed on negation. In the end it was difficult to find meaning in suffering for its own sake. All the wisdom the animals had received direct from the living world provided no answers; but Beth found solace in Jack's company. The game was acceptable if they played it together, and autumn could provide images to rekindle rapture.

Yet Chancellor's horses were aware that something had entered their lives to take away the still mornings when they had come together on the edge of mystery. Recollection of Tor Barton Springs sent the chestnut blossom pattering across Beth's thoughts. The sun shone and they were running around

368

the paddock: Princess and Bathsheba, Melody and her foal. Then the night was speaking to her and the curlews were calling as Iona ambled down the hillside. She rolled in the grass beside the hedge where the yellow hammer sang. The special somewhere lay behind a fold in the countryside or a bank of cloud, waiting. There the willow leaves were whitening and the dragonflies clicked and rustled over the reflection of boy and horse.

Coming out of action for a rest and refit gave the drivers a chance to scrounge extra fodder for the animals, but there was little to be had. Yet more draught and carriage horses poured in from the Remount Centre. They passed through the village, heads erect and coats all rain-glossed. The infantry coming up from base were also well-groomed.

The general service wagons, omnibuses and carts left deep ruts in the muddy streets which quickly filled with water. Then the rain passed leaving the day showery.

'Some of the lads have got Blighty leave,' said Milburn. 'Jammy bastards.'

The oil lamp and open iron stove smoked into the *estaminet*. Madame beamed through the fug and collected the money for a refill. She returned to the table holding the jug in both hands, but Jack waved her on. He sat in the corner trying to rough out a letter to Kitty, feeling lonelier than he had at the wagon lines. The timelessness was absent. He was in a small, stuffy room in a foreign country with a lot of strangers and an old lady who could speak no more than half a dozen words of English. Her feet rucked the newspapers which had been laid on the floor like lino, and the beer clouded and swirled in the glasses. Two of the subalterns called for cognac, using schoolboy French as they handed round cigarettes which were better quality than the usual 'issues'.

Three jugs were emptied before Sergeant Pike decided to sing. He had a pleasant tenor voice softened by the Devon burr:

My old man's a dustman,
He fought at the Battle of Mons,
He killed 10,000 Germans
With only a couple of bombs.
One lay here, one lay there, one lay round the corner;

369

And one poor sod with his leg hanging off
Was crying out for water.

Other voices joined the chorus:

Madame, your beer's no *bon*,
Madame, your beer's no *bon*.
Your *pomme de terre frites*,
They give us the squits,
Madame, your beer's no *bon*.

The proprietress who had heard it all before, continued to beam
and supply the ale. Then the Chagford boy took out his mouth
organ, and played a medley of sentimental songs and ballads.
Beer and warmth, safety and comradeship loosed the tears until
Pike guided the company back to cheerfulness when he
suddenly stood on the bench and gave them '*Après La Guerre*'
to the tune of '*Sous les Ponts de Paris*'.

Après la guerre finie
Soldat Anglais parti;
Mam'selle Fransay boko pleuray
Après la guerre finie.

Après la guerre finie,
Soldat Anglais parti;
Mademoiselle in the family way,
Bokoo de picaninnee

'*C'est seulement une farce*,' one of the subalterns explained, but
the proprietress never took offence. The words were un-
important and the tune pleasant. Out in the kitchen her sister
hummed to herself as she cooked the omelettes.

Pike was repeating the final verse when the door opened and
an officer entered with his trench coat slung over an arm.

'Don't stand,' he said smiling. 'Is that beer? God! I've got a
thirst on.'

The voice was enough. Before his eyes lifted from the letter
Jack knew it was Edward Daubeny crossing to the stove, the
three pips glinting on his shoulder. A lump came to Jack's
throat. He got to his feet, and stepping back to let Madame
through with her jug Daubeny caught sight of him. Pike and the
estaminet choir had begun 'Fred Karno's Army' which had

borrowed its air from 'The Church's One Foundation'.

> We are Fred Karno's army,
> The ragtime infantry:
> We cannot fight, we cannot shoot,
> What bloody use are we?

'They're in good voice, Jack.' His handshake was firm. For Daubeny the war, like life, was a question of reaffirming priorities, so it was easy to ignore the subalterns' glances.

'Captain Daubeny,' Jack grinned.

'*Acting* Captain, Corporal McKenna,' from a sardonic smile.

'Will you join me in a drink, sir?'

'Are you buying?'

'Why not? Doo beers, Madame sil voo play.'

'That's pretty good French.'

'All the lads can speak a bit of the Froggy lingo.'

Daubeny accepted one of Jack's cigarettes and said, '*Et deux cognacs aussi, Madame.*'

It transpired that his presence was no coincidence.

Dora had given him Jack's serial number, battery and brigade. The transfer was simple, considering the 'wastage' of officers in the regiment. 'Wastage' was Daubeny's expression. If was the official term to denote numbers of animals killed in action.

'But why my battery?' Jack said.

'You are minus a second-in-command I believe.'

Daubeny tried to blow a smoke ring and failed. His moustache was quite bushy and lent a solemn note to his countenance.

'Also Dora wants me to make sure you don't do anything daft. Remember our conversation on Goodrington Beach? I was more than a bit dingo then, coming home like that straight out of action. Well, don't try anything dodgy out here or they'll shoot you as a deserter. Have you found Beth?'

'Yes.'

'And you plan to walk off with her? Just walk on and on to, say, Brittany and get a boat to Ireland?'

'Something like that.'

'Forget it. It's too fantastic for words. They'd catch you and shoot you for certain. Then they'd send her back to the Front –

371

with no one to care whether she lives or dies.

'They can try.'

'Listen, Corporal, the woods round here are full of deserters who aren't going anywhere. You might crouch in a covert till the war's over but what about Beth? Stay put – there's a good chap. Keep an eye on her. After all, you know the ropes. You're her one real chance.'

They threw back the cognacs and sipped the beer.

'Christ!' Daubeny said, wrinkling his nose and shuddering. 'I'd forgotten how bad this is.'

'It's all right on the old *pommes frites*,' Jack grinned.

'You'll pull in your horns, then?' Daubeny pressed. He was reminded of converstions with difficult members of the school fifteen.

Jack nodded.

'Good show! Now where is this blessed roan?'

'Under cover for the first time in months. Up the road at the farm. Beth, Bathsheba and Solomon.'

'God Almighty! You're a magician, Corporal.'

'Will you have another cognac, sir? Those subalterns are giving us some funny looks.'

'Do you know them?'

'Yes – they're A1.'

'Subalterns generally are. Shall I call them over?'

'Why don't you go and join them? Tell them I was your groom or something back in Blighty.'

'Not my pal?'

Jack grinned again. 'We're all pals out here, sir, but you don't have to talk about it. That would spoil everything.'

45

Men and horses died in a landscape that grew darker and more alien as autumn progressed. Cold drizzle passed over the fields. The sky was grey, the earth grey and glistening. Across this desolation the horses journeyed. Stark perception of their plight kept them miserable although Beth had a little vitality now and shared it with her companions.

The fighting of mid-September had run through a series of attacks and counter attacks to a great artillery battle near the end of the month; but the heavy rains of October failed to wash away the confusion at the gun pits and wagon lines. Despite newspaper claims, the Germans could throw up a bombardment whenever they chose. On nights free of shelling, and there were many, tension persisted. Weariness was the one thing all men and animals at the Front had in common.

'The clocks go back in a couple of weeks,' Milburn said absently.

They were trying to dry the horse blankets in front of a bonfire of ammunition boxes. Rain slanted across a sombre afternoon. The desperation in Milburn's voice no longer surprised Jack for it was part of dugout life, like the odour of damp khaki and the itch of lice.

'I'd give anything to hear my old mum's clock ticking on the mantelpiece above a real fire.'

Jack did not reply. He was struggling to work out a way of rescuing Beth from the limber runs. Rain beaded the eaves of his helmet. Along the wall where the horses stood it hissed relentlessly.

Throughout the early hours shells had fallen close to the picket lines and a couple of animals had gone crazy and were shot. Life for the horses had become a continuous penance. Captain Daubeny's attempt to raise tarpaulin stables had met with his CO's disapproval. Men were out in the open, so were the guns. Daubeny's tarpaulins vanished to hide the eighteen pounders, and the animals were left to survive as best they could. Whenever they were at the lines Jack spent half the night changing their blankets and drying out the wet ones so that his team were not shivering when breakfast was served. The other drivers attempted to follow his example but most were as exhausted as their horses and by dawn the line was a chorus of coughing and wheezing animals.

The wind came off the ridge, wet and cold. Beth snorted a greeting and settled her gaze on him, stamping the rhythm of her pleasure. Watching them together Daubeny was saddened. On a surge of bitterness he saw God as a falsification of the human condition. Instinct made him cry out for justice and kindness, but he could not bring himself to approach Jack and speak to him. More than anything he was aware of his impotence which the siege guns, opening up in the west, accentuated.

At dusk the activity around the pickets was frantic as the teams were driven to the ammunition dump. Beth was in her usual lather despite Jack's weight on her back. During the afternoon meal five nines had fallen close to the road and all the horses were apprehensive; but Bathsheba's distress was heightened by illness. She gasped throughout the loading of the limber and Jack held her muzzle and spoke to her. That excitable temperament could not come to terms with the nightmare. Like Beth she recalled the happy times at the yard where the absence of suffering was a benediction. Shadows veiled the brilliance which she could never quite shape into a field. Even the love transmitted by her fellows failed to set her cantering beyond care if only for the time her eyes remained closed.

Rain swooped, blurring the lights on the horizon but not their noise. They passed a bogged down water cart up to its axles in mud. Light faded to pitch-black darkness, lit now and then by the flash of the field guns. The battery fired over a thousand shells in half an hour. The guns glowed and the fumes got into the horses' throats. Then the rain eased to reveal the moon behind thin cloud; but the mist wreathing the sandbags and barricades held its own sickly light.

Weighed down by wet topcoats the men emptied the limbers, crouching whenever a shell landed. Their faces would suddenly leap golden out of black as the guns barked and spurted flame. A downpour hammered the emplacements but the work continued.

The road back was a gleaming cat-walk of mud and flooded shellholes. Whenever the moon shone the landscape swelled and the sea of mud vibrated under a fresh barrage. One of the limbers took a direct hit and exploded leaving a heap of bodies and some smoke. Beth threw back her head and snorted. The men were dead and the sole surviving horse was quivering into stillness. More five-nines descended close at hand. Then Solomon flopped onto his side, dragging Grace with him. The moon chose that moment to sail free of the clouds. Jack, Milburn and the wheel driver gathered round the old horse.

'Jesus,' Jack spat through clenched teeth. 'Jesus Christ. Oh Christ, Christ.'

The shell cap had smashed Solomon's left foreleg below the knee, splintering the bone and almost severing the limb. He managed to sit back on his hindquarters but an attempt to stand brought him over on his side again. The rest of the team went berserk and Milburn and the other driver struggled to calm them.

Solomon breathed a high-pitched neigh of agony and raised his head, unable to comprehend and expecting help from the man crouching over him. Jack wiped the filth from the horse's nostrils. Blood oozed black into the black slime partly covering the wound. Solomon groaned. Sick with horror Jack turned to the subaltern but the young man was appalled.

'Do it, sir.'

Solomon's great brown eyes were full of question and pain. What have you done to me? they pleaded. Why am I here like

375

this?

'Sir.'

The eyes rolled but they held a glimmer of hope after the bullet had stilled Solomon's brain. Jack tipped back his helmet and shook his head. Beth was struggling to turn, perpetually shrilling her anguish, and the subaltern was troubled by this unexpected demonstration of grief.

Beth felt the past disintegrating and spinning away from her in fragments. She and Bathsheba lamented the passing of their stablemate. They swung their heads from side to side, and stamped their feet as Jack released the gelding from his gears for the last time.

The rain returned, washing the mud off Solomon's face. The drivers remounted and took the team forward. Half the sky was starry and moonlit, the remainder black. The shelling stopped. Through the hush came the gasp and snort of animals and Milburn blaspheming.

46

Jack and Daubeny had very little contact as autumn wore on. Daubeny did not regret acting on impulse; it was his nature, but apart from the horse and the memory of a few seaside summers he felt he had nothing in common with the Irishman. Sharing a love of truth was hardly the basis for a friendship rendered almost impossible by class barriers. McKenna had no interest in literature or art or anything vaguely intellectual. Daubeny did not regret coming to the Brigade. One corner of the slaughterhouse was very much like another. But it made things interesting, slightly noble, and Dora would be impressed.

And yet behind the excuses his respect for Jack endured. He continued to admire the horsemaster and the way he handled the picket line animals. The magic was raw and aboriginal, and it questioned his own culture which had shallow roots.

Seated alone in a corner of the mess, half-listening to the gramophone grate out something from 'Chu Chin Chow', he completed the poem.

> I can't see you, he screamed
> From behind the blood.
> I can't see you, Mother;
> But we were already sleeping
> In the mud,
> My brother, my brother,

And tomorrow fell
Then another and another.

The rest camp merely postponed the inevitable. Men sang the well-worn songs in the YMCA canteen. They played housey-housey and brag, attended awful concerts, drank in the fug of the *estaminets*, then went back to be killed. It was rather like a tragi-comedy performed in an asylum.

At a different time near the Rest Camp a thin woman offered her body for money. Jack grinned and dug into his pocket and gave her a handful of loose change before leading her to the door.

Outside he said, 'Go home, darling, and God go with you.'

'*Mais, m'sieur –*'

'No mays – just go.'

Oh Kitty. Let me lay my lips on your flower-scented hair. Reconstructing their lovemaking behind his eyes was never easy. The bath water beaded on her breasts, her lashes quivered, light streamed down her curves. He was consumed by the phantom of her beauty – the movement of an arm, the arching back, eyes full of his facsimile.

'Go home,' he choked.

Rain swept the tableland and the horses bowed their heads. Bathsheba gazed at the horse occupying Solomon's place. The loss of the gelding nagged away at her and she would not be consoled. Lifting her nose she whickered and waited for him to answer. The heartache was stubborn.

Rain continued to fall, heavy and silent. Now Bathsheba was refusing her food. Putting her in her gears Milburn was conscious of the piercing look she gave him. Jack let Beth stand close to the sick creature and bring her into silence. Right down the line horses were restless and ill. The Brigade veterinary officer despaired but did what he could, weeding out the worst cases for hospitalisation.

To this small corner of the Western Front came the staff officers. The drivers were loafing about unshaven in their jerkins and muddy puttees for the limber runs through the previous night had been particularly arduous.

'Good lord,' drawled the red-tab colonel. 'What is this, Daubeny – a tramps' convention? Get the riff-raff in line.'

378

'They've been up and down to the guns all night, sir.'

'That's no excuse for slovenliness. Put those men on a charge. Have I made myself clear?'

The colonel had cut himself shaving but otherwise he was perfectly groomed. The mud oozing over his polished riding boots delighted Daubeny and the subalterns.

'This really is a shambles. Can't you find any fatigues for these men? The brigadier hates idleness.'

'My drivers have come under enemy fire for three days in succession,' Daubeny said. 'They are exhausted, hungry and close to breaking.'

'Rot! If every CO along the Front thought like that morale would be nonexistent and the Boche would be in our trenches now.'

His inspection was memorable if only for the enormous fart released by a horse and the attempt of the entire parade to keep straight faces. All the colonel could do was pretend the incident had not occurred.

'Don't let these men go back to base for another dose of idleness. This sort of thing stems from slack command.'

Daubeny nodded and Sergeant Turnbull could see the jaw muscles twitching as the captain fought for self-control. The party moved across to the picket lines.

'It simply won't do, Daubeny,' the colonel said. 'These animals need grooming, and look at the state of their rugs!'

The horses stood in liquid mud. They were lifting their feet one at a time in an effort to ease their discomfort. A dozen or so were isolated from the others. Individual ailments included bog-spavins, cracked hooves, splints and poll-evil. Tissues and joints were inflamed, and the pus ran from head wounds.

'They aren't clipped,' the colonel said triumphantly. He pointed his riding whip at Bathsheba. 'Regulations insist all animals are clipped in November. November began three days ago. See that they are trace-clipped, Captain. I'll be back in a day or so, and God help you and your slackers if things haven't improved.'

'You clip them horses, sir,' Jack blurted, 'and they might as well lie down and die right now. Standin' out in all weathers with half their coat gone will finish them off.'

'Put that man under arrest, sergeant,' Daubeny barked.

379

'Bring him to my dugout as soon as the Colonel's gone.'

Walking back to the road and the staff officers' transport he said, 'I think, sir, what the corporal meant was the animals have pretty thick coats, waterproofed to a certain extent by their own oils. Clipping them will make them vulnerable to debility. The wastage here is phenomenal as it is.'

'Corporals are not running this show, Captain,' came the haughty reply. 'Clip them. The brigadier does things by the book.'

'With the greatest respect, sir, the brigadier does not have to stand out in all weathers, day and night.'

Colour suffused the Colonel's face. 'I shall be having strong words with your CO, Captain. Slackness cannot be tolerated.'

The horses remained unclipped. Major Dellow, the Battery Commander, was no fool. In a memo to Brigade he regretted the loss of clipping irons and noted tersely that there were more important jobs to be done than primping animals.

Enemy shelling accounted for only a small percentage of limber horse deaths. Standing in the rain at the lines, deterioration was rapid. They stood shivering under the wet blankets, lifting their feet endlessly until exhaustion claimed the weakest. The rain poured down and the shortage of food left them desperate with hunger. Some tried to eat their own harness and their neighbours' rugs. Those at the end of the lines gnawed the picket posts.

During the dark hours when even the guns were still the 'chug-chug' of hooves being withdrawn from the mud and set down again was a most harrowing sound. The drivers went from horse to horse offering words which had long ago lost meaning. The pavane of distressed animals lent a haunting sadness to the night; yet although each dawn produced its scattering of lifeless heaps, the dance continued.

Among the victims was Bathsheba. Weakened by exposure and grief she no longer wished to live. Eventually her heart broke and she keeled over and died without a sound. As gently as possible Jack removed her halter and scraped the mud off her face. Beth's head dropped and she pawed the ground.

47

Another gas attack, another night of rain and blackness on the limber runs, another box barrage, a direct hit on an ammunition dump and flame ascending. The hideously slow lurch of blind animals. Horses with influenza or pleurisy being carted away in ambulances; others receiving the bullet. The sky pressing down on the picket lines.

Then the weather suddenly brightened and aeroplanes and balloons were aloft, spotting for the artillery. Barrages became less haphazard and the Signals Officer in his forward position could supply detailed information to the guns. Gazing down from the cockpit of his aircraft the young British aviator saw a landscape born of some immense nightmare. Animals and men were crossing it, and shells were bursting above it but in the distance, east and west, the countryside was green.

They were rounding up sick horses for the veterinary hospital. The smell of chloroform drifted over the picket lines from the Dressing Station in the village and the drivers cursed the mud that had the consistency of glue. It sucked at their legs wherever the ground shelved to a hollow. They brought it underground on their clothes. Each side of the road the land had become a bog, but the morning was clear and frosty, the stillness broken by the thud of the pumps in the dugouts trying to lower the water level.

Beth had been resting behind the wagon lines and looked fitter than she had for weeks. Somehow Daubeny had obtained a load of hay and oats. The subalterns said it was his connections at Brigade but no one cared. It was pleasant to hear the animals chomping their fodder in the sunlight, and the larks singing again.

'Hark at the little beauties,' Milburn smiled, pulling on his pipe. 'What've they got to sing about?'

'It must be a relief not to know anything,' someone said.

'This can't go on forever. Jerry must be as cheesed off as us,' said Milburn. 'Poor old Jerry.'

'Why shouldn't it go on forever?' Sergeant Turnbull said. 'Hell's forever, ain't it?'

'We'll run out of animals,' Jack said.

'Then the sodding staff officers will get us –' as he said 'us' Turnbull stick a finger in his chest – 'To haul the limbers and guns. Further down the line I hear they're eating horseflesh regular.'

Jack buried his hands in his pockets and walked off.

'That's where most of your casters go, Irish – to the Froggy butchers or the regimental cooks.'

Towards the top of the picket line Milburn caught up with him and dragged his elbow.

'Turnbull was only having you on, son.'

'I know. He don't bother me. He's not a bad bloke.'

'What's up then?'

'I've got to get Beth off the limber runs before she joins Sheba and Solomon.'

'You can't steal a horse and just ride it away. They'd have thee as a deserter.'

'Then I'll have to do what I should have done before the bastards took her. Dora was right.'

'Dora?'

'My sister-in-law. She told me to cripple her but I couldn't. To me Beth's perfect. It's not just the way she looks, it's what she is. To interfere with all that purity would be evil.

'But if you cripple her she'll get the bullet.'

'I won't give her a bad injury – just something to get her sold off to a French farmer. Daubeny says that happens to a few casters. The farmers need work-horses and they don't eat everything on four legs. Anyway, at least she'll have a chance, Stan. Here she's doomed. I'll see to it on the run back tonight, or maybe I'll do something a bit more drastic a bit sooner.'

He passed a hand swiftly across his eyes.

'How is all this possible? Where's the sense in it?'

Beth opened her eyes and came back to the dusk. Stars shone from a blue haze. The bombardment had lifted but every so often the eighteen pounders banged. Coolly and methodically Jack went down the line loosing the halter ropes while the sentries huddled together sharing a cigarette. The animals retreated a pace or two, lifting their hooves high but remaining silent.

'And where do you and they go from here?' said Daubeny's voice. 'Paris? Timbuktu? Cloud bloody cuckoo-land?'

'Anywhere's better than here.'

Daubeny tugged at his coat collar. 'Have you considered the chaos a mass of strays would cause running about in our wagon lines?'

The sentries started down the slope towards them but he sent them back with a quiet command.

'The horses, McKenna. Return them to the line – now.'

'Or you'll have me shot?'

'Something like that.' Daubeny's voice hardened. 'Do it.'

Jack tied the first hitch. 'Jesus, but you're no different than the other bastards, mister. They bullshit you and you believe it or pretend to believe it. That makes everything fine and dandy. All the King's horses, the flag, the bloody Empire. Murderin' these animals don't matter so long as the village up the road is taken or that bloody wood or – or some other place. You weren't like this on the beach back home.'

'You cannot take off with a string of horses, not here. Back in Blighty your lunatic scheme had a slight chance but here you and I and everyone else – including the horses – are part of the show. We have responsibilities.'

'Have you told the animals, sir?'

'Jack,' Daubeny breathed. 'The guns need shells. The horses take them to the pits. It's the way things are – whether we like it or not.'

383

'You've changed your tune.'

'The situation is different. When you're in uniform you've no freedom of choice.'

'Tell the horses that. They don't understand.'

'Good. If they did would it be easier for them? Now let's bring this to an end once and for all. Don't try it again or I will personally have you tied to a wheel and flogged. No more talk. I'm tired of talk. Do you understand, Corporal?'

'Corporal, Captain, Yes sir, No sir – it's all a load of shit.'

Daubeny lit a cigarette. 'I'll forget that. See to the animals or you'll finish up before a firing squad or in the bullring. Not another word, McKenna.'

The horses settled into their dance even though the ground was quite firm and they only sank hoof deep. It was dark now and the stars were as big as they were over Cider Mill Tor. They pulsed around Beth's head. Then she saw Iona, Melody and Bathsheba among the ghost moths on the hilltop. She could smell the hill and feel its presence. Apple blossom was firming against the glow when the German strafe began and the road came under fire. The heavy guns had the range of all the approaches to the emplacements. During the fine weather the movements of British infantry had been charted by the enemy reconnaissance planes. Something was about to happen. On the edge of the village the sentries noted the barrage of coal boxes, four-twos and whizzbangs exploding over a wide front between the wagons and the pits. The infantry columns pouring forward to the battle zone were having a bad time.

Beth was quivering. He drew the curry comb over her body, feeling the bones where the flesh had once been firm and round. Sensing his heartache she lowered her head to his hands.

'Get her in harness, Jack lad,' Milburn said gently.

'I'm doing it tonight, Stan, on the homeward run. I mean it.' He produced the jagged shell splinter and returned it again to his greatcoat pocket.

Chance had been promoted to the lead position and she was in remarkable shape considering the way things were. Beside her Beth looked old, ready for the knackers, Jack thought. Oh no you don't God. Not her.

It was the last run of the night and dawn was close. They moved onto the road, starlight gleaming on helmets and harness

384

and the prairie of mud. Dreamily Jack wondered if the White Lady of Lansworthy could see as far as that bit of the world. Hail Mary, full of Grace, get St Francis to watch over my horse. For the love of God, I'll never ask for another favour. Harness jingled on the frosty air. Jack steered the team among the flooded shell holes and dead mules, following the subaltern who rode ahead tracing the route.

Fear took his breath away. He could hear the hollow ringing of his heart beneath the numbness. Dried mud made his topcoat stiff as well as heavy, and the sweat was cooling under his balaclava. Outside his discomfort the nightmare was busy. The limber behind them went off the road into a crater and between shellbursts men and animals could be heard screaming as they sank.

'Keep going,' the subaltern cried. 'The others will sort them out.'

'Like shit they will,' Milburn grunted.

The greasy side of the crater offered no purchase. Jack glanced over his shoulder from cold nausea. He could see nothing but knew what was happening.

'Keep going,' half sobbed, half snarled.

Dark figures were struggling to drag a mule out of the wayside slime. The animal was protesting. Hands fought to free the ammunition panniers which gave the mule a value above that of his life or carcass. Coal boxes droned in, fell and became flame that leapt on a crashing roar. The air was full of fumes and the stench of mud and decaying things. The cannonade crescendoed as the British eighteen pounders struck back.

Treading cautiously on the brushwood and duckboards which had been put down to make the approach to the emplacements possible, Jack's team toiled up to the guns. All the animals were lathered and steaming. By the orange light of gunfire Jack and Milburn stared at each other. The horses stood resigned to the violence breaking around them. What sort of wound? Jack thought, climbing onto her back and urging the team to the road again.

Low trajectory shells were arching over the pits and the incoming limbers caught some of the shrapnel. Curiously devoid of emotion Jack considered the horse's anatomy. A lame animal would be no use to a farmer, so any injury to the legs was out. Withers, croup, shoulders, stifle. Not her face. The empty limber bumped over the carcass of an animal. Dawn broke grey, misty and dry, and the Allied bombardment began with the mighty roar of siege guns. It produced swift German retaliation, forcing the battalions waiting to reinforce the impending advance to cower in the reserve trenches back from the eighteen pounders. Here they had a clear view of the limber teams crawling through the mud in the grim first light. The foremost wagon vanished on the edge of an explosion. More shells crashed down and the little column was hidden by smoke.

When it cleared some horses could be seen staggering about at a wayside littered with mutilated creatures and wreckage. Four black holes were filling with mud and water. More horses climbed to their feet and joined their companions but nothing living stirred on the road ahead or behind them. They were stranded in a sea of mud.

Jack recalled the descending whine and the flash that had lifted him off Beth. Then he was aware of nothing until he opened his eyes and heard the wild, low screaming. Something warm lay under his head. It was Chance's dead body. He raised himself on his elbows. Milburn lay a few yards away on his back in the mud making inhuman noises. His spectacles had been driven deep into his face.

'Stan.' Jack tried to get up but nausea and giddiness pinned him down.

For a long time Milburn screamed and all of a sudden stopped. Daylight swelled behind the smoke.

'Are you all right, Corporal?' the subaltern said, bending over him.

'Shall be in a minute, sir. A bit dizzy.'

'When you're fit we'll round up the horses – those that are left. All the men are dead except a couple of lucky beggars back there. They can't walk. It's Blighty for them.'

'My horse,' Jack whispered.

'Your team copped it badly, I'm afraid. Only one on its feet. A few of the others are in a bad state.'

He took out his revolver.

'Beth,' Jack breathed, struggling again to drag himself up.

'Lie still for a bit,' the subaltern said. 'You caught one on the head.'

386

The complaint of dying horses was beyond belief, and the officer left him and went to do something about it. The screams and groans were punctuated by shots. Eventually just one voice shrilled on but a moment later that was silenced.

The subaltern stooped over Jack.

'How are you feeling, old chap?'

'Could you help me up, sir? If I can get on a horse I'll be as right as rain.'

'Good show,' the young, smooth face smiled. 'Hang on, I'll put this away.'

He straightened and was returning the Webley to its holster when the shrapnel ripped through his spine killing him instantly. He crumpled rather than fell and lay curled up like a sleeping child. Jack turned away, the corpse stench of mud in his nostrils. A curious mixture of Maconochies and bully beef gushed from his nose and mouth. The shell splinter had opened his forehead to the bone. His helmet was gone and blood dribbled into his eyes. He pawed at them, letting the dizziness do as it pleased. The chill of muddy water crept over his flesh and he began to shiver. There was no need to get up; nothing to get up for. He blinked his eyes on the redness clogging his lashes.

48

A few hours before Jack's team made its run Arthur Lacey's war took a new twist. His descent into nightmare since the heady summer of 1914 had been rapid, and two years of bluff and terror had pushed him close to breakdown. Yet he survived even the first days of the Somme offensive where luck carried him across No Man's Land and back again. At the Front everyone except the lunatics was afraid so Lacey's cowardice went almost undetected among those who were constantly struggling through their own fear to meet the demands of trench warfare. A Blighty wound which turned septic kept him out of action until November when France reclaimed him.

His regiment was in the front line and Lacey did his best to avoid action. He reported sick three times claiming to be suffering from dysentery, then a chest infection and finally dizziness and blackouts. The medical officer marked him down as a slacker and one starry night he found himself on the fire step of the forward trench, his body pressed against the sandbagged revetment, waiting for 'a little remedial treatment'.

He and another private named Chard were going on a scouting expedition into No Man's Land with Lieutenant Nicholson. The sergeant-major had insisted he volunteer. Lacey groaned and bit his sleeve to try and stop his teeth chattering. Sweat beaded the face he had blackened.

Other raiding parties were busy beyond the barbed-wire entanglements. Star shells burst and light wobbled on its descent. The staccato 'tic' of Maxims prickled his scalp. A rat rustled along the parado wall behind him, a man called softly from sleep, the pumps pounded away in the dugouts but the duckboards were awash. His legs were wet and freezing to the knees.

'Right,' Nicholson whispered.

They went over the sandbags on their bellies, using knees and elbows to get them past the forward sap. The path through the wire was not a dead end and the subaltern breathed a sigh of relief as he led his men into the shell hole and two feet of water that stank like a gangrenous limb. Verey lights flared and the German machine guns raked gulfs of darkness which moved after the light had died.

Lacey had never felt more vulnerable. They were in the middle of No Man's Land, close enough to the German trenches to catch snatches of laughter and conversation. Lacey was no longer a human being. He was a mass of sensitive vitals in a sack so frail a raindrop could have penetrated the skin. Peering from another shell hole he saw the crosslines of the German wire.

What the hell were they doing in that place? Close at hand the rats had quarried into corpses to release a sweet putrescence. Into me, Lacey screamed silently, feeling reality crumble away. Then he knew what the subaltern intended. The mad bugger was going to have a go at wiping out the machine gun nest with grenades. That would make them a target for every trigger-happy Hun in their line. Get out of this one, Arthur, said the voice in his head. Luscombe's voice, he mused; an irritating snigger. Through the fog of disbelief he could see the German smiling down his Maxim, waiting for Arthur. Every nasty thing in the world was waiting for Arthur.

Nicholson and Chard were about to wriggle forward again. The wind sang in the barbed wire; Lacey's face was a mask of sweat and his knees were lifeless. More lights drifted down the sky, bathing the landscape in a maggot glow. A rat ran over his hand and he choked back his cry of horror. The shell exploded, filling the air with shrapnel but his head was already down. Chard had been on his hands and knees peering over the rim of the crater at the moment of detonation. The small black holes in his face and throat were clues to how he had died. One of our shells, Lacey reflected without emotion. He was safe and comfortable. Bringing his knees up to his chin he assumed the foetal position.

'Get out of there – you damned coward,' Nicholson slurred.

The subaltern knelt on the edge of the crater and when the next Verey light fell Lacey saw blood glistening on the face snarling down at him. Nicholson held the wreckage of his left arm across his chest.

'Lacey.' He waved his revolver as numbness spread. Then the side of the crater collapsed and he slid gently face downwards into the morass. Raising himself on his good arm he tried to shake the mud from his eyes. For a second or so he was a melting chocolate man, with his mouth opening and closing.

'I'll see you court martialled,' from a gurgle of bitterness. 'You damned coward.'

'Tidn my fault,' Lacey wailed.

Nicholson's strength gave out and he vanished to emerge once more spitting mud. Lacey leaned over and pressed down on the helmeted head with all his weight and it subsided noiselessly. For a moment an arm flailed then Nicholson lay still. A swirl or two broke the surface, bubbled briefly and left the gruel flat and calm; but Lacey continued holding the corpse under until his muscles ached.

Afterwards he rested and considered his next move. On a flash of inspiration it came to him. Slithering and grunting he hauled Nicholson's body clear of the crater and slung it across his shoulders, keeping as low as possible. Shells crashed down in a random barrage on the German trenches, and as the smoke spread he came staggering to the barbed wire in front of his own lines. A star shell descended but the gap in the entanglement was close now. Then a bullet crunched into the corpse shielding his back. The sniper was hampered by the smoke and Lacey was clear of the wire before the machine gun crew spotted him. The Maxim opened up as he struggled over the last few yards. Suddenly there was a searing pain in his right leg but his impetus carried him and the body over the parapet into the trench.

'Bloody well done, lad,' the sergeant-major grunted, rolling up the greatcoat and placing it under his head.

'Lieutenant Nicholson?' Lacey gasped.

'The officer is dead, but it was one hell of a brave effort.'

Lacey nodded and groaned. The pain pulsed from the black cavity that had once housed his right kneecap.

'Chard bought it, too,' he managed, refusing the cigarette.

'That leg is your ticket out of the shit – for good. So cheer up, lad. There are worse ways of gettin' home.'

'Home,' Lacey murmured.

'You're one of them khaki heroes newspapers write about,' the sergeant-major said.

And Lacey went down the heroes' trail, stage by stage, with the nightmare ebbing the further he travelled from the Front. Stretcher bearers brought him to the Aid Post for iodine and bandages; then he was carted to the Advanced Dressing Station and on to the Casualty Clearing Station for surgery. Here he lost a limb and gained the Military Medal. During his convalescence he was to dwell often on this stroke of good fortune. Almost everyone he knew had two legs but the medal and the crutches set him apart.

49

Something warm and moist fluttered over Jack's face. He tried
to open his eyes but the lashes were gummed-up with blood.
Beneath his head Chance's body was no longer warm. He
sighed, waiting for Sean to kick out in sleep or his mother to cry
from the adjoining bedroom. But he wasn't at home. The
miserable truth seeped through with the stink of mud. He was
cold and wet and his head ached. Maybe if he lay there long
enough he would become part of the dream. At the top of the
terrace the band was playing and the skipping ropes beat out
their rhythms. He could smell the Sunday breakfast, hear the
bacon crisping.

The warm moistness on his face made him conscious of his
wound. Working his eyelids free he saw Beth's muzzle a few
inches from his nose. Gently she nudged him. The nausea
passed and he could stand without feeling giddy. Around him a
bloodless sun was picking out the wreckage left behind by the
strafe that continued blighting the landscape.

Jack blew on his fingers and tugged off his balaclava. The
horses broke from light that dilated and dimmed, great silver
creatures bounding across the mud. And he remembered with
sadness the silver horses running through the childhood dream
– star horses bursting from the sky, the wetness of birth
glistening on their coats. He was walking towards the hills

again, watching the horizon retreat and beckon. Beth stared at him while the thunder of the guns rippled across their thoughts. Her eyes were placid, and the sunlight reflected in them was also turning the mud on her body to silver.

Horses dragging their traces gathered around her and stood waiting. Some were wounded, all were shocked. Elsewhere the more seriously injured animals cried out for release. Taking the dead officer's revolver Jack went among them and ended their suffering. Then he hauled himself onto Beth's back and rounded up the rest of the strays until over a dozen were ready to be led to safety.

Their progress was watched by the infantry herded into the reserve trenches. As the little group picked a path among the debris and shell holes every man watching them willed their escape.

Beth splashed along the road, holding her head erect. Sunlight falling horizontally across the mud raised a silver fire, but Jack's hand lay on her neck and the brightness held the shadows of themselves. Shining animals flashed through the dusk to ridges of brilliance that sighed and fizzed and faded. She was weightless, taking the shift of glare in her stride on a journey without reason or destination.

A horse left the road and vanished in a flooded crater. The low, nasal trilling ended abruptly. Four-twos began to fall again. Beth's stride lengthened and she went in and out of the mud like a filly. The carousel horse, Jack thought and there was Kitty on the roundabout, rising and falling until she disappeared. The earth lifted and roared and he was down in the mud unable to hear anything save the thrum of life at the base of his skull. The feeling had gone from his back and his chest was cold. Each breath was a jolt of agony. Not yet, he said to himself. Please, not yet. Beth was on her knees beside him and a groan rose from the trenches as the smoke cleared. Two animals lay motionless, another was on its back, legs thrashing, and the driver had gone. Then Jack was up, coaxing Beth to her feet, deaf to the cheering soldiers.

She had lost an eye and the left side of her face was a sticky mask of blood.

'They've made such a mess of you,' Jack choked. 'Come on, my lovely – let's get you out of here.'

At birth we are given the whole world as a gift. Yes, he grinned, yes. Nothing had changed. But oh God never to see another spring or Kitty's face or the bay full of stars! He tried to lift a hand to his forehead but the movement fanned the pain in his chest and he coughed blood. His mother smiled in her white gown from under the white parasol. Then the carriage glided by.

'Mother.' The blood frothed between his clenched teeth and dribbled down his chin. Shells exploded nearby but beyond the wood the ground was firmer and the road jammed with ambulances and limber teams bound for the pits. Everything came to a halt. Men drew rein and stared in horror at the apparitions galloping towards them. The rider and his horse were grey but their faces were blood-smeared red. At their heels stampeded six or seven loose animals, madness staring from their eyes.

Daubeny knew it was Jack and Beth. They passed in a flurry of mud and spray, and he spurred his horse after them. It was beyond commands or threats or words of any sort. The horses went unchallenged through the wagon lines and met the road a little south of Hédauville. Here a military police patrol tried to stop them only to be brushed aside.

'Animals for the veterinary hospital,' Daubeny shouted. Now they were running west over plashy meadows, pounding through the sunlight into the start of the British bombardment. The siege guns roared and the sky was racked by the rush and drone of shells. Lather covered Beth from head to tail but she had no desire to rest. Over the low hedge she flew and ran on towards the village that was there behind the apple trees.

'Jack,' Daubeny cried, overtaking him and grabbing Beth's bridle; but Jack's chin was down on his chest. Beth turned and whinnied before she was pulled up under the apple boughs. A handful of curled, yellow leaves idled down the windless air and Jack followed them into the grass. He could hear the voice but not the words. Kneeling beside him Daubeny saw the darkness on his face and the eyes round and full of agony. The world went up and down and Jack was riding it like a horse out of torment.

'Jack.'

Blood from the wound in his back flooded both lungs, cancelling breath and pain. The White Lady fell, blotting out the sun and sweeping him with her into darkness that glowed.

Daubeny closed the eyelids and still on his knees lit a cigarette. Jack's features had relaxed but his hands were clenched on the grass blades. Lice slowly uncurled from the sleeves of his greatcoat and crawled over his knuckles. Daubeny's cigarette descended to crisp them into crumbs of charcoal.

When he got to his feet he saw the old people and children among the horses.

'*Il est mort?*' demanded the little girl. She had a pale, serious face and long brown hair.

Daubeny nodded.

'*Mon frère est mort aussi.*'

Again Daubeny nodded. 'Please fetch the priest – *le curé, s'il vous plaît. Mon ami est Catholique.*'

He looked about him. Whatever spirit presided over the Western Front it was not a familiar deity. He closed his eyes, hollowed his cheeks and inhaled. The gunfire brutalising the morning angered him. 'Our Father which art in heaven.' He looked up at the sky. There were no birds.

The children fed handfuls of grass to the horses, withdrawing their fingers quickly for fear of a nip. But Beth stood absolutely still over Jack, her head lowered and her breath ruffling his hair. She uttered no sound yet Daubeny could feel the intensity of her grief. Her entire world had gone. Slowly then she walked around the body, nudging it in a silent plea for him to come back to her. Later, when they had carried Jack away, she resumed her vigil while the leaves fell and the thunder of the bombardment peeled between the Ancre and the Somme.

A one-eyed horse could pull a plough or a muck cart or turn the wheel of a cider press. Daubeny had the vet brand her as a caster and made sure she went to a good home in the village where Jack had died.

'If I survive I'll come back for her,' Daubeny said. 'Do not part with her, *m'sieur*. Have I your word of honour?'

The old farmer smiled. '*Ma parole, m'sieur,*' and they shook hands.

'Take this money and look after her, please. I will help feed her for as long as I am able. Meanwhile she is in your care.'

The bombardment was over. Little, it seemed, had been gained by the fresh offensive. He stood in the rain beside Jack's grave. The children had laid bunches of flowers at the foot of the wooden cross. But the soil was grey, not red like the Devon plough and the robin's song in the failing light was poignant to the extreme.

50

Life at Number Eight Angarrick Terrace continued although the blinds were down in the front room window. The children still played around the lamp post after dark, Dando was taken for walks and the Salvation Army band struck up every Sunday morning. It was this uninterrupted flow of the ordinary that distressed Mary McKenna. She sat by the fire, gazing at the things his eyes had rested on: the wallpaper, the range, the teapot, dishes, jars, cruets, the knocked-about furniture. Wearily she picked up the sugar bowl and dropped it in the hearth where it shattered. For a moment she stared at the pieces. The thing would not have life while he lay dead. A plate was next to go and the destruction would have continued if Sean and Kitty had not restrained her.

Mary needed no persuasion from Father O'Driscoll to believe Jack was with Michael at Jesus's right hand. She had a clear picture of heaven printed on her mind. There was God and the saints on a mountain like Brandon, only the top was white with the purity of the Host. The rest of heaven was like the Dingle Peninsula, surrounded by white clouds and ringing with the hallelujahs of the righteous. Her mother and father were there chatting to St Patrick, but St Francis was listening to Jack and smiling.

Then the sickness and grief swelled and swamped

everything. She would rock back and forth, eyes closed, reliving the moment the official notification had arrived: a sharp rap at the door, Blanche's bare feet padding on the lino, voices, a cry. The horror caught her again and the colour vanished from her face. The words swam before her but he was alive despite the piece of paper she had crumpled and tossed aside. He was a child again and safe from it all there with his head tucked into the folds of her skirt. Not gone forever. Forever. She rocked and moaned and the girls stared at her unable to do anything.

Kitty's stoicism surprised everyone but most of all Dora. She bore the loss well for in her heart she had known Jack would never return once the war got its hooks into him. Old Chancellor had visited the house full of guilt to speak of the dead heroes and tell her she would be getting a small pension from the store.

Edward Daubeny's news that Beth was alive on a French farm left Kitty unmoved. Again it seemed inevitable – Jack dead, the horse alive, she and the baby alone. Father O'Driscoll could not explain any of it, and 'God moving in a mysterious way' was no consolation. But Mary McKenna knew that if the horse lived then so did part of her son. She knew it from an instinct whose roots ran deeper than her faith, right back to the folk history of Ireland. Man and horse, woman and hawk, all one in the spirit-life creatures shared. So she smiled and patted Dando's head.

The seasons passed, and the war continued, measured by other battles; but nothing that was to come could match the prolonged slaughter of the Somme.

Three springs after Jack's death there were many crosses in the paddock beyond the apple trees. Fallen blossom lay on the graves and a blackbird sang in the orchard. Beth's ears twitched as she caught the melody on her return to evening grass. Her workmate was an old Percheron cross named Marie who was forever seeking to comfort her. Yet Beth's habit of standing perfectly still every dawn and dusk, like a creature expecting to find something in the bottom of the sky, baffled her companion and the farmer. She had a vague recollection of Jack lying in the field with his eyes closed. Where had he gone? When would he return? This time there was no certainty of reunion and she was low.

The farmer treated her well despite the shortage of hay and oats, and Daubeny's visits made her perk up until she discovered the voice calling her name was not the voice she craved. But her mane and feather had grown again and she had lost some of her thinness. When the work day was over she would permit the farmer's grand-daughter to groom her. Then the scent of apple blossom would resurrect the vision of the other orchard at the top of the Devon valley. The curlews passing between the Ancre and the Somme called their sweet double-notes and opened the heartache. Larks were aloft and singing, and the chalk dust drifted over the countryside, hazing distance. Munching her way across the paddock she did not know Jack was there under one of the crosses. She thought of him alive in the good place and was desperate to join him. All the animals lost to her now would have gathered on the hill under the star-dance, and he would come up from the orchards calling her name to put her in harness and take her to the yard.

Dora and Edward strolled together along Station Lane and went through the gates into Chancellor's stables. Old Bob sat in the tackroom by himself. He greeted them warmly and they spoke of the war and how things were before 1914. The old man was struggling to come to terms with the enormity of the holocaust.

'Most of them have gone. Tom Palfrey was gassed at Passchendaele and he's an invalid; the Dunsfords, Drew, little Charlie Wotton, Moony, Ginger, some of the other stable boys and Jack, all daid and buried. I doan know what to make of it. All they harmless men and boys and horses.'

He hung his head. 'Bliddy war. Bliddy waste. Still, it made a few unlikely heroes. Who would've thought that ornament Lacey would go and get chopped up tryin' to save an officer? I never thought he had it in him. Do'ee know they've made un landlord of the King Bill? Tidn the King Bill now, of course, because the brewery have renamed it "The Lord Kitchener".'

Dora turned away in disgust. 'After that prize idiot!'

Edward walked her down to Lansworthy Beach, through the drizzle of early May.

'Jack didn get a medal,' she said in a small, unhappy voice. 'I can't bear to think of that boy and all the others under the soil out there.'

'A medal is the last thing Jack would have wanted.'

'Did he suffer, Edward?'

'Lord no! He went out like a light, peaceful as a lamb.'

She looked at him and he averted his eyes.

'Tell Kitty, please. It's the best sort of lie.'

'Will you marry me, Dora?'

'No – and in your heart you don't want me to.'

She smiled and kissed him. The wet, gritty sand crunched under their boots. Gulls swooped around the pier where a child was flying a kite.

'I shall go to London and push the cause. We can see each other often. Please,' she added firmly, 'don't go on about it, Edward. That kind of marriage could never work. Love isn't enough. I'm not ready for domesticity and I certainly couldn't put up with the sort of social daftness your sister and her set pursue. Come on,' from a smile now as his face dropped – 'you'll get over it. You've got your chums and cricket and your books and things.'

'But I haven't got you.'

'I can't see myself as something for the trophy cabinet.'

She laughed and he cupped her lovely, expressive face in his hands.

'Honestly, Edward, I'd make an awful wife – ask Kitty. All I want to do is lug my soap box round street corners preaching to all them deprived slum dwellers.'

'Sounds beastly depressing.'

'But a little more fulfilling than working out menus for dinner parties or scolding nanny for slackness in the nursery.'

Under the pier they were out of the rain. Part of the luminosity the sky borrowed from the sea flushed the shadows.

'There was a letter addressed to me in Jack's things,' Edward said, taking it from his wallet and handing it to her.

'"Dear Edward",' Dora read. '"If I cop a bad one I'd like you to try and bring Beth home. I hope I can get her out of this mess but she won't have those green pastures until she is back in Clennon Valley. If I can't see this through I hope you won't let her down. I made her a promise. Best of luck, Jack McKenna."'

Her eyes lifted to his face. 'What will you do?'

'Go to France and bring Beth home. I would have done it

Even if he hadn't asked. Chancellor wanted to pay my expenses but that's out of the question. I need to do this for my own sake. Apart from anything else I've been wondering what it would be like to make that journey free of terror.'

'Was it always bad?'

'Always. Going back off leave was the worst part of the business.'

She slipped her arms round his neck and kissed him, feeling the tears pricking the back of her eyes. Yet he was not free of trauma. On the ferry old memories and fears crowded in: the smell of damp greatcoats, sweat and cigarette smoke, the coughing and nervous laughter while the sea slid by. He recalled the stark misery on his mother's face as she raised it for the parting kiss. All suffering came to a head during the journey from sea port to front line destination. Once there the war exercised its tyranny on the consciousness.

His hand shook so badly the match went out. He struck another and managed to light the cigarette. The track west of Hédauville carried the scars of bombardments but the taxi was driven with lunatic sang-froid. Sitting in the cab Daubeny wondered how long the vehicle could take such punishment. He began to giggle hysterically while the driver cursed the dust and *les Anglais*.

Après la guerre fini
Soldat Anglais parti.

The tears streamed down Edward's face. Like a mirage the village grew on the horizon. First there were the fields and lines of peasants hoeing crops, then the paddock which had become a cemetery for British soldiers, and finally the orchards, farms and houses.

'*Elle est une mignonne, m'sieur,*' the farmer said. '*Très belle et gentille, et un peu ètrange.*'

'*Etrange?*' said Edward with a lift of the eyebrows.

The priest accompanying them tried to explain.

'After the work is finished she rests absolutely still and goes inside herself.' He tapped a fingertip against his temple. '*Où le rêve commence.* She is a strange animal.'

Edward nodded, and that was how she was when he came to the cemetery. She stood in the grass, unmoving, waiting on the threshold of dream. She was haggard, half blind and one of her

401

knees was swollen. He drew the flat of his hand down her neck.

'Bethlehem.'

At the sound of her name she swung her head to look at him, but it was not Jack and her interest died. She stared into the dust haze, shutting out the rest of the world. Daubeny lingered for a while beside Jack's grave and said as much of the 23rd Psalm as he could remember.

> The Lord is my shepherd, I shall not want.
> He maketh me to lie down in green pastures;
> He leadeth me beside the still waters.
> He restoreth my soul . . .

Maybe, he reflected, the war had achieved something, if only to sweep away well-worn deceits from so many smug corners. To be alive in that field was a privilege. To be alive and warm and free from terror.

Brought back to Tor Barton she hobbled awkwardly into the sunlight on Cider Mill Hill, and the farm horses gathered to sniff her. She was recognised by some of the older animals who populated her interior vision of the past. At dawn the curlews called and she waited for the sun to climb out of the bay.

'Bethlehem. My Beth.'

But where was he in this place which breathed peacefulness and was alive with his love? Kitty and her son came to make a fuss of her.

'She's yours now, my dear,' Chancellor said. 'This is her home and when the little boy is big enough he can ride her. Jack did. Jack was a bundle of mischief.'

'A bliddy nuisance, sir,' Trant said from a bleak smile.

'She's still his horse,' Kitty said, stroking Beth's face.

Walking home over the water meadows she wept for all that would never be again: his body laid on her own, his smile and voice, and the brightness of his eyes in those summers they had shared. The curlew calls followed her down Tanners Lane but she did not hear them.

And Bathsheba, Solomon and those the mud and noise and cold took away, they were there with her in the grass and sunlight. Was the wind a dream – the warmth and greenness merely shadows of what had risen from his love? She turned and lifted her head when he called; and they came, the mares and geldings, arching their necks and loosing their manes. They lived in her and were the grass and the summer rain and the sun that never ages.

She lowered her muzzle to the meadow and Solomon was not sitting in the greyness waiting to be led out of pain. The wind sent the shadows swimming around her.

'Beth. My Beth. Walk on, girl. Walk on.'

Muffled hoofbeats announced the arrival of the farm horses. Solomon, Bathsheba, Melody, Iona. She started forward, her whole body vibrant with recognition. He was on the tor against the sun, part of the brilliance. The horses thundered up to brush her flanks with their bodies. Beth's lashes descended and her chest heaved. All about her the grass whispered her name, and the fields ran with the life of summer down to the sea.